EX
LIBRIS

Romance Treasury

THE ROMANCE TREASURY
ASSOCIATION

NEW YORK · TORONTO · LONDON

These stories were originally published as follows:

MASQUERADE
Copyright © 1966 by Anne Mather
First published by Mills & Boon Limited in 1966

RATA FLOWERS ARE RED
Copyright © 1969 by Mary Moore
First published by Mills & Boon Limited in 1969

THE UNKNOWN MR. BROWN
Copyright © 1971 by Sara Seale
First published by Mills & Boon Limited in 1971
under the title *Mr. Brown*

ROMANCE TREASURY is published by:
The Romance Treasury Association, Stratford, Ontario, Canada

Editorial Board: A. W. Boon, Judith Burgess, Ruth Palmour and
Janet Humphreys
Dust Jacket Art by Muriel Hughes
Story Illustrations by Muriel Hughes
Book Design by Charles Kadin
Printed by Kingsport Press Limited, Kingsport, Tennessee

ISBN 0-919860-23-0

Printed in U.S.A.   A024

CONTENTS

Page 11

MASQUERADE
Anne Mather

Page 205

RATA FLOWERS ARE RED
Mary Moore

Page 349

THE UNKNOWN
MR. BROWN
Sara Seale

MASQUERADE

MASQUERADE

Anne Mather

When Samantha Kingsley reached 21, her world turned upside down. Whisked away from Italy to London by the terms of her father's will, she met the mother she had never known.

The discovery that her mother was a famous and glamorous actress, as well as an extremely hard and selfish woman, was shattering — and Samantha hated the sophisticated, artificial life her mother led.

Only two people mattered in Samantha's new world — her grandmother and the disturbing Patrick Mallory, a lawyer she had met on her flight to London.

But what chance was there for any relationship to develop between them when her mother refused to admit in public that her daughter was a day older than sixteen!

CHAPTER ONE

The letter from England arrived only one month after the sudden death of her father. Samantha was still living in the shocked daze that had taken hold of her when she had heard that her father's car had crashed on the autostrada while he was driving from Milan to Bologna. A sudden puncture of a front tire had caused the old sedan to skid dangerously, crossing the dividing lanes and colliding with a tour bus coming from the opposite direction. The passengers on the bus had been shocked but unhurt. John Kingsley was dead.

Samantha was desolate; she had lived here so long in the small Italian fishing village of Perruzio with her father, sharing the villa and sharing his life. They had been so close. Too close; for now that he was dead she felt she had no one. Even old Matilde, who had been housekeeper at the villa for as long as she could remember, could not make up for the emptiness she felt inside. She thought she would never feel secure or happy again.

John, she had always called him that, had been to Milan to open his first exhibition of sculptures. For years, his talent had gone unrecognized. Then a visiting art enthusiast had been impressed and had arranged for John to have this exhibition in Milan. He had been there two weeks, writing home to tell Samantha of the success he was having; the commissions he was hoping to fill. He was driving home when the accident occurred. Samantha reflected bitterly that it was ironic that he should be cut off

11

from life just when all he had ever worked for was being realized.

The funeral had taken place in Perruzio, with all the villagers turning out to the little church where the Catholic father had said the Requiem Mass. They were all so friendly, so sympathetic, and yet Samantha could hardly bear their kindness. She only wanted to be alone, to grieve in private.

Her father's affairs were in a sorry state. The villa was rented. Although the exhibition was the beginning of his success, as yet there was little to show for all his years of work. He had had a small military pension, but that had died with him. After the funeral was paid for there was very little left for Samantha. For the time being she was content to stay on at the villa, but she knew it could not last. Soon she would have to do something. Get a job, or alternatively accept the offer she had already been made. Her thoughts shied away from this inevitable conclusion. For, after all, what job was she equipped to perform? She knew some typing and could look after a small house. She could cook a little, but she did not think these attributes amounted to much in a modern world where every girl seemed to provide herself more than adequately to fit any position.

And now, this letter had arrived from England; the country she had never really acknowledged as her birthplace. She had lived in Italy since she was four years old and spoke Italian like a native. This was the only country she really knew although her father had always insisted that they speak English when they were alone together.

John had told her that her mother had died when she was a baby and that she had no other relatives. He had left his life in England and come to Italy after her mother's death to enable him to have the time and inspiration for his work. They had never had much money, but what they had had sufficed. Life was cheap in the fishing village. Fish was plentiful and easy to obtain. Matilde made all their bread. They grew vegetables in the small garden on the cliff top, and Samantha had always been content.

She turned the letter over in her fingers before opening it. It was an expensive envelope, that much she knew and was doubly intrigued to learn its contents. It could only be from some friend of her father's in England who had heard only recently of his death.

The letter that emerged from the envelope was written on headed letter paper, with the address Daven House, Daven, Wiltshire in tiny, gold letters.

Frowning, Samantha turned to the end of the letter to read the signature. It was simply "Lucia Davenport."

With a characteristic shrug of her slim shoulders, Samantha began to read from the beginning.

"My dear Samantha,

Since being informed, a few days ago, of my son-in-law's tragic death, I have made arrangements for you to return to England. Of course, you must return here. We are your family and we want you. I am your grandmother, and since Barbara still refuses to act as a mother should, I myself will avail you of the facts.

Whatever your father may have told you to the contrary, your mother is very much alive. I suspect you are unaware of this. I will explain more fully when we meet. I am an old, old woman, my dear, and it would give me delight to have you come and live with me at Daven. My existence is now somewhat dull, but I would like to have a young person like yourself around me. I would try to see that you did find enjoyment and entertainment in spite of this.''

Samantha stared at the letter in amazement. Her legs felt as though they would no longer hold her, and she sank down weakly on to the arm of a nearby chair, astonishment vying with disbelief. Could it possibly be true? Or was this someone's idea of a cruel joke? With trembling fingers, she turned the page and read on:

"When your father's lawyers contacted me, as your father had left instructions that they should if anything should happen to him, I immediately sent instructions for your journey to London. I myself will be in London to meet you, if you will let me know the date and time of your arrival.

Please do not think too much about this until we meet. You cannot possibly understand anything until the full facts are explained to you. Simply rest assured that we will welcome you here.

Yours affectionately,
Lucia Davenport.''

Samantha could not restrain the gasp of pure bewilderment that escaped her. She replaced the letter carefully in its envelope and stared unseeingly into space.

Could it possibly be true, she asked herself again. Had she indeed been living a lie all these years? Was her mother really alive? And if so, why had she never contacted her? And yet, if it was not true, who was there to do such a thing to her?

No, she decided at last. It must be true.

She reached to the carved cigarette box that her father had made and extracted a cigarette. Lighting it she pondered on the turmoil that had now invaded her brain. Suddenly her empty life was full again. Full of strangers, claiming to be relatives. A grandmother; a mother! Could she possibly have any brothers or sisters?

A hundred and one questions buzzed around in her head, and she had no satisfactory answers to supply to them. The only way she would ever know would be to go to London as this "grandmother" of hers suggested and find out for herself.

The thought of uprooting herself from all that she had held dear all these years was a terrifying one. How could she leave Matilde? Of course, Matilde did have a sister who lived in Ravenna, not far away from Perruzio, but was it fair to expect her to leave, just like that?

And what if she did not like these strange new relatives? After all, they had not cared about her until now. Why had John kept it all such a closely guarded secret? She had thought they had no secrets from one another, while her father was withholding something that could change her whole life!

She shivered although the day was already quite hot. She rose and crossed the polished wooden floor to the French doors that opened onto the veranda, that overlooked the almost white sands of the beach, lapped continually by the smooth, creamy surf of the Adriatic. It was all so beautiful that it took her breath away. To leave all this, for some cold, gray English town, where the sun never shone and where people could not go out without their raincoats! John had painted a very gloomy picture of the country of her birth, but after all the secrets he had withheld, she wondered now whether London was indeed as bad as he had painted it. If there had been something there which he hated; something he had come to Italy to get away from, might he not see it with very different eyes from hers?

For the time being she felt she could not share her news with anyone. It was too sudden; too difficult to explain, even to Matilde.

Stubbing out her cigarette she turned and recrossed the room. She walked down the tiled passage to her bedroom and stripped off the old jeans and sweater that were her only attire. She pulled on a diminutive bikini that she had made herself and caught up her long, silky hair in a ponytail.

She left the villa, crossing the veranda and descending the sloping cliff to the beach. She ran eagerly into the warm ocean, allowing the cooling water to swirl over her head for a moment, before surfacing and swimming strongly through the waves. She swam almost every day. In the water she could escape for a while the implications of the fateful letter. Soon she would have to go back, to tell Matilde and ask her advice. But for now, she forgot everything but the warmth of the sun and the sense of well-being the water always gave her. She was not aware that, for the first time since her father's death, she had cast aside her melancholy.

She was a strong swimmer, and looking back toward the shore she realized she had come farther out than she had planned to. Turning, she saw the stocky figure of a fisherman watching her. She waved, recognizing him. She soon reached the shallows again and waded up out of the water onto the beach.

Benito Angeli stook watching her as she approached him; his eyes warm and desirous. She was so fair, this English girl, with the silky mass of her hair falling wetly about her shoulders. Her green eyes surveyed him smilingly, and as she was a tall girl they were on eye-level terms.

"You are better, eh?" he asked in Italian. Samantha nodded. Although it was unlikely Benito would ever leave his native village, she had been teaching him English and she said now, "Yes, thank you, Benito," and he grinned sheepishly.

"It's no good," he went on in his own language. "I'll never learn."

"You won't if you don't try," she replied in Italian now, and loosening her hair from its restraining band she flung herself down on the sand and stretched luxuriously. "The water is delicious!"

Benito knelt beside her. "You swim too far alone," he remarked.

"I know." She sighed and looked suitably chastened. Benito was puzzled. Since her father's death Samantha had had no time for idle chatter. But today, she was different.

Samantha, as though reading his thoughts, said, "To be quite honest, I'm a bit bemused. I had a letter from England this morning."

"England?" Benito frowned. "You know someone in England?"

"Apparently so," replied Samantha, rolling onto her stomach.

"Someone who knows your father?"

"Yes . . . at least 'knows' is rather an understatement." She shook her head.

"So? Tell me, who is it from?"

He allowed himself to relax beside her, his fingers straying caressingly over her bare back.

But Samantha was not in the mood for that, and she rolled restlessly away from him and sat up.

"Don't," she said, irritatedly. "I'm serious. The letter was from my grandmother. Now do you understand?"

Benito lost his lazy air. "Your grandmother! But your father said that you had no relatives!"

"I know." Samantha hunched her shoulders. "But it seems I have. That is, unless someone is having a joke at my expense. And that's not all. I also have a mother!"

"*Madre di Dio!*" Benito gasped.

"Yes, that's exactly how I feel. So you see, I am presented with a problem."

"And that is?"

"My grandmother wants me to go to England."

"No!" Benito looked angry. "But you are not going?"

Samantha sighed. "I haven't made my mind up yet."

Benito leaned toward her. "Cara, what about us? You know how I feel about you. I thought . . . I hoped . . . that soon now. . . . "

Samantha nodded. "I know."

She had been left in no doubt as to Benito's feelings. They had grown up together. They had always been in each other's company. He had taught her to swim, to handle a boat as well as any boy, to fish. John had not objected, although at times her father had been a little obtuse where Benito was concerned. He had not been able to see what was happening under his very nose. Perhaps, Samantha reflected, he had thought they were too close for anything emotional to come of it. But in Italy, it was the natural thing that children brought up together should marry, and Benito had never made any secret of his feelings. Benito's family expected the match. Already there was talk of a small cottage becoming vacant in the village that would suit their needs. John Kingsley's villa had too high a rent for any of the village folk and anyway, Benito would want to remain in the bosom of his family.

And Samantha had always enjoyed their company. She adored the children; Benito's nephews and nieces, but marriage was such a big step. In no time at all she could see herself with a family of her own and no possible chance of ever leaving the village again. Was this what she wanted, she had asked herself time and time again, and had always come up, unsatisfactorily, with the same answer. What other choice had she? Now that John was dead the problem had become daily a more difficult one. This letter had opened new doors, shown new horizons. Although the idea of leaving was frightening, she felt sure that this was her opportunity to see something of the world. How could she explain all this to Benito, though? How would he ever understand? He was content to live in Perruzio. He had a good life. He belonged with his family. And so might she belong with hers.

Benito had always taken her acceptance for granted and now to be confronted by this new Samantha was disconcerting for him.

"Why have they never come to see you?" he asked suddenly. "Why did your father say your mother was dead?"

"I don't really know," she admitted, sighing. "Perhaps as far as he was concerned, they were. But my grandmother was contacted by my father's lawyers, so he must have decided that should anything happen to him, I was to know the truth. Of course, he would never think that anything would happen so soon. He was only a young man, after all."

"But what about me?" Benito rose to his feet. "Surely your father knew about us?"

"He knew, and yet he didn't know," murmured Samantha. "Benito, I don't think Father thought that there was anything more than friendship between us."

Benito turned away. "And you let him think that?"

Samantha rose too now. "Of course not. I told him that we were very fond of one another. . . . "

"Very fond?" Benito spread wide his hands helplessly. "I adore you."

Samantha compressed her lips. "I know, I know."

"But you are going to let this new family of yours take you away from me," he exclaimed angrily.

Samantha put her hands over her ears. "Don't! I don't know yet."

Benito looked belligerent. "I won't let you do this to me!"

Samantha turned and ran up the cliff to the villa, without answering him. Benito ran after her, and as he was not tired from swimming caught her easily.

"This is your home, *carissima*," he murmured, in another tone.

Samantha looked gently at him. "It's the only home I've ever known," she whispered.

"And so?"

"I still can't quite take it in," she said. "Try and understand, Benito. How would you feel if you suddenly learned that your mother was still alive after you had thought her dead for all these years? I'm 21 now. I've never known what it's like to have a mother. Naturally, I'm curious to see her. If only to find out what kind of a woman could desert her child to the extent that my mother has done. It must be at least 17 years since she saw me."

She felt a lump in her throat at this thought. Then she looked at Benito. Standing beside her in denim pants and a rough shirt open at the neck, he looked dear and familiar. She wondered why she was allowing the letter to come between them. If only it had never arrived! It would have been so simple to marry Benito and have his children.

Living in Perruzio there would be no complications in their lives. Just as his parents had lived before them.

She slid her arm through his. "Don't rush me, darling," she murmured.

He looked dejected for a moment and then pulled her to him to press his lips to hers, his rough hands encircling her slim throat.

"Si," he said softly. "I will give you time."

They walked on up the cliff path until they could see the villa, lying peacefully as ever in the sunlight. But, to their surprise, there was a low, black limousine parked at the entrance.

Samantha looked at Benito and raised dark eyebrows. Benito shook his head in reply.

"Are you coming in for some coffee?" she asked.

Benito smiled slightly. "I think I had better. We must find out who your visitors are."

Matilde was in the hall when they entered the door. An elderly woman, her long black hair twined always into a bun on the nape of her neck, she looked at Samantha with relief in her face.

"You have company," she said softly in Italian, indicating the door of the lounge where earlier Samantha had read the stupendous news. "From Milano."

Samantha frowned. The day was gradually taking on the aspects of a dream. First the earth-shattering letter and now some strange company. Her limited existence was widening alarmingly.

Benito waited in the hall while Samantha went to change and put on a dress. She returned only a couple of minutes later, having towelled her hair almost dry and donned a simple shift of yellow cotton, another of her own creations. There had not been much money to spend on clothes, and she had found that buying material in the market and running it up herself left more for essential commodities.

"Do I look all right?" she whispered to Benito, and he nodded. To his eyes she would look good in anything. Just to look at her sent the blood pounding through his veins; his heart thumping wildly. Soon, oh! soon, she must marry him. He could not wait much longer. He wanted her passionately. With her fair skin and almost white hair she was so different from the dark-haired girls of his own race. He had delayed too long already. Had they already been married when the letter came this morning, she would not have been able to talk to him as she had done. She would have been his wife, his property, and, most probably, the mother of a *bambino* by now.

Together they entered the lounge to find two men seated in opposite armchairs, smoking and drinking the strong coffee that Matilde had brewed for them. They were both much older than the two young people, the younger of the two being about 50 years of age. They rose to their feet politely at Samantha's entrance, and the older man came to greet them.

"Miss Kingsley?" he asked, in heavily accented English.

"Yes." Samantha shook hands cautiously. They looked all right, so she supposed that as they came from Milan, they must be business associates of her father. Perhaps they had something to do with the exhibition.

"My name is Arturo Cioni," went on the man, "and this is my brother Giovanni." He smiled. "We are your father's lawyers." He hesitated. "Do you speak Italian, Miss Kingsley?"

Samantha smiled and nodded. "Yes. Do speak in your own language if it is easier for you."

"Good." The man continued in Italian. "We have had

a communication from your grandmother in England. I understand you have had the same. Yes?"

"That's right," Samantha nodded. "It arrived this morning. I must confess I knew nothing at all about having any other relatives. My father did not tell me."

"Yes, I know. But now your grandmother has instructed us to arrange for your flight to England. Was this explained in your letter?"

"Yes. I haven't recovered from the initial shock yet."

"Very understandable," said the younger man, speaking for the first time. "I always advised your father that you should be made aware of the facts in case such an unfortunate contingency occurred. I think he found it hard to tell you. You had lived so long without this knowledge. I also think he was a little afraid."

"Afraid?"

"Yes. You were his only reason for living. Had you known that you had a mother in England, you might have insisted that you return there directly and see her. He might also have feared you would prefer her life to his."

"Oh, how could he have thought that? He knew I adored living here. I would never have left him." Samantha felt quite distraught.

"Please. Do not distress yourself unduly. Your father died a happy man. He never told you, and your life was his to mold as he wished. I think that was all he ever asked."

"Yes." Samantha was unsure.

"Now. Let us get down to details," said Arturo Cioni, in a more businesslike manner. "Your grandmother wants you to fly from Milan to London as soon as possible. Naturally your affairs here will be tied up quite easily. Anything further you need to know can be explained to you. The villa is too big for you to rent alone. Surely by now you must have made some plans for your future."

"Not really," murmured Samantha weakly, sinking down onto a chair, her face pale. Suddenly she felt the enormity of what was expected of her sweeping over her, and she felt quite faint.

Benito, familiar with the whereabouts of everything in this room, crossed to a small cabinet and drew out a bottle of brandy that her father had always kept there for medicinal purposes. He poured a little into a glass and returned to Samantha, handing her the glass tenderly.

"Drink," he murmured softly. "It will make you feel better."

Samantha obediently sipped the fiery liquid and felt it burn its way down into her stomach, warming her chilled body.

"Forgive me!" exclaimed Arturo, looking anxiously at her. "This must all have been a great shock to you. I am a clumsy oaf. I have tried to rush you. It is simply that your grandmother put such a sense of urgency into her communication that we lost no time in putting her plans into operation."

Samantha stiffened. She wondered how great the gulf between her parents must have been. Knowing how sensitive John had always been, her mother must have hurt him immensely for him to pack up and leave the country like that.

"Yes," she said at last, sipping at the brandy. "I understand. And . . . and he thought I should go to England when he died for all he never went back."

"Time changes many things," put in Giovanni. "Circumstances change even more. He knew that whatever you shared could not go on forever. One day you would have to know the truth and then decide for yourself. What else can you do? Have you a job in mind?"

"We are betrothed," said Benito, looking fierce. "Is this not job enough? Is her future not secure in my hands? Why should some stranger provide for her what I can provide and more besides?"

"Benito!" said Samantha, sighing. "Please! We are not betrothed. Not yet. I must have time."

Arturo shrugged. "Should you decide to stay in this country, *signorina*, I will inform your grandmother to that effect. You need not write or communicate with her in any way if you do not wish to do so. It is in your hands. You are of an age now to please yourself, one way or the other."

Samantha ran a tongue over her lips. "Naturally, I am curious," she said. "Do you know why my mother and father separated?"

"They divorced," said Giovanni. "That is all we can tell you. Your father confided in us, but we do not know the whole story. You must find that out for yourself."

"I see." Samantha finished the brandy and put the glass down. She looked thoughtfully at Benito. He looked solemn and very angry. She could tell this from the way his eyes flashed when he looked at her.

Samantha bent her head for a moment, twisting her fingers together, and then said; "It is nearly lunch time. Will you stay for lunch?"

"That is very kind, *signorina*," said Giovanni, smiling. "We would be most grateful."

"And after lunch, I will give you your answer," said Samantha firmly.

Matilde was in the kitchen when Samantha went in search of her, leaving Benito to entertain her guests. She perched on the board at which Matilde was working and slowly began to explain all that happened. Matilde did not interrupt. She was a very comforting presence, and Samantha knew she would miss her terribly if she did decide to go away.

As they washed and prepared a salad, Matilde looked questioningly at the girl.

"And you will go to England?" It was a statement more than a question, and Samantha looked surprised.

"Do you think I should?"

Matilde shrugged. "I do not know, Samantha. I only know that if you do not you will spend the rest of your life wondering whether you should. What is there for you here? Marriage with young Benito. Five years marriage, and who knows? You may find your life is not as full as you had thought. There would be no escape. Our faith does not recognize divorce. Once married you stay married for many, long years. Be sure before you commit yourself to such a sentence."

"Oh, Matilde. You make it sound so dreary."

"And isn't it? When you are young and have the world before you, is not anything humdrum dreary? Will you really be contented with half a dozen *bambini* to look after? Benito is a good man. You could do no better in this village. But Benito is Italian. You are not. Never forget that. Whatever you have done in the past, however much you speak the language and become one of us, you are still English. I am sorry to sound disparaging, Samantha, but I think you know I am right. Your mind is not really undecided. Only your heart is fickle. You want the best of both worlds. You would like to be married, for a time, but this is not what marriage is for. Marriage is giving yourself into another's keeping forever. For as long as you live. Always remember this. No matter where you go, or who you marry."

Samantha looked pensively at the older woman. "As usual, Matilde, you are right. But what about you? What will you do?"

Matilde smiled. "I am getting old. Too old to mind giving up my work. My sister is a widow. She lives alone in Ravenna. She will be glad of my company. She is not a poor woman. We will not starve. Do not worry about me, Samantha. Worry for yourself. Go and get what you want and hold onto it. Never be content with 'second-best.' Just tell yourself, you are as good as anyone else, and you cannot go far wrong."

Samantha smiled. "All right, I'll tell the Cionis. And thank you for your understanding. I'm going to miss you."

"If you come back, come to my sister's in Ravenna. We will make something out. Don't worry. Be strong and honest, and you will survive. In life, strength of mind and purpose solves most things. Don't be a child. You are a young woman. Act like one and be independent."

Benito was sitting moodily on the veranda, when Samantha went to tell him that lunch was ready. He looked up dejectedly at her approach, and she felt guilty that she should be the cause of his depression.

"You're going, aren't you?" he said accusingly.

Samantha shrugged her shoulders. "I have to, Benito."

"I don't understand you, Samantha. I always thought I did. I was wrong."

Samantha spread her hands helplessly. "Would you want me to marry you and spend the rest of my life wondering whether I had done the right thing?"

"Of course not, but before this letter came there was no doubt."

"There was no alternative either," she reminded him,

awkwardly. "Please, Benito, try to understand. I've never left this country since I was four years old."

"I have lived here all my life."

"But you're Italian."

"So will you be, when you become my wife."

"In name only. Benito, I'm English."

"I've never known it bother you before."

"Oh, Benito, try . . . try to understand. I do think a lot of you, but if I go away I will be able to see things in perspective. If I love you, I will come back. You know that. If you love me you must know that love does not die simply because the two people concerned are separated."

Benito frowned. He knew she was right, and yet he was also afraid of what the separation might do. He was not as sure of her as he was of himself. He could see that she genuinely did not want to hurt him. Yet if she did go, would he ever see her again?

"If you are determined, there is nothing I can do to stop you," he said coolly.

"There is," she said desperately. "You could give me an ultimatum. I don't think I would dare to refuse you then."

Benito sighed and shook his head. "No, of course you are right. I could not force you into such a position. You are a free woman, Samatha. But please come back to me."

Samantha flushed. "Oh, Benito, when you look at me like that, I wish I had never even seen the letter."

Benito pulled her to him. "So do I," he groaned, as he pressed his lips to her hair.

"And now," he said, at last, "you must tell the Cionis of your decision."

"Yes," Samantha nodded. "And soon I'll know the secret of why my mother acted as she did. I only hope she is not as horrid as she sounds."

CHAPTER TWO

Patrick Mallory crossed the smooth tarmac of Milan airport. Ahead lay the gleaming aircraft that was to transport him back to London and the busy life from which he had enjoyed a brief respite. He always regretted leaving Italy after staying there for some time. It was his mother's country, and he had spent four idyllic weeks with her in their villa on the shores of Lake Como, soaking up the sun and relaxing completely. His life in London was hectic and sometimes nerve-racking. This holiday had been a godsend. Now he had never felt better. He looked tanned and fit and was ready to assume the responsibilities that were waiting for him in England.

He was a tall lean, attractive man in his mid-thirties. His hair was very black. His olive complexion owed much of its darkness to his being half-Italian. His eyes were hazel, tinged with tawny lights, his expression was rather cynical. He had not the kind of square-cut good looks that are generally called handsome, but he had a whimsical charm that in itself was much more magnetic. He was quite aware of the effect he had on members of the opposite sex and could use his charm to good advantage if it suited his purpose. He had not lived 36 years without knowing a great many women, but so far he had found them monotonously the same. Plenty of the village girls

Running a restless hand through his short hair, he mounted the steps to the entrance of the airplane, smiling

his warm, attractive smile and causing the young stewardess to become blushingly confused.

She directed him to his seat. Putting down his briefcase
beside him he stretched his long legs luxuriously. Now
that he was actually almost on his way, as it were, his
mind was already leaping ahead to London and to his
immediate plans on arrival. There was the new play, for
example. That might take some re-writing to fit the stage.

Reaching up a lazy hand, he loosened the top button of
his shirt beneath his impeccable tie. It was hot in the aircraft. It would be cooler when they took off. At least the
journey required no further effort from him. He could sit
back and enjoy it.

His thoughts turned to the woman who had been occupying much of his mind during the holiday. She would be
waiting for him in London. He wondered whether it was
time he started thinking seriously about settling down. A
bachelor life was fine, but the idea of having a settled
home appealed to him. His mother had said much the
same thing to him when they had discussed his life. She
wanted him to have children. His sister was married with
six children and had been married now for over 18 years.
Of course, Gina was ten years his senior, but he ought to
be turning his thoughts in that direction, he supposed.

He looked casually out of the window, surveying the
airport buildings. Already it was nearly time for take-off.
He was glad his mother never insisted on coming to the
airport to see him off. He detested long farewells, particularly those made in public.

His attention was caught by two young people by the
gate that led over to this aircraft. The young man was
obviously upset and was trying, rather unsuccessfully Patrick thought, to hold the girl tightly to him and kiss her.
Eventually he succeeded in his objective, but the girl

broke away almost immediately and darted from him, and across the tarmac to the waiting plane. Apparently the young man had come to wish her goodby and things had become emotional and out of hand.

Patrick felt amused. The girl looked English, but you never could tell these days. It could have been a holiday romance that had blossomed swiftly in the hot sun, or she could be an Italian leaving home for the first time for some reason. They were too intense, thought Patrick cynically. Why did young people always seem to feel things so intensely? He never had, at least he could never remember having done so. Perhaps he was singularly lucky, or alternatively not the sort of person to feel emotion deeply. At any rate, no woman had ever made a fool of him. He lit a cigarette. Well, he was glad he was past the stage for hearts and flowers. If he married, and it was a big "if," it would be for practical reasons, not emotional ones.

A few moments later the girl came down the aisle with the stewardess and was deposited on the seat beside him. He looked at her with interest. At close quarters she was remarkably attractive, and he liked the way her hair fell straightly to her shoulders.

At first she was unaware of his scrutiny. She was too absorbed by her own feelings, and he was able to regard her openly. He noted the long, curling black lashes, the tanned yet creamy complexion and the slight tip-tilt of her nose. Her dress was not fashionable. Her shoes were flat and uninteresting, but in the right clothes he thought she would be quite arresting.

Suddenly, she became aware of him and looked abruptly at him. For a moment, Patrick held her gaze and then withdrew his eyes. Her clear expression did not embarrass him, but the girl's face suffused with color, and she twisted the strap of the purse in her lap.

A few minutes later, the engines roared to life, and the sign requesting passengers to put out their cigarettes and fasten their safety belts flashed ahead of them.

Patrick fastened his safety belt with the ease of long practise, but the girl fumbled awkwardly with hers. Patrick, unable to prevent himself, took the straps from her unresisting fingers, and fastened it securely.

"Thank you," she murmured, showing even white teeth, as she smiled shyly at him.

Patrick merely smiled in return and stubbed out his cigarette. The aircraft began to move with slow, deliberate grace, and soon they were taxiing along the runway.

The girl gripped the arms of her seat tightly, and Patrick found himself watching her again. She was obviously terrified, and for once he felt something akin to sympathy. Usually he had no time for nervous passengers.

"Relax," he said easily. "We're almost airborne. Is this your first flight?"

She nodded. "As far as I know," she replied. "I'm rather a coward, I'm afraid."

Patrick shrugged his broad shoulders. "I guess we all are at times. Take-offs can be frightening, if you're not used to them." Then he looked up. "There, it's over. You can unfasten your safety belt now."

"Oh, thank goodness." She released the strap and relaxed in her seat.

Patrick unfastened his own and then said, "Do you smoke?" He offered her his slim platinum case, with the engraved monogram.

"Thanks." She took one and leaned forward to apply the tip to his lighter. Then she lay back again and looked speculatively at him.

Patrick lit a cigarette for himself and wondered, half-amused at his thoughts, why he was taking such an inordinate interest in this girl. He rarely struck up conversations on airplanes, as they had a habit of becoming a bore. Besides, well-known as he was, people usually had ulterior motives in speaking to him. He had grown wary of the casual remarks passed to him and usually spent journeys either reading or studying some aspect of his work.

But the girl did not somehow come into this category. She did not appear to recognize him and was certainly unlikely to be connected with the theater, dressed in such an outmoded way.

He drew on his cigarette and looked again at her.

"What's your name?" he asked idly, his eyes narrowed.

"Samantha Kingsley," she replied at once. "And yours?"

"Oh!" Patrick hesitated. Now for it! Even if she did not recognize him, the name might mean something to her. "Patrick Mallory," he said reluctantly.

If he had expected a reaction he was disappointed. It was obvious his name meant nothing to her. He sighed gratefully. Although he never lied about his identity it was a pleasure to meet someone who knew nothing at all about him. "Are you going to London?" he asked.

"Well, to begin with, but not exactly there. Wiltshire. Is that near London?"

"Reasonably so," Patrick nodded, amused by her expression. "You don't know much about England, do you? I thought you were English."

"I am. At least, I was born there, but I've lived in Italy since I was four years old."

"Oh, I see." Patrick frowned. "And you've never been back?"

"No. Never. My father preferred not to do so." Samantha was silent for a moment, and Patrick had the feeling that she was withholding much more than she had told him.

"And your father?" he probed, curious about this girl and unable to stop the question. "Is he not going with you?"

"No. My father is dead. He was killed over a month ago."

Patrick frowned again. "I'm sorry." He studied his cigarette for a moment. The name Kingsley rang a bell somewhere. Now she had told him that her father had been killed, he remembered where he had heard it. "John Kingsley," he said slowly. "Your father wasn't John Kingsley, was he?" Samantha's eyes widened.

"Why . . . why, yes. Did you know him?"

"No, not exactly. I met him in Milan at the exhibition. It was an excellent show. That must have been just before. . . . "

Samantha sighed. "Yes, it was. I'm still a bit dazed about it. And . . . and you liked the sculptures?"

"Oh yes." Patrick stubbed out his cigarette. "Very much. And so now you are an orphan?"

Samantha hesitated. "Not exactly." She halted awkwardly.

Patrick glanced curiously at her, and then seeing that she obviously did not want to talk about her immediate future, he changed the subject.

They talked about general things, books, art, music. Patrick was not bored by her shy conversation. It was so refreshing to find a girl as comparatively untouched as she seemed to be.

"Tell me," she said suddenly, "what do you do?"

Patrick lit another cigarette reflecting that he was smoking too much. The brief respite gave him time to think.

"I'm a writer," he replied, without qualification.

Samantha frowned, wrinkling up her brow. "What do you write?"

Patrick shrugged. He had no wish to become embroiled in a conversation about his work. His relief was overwhelming when the stewardess appeared at their side and asked them if they would like a drink.

Samantha looked up in surprise. This was all quite new to her. It was almost lunchtime, already.

"I'll have a tomato juice, please," she said quietly, but the stewardess had eyes only for Patrick Mallory. She knew only too well who he was, and the influence he had in the theater. Besides, his physical attributes alone were a challenge in themselves to any woman.

"What will you have, Mr. Mallory?" she was asking gushingly.

Patrick looked up, his lazy eyes amused. "Scotch," he said easily. "And bring this young lady a sweet sherry instead of tomato juice."

Samantha stared at him in surprise. With obvious reluctance the stewardess moved away.

"You don't object, do you?" he asked half-mockingly.

Samantha shook her head slowly. "No, I suppose not." She bit her lip and looked thoughtfully at him. "Why did that stewardess act so strangely?"

Patrick grinned. "Strangely?" he mocked.

"Yes. You must know what I mean. She . . . well. . . . " She flushed.

Patrick looked at her through a haze of smoke. "When you get a bit more experienced, you won't ask questions like that."

"Won't I?" Samantha shrugged.

Patrick laughed softly. "Here are the drinks. Cheers."

"Cheers," she echoed slowly and sipped her sherry.

Lunch was served soon afterward, a delicious meal although it had all been pre-cooked. Samantha looked out on the fluffy, cotton-wool world of cloud below the aircraft and wondered why people made such a fuss about flying. There was absolutely nothing to be seen, and it did not seem so much different from bus-riding at home.

Home! She sighed. She had to stop thinking about Italy as her home. Soon Daven House in Wiltshire was to be her home. There was no going back. If she returned to Italy it would be to marry Benito, but, as the distance between them increased, she felt the ties between them decreasing.

She took the opportunity after lunch of going back to the ladies' room. She washed her face and hands and combed her hair. The eyes that stared back at her through the glass were scared eyes, and she inwardly chided herself. Why should she feel scared? After all, she had nothing to be ashamed of. It was these women she was going to meet today who ought to feel ashamed.

Stiffening her shoulders, she walked back to her seat to find Patrick Mallory absorbed in some papers he had extracted from his briefcase. He did not even glance at her as she reseated herself beside him. Samantha found her thoughts returning to the problem of the next few hours. She felt that she was gradually becoming more and more nervous, and she would be glad when this day was over at last.

Her eyes strayed once more to her companion, as though drawn to him. In profile his features were just as attractive. From his immaculate tailoring and ease of manner she guessed he was a man who knew the world and what life was all about. He looked quite young, and she speculated about his exact age. He must be about 30 she decided, and wondered whether he was English. His name was English enough, and yet there was something slightly alien about his dark complexion and tawny eyes. Cat's eyes, Samantha thought. Like those of the tiger she had once seen in a traveling circus. Pondering, she wondered whether he was virtually quite as dangerous. He was very easy to talk to. She could understand a woman enjoying the attention he would devote to her. He treated Samantha rather like an overgrown schoolgirl, and she wondered whether she acted that way. It was disconcerting to find that after having thought yourself quite grown-up, a man like this man could make you feel quite gauche. It was apparent that the men of the village could hardly be compared to Patrick Mallory.

He was a writer, too. She wondered what he wrote. He had not wanted to talk about that. But the stewardess obviously knew him, and he *had* expected her to recognize his name.

From these thoughts she returned to thoughts of Benito. He had insisted on coming to the airport to see her off and had made the scene she had half-expected. After his early capitulation he had changed to become sullen and resentful. Samantha suspected that his family was to blame. They had not taken kindly to her plans for going to England. His mother had been quite blunt.

"Benito needs a wife," she had said. "Not some fly-by-night creature who goes shooting off to England at the whim of a relative she has not seen for 17 years. Don't blame Benito if he finds someone else while you are away. Plenty of the village girls would give their right arm to have your opportunity with him."

There had been more in this vein, and Samantha had left, knowing that it was very unlikely that she would ever go back. That was partly why she felt so scared. She had burned her boats. The villa had been rented by a young couple from Ravenna, and Matilde had gone there to live with her sister. At the moment she felt in transit. She had nothing left for her in Italy and ahead? Who knows!

She was roused from her reverie by Patrick Mallory. He offered her another cigarette and then said,

"You were very thoughtful, just then."

Samantha smiled rather wistfully, Patrick thought.

"Yes." She smiled. "Have you finished your work?"

Patrick shrugged. "I don't suppose I shall ever be finished," he replied enigmatically.

Samantha digested this and then said, "How much longer now? Before we land I mean."

Patrick glanced at his watch. "Only about a quarter of an hour. Is someone meeting you?"

"Yes. My grandmother."

"I see. And are you going directly to Wiltshire?"

Samantha shook her head. "I'm not sure. My grandmother is staying at the Savoy at the moment, so I don't really know what her plans are."

"Is she indeed?" Patrick was impressed. This rather shabby little creature did not look the type to stay at the Savoy, but of course, appearances could be deceptive. "I hope you find London to your liking."

"Do you like it?"

Patrick raised his dark eyebrows. "It's a place to work. I prefer somewhere quieter when I have the time."

Samantha frowned. "Oh dear. I hope I shall like it."

"Is it so important?"

She clasped her fingers together. "Terribly."

Patrick was more intrigued than ever, but he contained his natural curiosity. As a writer he was interested in people and he found Samantha a fascinating subject. She was so unspoiled. It would be a pity if the life she was so ardently hoping to enjoy changed her natural acceptance of life.

It was one-thirty, London time, when the aircraft touched down. Samantha lifted the light, poplin coat that she had had lying beside her and walked shakily toward the exit of the airplane. Patrick followed her and was amused at her expression as she felt the cold inrush of air from outside the aircraft. It was a chill September day, and Samantha hurriedly pulled on the light coat, shivering.

Patrick smiled down at her. He made her feel quite small, for he was easily six feet in height and had broad shoulders tapering to narrow hips. "This is quite mild, you know," he remarked mockingly. "Wait until you experience an English winter!"

She looked up at him. He seemed to be her last contact with the familiar things of her life. "My father always said it was a cold climate," she murmured in a small voice.

Patrick felt something stir inside him. He could not understand what it was, but he suddenly felt responsible for this girl. She was not small or clinging, and yet she had a wistful air. He thought she would soon lose that gentleness in the bustle of this busy city.

They descended the stairs and crossed the space to the airport buildings. Formalities separated them, and Samantha was so busy with the unfamiliar procedure that she found she had lost sight of Patrick Mallory. Immediately her heart began to thump wildly, and a kind of panic invaded her system.

She looked around, searching for a sight of him, when a hand touched her shoulder. She swung around to find him behind her. She ran her tongue over her lips and sighed in relief.

"I . . . I . . . thought you'd gone," she whispered, thankfully.

Patrick looked solemnly down at her. "And?"

Samantha bit her lip. It seemed silly now that he was here again. "N . . . nothing," she said awkwardly.

"Come on. Let's go," he said softly and taking a grip on her arm above the elbow he urged her through the reception lounge and out into the hallway.

A man in a chauffeur's uniform was eyeing them strangely and Patrick said, "Do you suppose he is some connection of your grandmother's?"

Samantha shook her head. "I've no idea. Should I ask him?"

Patrick grinned. "Hardly. Look, wait here. I'll ask him."

"Your carriage awaits," he remarked dryly. "Are you all right?"

"Oh yes, thank you." Samantha looked up at him. "Thanks for all your kindness."

"Think nothing of it," he remarked easily. "You'll be fine. And don't worry. Everything is for the best, you know."

Samantha managed a small smile and then turned and followed the chauffeur across the wide hall and out into the sweep of road behind it. A massive old Rolls-Royce awaited her. She was assisted into the back by the man who had introduced himself as Barnes, her grandmother's chauffeur and handyman.

The chauffeur went to stow her case in the trunk and Samantha sat in the back feeling isolated. She would have liked to have asked to go in the front, but Barnes looked such a disciplinarian that she decided against it.

She was disappointed that her grandmother herself had not come to meet her. She had needed that feeling of being wanted. Now all she had was a lonely seat in the back of the huge car and only Barnes for company.

In front of the Rolls, a low blue Jaguar awaited its occupants. As Samantha waited she saw Patrick Mallory emerge from the building with a small, slim blonde clinging to his arm.

The woman was one of the most beautiful Samantha had ever seen. Her hair was short and curly, and she was wearing a wonderful leopardskin coat. She was small and daintily proportioned. Everything Samantha was not.

Samantha felt her heart turn over sickeningly and wished Barnes had driven directly away. This was something she had expected, and yet now she was seeing it she felt a pang. Of course it was to be expected. He was a sophisticated man of the world. There would be plenty of women in his life.

Barnes got into the driving seat at that moment, and the car was set in motion. Samantha leaned back against the upholstery and sighed. She had no wish for Patrick Mallory to see her. Besides, he would probably have forgotten all about her by now.

Barnes lowered the glass partition and said, "Did you have a good journey, miss?"

Samantha roused herself to reply. "Yes, thank you."

Barnes concentrated on his driving and, for the life of her, Samantha could think of nothing further to say. He would probably think her stupid, but it had been an exhausting day, both physically and mentally. She needed time to collect her thoughts.

They drove swiftly and silently after that. Samantha had a confused impression of a gray, overcast sky and tall, sometimes grimy buildings. There seemed to be hundreds of cars, all going the same way. The sense of urgency communicated itself to her. There was a hustle and bustle she had never experienced before. Yet, for all that, she found that now she was actually in England she did not feel a stranger. After all, this was her homeland. She was English, even if she felt and spoke more like an Italian.

When the car turned into the courtyard of the Savoy Hotel, her underlying fears crystallized into actual terror, she could hardly force herself to get out when the door was opened for her.

The chauffeur followed her inside and spoke to the receptionist.

"Will you see that Miss Kingsley is taken up to Lady Davenport's suite?" he said smoothly, and Samantha's eyes widened. *Lady Davenport*. Her grandmother was *Lady Davenport*. Her stomach turned over. This was even more frightening than she had expected.

One of the bellboys took her suitcase and asked her to follow him into the elevator. Speculative eyes watched their progress. Samantha was made uncomfortably aware of the limitations of her poplin coat and flat-heeled shoes.

The elevator halted on the second floor, and she was conducted down the corridor to her grandmother's suite. The bellboy waited until a maid opened the door, and then Samantha was left in her charge.

By this time Samantha felt like a parcel that was being handed around from person to person and felt sure her grandmother must be quite an awe-inspiring person.

However, she seemed to have reached her destination, for the maid took her coat and said kindly, "Sit down, won't you? Lady Davenport will be with you directly."

"Thank you." Samantha complied with her instructions and seated herself on a low couch. The maid left the room, apparently to inform Samantha's grandmother that she had arrived. Samantha looked around her with interest. It was a massive room, beautifully decorated, with a thick carpet fitting into alcoves. The furniture was expensive and luxurious. The room was heated and wonderfully warm after the cold air outside the hotel.

A few moments later a door opened, and Samantha rose tremblingly to her feet as an old lady came into the room, leaning heavily on a stick. She was very small and fragile looking, with gray hair and a lined face. She was dressed fashionably in a mauve silk two-piece and her eyes, which were a definite blue, twinkled a little.

Samantha stood before her, wondering what she should do or say. Lady Davenport smiled. She had a warm, gentle face, and Samantha felt some of her trepidation leave her.

"My dear," she said softly. "Samantha, you're here!"

"Grandmother," said Samantha slowly. "It sounds so strange, I never knew I had any other relatives."

The old lady made her way across the room until she was close to her and then said, "You may kiss me, my dear."

Samantha bent and touched the soft cheek with her lips. Then the tension she had been feeling snapped, and she put her arms around the old lady and hugged her, feeling tears coming to her eyes.

"There, that's better," said Lady Davenport, her own eyes a little moist. "Shall we sit down, my dear? My legs are not what they used to be."

They sat, side by side, on the couch. Lady Davenport looked at her thoughtfully.

"You're much more like John than Barbara," she said, at last. "Oh, Samantha, you've no idea how I've longed to see you."

"But why . . . ?" Samantha halted.

"Let's have some tea first, and then we can talk."

The maid brought in a tea trolley, and for a while the

clatter of the cups and the tinkle of spoons on bone china silenced both of them. They each seemed to be studying the other. Both had so much lost time to make up.

When they were finished, her grandmother offered Samantha a cigarette from an onyx cigarette box. After it had been lit, Lady Davenport lay back against the damask upholstery.

"And now! You feel refreshed?" she asked.

"Yes, thank you," said Samantha, smiling.

"I was sorry I could not meet you at the airport, but I have a little trouble with my old body. My doctor insists that I rest after lunch every afternoon. Did Barnes find you satisfactorily?"

Samantha smiled reminiscently. She was thinking again of Patrick Mallory. "Yes, he found me," she replied quietly.

"Good." Lady Davenport bit her lip. She was obviously finding it difficult to begin. At least, Samantha thought, she was no ogre. She was a sweet old lady, but where was her mother?

"I suppose I must begin by telling you about my daughter," said Lady Davenport slowly.

"My mother?"

"Yes, your mother. Barbara." Lady Davenport sighed. "Your mother is my only child. She was born when both Harold and I were past believing we would ever have any children. I'm telling you this because Barbara was always spoiled, and I'm afraid Harold and I were to blame. She grew up accepting everything as her right. When she met your father she wanted him, too. She was 18 at the time and far too young really to know her own mind. They were married two months later. It was just after the war as you know. Barbara was an up-and-coming actress in a London repertory company, mainly entertaining the troops and going on tours. You know the sort of thing. Your father was in the Navy and looked very handsome in his uniform. Lots of couples were getting married at that time, and Barbara was so sure she was in love. Naturally, soon after the wedding John went back to sea, and they saw little of one another for some time. By then you were a little over a year old." She paused and twisted a ring around her finger.

"When Barbara found she was pregnant in the first place she was furious. She had to leave her career and come home to Wiltshire. After you were born, she could not wait to get back again." She frowned. "Oh, my dear, I'm sorry about this, but you were an encumbrance."

Samantha felt the tears come to her eyes, but she forced them back. "Go on," she said, longing to know and yet dreading the inevitable.

"When John was demobbed, he came home to find you living at Daven with me, and a nursemaid, of course, and Barbara back in London. I did not mind. You were a delightful child, and I thought the world of you. Unfortunately, John did not see it that way. He thought, and naturally so, that Barbara herself ought to have care of you. Before the war he had been a schoolmaster. He had seen the result of this kind of upbringing on a child whose parents were separated. At any rate, he took you away from me and got an apartment in London. For a while the old attachment seemed to work on Barbara. John was so masterful and still a very handsome man. For a while she did only bit-parts and looked after you and lived with John.

"I was sure everything was going to turn out all right, now that John was home again. Barbara seemed happy enough. . . . " She sighed. "I'm sorry, my dear, but I must be frank. John found out she was having an affair with a film producer. He had probably promised her all sorts of parts in his films. He was a married man too." Samantha felt dreadful. Was this the mother she had so urgently wanted to meet?

"By then, you were nearly four. John refused to speak to Barbara after that. Without our knowledge, he sold everything he could lay his hands on, drew his savings out of the bank and disappeared, with you. Later his lawyers contacted us from Milan to say that he was living in Italy and did not wish to let us know his address.

"Barbara seemed not to care, and without her support there was little I could do. She began getting bigger and better parts. As the years went by she became famous. Now she is able to choose her own parts. She is a remarkably good actress, whatever her faults may be."

"I can't believe it," exclaimed Samantha. "How could she do such a thing?"

"Barbara is wilful and single-minded. She always intended being a success and has succeeded in her object. She likes men. There have always been men hanging around her. She's like a child in many ways. She does not want to grow any older. The eternal Peter Pan."

"But she must be quite old. I'm 21."

"Yes. She will be 40 next birthday. But I defy anyone to guess her age correctly."

"You still love her?" exclaimed Samantha, in wonderment.

"Yes, I love her. She will always be my daughter, my only child. My husband died when she was only seven years old. I blame myself really for the bad things she has done in her life. I was too easy with her. I denied her nothing."

Samantha shook her head. "And . . . and did they divorce?"

"Oh yes, there was a divorce. John's lawyers had plenty of evidence. It was undefended and hushed-up. It was all over before she became famous. No one today knows anything about it."

"Oh!" Samantha was silent for a moment. "I'm afraid I've never heard of her. What does she call herself. Barbara Davenport or Barbara Kingsley?"

"Neither. Her full name is Barbara Harriet Davenport. Her stage name is simply Barbara Harriet."

"I still don't know anything about her."

"No. Well, you have lived a rather sheltered life, haven't you. I doubt very much whether John would have risked your seeing much about her."

Samantha felt herself shiver involuntarily. Altogether she did not much like the sound of her mother. She supposed it was natural that her grandmother should be able to see Barbara's side of things, but from her own point of view Barbara had behaved abominably. She seemed to care for no one but herself.

"So she has never married again?" she asked now.

Lady Davenport shook her head. "No. She has never felt the desire to tie herself completely to one man. At least, she hadn't. I think she is feeling a little differently now. There is a man. . . . Well! That can wait." Lady Davenport frowned, and then straightened her back. Taking one of Samantha's hands she said, "My dear, there is something more you have to know."

"What else?" she asked cautiously.

"Well, as I have told you, Barbara is a very famous actress today."

"Yes."

"And as such, she must appear to her public as a young and attractive woman."

Samantha frowned. As yet she could not see what all this was leading up to.

"Go on," she said. "Has she refused to acknowledge me as her daughter?"

Lady Davenport smiled wryly. "You are becoming wary, Samantha. I'm sorry about that." She sighed. "No. She wants to acknowledge you as her daughter."

Samantha swallowed. "So where is the problem?"

"You are 21 my dear. That is the problem. Everyone would know, if she told them your age, that she was much older than she has claimed to be."

"Oh lord!"

"Samantha dear, try to understand. Barbara looks very young. At most she could be taken for 32 or three."

"So! What is your suggestion, or should I say Barbara's suggestion?"

"She wants you to agree to being a teenager. . . . "

"A teenager!"

"Yes. Shall we say . . . 16 or 17?"

"Absolutely not!" Samantha was indignant. "How can you ask me to do such a thing, after the way she has acted all these years? No, I refuse."

Lady Davenport sighed heavily and sank back against the couch.

"I told her you would not agree," she said weakly.

"Well, why should I? I owe her nothing. Nothing at all."

"I agree with you, my dear, but those are the only terms on which she would agree to me having you here. You haven't heard everything yet. You are to live with me at Daven. You will only be in town very occasionally. It is only on these occasions when you need to be a teenager. Back home in Daven you will be able to be yourself. It is a quiet village. No one need know your true identity, if you don't wish it so." She took Samantha's hand again. "Is this so much to ask, for myself? It was my idea that you come here. For so long I have wanted to know you. I'm a lonely, old woman, Samantha. It would give me great pleasure to have you with me. Is there so much for you in Italy, that you cannot give it up?"

Her words brought Samantha up with a start. It seemed that there was very little for her in Italy. She had never expected such a thing as this to happen. She had been quite confident that her family would like her, she realized now. Her only concern had been that she might not like them. Now, knowing the devious methods her mother had used all these years, it was not really surprising that such a proposition should be put to her.

She looked gently at her grandmother. Whatever Lady Davenport's faults had been, she was a sweet and loving old lady. Samantha felt sure she could grow to love her too. They had so much to say to one another, she half wished she had no mother to complicate matters. She could have lived with her grandmother quite happily without any qualms.

"And if I still refuse?" she asked. "Why couldn't we live in Daven and forget about Barbara's schemes?"

"Harold, my husband, left the house at Daven to Barbara. He left sufficient for me to live on comfortably, but the bulk of the estate is your mother's. She could make my life a misery, if I disobeyed her wishes. As I've said, Barbara is a very single-minded person. If she is not crossed, she is charming enough. I'm too old now to start crossing swords with her, I'm afraid, and she knows it."

Samantha was genuinely shocked. "Why, that's terrible!" she exclaimed, a feeling of protectiveness toward her grandmother sweeping over her.

"Yes, well, I've told you the situation. That's how it is."

"But why, if she doesn't want to have a daughter of 21, why does she want to acknowledge me as her daughter, at all? Surely I could be a distant cousin, or a close friend . . . anything."

Lady Davenport shrugged. "That is Barbara's problem, not mine. I only know that she wants you . . . but as a teenager. Now, are you agreeable or not?"

Samantha rose to her feet, feeling slightly nauseated about the whole affair. The problem was really quite a simple one. Either she agreed to Barbara's schemes or she could pack her bags, metaphorically, and go.

She felt that, were she better acquainted with this country, that was exactly what she would do. But in her case, Italy was more welcoming.

Then there was the problem of what she could do. She was more than ever convinced that marriage to Benito was not the answer. He attracted her physically, but possibly only because they had been brought up in such close contact with each other.

And finally there was her grandmother. Try as she might, she could not rid herself of the feeling that she was needed here. Lady Davenport was very old. Might it not be kinder to her to agree to Barbara's plans, and then later, when Lady Davenport could not be hurt, explode her plans in her face?

Had she the right to leave her only relatives, however tardy they had been in the past? She was needed now, albeit cunningly. Since her father died, no one had needed her.

She turned back to her grandmother, sitting hopefully watching her.

"You are young" said the older woman quietly. "Couldn't you afford a few months, a couple of years at most, out of your life?"

"I feel like a publicity gimmick," said Samantha at last. "If I agree, do you think I could look 16?"

Lady Davenport smiled. "Easily. At the moment you look little older, Samantha; your life has been calm, untroubled. Your face shows none of the stresses and strains evident in the faces of some young people. Teenagers today are a provocative bunch at best; you might even find you enjoy it. I promise you, you will not find life dull."

Samantha wondered what her father would think of her if he knew. After all, it was he who had virtually sent her back to her mother. She guaranteed he would never have agreed to anything of this kind. Subterfuge was abhorrent to him. And yet, her mind argued, had he not practised a certain kind of subterfuge himself, allowing her to believe her mother was dead when actually she was very much alive?

"All right," she said at last, "I'll agree. At least for now. I won't guarantee my actions until I try out this masquerade."

"Oh, my dear. I'm so glad, and so grateful. You've made me so happy." There were tears in Lady Davenport's eyes. Samantha felt glad she was able to make at least one person happy.

"And now," said Lady Davenport, "we can get down to details."

"What details?" Samantha was puzzled.

"Well, I'm afraid that Barbara has already given it out that she contracted a secret marriage, years ago, when she was 17. You were the outcome, and your existence was kept a secret so that you might grow up without the usual hoo-ha attached to children of famous people."

"Wait a minute." Samantha frowned and stared at her grandmother. "How could she give that out? She didn't know that I was going to agree."

Lady Davenport looked uncomfortable. "My dear Samantha, Barbara banked on your acceptance of her plans. No one ever refuses her anything."

Samantha shook her head. "Oh, God, so I'm just another pawn in her game."

"Don't, please, Samantha. Let it go. You won't regret it, I promise you."

Samantha was not convinced, but as the whole plan had her head in a spin already, she could not voice her objections. She felt heartily sick of the whole business and wondered what was behind it all. There must be something. From what she had gathered about her mother, Barbara never did anything without good reason.

"And when do we leave for Daven?" she asked now.

Lady Davenport looked thoughtful. "Well, not for a week or so, I'm afraid. Barbara wants to have time to introduce you to her friends. She has planned parties, dinners, etc. When we leave, you will not need to worry about coming back to London for some time."

"I see." Samantha bit her lip. Dinners, parties! And she was to be 16 again!

CHAPTER THREE

The next morning Samantha awoke in an enormous bed, with soft sheets and a creamy silk bedspread. For a moment she lay wondering where on earth she was. Then it all came flooding back to her. She was in England. She was staying in London with her grandmother, and today she was to meet her mother for the first time in 17 years.

At the remembrance of this, she turned over and buried her face in the pillow. It was no more palatable today than it had been yesterday.

Last evening she had spent alone with her grandmother. Lady Davenport had said that Barbara had an important engagement and would not be around to greet her daughter until the following day. To Samantha, tensed and curious, this in itself was revelation. Had her mother no interest in her at all?

This morning Lady Davenport had said they were to go shopping. Samantha had to be fitted out with suitable clothes, and her hair must be shampooed and set. To Samantha, who had never seen the inside of an expensive London salon, this was to be a terrifying experience. She had asked why she could not set her own hair as she had always done in the past.

Lady Davenport had smiled. "My dear, you must get used to the idea that you are now a comparatively wealthy young woman. As such you do not 'do' your own hair. You have it shampooed and styled regularly at a salon. You must never be seen looking disheveled or untidy."

Samantha had still thought it was an unnecessary expense, but had refrained from making any further comment.

Now she slid eagerly out of bed, glancing at her watch as she did so. It was already eight-thirty, and back home she would have been up and breakfasted by now. "Back home!" She sighed. Would she ever get used to calling London her home? It seemed unlikely at that moment.

She was bathed and dressed by the time the maid knocked and brought in her breakfast tray.

"Oh, miss, you're up!"

"Yes." Samantha looked anxious. "Does it matter?"

The maid smiled. "Bless you, no, miss. But I was surprised, that was all, I thought you would have been tired after your journey yesterday."

"Oh, I'm all right. This looks an enormous breakfast."

"Why, it's only cereal, bacon and eggs and toast!"

Samantha smiled. "I've been used to managing on rolls and butter. My ... my ... I've been told about this English meal." She had nearly said her father, and she swallowed hard.

"Well, you do your best," said the maid easily, not noticing any change in Samantha's expression. "Lady Davenport said to tell you that she will be up and ready for your shopping expedition at ten o'clock."

"All right. Thank you."

Samantha ate her breakfast on the table below the window in her room and looked out on the busy thoroughfare below. Already the surrounding buildings were giving her a closed-in feeling. She would be glad to get out and see something of the town.

She dressed in the dress she had worn the previous day. Compared to her grandmother's expensive clothes her things looked shabby, and her underwear had seen better days. It was embarrassing to feel like this. But she had naturally assumed that her grandmother would be very much the same as herself. She had certainly never dreamed of having a member of the nobility for a relative.

Lady Davenport emerged promptly at ten in a town suit of light, Donegal tweed. She looked small and elegant. Samantha envied her her assurance. Beside her she felt gauche and bulky, and much too tall.

"Do not slouch, my dear," said Lady Davenport, studying her severely. "You are tall, yes, but that is something to be proud of. You will soon be wearing high-heeled shoes that will add a couple of inches to your . . . what . . . five feet five?"

"Five feet six," said Samantha quickly.

"Very well. That will make you five feet eight. If you find yourself with smaller people, do not stoop to their level. Let them look up at you. You have the advantage. Use it. Don't pander to yourself."

"Yes, Grandmother," said Samantha dutifully and smiled. "You're quite severe when you're roused, aren't you?"

Lady Davenport chuckled. "It depends who I am with. Now, shall we go? Barnes is waiting for us."

The Rolls awaited them in the courtyard. Samantha helped Lady Davenport in, before following her. Barnes shut the door and then walked around and climbed in himself. Now that they were on their way, Samantha felt excited and stared unblinkingly out of the car window, not wanting to miss a thing.

They crossed part of London, Barnes, on Lady Davenport's instructions, driving around Piccadilly Circus so that Samantha could see the statue of Eros.

"You will have to go sightseeing properly one day,"

said Lady Davenport. "Do you know much about London?"

"Well, I know about the Tower of London and Buckingham Palace," Samantha replied. "My father told me quite a lot really. He loved the museums and the art galleries. He once took me to Rome to see the Colosseum and the Vatican."

Her grandmother smiled. "And did you like these sort of things too? The art treasures of the world?"

"Oh, yes. I would like to explore London, really. There are heaps of things I want to do."

"Well, you will have plenty of time."

"I know, and for that I'm grateful. At the bottom of me, I've always longed to see this country. Only circumstances sometimes contrive to make you believe differently."

In a store that Lady Davenport patronized, off Bond Street, Samantha really found what it was to have money. From the outside the store had looked ordinary enough, but inside a whole new world opened out for her.

It was called, simply, "Hélène," but it was one of the most expensive dress establishments in London. Inside the door, Samantha's feet sank into the pale, mauve carpet, while the hangings and furniture deepened to a richer purple. They were shown into a salon and were attended by Hélène herself, who turned out to be an elderly Frenchwoman, with hands almost crippled by arthritis.

Samantha was stripped down to her undies and measured and weighed up intently. Unused to undressing in front of anybody, she felt embarrassed, stupid, and wished it would soon be over.

"Your granddaughter has a wonderful figure," remarked Hélène. "Tall and slim, but rounded. There are no angular bones to disguise."

Lady Davenport looked pleased. "Exactly what I myself thought," she said, smiling. "I think she will dress well, don't you?"

"But of course. Our new designs, slanted toward the younger woman, will suit her admirably. She is 16, you say?"

"That's right." Lady Davenport did not sound at all perturbed, but Samantha felt herself blush scarlet.

They spent over two hours in Hélène's establishemnt. By the time they emerged, Samantha felt as though she would never feel modest again. Gone were her old cotton underclothes, and in their place were the sheerest nylon garments she had ever imagined.

Suits, dresses, cocktail numbers suitable for a teenager; one long evening dress for special occasions, skirts, slacks, blouses, sweaters. Samantha's head spun from the enormous amount of clothes that had been hastily slipped over her head and examined critically. Then there were tights; dozens of pairs, and shoes to match every outfit. She could not help feeling thrilled to own so many beautiful things and to know she need not make any more clothes for herself, at least for years.

Barnes had packed piles of boxes into the trunk of the Rolls, but what were left were to be delivered later in the day. Samantha was now dressed in an orange knit suit, with a pleated skirt and a loose jacket top, that left her throat bare. Her old clothes had been left at the salon, apparently fit only for throwing away. Even her shoes had been replaced by squat-heeled, cream pumps.

The difference in her appearance was staggering, and she had stared in amazement at the transformation as it was taking place.

Lady Davenport was assisted into the back of the Rolls. After Samantha had joined her, she said "And now, your hair."

Samantha ran a questing hand over its silky softness. "What do you intend shall be done with my hair?" she asked, reluctantly.

Lady Davenport smiled. "Don't worry, my dear, nothing much. Teenagers these days wear their hair long, but it is a little ragged at the ends. I think Raphael might make it a little more stylish. Bangs, I think. Much deeper than the ones you have at the moment. To draw attention to those beautiful eyes."

Samantha colored again. She was unused to being paid any kind of compliments of this sort.

Raphael's salon was not far away. Lady Davenport left Samantha there, after going in with her and ascertaining that Raphael himself should attend to her, and that he knew exactly what was needed.

While Samantha was under the dryer, she was given a manicure, and her skin was tested with several different creams. Finally she was made up by the skilled assistant. When Lady Davenport arrived to collect her she clapped her hands in delight.

"Marvelous!" she exclaimed. "My dear, you look wonderful."

Samantha was not so confident. She felt awfully like a guinea-pig, but her grandmother was deriving so much enjoyment from the affair that she could not fail to respond.

They returned to the hotel for lunch and had it downstairs in the restaurant. Samantha attracted a great many interested glances from the other diners; Lady Davenport smiled a little wryly now.

"I think perhaps it is just as well that you are supposed to be only 16," she said thoughtfully. "I don't think Barbara had any idea you would turn out to be so lovely. Indeed, you are the perfect mixture of both John and Barbara. You have her looks in many ways, and yet you are much taller than she is. Your eyes are certainly more like John's.''

Samantha looked down at the grilled salmon on her plate.

"How much longer will it be before I meet my mother?'' she asked.

Lady Davenport glanced at her watch. "Barbara said she would arrive some time this afternoon. She rarely gets up before lunch time when she is not working, and at the moment she is between plays. She has just completed a six months' run on Broadway and is resting for a month or so, before going into rehearsal for a new play, due to open in the West End.''

"I see.'' Samantha nodded. "And when does she expect to start exhibiting me in public?''

"Please, my dear, don't look at it like that. I'm not sure, anyway. It may be this evening, but I doubt it. Tomorrow evening she is giving a cocktail party at her apartment, before dinner, so possibly that is when you are to make your debut.''

"Why don't you stay at her apartment, while you are in London?''

"Well, Barbara's pace of life would not suit me, my dear. She may keep late mornings, but they only match her late nights. She is rarely in bed before the cock crows, as the saying goes.''

Samantha, who had been used to both retiring and rising early, wondered whether she herself would be expected to keep these hours.

After lunch was over, they went up to Lady Davenport's suite. The boxes from Hélène's had all been unpacked by the maid, whose name, Samantha had found, was Emily. She had been with Lady Davenport for over

20 years. Samantha wondered what her reaction to all this deception was. She must have known Samantha as a child, too, and would be in no doubt as to her real age.

But Emily kept her own counsel. If this piece of intrigue was to please her mistress, she was not the one to spoil things. She adored Lady Davenport and would do nothing to hurt her.

Lady Davenport retired to her room to rest for an hour and Samantha was left to her own devices. She lit a cigarette and lounged on the couch, reading some magazines that Emily provided for her. She was restless, and could not decide whether she wanted her mother to arrive or not. She felt a faint revulsion toward her already, and she did not wish to feel any worse about it when she met her. She hoped that Barbara had mellowed with age, but from what her grandmother had said, that did not seem likely.

The door behind her opened, and Samantha swung around, expecting to see Emily. Instead she was confronted by a small, exquisitely lovely woman, with short blonde hair and blue eyes. She was dressed in a clinging suit of crimson velvet and looked vividly exotic as she leaned back against the pure whiteness of the door.

Samantha realized this could only be her mother and rose involuntarily to her feet. Later as she came to know Barbara better she realized that Barbara had planned such an entrance as this. She knew perfectly well how outstandingly beautiful she looked against the background of the door. Her daughter was intended to see her this way for the first time. Around her neck was a necklace that sparkled brilliantly, while diamond studs glinted in her ears.

"Well," she drawled slowly. "So you are Samantha!"

Samantha felt herself trembling. The moment had

come and she was practically speechless. "Yes," she managed quiveringly. "And you . . . are my mother."

"Obviously." Barbara straightened and walked negligently across the room. "Well, Mother has certainly worked wonders with you. You look quite . . . attractive."

Samantha felt her body coming back to life. Her mother's half-sardonic remark had brought the resentment she had been feeling back to the surface.

Barbara halted a few feet away from her and said, "You'll forgive me if I don't kiss you, won't you? Kissing women is not a habit I enjoy. Besides, there has been too much between us for too long for there to be any real affection between us now. We couldn't possibly feel as any natural mother and daughter should feel. I'm sure John put paid to any ideas you may have had about me."

"He told me you were dead," said Samantha in a cold, little voice.

Barbara smiled at this. It did not disturb her one iota.

"Did he, indeed? Well, he certainly wasn't taking any chances, was he? Was he afraid the same thing might happen again, I wonder?"

"There was no fear of that," retorted Samantha heatedly.

Barbara smiled again, more broadly. "Oh really! And are you such a woman of the world that you can pass judgment, just like that?"

"I don't know what you mean, but I think you behaved badly." The words were out before Samantha could prevent them.

"Do you, indeed? And have you never been attracted by a man who seemed slightly out of reach?"

"No."

'Of course, you wouldn't have." Barbara's voice was

bored. "But you would hardly find any eligible men in a village in the middle of nowhere."

"We lived in a beautiful village," retorted Samantha angrily. "We were very happy together. I never needed any other man."

"How charming!" Barbara turned away, and as she did so, something about her struck Samantha as being familiar. It was strange, as they could not possibly have met before, and yet there was something about her. . . .

"Well, I suppose Mother has explained the position," said Barbara now. "Are you agreeable?"

"Obviously," returned Samantha. "Or I shouldn't be here should I? Wasn't I to be shipped back where I'd come from, if I refused?"

Barbara laughed softly. "My dear, don't hate me so much. I am your mother after all, and I don't want anyone to think we don't like each other."

Samantha took a cigarette from the box on the low walnut table and lit it abstractedly.

"Do you smoke much?" asked Barbara thoughtfully.

"Why?"

"Well, my dear, you won't be able to smoke in public, will you?"

Samantha frowned. "I don't smoke a lot," she said bluntly. "And I'm seriously considering whether to go through with this."

"I shouldn't change your mind, now, my dear. After all, think of all the money that has already been spent on you. Mother did take you shopping, didn't she? That suit looks like one of Hélène's creations."

Samantha pressed her lips together mutinously. Of course, her mother was right. Lady Davenport deserved some consideration. After all, had it not been for her

Samantha would never have agreed to this in the first place.

"Yes, it is," she said now, staring angrily at the other woman.

"I thought so." Barbara smiled. "Do relax, darling. I haven't committed a murder, you know. John probably lived a much happier life alone than he could ever have done with me. We just didn't mix. Like oil and water."

Samantha thought how hard Barbara was. She was used to people being open and frank about everything. If Barbara believed that, she was practising the art of self-deception. Perhaps she did that all the time. Or had she really no conscience? It seemed this was nearer the truth.

"Now," Barbara lounged onto a low chair, removing her gloves, "I want you to call me Barbara. I'm sure you'll find it much more to your taste, too. You could hardly call me Mother after this, could you?"

"Frankly, no." Samantha felt disgusted.

"Good. What did you call John?"

"John."

Barbara smiled. "How amusing! You must be one of the few children who have called both your parents by their Christian names."

Samantha drew on her cigarette and walked over to the window. Barbara watched her speculatively. Her eyes narrowed. Samantha was really not at all what she had expected. She was much lovelier than she had ever imagined. And her height gave her an added advantage.

Still, reflected Barbara brightly, most men preferred a woman to be small and dainty like herself. Samantha could never bring off the kittenish things she could.

But her hair was a glory of gold and silver. Barbara wished her own hair would stay that way without the innumberable rinses she had to have nowadays, to rid herself of the few gray hairs.

Samantha for her part was wondering how she was going to stand this continual bickering with her mother. It was a kind of polite bickering, that was true, but there was no love lost on either side. To Samantha, who had come to England prepared in part to accept her mother unconditionally, this was doubly unsteadying, and she felt out of her depth.

She could understand slightly that it must be frustrating for Barbara to look so young and yet be verging on 40. Had she been welcomed, as she had expected to be, she might have agreed willingly to this scheme. But after learning about the past history that had led up to her father's exile, she could not help but feel differently. And now, to be confronted by this cold, calculating female, who seemed unable to have any normal parental feelings, the world seemed a very hostile place indeed. She reflected that in 24 hours, she had had her childish dreams burst like balloons before her eyes. Already she felt older, more mature, and certainly more wary.

She was inestimably relieved when, a few moments later, Lady Davenport emerged from her bedroom. She stopped abruptly at the sight of her daughter.

"Barbara!" she exclaimed. "You're much earlier than I expected."

Barbara had crossed to a table on which was a tray containing an assortment of drinks. She was in the process of pouring herself a whisky when her mother came in.

"Yes, I am, aren't I? I couldn't wait any longer to meet my charming daughter."

Samantha turned away at this.

Lady Davenport bit her lip and looked questioningly at them. The atmosphere in the room was not pleasant, and she was wondering what had been said to make Samantha look so weary and dejected.

"Well," she said, "don't you think you have a beautiful daughter?"

Barbara turned around holding her glass negligently. "Yes, indeed. In fact, she's quite a surprise in many ways." She sipped her drink, eyeing her daughter mockingly over the rim of the glass.

"I . . . I think I'll take a shower," said Samantha suddenly. "You don't mind, do you, Grandmother?"

Lady Davenport hid her anxiety. "Of course not, my dear. Go ahead."

"Thank you." Without a backward glance, Samantha left the room and, after the door had closed behind her, Lady Davenport looked at Barbara.

"What have you been saying to upset that child?"

Barbara laughed softly. "Mother, we only met a few minutes ago. What could I say?"

"Knowing you as I do, a few minutes could seem a lifetime," returned Lady Davenport heavily, sinking down onto a chair.

"You're exaggerating as usual," remarked Barbara coolly. "Tell me, did she take much persuading?"

Lady Davenport frowned. "Yes, a great deal of persuading. She is an attractive girl. Would you care to pretend to be a girl again, and waste the fullness of your youth?"

"No," admitted Barbara slowly. Then she reached for a cigarette. "But needs must when the devil drives."

"So long as it's not Barbara Harriet who gets hurt," said her mother bitterly.

"Well, darling, in the long run, if I get hurt, you do too." She smiled again. "I'm rather proud of myself really. This way I'm killing two birds with one stone."

"Must you talk in adages?" asked her mother crossly. "I only hope you're right, though. I dread to think of the publicity if. . . ."

"Relax." Barbara sank onto a low chair. "Everything is going to be fine, you'll see."

Barbara was gone by the time Samantha returned to the lounge and she could not help but feel relieved. With her grandmother she felt at ease, but Barbara caused dissatisfaction and distrust.

Lady Davenport had some news to impart, however. "Barbara is giving her cocktail party tomorrow evening as I intimated to you earlier," she told her granddaughter. "We won't see her this evening. She has another—well, appointment."

"With this man she's involved with?" asked Samantha dryly.

"You could say that, my dear. Now, don't be bitter. We have the evening to ourselves, so I have decided we will get tickets for a play and have an evening on the town. Does that sound appealing?"

Samantha's face changed. "Oh, yes, it sounds wonderful!" she exclaimed. "What are we going to see?"

They eventually decided upon a play that had been running for a couple of months with good reviews. With Lady Davenport's undoubted influence they were able to obtain two seats in the stalls.

Samantha wore one of her new dresses; a long, severely styled caftan, whose stand-up collar gave her a medieval appearance. She left her hair loose, and Lady Davenport loaned her a fur stole to drape over her arms. Then she smiled affectionately at her.

"You look lovely, my dear," she said warmly. "Oh,

Samantha, we are going to have some good times together. Will you find it worthwhile?"

Samantha flushed. "I'm doing this for you," she said softly. "And of course it's worthwhile. Just meeting you has made my life have purpose again."

During the course of the play, Samantha found herself remembering Patrick Mallory. Yesterday, so many things had happened to put any thoughts of him out of her mind. But now here, in the comparative quietness of the theater, she recalled how kind he had been to her. She wondered if she might possibly meet him again, but such an event seemed unlikely. London was such a huge place. Besides, if all went according to plan, she would not be here much longer, but at Daven, with her grandmother.

She sighed and Lady Davenport glanced quickly at her. " Are you bored, Samantha?" she asked, in a low voice.

Samantha smiled. "Of course not. I was thinking, that's all."

"In the middle of the play! That doesn't sound encouraging."

Samantha squeezed her grandmother's arm. "All this is quite new to me," she murmured gently. "Even now, I find it difficult to accept everything that has happened."

Lady Davenport patted her hand. "We have a lot of lost time to make up," she agreed. "But are you really enjoying yourself?"

"Immensely," replied Samantha truthfully, and thereafter concentrated on the actors on the stage and put all thoughts of Patrick Mallory out of her mind.

The evening ended with supper at a small but discreet restaurant. They eventually returned to the hotel at midnight. Lady Davenport was looking a little strained, and Samantha helped her gently along to their suite.

"I think I shall have a little rest in the morning," said

Lady Davenport wearily. "If you want to go out, Samantha, before I'm up, do so, but don't get lost, will you?"

"Of course not, Grandmother. It's been a marvelous evening. Thank you."

Lady Davenport smiled. "It's been marvelous for me, too." She kissed Samantha's cheek. "And now . . . bed! Goodnight, my dear."

"Goodnight. Grandmother."

Samantha went to bed too, but not to sleep. She lay awake for hours, the excitement of the evening having left her mind too active for actual slumber. It was four before she actually slept. When Emily brought her breakfast in at nine o'clock, she felt as though she had not slept at all. Mixed with her thoughts of the new things that had already happened to her was the trepidation she was feeling at the thought of Barbara's party. She wondered who would be there.

She dressed after breakfast in dark blue slacks and a blue Italian overblouse. She tied her hair up in a ponytail and, after inquiring of Emily how her grandmother was feeling this morning, pulled on a short sheepskin jacket and left the hotel.

Outside in the Strand, a cool wind was blowing, but the sun was trying to break through and the air was invigorating. Samantha reveled in the feeling of freedom she was experiencing and buttoning her coat set off to walk in the direction of Trafalgar Square.

It was all enormously exciting, and she could see much more on foot than she had seen from the car. She stood and watched the fountains, smiled at the statues of the lions and continued on toward Admiralty Arch.

The Mall stretched ahead of her. Noticing the park on her left she decided to walk through it toward Buckingham Palace. Although it was still comparatively early, there was an amazing amount of traffic to Samantha's eyes. The peace of the park made her think of the quietness she had know in Perruzio.

She stood for a while on the bridge that spanned the lake in the park and watched the ducks gliding about the smooth surface. Then she continued on toward her goal; the palace and the Victoria Memorial.

Then with a sigh she turned and made her way back down the Mall. Although she had felt tired when she awoke, her tiredness had left her and she felt exhilarated.

She was crossing to the elevator back in the hotel when a voice hailed her. She swung around. It was a man's voice and as far as she knew, she knew no men in England.

A man of medium height and build was coming toward her. His fair hair was tinged with gray in places, and he looked about 40, Samantha thought.

"Yes?" she said curiously. "Can I help you?"

"You are Barbara Harriet's daughter, aren't you?"

"Yes, that's right. But who are you? Why are you speaking to me?"

The man smiled, turning his harsh face into a more human countenace. "My name is Martin Pryor. I'm a . . . friend of your mother's."

"Oh, really. And how did you know I was her daughter?"

"You're rather like her," he replied, and noticed with shrewd eyes the way Samantha looked a little startled at this. "Would you like a drink?"

Samantha looked up at him with surprised eyes. "I'm not 18 yet," she replied smoothly, not quite liking his manner.

The man half smiled at this, and Samantha felt uncomfortable.

"Look," he said, "it's nearly noon, but how about having some coffee in the lounge? I'm sure I could arrange it."

"I'm sure you could," remarked Samantha coldly. "However, I'm not in need of any refreshment at the moment, thank you. If you will excuse me. . . . "

"Hey, wait a minute. I've been waiting here over half an hour to see you."

"Have you?" Samantha frowned. "Did you contact my grandmother to let her know you were here?"

"Actually, no. When I arrived I asked to speak to you and was told you had already left the hotel. I decided to wait."

Samantha looked sceptical. "Well, surely anything you have to say to me you can say right here, in the foyer."

"Okay, okay. Let's sit down."

After they were seated he said, "I suppose I ought to tell you I'm a newspaper reporter."

Samantha stiffened. "Indeed you ought!"

"Don't freeze up on me, honey. I only want a story from you. Like how long have you been living in Italy, and how well do you know your mother. . . . "

Samantha rose to her feet angrily. "I don't intend discussing my private affairs with you or anyone else," she said coldly. "Now you really must excuse me. I have things to do. . . . "

She turned and strode away. Martin Pryor lay back in his seat and watched her with an amused look in his eyes. So that was the 17 year-old daughter; or had Barbara said 16? Either way, she was a very self-possessed teenager. He smiled, rose to his feet, and walked into the bar.

"Good afternoon, Mr. Pryor," said the bartender. "Your usual?"

Martin nodded. "And have one yourself, Harry."

"Thank you, sir. Did you see Miss Kingsley?"

"Yes, I saw her." Martin sipped his drink. "Barbara has certainly produced a beautiful daughter, hasn't she?"

Harry grinned. "If you say so, sir. I must say I've not seen much of her."

"No, you wouldn't have."

Meanwhile, Samantha had reached her grandmother's suite and when she opened the door she found Lady Davenport seated at a bureau, writing a letter.

"Oh!" exclaimed Samantha, as she entered. "Grandmother, do you know a man call Martin Pryor?"

Lady Davenport swung around. Her face was disturbed. "Yes, I know him, child. Why do you ask?"

"Because he's just waylaid me in the foyer and started asking questions about me and Barbara."

"Oh, dear." Lady Davenport frowned. "And what did you say?"

"I refused to answer. I didn't like him at all. He seemed too confident for my liking."

Lady Davenport smiled wryly. "Martin Pryor is very confident. He is also one of the most influential men in Fleet Street. He writes a gossip column for the *Ambassador*. The whole paper is slanted at famous people. His column is the Mecca for anyone wishing to make their name known to the public. Everybody reads it." She turned back to the bureau so that Samantha could not see her face. "It is especially enlightening about any scandal in the film or theater world."

"I see. I suppose he is one of the people who would make a feast about Barbara having a 21-year-old daughter."

"Precisely." Lady Davenport turned back to her granddaughter. "You did perfectly right, downstairs. Never say anything unless you have been briefed first.

Statements made to the press can be misconstrued and quoted out of context."

"All right, Grandmother, I understand. Have you had lunch, yet?"

"No. We'll have it up here. Ask Emily to see about it, will you, dear?"

Samantha nodded and Lady Davenport smiled. "Are you looking forward to the party this evening?"

"Not particularly. It's quite frightening."

"Nonsense. Remember, however you may feel, people will want to meet you simply because you *are* Barbara Harriet's daughter."

"I know. That's what bothers me." Samantha managed a smile. "Anyway, it will soon be over."

"It will only be the start," replied her grandmother, sighing. "You are in for quite a lot of publicity, one way and another."

It had been arranged that Barnes should take Samantha to her mother's apartment that evening at about five-thirty. The party was due to begin at six, but Barbara wanted Samantha there in good time to show her the apartment and to give her her instructions. Samantha felt like a maid who had been hired for the evening to act as Barbara's daughter, and who had to learn her lines beforehand.

She was dressed this evening in an apricot knit that hung straight to her hips, only to fall into a thousand tiny pleats from there to the hem.

She wore a brown corded velvet coat over her dress and dark brown shoes. Her hair was left loose, and she looked young and lovely.

Barnes had become more relaxed with her now, and they chatted quite amiably on the way over to Barbara's apartment in Belgravia, thus relieving Samantha of her tension.

Barnes left her in the entrance hall. He told her to take the elevator up to the third floor and walk along the corridor until she reached number 33.

"Miss Harriet will be waiting for you," he said. "Good luck!"

"Thank you," Samantha smiled. "I'm going to need it!"

The elevator was a contraption that Samantha had never used alone. It was rather terrifying to press the button and then leave herself solely in the hands of the mechanism. However, the elevator was well adjusted. In no time at all it had stopped at the third floor, and the doors slid back to allow her to get out.

The corridor was carpeted, and she walked slowly along it, looking at the numbers on the doors. Thirty-one, 32, 33. She was there!

She tapped lightly and then discovered that there was a bell. She pressed the bell just as the door was opened by a uniformed maid.

"Oh, I'm sorry," she said confusedly, feeling that his was a very poor beginning. "This is Miss . . . Harriet's apartment, is it not?"

"That's right," said the maid uncompromisingly. "You must be Miss Kingsley."

"That's right. My mother is expecting me."

"I know. Come in!"

Samantha stepped inside onto a black pile carpet. It was so stark that she stared in amazement and had to force her eyes away as the maid urged her into the room.

The room itself was like an advertisement for modern living. The astonishing black carpet was relieved by pure white, velvet curtains hanging across the massive window that ran the length of one wall. The furniture was futuristic and uncomfortable-looking; white leather armchairs and an ebony cocktail bar, basket-weave loungers in black and white stripes, and low coffee tables designed in a kind of stonework into the shape of huge hands.

Samantha felt as though she had accidentally stepped into a store window, so bare of human habitation was the room. Its white walls were relieved only by carved plaques in a variety of colors. It was a long, high-ceilinged room and several doors opened from it, although all were closed at the moment. At the opposite end of the room to the window were French doors that apparently led out onto a balcony. After the maid had departed to advise her mother of her arrival, Samantha gravitated in this direction and tentatively tried the handle.

The French door opened, and she emerged onto a wide balcony that overlooked Belgrave Square. She was breathing in the refreshing air, when a voice behind her made her jump.

"Admiring my view?"

Samantha swung around. Barbara was standing in the doorway, dressed this evening in a black cocktail dress of heavy silk that clung to every lissom curve of her small body. Samantha stared at her. She looked so lovely. How could she be all bad?

"Yes," she said at last. "I gather I'm the first to arrive."

"Yes. Come along to my bedroom and take off your coat. Clyde can brush your hair, too. It's a little windswept."

"Clyde? Was she the . . . person . . . who let me in?"

"Yes. Did she antagonize you?"

"A little."

Barbara smiled. "Clyde's all right, when you get to know her. Come along."

Barbara's bedroom was a pleasant oasis after the desert of the lounge. Here the carpet was palest pink while the drapes were rose-colored brocade. The feminine divan was upholstered in cream and rose-colored satin. Samantha felt this room was less of a showpiece.

Clyde combed her hair and put a little spray on it to keep it in place, while Barbara complimented her on her choice of dress.

"It's the perfect thing for a party of this kind," she approved. "Naturally, my dear, you won't be able to drink any alcohol in public, so shall we have a small cocktail now before the others arrive?"

"Thank you," Samantha nodded.

"Good. Clyde, bring the drinks in here for us, will you? We don't want anyone to arrive unexpectedly and find my teenage daughter indulging in secret drinking."

After Clyde had gone Barbara continued, "And this way, if anyone does arrive we shall both emerge from the bedroom together. Everyone will think we have been exchanging girlish confidences."

While Barbara and Samantha were in the bedroom, Clyde set out the cocktail glasses and provided trays. On a low table she produced for the purpose were set sandwiches, cocktail sausages on sticks, canapés, small slices of toast spread with caviare; everything anyone could wish for at an intimate affair of this kind. The drinks were many and plentiful. By the time the doorbell rang to admit Barbara's first guests, everything was in order.

The first people to arrive were Annabel and Charles Barratt. Charles was Barbara's agent and his wife was much younger than he was. Annabel chatted away quite charmingly to Samantha, asking about the sheltered life she had led in Italy, and how she was enjoying London.

Samantha had been briefed that she was supposed to

have been brought up by an elderly nursemaid in Italy, educated at a convent (which was in fact true), and had been brought into society now at her own suggestion. Barbara was supposed to have been keen on a finishing school, but she, Samantha, had persuaded her mother to allow her to come to London.

After the first few explanations, Samantha found herself slipping easily into the part and presumed it must be her maternal forebears. After all, Barbara must have received her talent from somewhere.

There were several couples at the party who were associated with the theater, and after the early introductions Samantha lost track of names. Two young men of about 18 arrived about half an hour after the party had begun. Barbara brought them straight over to her daughter.

"Samantha," she said, "I want you to meet two friends of mine. Ken Madison and Andrew Frazer."

Samantha smiled and shook hands with the two young men. Then someone else arrived and Barbara excused herself to greet the newcomers.

Andrew Frazer was by far the most attractive of the two. As Ken Madison seemed more interested in speaking to Barbara's agent than he did to Samantha, Andrew was left alone with her.

"Would you like another?" asked Andrew, indicating the glass of pineapple juice in her hand. "What is that? Gin?"

"You must be joking," exclaimed Samantha, laughing. "My mother would never allow me to drink spirits . . . at my age," she added mischievously.

"Of course," Andrew grinned. "Sorry."

He helped himself to a cocktail, and then taking her arm drew her over to a low couch, and they sat down together.

"Now," he said, "tell me all about yourself."

Samantha smiled "My life hasn't been very interesting. Tell me about you. What do you do?"

"Well!" Andrew leaned his head back against the leather upholstery. "Ken and I do a double act together, actually. If it wasn't for the fact that you have lived in Italy all these years, I venture to say you would have heard of us. We call ourselves the Kendrews. Get it?"

"Yes. Very good. Do you sing?"

Andrew chuckled. "Yes. With guitars, the lot. It's the current craze here, or didn't you know that either?"

"Oh, yes. I know that there are a lot of young men about with . . . er . . . groups. Isn't that right?"

"Yes. Well, we're a group of two. We have a drummer, Ricky Land, but he's a bit of a drag. . . . "

"Drag?"

"You know . . . er. . . . Slow-witted. Right?"

Samantha found she was enjoying herself. "And don't they all wear their hair long? Yours is . . . well . . . pretty long, but not as long as some I've seen in the papers since I've been here."

"Yes, well, to be quite honest, my mother doesn't like it much." He said this last rather mournfully.

They talked for a while about different things. Samantha repeated her story again and watched her mother out of the corner of her eye. She seemed very popular. She wondred how many of these people liked her for herself, or for the fact that she was a famous actress and consequently influential.

Barbara kept coming over to her daughter, behaving, Samantha thought dryly, like the affectionate guardian she was supposed to be. She was clearly pleased that Samantha had found someone to entertain her and thus did not need her mother's constant attention.

Samantha felt quite cynical herself, thinking like this. How greatly her world had changed since the flight over from Milan. She had been virtually a child then, she realized that now. After having to accept the unpleasant things she had had to accept since her arrival, she felt differently.

She also knew that as the hours went by the circumstances of her acceptance in London mattered less to her. She felt that what must be, must be. She might as well enjoy it as cause herself a lot of unnecessary heart-searching.

The room was now full of people, and Samantha wondered whether her mother was going to introduce her to the man who her grandmother had said was becoming the big thing in her life. She had been introduced to several unattached males, but Barbara had made no particular significance between them. Surely, with her volatile nature, she would if there was someone special.

The doorbell pealed again, and Barbara went to answer it. Samantha looked up idly, expecting to see yet another couple of visitors, who were this time apparently very late. She could hear her mother's vivacious chatter and saw that the visitor was standing with his back to her, removing his coat.

Her mother looked completely unlike herself. She was so *animated*. Up till now, Samantha had thought nothing could disturb her.

The man turned around and Samantha felt all the color drain out of her cheeks. Andrew, who had been looking at her and talking about the current crazes in dancing, frowned.

"Say, is anything wrong?" he asked anxiously. He looked up. "You look awful pale."

Samantha shook her head. "I'm fine."

"Well, that's my uncle who has just arrived, if you're interested."

"Is it really?" Samantha forced herself to remain calm. "Who . . . who is he?"

"Gosh, you have been out of touch. He's Patrick Mallory. He's a playwright, a very famous playwright. He's the one who is writing this new play for your mother."

So that was what he wrote!

"Oh!" Samantha swallowed hard.

"Do you want to meet him? I guess Barbara will be bringing him over. He and Barbara are like that." He crossed two fingers together.

"Oh!" Samantha felt stupid, but just for the moment she was speechless.

Her eyes were drawn irresistibly toward him. He was smiling his lazy smile and talking easily to her mother and to a few of the guests who had joined them. Samantha thought he looked wonderful. He was dressed in a charcoal gray lounge suit. His dark hair was combed immaculately, and his tanned complexion was arresting among so many lighter-skinned men.

She felt her stomach lurch sickeningly. Could this be the man her mother intended to marry? Surely not! And yet she was sure he was. Barbara had certainly never acted so warmly toward anyone else. In fact, Samantha thought dryly, Barbara was acting completely out of the character that her daughter had built up about her. She was flushed, charming, and utterly feminine. Gone was the cold creature of a couple of hours ago. Here was a young and alluring woman, doing her best to enslave a man.

Then on the heels of these speculations she remembered her own position. She was supposed to be 16 years old. She would be introduced to him as Barbara's 16-year-old daughter! All her old inhibitions returned. If only Barbara had accepted her as she was!

And yet why should she be so concerned about her age? Whatever age she might be, no man would give her a second glance while Barbara was around. And Barbara intended to be around. Of that she had no doubt. There was possession in every line of her mother's body as she clung shamelessly to Patrick Mallory's arm.

She sipped her drink and tried to readjust herself. Andrew had resumed his conversation. She presumed the color must have returned to her cheeks. She still felt shocked, but the first onslaught had passed.

"Tell me," she said, unable to leave it alone, "how ... how old is your uncle? I gather he's not married."

"No, he's not married. Patrick's about 37, I think. Why?" He laughed. "Do you find him attractive? Most women do. You're a little young, perhaps. Maybe you haven't reached that stage yet."

Samantha managed a smile. "Oh, I wouldn't say that. I think he is very attractive."

Andrew grinned, more broadly. "How about me? Do you think you could stand an evening out with me? On your own, of course."

Samantha relaxed a little. "Oh, I should think so. Are you inviting me?"

"Of course. Just name the day."

They were laughing together when something else struck Samantha. Now she knew why her mother had looked so familiar to her. She had been the woman with Patrick Mallory, the day they arrived from Milan!

That hurt. It really did. That Barbara should come to the airport to meet Patrick Mallory, probably knowing they would arrive on the same plane. Yet she had made no attempt to locate her own daughter. How inhuman had she become?

Samantha swallowed hard again. She had to keep calm, at all costs. To give way to the feeling of hysteria she was feeling would be foolish and futile. Barbara was too sure of herself to care what happened to her daughter. She was cold; completely devoid of any normal feeling.

That Patrick Mallory should be famous was really no surprise. It explained the way he had half-expected her to recognize his name; the reason for the stewardess's fawning attitude.

But that Barbara should know him so well! That was the horrible part. He must be the reason why Samantha had seen so little of Barbara since her arrival. They must have spent hours together. Did he love her? Did he make love to her?

She nearly jumped out of her skin when Barbara's voice spoke close to her ear.

"Darling, I want you to meet a very, very dear friend of mine."

Samantha rose to her feet. She felt as though she towered over Barbara's trim daintiness. Patrick Mallory was still so much taller than she was that she did not feel the disadvantage. She looked up at him defiantly and heard his sharp intake of breath.

For only a moment, his eyes mirrored his disbelief, and then Barbara took over, saying, "Patrick darling, this is Samantha. I would say little Samantha, but as you can see, she is certainly not that."

Samantha was flushed, and, at her mother's words, her color deepened.

Patrick Mallory, however, had regained his composure and replied, "She's quite a beauty, Barbara. You've been hiding your light under a bushel, all these years."

Barbara had not expected quite this sort of remark from him, but she quelled her own irritation and continued, "It's been so wonderful, having her back again."

"I'm sure."

Samantha's fingers clenched around her wine glass. His sarcasm was so evident she was sure that Barbara must hear it. But Barbara seemed not at all perturbed and went on, "Is Andrew looking after you, darling?"

Andrew grinned. "Sure thing. Hi, Pat."

Patrick smiled warmly at his nephew, and Samantha was sure these two were good friends.

"I'm enjoying it," said Samantha awkwardly, feeling that she should say something. "I hear you're a playwright, Mr. Mallory."

Patrick ran a tongue over his lips. "Yes, that's right. What . . . er . . . what do you do?"

"Why, nothing," exclaimed Barbara playfully. "Darling, you mustn't tease Samantha. She's going to live with Mother at Daven. Won't that be nice for her?"

Patrick shrugged his broad shoulders. "If Samantha is your daughter, Barbara, I should have thought she would have preferred the bright lights to stagnation in the country," he said.

Barbara pressed her lips together for a moment, and Samantha could sense her impatience. "Darling, you must remember, Samantha is only a child."

"Teenagers are grown up these days," retaliated Andrew. "I'm only 18 myself, and if I can vote I'm not just out of the kindergarten."

Barbara's lips thinned. "You all seem determined to decide Samantha's future for her," she said with assumed tolerance. "Perhaps you should ask her where she wants to live."

Patrick looked at Samantha. "Perhaps we should. How about it, Samantha? Does the quiet life appeal to you?"

Samantha hesitated only momentarily, conscious of Barbara's narrowed, wry gaze upon her. "I . . . er . . . I've never been to Daven . . . at least, not for years," she hurried on. "My grandmother says there are horses there, and I'll have them to exercise . . . and the countryside to explore. . . . "

Patrick's eyes were sardonic. "But will you like it?"

"Of course she will!" Barbara's temper was obviously fraying. "Come along, Patrick, there are several people I want you to meet. . . . "

Patrick allowed himself to be drawn away, but Samantha was aware of speculation in his baffled gaze. If only she had not met him on the plane, how much less complicated things would be. Barbara was not going to be at all pleased if it came out. How would she explain to Patrick that she had met him from the same plane as her daughter arrived on without bothering to contact her own flesh and blood?

And then there was the problem of Samantha's father being killed only recently. How would Patrick reconcile that with the information that Barbara had given that her husband had died years ago?

Talk about a tangled web, she thought wearily. This was going to be a veritable ravel.

And last but not least, there was her age. She might have looked younger on the plane, but what about the sherry he had ordered for her? Thank goodness, she had ordered tomato juice to begin with. At least that was non-alcoholic.

Andrew could not understand her agitation. She stared continually at her drink and seemed to be paying little attention to him.

"I'm sorry," she said at last. "I was thinking. It was very rude of me. Do go on."

They talked for a while and then wandered out onto the terrace. Although the doors had been opened, no one else had braved the cold evening air. Samantha found it invigorating after the heat of the room. She was still wondering how she was going to tell Barbara that she had spoken to Patrick Mallory before tonight. They had both acted as though they had never seen one another before, but that was as much his fault as hers. He could easily have said that they had met on the plane. Why hadn't he?

Andrew leaned on the balcony rail.

"It's not a bad evening," he said. "What are you dong after this affair?"

"I hadn't really thought about it," replied Samantha truthfully. "Why? Have you any suggestions?" Just at the moment the idea of escaping from all these people seemed a pleasant one.

"Yes. Ken and I are free this evening. How about spending the evening with me?"

"Well, I would have to ask my mother," said Samantha slowly. "And there's my grandmother to consider."

Andrew grinned. "Don't I rate as more interesting company than her?"

Samantha smiled. It was nice to relax and forget her troubles. Andrew was so uncomplicated. He accepted her for what she was, without requiring any explanations.

"All right," she said. "I'll call Grandmother later, after I've asked Barbara."

"Barbara?"

Samantha shrugged. It sounded so cold somehow. Not at all like when she had called her father John.

"I mean Mother, of course. She asked me to call her

that. Everyone does, and it sounds so ancient for her to be called 'Mother.' She looks so young.''

Andrew accepted this. He was used to the casual modes of address used among theater people.

''Good. That's settled, then. I know a disco club where the music is really way out. Can you dance?''

Samantha laughed. ''No, but I can learn. I'm sure you'll make a marvelous tutor.''

''And just what is he going to teach you?'' asked a lazy voice.

Samantha swung around. Patrick Mallory was leaning indolently against the frame of the French doors. He held a drink in one hand, and his expression was sardonic.

Samantha glanced at Andrew. ''We . . . er . . . we're going out together this evening. Andrew is going to teach me all the new dances.''

''Is he?'' Patrick straightened up. ''I thought you might like to have dinner with your mother and me. After all, we ought to get to know one another better, don't you think?''

Samantha felt the hot blood surge to her cheeks. She had no desire to spend an evening with them! Heavens, the pitfalls that lay ahead were already too close for her liking. She had no desire to expedite confession.

''What! Spend an evening playing gooseberry? Not likely, Patrick. She's coming out with me. Besides, haven't you anything more exciting in mind, for your own amusement, of course?''

Patrick was not disturbed. He smiled his attractive smile and said, ''What do you know about my amusements?''

Andrew chuckled. ''Not as much as I'd like, believe me.''

At that moment Barbara emerged from the French

doors. "Patrick, what are you doing out here? I've been looking for you? Oh!" She saw her daughter and Andrew. "Am I interrupting something? You all look rather conspiratorial!" Her smile was a little fixed.

Andrew glanced wryly at his uncle, and Patrick said, "I've been suggesting that Samantha might like to have dinner with us this evening, but Andrew had other ideas."

"I should think so, too," exclaimed Barbara, with scarcely concealed intolerance. "Darling, Samantha has to make her own friends. She's too old to want to come along with us!"

"She just might enjoy it," remarked Patrick sardonically. "To listen to you, Barbara, banishing your daughter to Daven as soon as she gets home, refusing to invite her to join us for dinner, anyone would think you didn't want her around!"

Barbara's face suffused with color, and Andrew turned away to hide his amusement. Of all the men Barbara had known, only Patrick had ever treated her like this.

"That's not the point!" Barbara rushed into explanations. "The places we go would bore Samantha. Andrew's much more likely to know what she would enjoy."

Patrick raised his eyebrows, and Andrew's eyes twinkled. "Get the message, Pat?" he asked mockingly, and Patrick grinned.

"I think so," he murmured, his eyes flickering over Samantha with disturbing intensity. Turning, he took Barbara's arm, guiding her back into the lounge. He said something to her in an undertone, but they could not hear her reply. However, Samantha was sure it would be something vitriolic. Barbara had never looked more furious, and it was evidently a novel experience for her to have someone else in the limelight while she was around.

The cocktail party ended soon after seven. As Patrick Mallory had departed at least half an hour before that, Samantha was quite glad to leave with Andrew at his suggestion. She told her mother she was leaving, but from Barbara's smoldering eyes she gathered she was not in her good books. In fact, Samantha was sure that, had they been left alone together, Barbara would have vented the whole force of her temper on her. As it was, she was forced to appear at least outwardly composed. Only Samantha saw the fury behind her eyes.

Andrew took her to a coffee bar in Chelsea. As he had said, the music was outrageous, with a rock group hammering out tune after tune. The young members of the club spent their time gyrating madly to one dance after another. To Samantha, it was all astonishingly new, and she could not believe that she was expected to get up and dance in like manner.

When Andrew was recognized, a guitar was thrust into his hands, and he was expected to sing. Samantha was amazed, but when he began to sing the type of folk songs that he and Ken Madison had made famous, she was absolutely enthralled. When he returned to their table she caught his hand enthusiastically.

"You were great!" she exclaimed.

Andrew grinned. "Come on," he said. "Let's dance. And this time we'll dance together. Right?"

"Right."

She enjoyed dancing with Andrew. He held her close against his thin frame, and his boyish charm enveloped her. She found herself thinking as a 16-year-old might think and was amused at the swift transition in herself. A couple of hours ago with Patrick Mallory, she had wanted to be a woman of his set like her mother. Now with Andrew she was reverting to a teenage outlook.

At the memory of Patrick Mallory, her new-found contentment partially evaporated. Try as she might she could not rid herself of the magnetic attraction he held for her. Andrew was nice; he was amusing and obviously not without experience with girls. But Patrick Mallory was a different matter. He, too, would be experienced, and from the rather jaded expression he sometimes wore, his experiences had not all been pleasant ones. But the charm of his dark good looks and lazy eyes, combined with his cynical outlook were a challenge to any woman. Samantha felt all woman in his presence.

"What are you giggling about?"

"Oh, nothing, really," she said, sighing. "Patrick Mallory is a very attractive man, isn't he?"

"Oh lord!" Andrew stared at her. "He's far too old for you."

"I know, I know. I was simply being objective."

"Were you?" He sounded sceptical.

"Are you an only child?"

"Me?" he exclaimed. "Heavens no. I have two brothers and three sisters, inclusive of one set of twins. Why?"

"Is Patrick your mother's brother?"

"Yes. My mother's name is Virginia, but she usually gets Gina."

"Are you the eldest?"

"Yes, we're quarter Italian. Pat and my mother are half Italian."

"That explains your uncle's dark complexion."

"Oh, yes. My mother's fairer. She takes after their father. He was partly Irish, by the way. Quite a complicated heritage, isn't it?"

"And you? With a name like Frazer, is your father a Scot?"

"Partly." Andrew laughed. "What's it like to be a thoroughbred?"

Samantha laughed. It was a pleasant uncomplicated evening, and she enjoyed herself. However, she was exhausted when she reached the hotel. To her surprise her grandmother was waiting up for her. When she had called earlier to ask her permission to go out with Andrew her grandmother had said she would have an early night.

Now she said, "Did you have a good time, my dear? You look radiant. You must have enjoyed yourself."

"I have," exclaimed Samantha. "But it's very tiring."

Lady Davenport smiled. "I expect it is."

"Why did you wait up?" Samantha was curious. "Weren't you tired after all?"

Lady Davenport bit her lip. "I wanted to speak to you, Samantha. Barbara . . . Barbara came around here this evening. She was in a temper."

Samantha stopped what she was doing. "Why did she come?"

"She was apparently furious because her current . . . admirer . . . had let her down."

"Patrick Mallory?" Samantha stared at her grandmother.

"You know him?"

"I met him this evening. Didn't she tell you?"

"Well, yes, actually, she did. Darling, did you say anything to generate such emotion? She was in a flaming temper. She said that you made her look a fool."

Samantha's eyes widened. "For heaven's sake! She made herself look a fool. Doesn't she have any pride?"

"It's been a new experience for her, to find a man who is not immediately enslaved by her," replied Lady Davenport. "Patrick Mallory seems to be playing the game rather coolly."

"He would," murmured Samantha under her breath, unaware that for all her grandmother's worried words, she herself had felt a surge of relief . . . or something akin to it . . . that her mother had not been able to spend the evening with Patrick Mallory.

"Well, anyway, Samantha, do be careful what you do in your mother's presence. I don't want you to be hurt, and Barbara can be a tigress when she is crossed."

"But I don't see that I did anything," exclaimed her granddaughter. "I've just spent the evening with Andrew Frazer. He's apparently Patrick Mallory's nephew. What was wrong in that?"

"Nothing. I understand the cocktail party caused the disturbance. She seemed to think you were laughing at her. Were you?"

Samantha sighed. "Not really. Oh, Grandmother, if you could have seen the way she tries to possess that man! He simply didn't seem to like it. It was her own fault if he chose to spend his evening elsewhere. She tries to dominate him. I don't think any woman could dominate Patrick Mallory."

"Evidently not. All right, Samantha."

Samantha hesitated a moment. Should she tell her grandmother about her meeting Patrick Mallory on the plane? She supposed she ought to, but she could not find words to begin something like that tonight. She was too tired. Too weary of all the intrigue, secrecy, and hateful deception.

"Do you mind if I go to bed now?" she asked quietly.

Lady Davenport smiled and shook her head. "No, dear. Of course not. I'm sorry I had to spoil your evening by this conversation."

"You haven't," said Samantha gently, bending to kiss her grandmother's soft cheek. "Goodnight, darling, and don't worry. I think I've grown up enormously since our first interview. I'm confident everything is going to turn out for the best."

Her grandmother pressed her hand. "You're a great comfort to me, Samantha. I'm glad your father decided that you ought to come here."

Samantha chuckled. "So am I! It's proving quite an experience, one way and another."

CHAPTER FOUR

Lady Davenport went out the following morning quite early. She told Samantha she was going to see her lawyer, and Samantha was left to her own devices. She felt sure that Barbara would appear before the morning was over, demanding an explanation of some kind. She decided to go out instead and postpone the row that would surely be coming.

She dressed in green slacks, a red bulky sweater, and slipped on a hip-length llama coat that was soft, warm, and casual. She was about to leave the suite when the telephone rang.

Shouting to Emily that she would answer it, she lifted the receiver.

"Lady Davenport's suite," she said. "Can I help you?"

"Indeed you can."

Samantha felt her heart turn a somersault. It was Patrick Mallory's voice. It was unmistakeable, so deep and warm and lazy.

"Oh, good morning, Mr. Mallory," she said unsteadily. "Do you want my mother? I'm afraid she's not here."

Patrick interrupted her. "No. It's you I want to speak to. Didn't you expect it?"

Last night she had, but this morning she had almost forgotten in the hurried avoidance of her mother.

"I expect so," she replied with a sigh. "I suppose you want an explanation. I don't really know where to begin. . . . "

"No, I should imagine it would be a difficult subject to broach. Look, I don't want to hear any confidences over the telephone. I want to see you."

Samantha subsided onto a low chair. "Oh, do you?"

"Yes. Now. Immediately. What are your plans for today?"

"Well . . . er . . . Andrew said he would call. I don't know what my grandmother is doing. She has gone to see her lawyer this morning."

"Good. That means you're free."

"I suppose I am. Why? Are you coming around here?"

"Oh no." She heard him laugh softly. "I imagine Barbara will be appearing there some time today. I have no desire to have our conversation broken by the advent of your dear mother."

"Well, what do you want me to do?" Samantha felt disturbed. She was not even sure she ought to see Patrick Mallory at all, but how was she to refuse?

"I really don't know whether I should discuss anything with you, without my mother's consent . . . " she continued slowly.

"If you don't discuss this with me, I myself will have a few choice words with your mother," retorted Patrick, in a voice that was quite cool now and curtly demanding.

Samantha had every belief that he would do just that thing. Her nerves were straining already. She was being placed in an intolerable position. The fact that he was creating that position did nothing to endear him to her. She was feeling quite angry herself now, and she said, "All right, Mr. Mallory. As you seem to be holding all the cards, what do you suggest?"

"That's better. Relax, Samantha. I'm not going to eat you, you know, even if you would prove to be a delectable dish. I want you to come to my house."

"Your house!" Samantha was staggered. "You have a house in London."

"Obviously," he returned dryly. "The address is 34 High Tower Road. It's off Great Portland Street, do you think you can find it?"

Samantha bit her lip until it bled. "I should imagine a taxi driver might know where that was," she remarked dryly, and he laughed.

"Oh, Samantha, you have changed. A week ago, you wouldn't have known how to get a taxi."

"People change," she replied tartly.

"Yes, they do." He seemed to wait for her to reply, and when she did not do so, he continued, "All right, I'll expect you in a short while."

"Yes, Mr. Mallory," she said quietly and hung up.

The commissionaire obtained a taxi for her, and soon she was on her way. She was quite calm, although the butterflies in her stomach were not to be denied. If she gave way to panic she would be lost. She had to conduct this interview in a manner that Barbara would approve of. She did not want to appease Barbara, but her grandmother deserved her consideration. Patrick Mallory must be made to see that she was not to be intimidated.

High Tower Road turned out to be a row of impressive houses with basements and at least three stories with tiny attic rooms peeping out of the roofs. She had to admit it was an attractive area, and she speculated on the price of the houses. Several thousands, she presumed. How nice it was to be affluent!

Number 34 had a white door and a brass knocker. She paid and dismissed the taxi driver before climbing the three stone steps. She lifted the knocker, let it fall, and then waited, nervously now, hands in the pockets of her coat.

It was quite a mild day, but Samantha was still not used to the sudden change of climate and consequently still felt cold. She supposed she was lucky she had not developed a chill or influenza, considering the weather, after her life in Italy.

The door opened, and an elderly woman stood there. She was dressed in black and was wearing a checked apron. so Samantha supposed she must be his housekeeper.

"I . . . er . . . I've come to see Mr. Mallory. He is expecting me," she said.

The woman smiled warmly. "Oh yes, you must be Miss Kingsley. Come along in, miss. I'll show you to his study. He's waiting for you."

The central heating of the house was a pleasant change after the cool air outside. Samantha loosened her coat, looking about her with interest.

The hall was paneled in a dark oak wood, and the carpet underfoot was a dark red. A high window above the door let in plenty of light so that the hall was not dull, but merely subdued and restful. Several doors opened from the hall, while a corridor seemed to lead along to the kitchen quarters.

A wide staircase led to the upper floors, several paintings mounted with the paneling. Paintings of men and women, dressed in the garb of days gone by. Darkly handsome men with black eyebrows that somehow resembled Patrick Mallory; pale waxen-cheeked women, with children gathered about their feet.

"This way, miss," said the housekeeper, bringing her back to earth.

Samantha smiled and followed the woman across to a door at the far side of the hall, below the curve of the stairs.

The woman knocked, and at the sound of a low, "Come in," she opened the door.

"Miss Kingsley, sir," she said and ushered Samantha into the room, going out herself and closing the door behind her.

Samantha felt like a wrongdoer up before the judge, but she straightened her back and walked decorously into the room.

It was a very attractive room. After the stark modernity of her mother's apartment, she had expected something in like manner of Patrick's house, but she could not have been more mistaken.

This room, like the hall, was paneled, but there were cases of books lining the walls. It struck her as being more in the nature of a library than a study.

The room was dominated by a massive mahogany desk, that stood square in the center of the russet and green carpet. Heavy curtains of a golden-colored velvet hung at the tall windows, while the seating arrangements comprised deep, leather armchairs with green, upholstered backs that looked well-used and superbly comfortable.

It was a warm, light, reassuring room. Only the typewriter that stood on the desk lifted one into the twentieth century. No telephone was here to disturb anyone who happened to be working. Samantha could imagine Patrick engrossed in his work, to the exclusion of everything else. Everything he did he appeared to do with a single-minded approach, like this summons to her to appear before him at once.

Patrick rose from behind the desk to greet her, his tall, broad-shouldered body seeming to minimize the generous proportions of the room. He was dressed this morning in tight-fitting dark slacks and a light wool shirt of royal blue, open at the neck, revealing the darkness of the hairs upon his tanned chest. Every part of him seemed to be darkly tanned, and Samantha presumed he must have spent the whole of his holiday, for she presumed he must have been in Italy on holiday, soaking up the sun. He was so attractive to her that she found herself blushing for no apparent reason and was immediately put at a disadvantage.

"Hello," he said, his eyes appraising. "How are you this morning?"

Samantha toyed with the buttons of her coat. "I'm fine, thank you."

"Take off your coat," he advised easily. "It's warm in here. You can, you know. I won't frighten you so much that you have to make a hasty departure."

Samantha sighed and slipped off the coat, allowing him to take it and put it over a chair.

"That's better," he said. "Sit down. Would you like a cigarette? Mrs. Chesterton will bring us some coffee in a short while."

"Thank you." Samantha had taken the cigarette before she thought about her actions, and she glanced up at him to see whether he had been expecting any reaction from her. He merely smiled his lazy smile. Samantha sighed and took a long draw on her cigarette savoring the relaxation it engendered.

Patrick reseated himself, only this time it was in the opposite armchair to hers, so that his eyes were continually upon her. He had the longest eyelashes of any man she had ever seen. At times when his lashes veiled his eyes, she was sure he was studying her through them, without her knowledge. His presence disturbed her more than she liked to admit, and deep in her stomach she felt the beginnings of the fear she was later to realize. She was beginning to like him too much! Much too much, and like was such an insipid word to apply to a man like Patrick Mallory. She was sure a woman would either love or hate him. Last night Barbara had been an example of that fact. She had hated him, for the indifference he had shown her. This morning, when Samantha had the telephone call from him she had hated him too, for forcing her hand.

Now her feelings had changed. In his presence, with his attention directed at her, she felt entirely different. His charm worked with practically anyone, she realized that now. She was no more likely to remain immune than anyone else. It was terrible to feel this way, particularly as she knew he was simply baiting her by making her come here and that her mother had much more chance of appealing to him in this than she had herself.

Everything about him seemed to mock and taunt her, and she moved restlessly, saying "Can't we get this over with? I'm sure you're simply longing to make me squirm."

"Now why should you imagine that?" he asked mockingly. "Samantha, honey, we were friends on the aircraft. Or so I thought. How was I to know you would appear as the daughter of the woman I . . . ?" he halted.

"Go on. You what?"

Patrick smiled. "Later. First of all, I want to know why Barbara is spreading the rumor that you've been living in Italy with a nursemaid, when actually you've been living with your father? And another thing, if John Kingsley was your father, why does Barbara say he died years ago?"

Samantha ran a tongue over her dry lips. "Well, my parents were divorced. That's the truth of the matter. Oh, Mr. Mallory, Barbara doesn't want any adverse publicity from this. Just imagine what would happen if it was discovered that my parents were divorced and that I had been living with my father all these years . . . "

"Yes." Patrick exhaled a cloud of smoke from his cigarette slowly. "So. That is the reason for all this intrigue?"

"I suppose so."

Patrick frowned. "That still leaves something else you said."

Samantha sought about in her mind, trying to remember what had passed between them.

"What was it?" she asked in rather a small voice.

"You said, if I remember correctly, that you had never been in England since you were four years old. You also said that your father preferred not to do so. Now I can understand that your father might find another country more to his liking after his unfortunate experiences here, but what puzzles me is how often have you seen Barbara during these past years? It can't have been very frequently with all her commitments."

"No, not very frequently," replied Samantha, wishing she didn't have to lie to him.

"And Barbara treats you like a long-lost daughter." He smiled sardonically. "My God, what an actress she is! No wonder she doesn't want this broadcast. I can imagine Martin Pryor making a feast out of it all."

"Martin Pryor!" Samantha's eyes widened. "Do you know him?"

"Everyone knows Martin Pryor," remarked Patrick dryly. "For their sins."

"I see. He contacted me one day. He started asking me questions about my life in Italy."

"Did he? I wonder why? Probably pure curiosity."

"Well, it doesn't matter now, does it?" she asked, sighing. "You know now, so soon everyone will."

Patrick frowned. "Indeed. And who is going to tell them?"

Samantha flushed. "Well, I thought—"

"Did you?" Patrick raised his dark eyebrows. "Then you thought wrong. I have no intention of denouncing Barbara to the world. Why should I? It's not really any concern of mine. If she chooses to keep her marriage secret, I won't care."

Samantha stared at him, a feeling of relief overwhelming her.

"But . . . I thought when you asked me here today—"

"—that I was going to get a certain form of enjoyment out of making you squirm. I know. Well, that was not my intention. I'm a writer, Samantha, and people interest me. I was also curious to know the reason for such subterfuge. It does not really surprise me. Whatever you might have assumed to the contrary, I find Barbara Harriet quite a transparent personality. After all, as I remember, she met me at the airport, the same day and time as you were arriving. That's something else that betrays the sort of woman she is."

Samantha felt somehow dejected. She had thought that Patrick might discover her mother's true feelings in this matter, but to find that he already had made quite a shrewd assessment of her character was disappointing. After all, his assessment of her could not be entirely based on the few facts that had come to light within the last couple of days. From his manner of speaking it would seem that he had already summed Barbara up, long before Samantha appeared on the scene. And in spite of this he apparently still found her very attractive.

"Tell me," she said suddenly, "why didn't you admit you knew me last night?"

Patrick laughed softly. "Oh God, if I'd done that, your

life would have been hell on earth! Particularly in these circumstances. As it is, I don't think Barbara is particularly pleased with you for all the attention you received last night. After all, 16-year-old daughters are supposed to stay in the background. You really are 16, I suppose. Or is that another fallacy?"

Samantha hesitated. It would be so easy to admit to her real age. She was sure he would not tell anyone, but that would age Barbara considerably. Although she was nothing as a mother, Samantha could not betray her so blatantly, whatever her own feelings in the matter.

"It's no fallacy," she said slowly.

Just then Mrs. Chesterton tapped at the door, and a few moments later entered with a tray of coffee and biscuits that she placed on Patrick's desk.

She left the tray and, after she had closed the door, Patrick said, "Will you pour the coffee? Or shall I?"

Samantha rose to her feet, glad of the diversion. "I will," she said and busied herself at the tray.

After she had given him his coffee, she poured a cup for herself, added sugar and cream and then reseated herself, albeit a little nervously.

"Having rid ourselves of that topic, let's talk about something else," he said, smiling lazily.

"Such as what?"

"Well, let me see. How are you liking England, for a start? Did Andrew give you a good time last evening?"

"Oh yes." Samantha was enthusiastic. "He sang, too. He's very good, isn't he?"

Patrick grinned. "If you like that sort of thing."

"I gather you prefer more sophisticated entertainment."

"Well . . . " Patrick looked amused, "I am a little older, you know. Have you been to the ballet yet?"

"No. We went to see a play, Grandmother and I, one evening."

"You must go to the ballet."

"Yes, I think I would like that. I'd also like to see one of your plays," she added a little naïvely.

Patrick looked even more amused. "Would you? Well, I'm afraid you will have to wait until December. The new play opens on December 15 at the Grosvenor Playhouse in the West End. Your mother has the leading role, so I imagine you will come to the first night. That is if you haven't vegetated at Daven by then."

"Oh! Aren't there any of your plays in London at the moment?"

"I'm afraid not. The last one closed about six weeks ago. It's at present touring in the provinces."

Samantha felt disappointed. She had been looking forward to seeing something he had written.

"You will have to contain your curiosity," he remarked dryly. "Tell me about your life in Italy. I'd like to know what you did with yourself."

"Would you?" She looked doubtful. "It was a very simple life really. We lived at the villa. Father worked while I simply spent my time helping him with his correspondence and sometimes helping Matilde with the housework. Nothing to interest you."

"I wouldn't say that," he murmured lazily. "My mother lives in Italy. She has a villa near Lake Como. I spent the last month with her. Don't you miss the climate?"

"I suppose so. Although since I arrived I've been too concerned with . . . other things."

"I can believe that," he said, sarcastically she thought. "And when do you go to Daven?"

"I don't know. In a week or so, I would think. Grandmother doesn't really like the hectic world of London. She says she prefers the peace at Daven."

"Well, surely you could stay on here and live with your mother for a while. After all, she has plenty of room at her apartment."

"I don't think Barbara—I mean—" Samantha halted rather helplessly.

"Maybe not. We'll have to ensure that you enjoy the part of your visit that is left then, won't we?"

"We? I mean you?" Samantha was staggered. "Who do you mean?"

"I mean myself . . . and Barbara."

Samantha felt her heart thumping wildly. To imagine herself spending an evening with Patrick Mallory seemed unlikely. Surely he could not be serious. And even if he was, Barbara would never allow it.

"Wouldn't you like to go out with me?" he asked mockingly. She felt sure he was quite well aware that she would love to do so.

"Well . . . yes, I suppose so. But I don't think my mother would agree."

"Not even if I invited her too?"

"Oh!" Samantha's heart subsided again. Now the idea was not at all appealing. To spend an evening with Patrick Mallory and her mother would be like playing the eternal gooseberry. They were so much older and more sophisticated than herself. Having to behave as a 16-year-old was infinitely worse than being her own age. She would have to drink lemonade or Coca-Cola and only smoke if her mother permitted her to do so.

"I can see the idea doesn't appeal to you," he remarked. She realized he had been studying her expressive face. She felt he could read her thoughts, and she swallowed hard and said, "I don't think either of you would enjoy having me tag along," she said quietly. "Besides, Andrew has promised to call me some time today. He wants to take me out while I'm in London himself."

"I know. He called me this morning before you arrived. He seems quite smitten for once. Only don't take him seriously, will you? Andrew is not recommended for his constancy."

Samantha rose to her feet and replaced her coffee cup on the table.

"Thank you for the coffee, Mr. Mallory," she said stiffly. "And for your understanding. I must go."

He smiled and rose also. He was very close to her, and she could smell the faint, male fragrance about him, mingled with the scent of shaving cream and good tobacco. His nearness disconcerted her, and she felt her heart begin its wild tattoo again. Why did he affect her in this way? Like the heady champagne that she and her grandmother had consumed the other evening at supper.

"Don't go cold on me, Samantha," he said softly.

"I don't understand you," she said uneasily. "I think you're laughing at me."

He smiled, and it was the most attractive smile she had ever seen. There was no mockery in it, merely a warmth and understanding. She moved swiftly away from him.

"I . . . I have to go. Goodby, Mr. Mallory."

"*Au revoir*," he corrected her lightly, and moving quickly himself he opened the door to allow her to precede him into the hall.

Patrick Mallory drove his Aston Martin into the quiet mews yard off Kings Road in Chelsea where his nephew Andrew and Ken Madison shared an apartment. The mews was small, and he had to maneuver the big car expertly to circle the central railings within whose protective spikes a lonely poplar spread its branches, thus giving the mews its name.

The apartments opening onto the mews were quite expensive, for all their diminutiveness, and were in the main occupied by theater people with an occasional artist thrown in for good measure.

Patrick parked the car and slid out, feeling the cool breeze strong upon his bronzed face. Today, dressed in a thigh-length, thick, camel coat, and a dark blue suit, he looked every inch the successful man he was.

He left the car and crossing the yard mounted the outside staircase that led to his nephew's apartment. All the apartments were self-contained, and each had its own entrance.

He had a key to Andrew's, opened the door, and entered without ceremony. The door opened into the lounge, and as it was only ten o'clock in the morning, the lounge was deserted.

He pocketed the key after closing the door behind him and crossed the lounge to the door leading to Andrew's bedroom.

Opening this door, he looked in. Andrew was buried under a mound of blankets and had apparently not heard Patrick's entrance.

Smiling, Patrick crossed to the bed and, bending over his nephew, he said loudly, "Good morning, Drew."

There was a muffled gasp, the covers were bundled over, and Andrew's head appeared.

"Lord!" he exclaimed. "Do you want me to have a heart attack? Coming in here in the middle of the night!"

Patrick straightened up. "I'll have you know it's ten o'clock. It's time you were up and about. It's a beautiful, fresh morning."

Andrew groaned and sat up in the bed, weakly. "And

since when have you known what the weather is like at this hour?"

"Since today," replied Patrick easily. "Come on, I want some coffee. I don't intend making it myself."

"Then why didn't you wake Ken? He's much more likely to appreciate your company than me, at this time in the morning."

Patrick grinned, loosening his coat. "What an uproarious welcome! What time did you get to bed last night?"

"This morning," corrected Andrew, sighing. "About four o'clock. We went to a party. . . . "

"Oh!" Patrick nodded. "Anyway, come on. I'm serious about that coffee."

With a resigned expression on his face, Andrew slid out of bed. He was wearing only pajama bottoms, and he reached for a thick, dressing gown that was draped over the end of the bed.

Patrick walked back into the lounge and from there through to the minute kitchen. He filled the coffee percolator and by the time he returned Andrew was in the lounge searching for a cigarette.

Patrick offered him his case, and then sat down onto an armchair.

"And what's troubling you, so early in the morning?" asked Andrew as he drew deeply on his cigarette.

"There's nothing troubling me, exactly," replied Patrick. "I want to talk to you about Samantha Kingsley."

Andrew stared. "Samantha!" he ran a hand over his ruffled hair. "I haven't seen her since the night of Barbara's cocktail party. That must be about four days ago."

"I know."

"Well! So where do we go from here?"

"Have you tried to see her?"

"Sure. Are you kidding? She's a nice kid. I liked her a lot."

"I thought you did." Patrick frowned.

"Have you seen her since then?"

Patrick's frown deepened. "Not exactly, no."

"Have you seen Barbara?"

Patrick studied the glowing tip of his cigarette. "Well, I've seen her. But I haven't taken her out, if that's what you mean."

Andrew was transparently puzzled. He couldn't understand Patrick's interest in a 16-year-old girl like Samantha. Of course, she was Barbara Harriet's daughter, but of late he had thought Patrick was losing interest in Barbara. Before his holiday he had not gone out of his way to see her. Her pursuit of him was becoming ludicrous in their circles. And Patrick did not like to be pursued. He liked to do the pursuing himself. That was where so many women failed with him.

Patrick, seeing the concern on his nephew's face, smiled suddenly.

"All right, Andrew, don't get worried. I'm not going overboard for a teenager, if that's what you think. I am concerned about Samantha, though."

Andrew heard the percolator and walked into the kitchen to get the coffee. When he returned with the tray, Patrick said, "I met her on the plane coming over."

Andrew's eyes widened. "From Milan?"

"Yes."

"But at the party you never acknowledged that fact." He frowned. "Neither did she, for that matter. Come to think of it, though, when you arrived, she did go rather pale. I wondered why, at the time."

Patrick shrugged. "There were reasons that I don't intend to divulge here; why we preferred to appear strangers."

"But why?" Andrew shook his head as he handed Patrick a mug of steaming liquid.

"As I have already said, that's our affair." Patrick grimaced. "There's no great secret, believe me. It's Samantha's affair, not mine. The reason I came here is because I want you to do something for me."

Andrew looked wary and slowly seated himself on the arm of a low chair. "You surprise me," he said dryly. "I thought you'd come here out of the kindness of your heart!"

Patrick looked amused. Then he said, "When you tried to see Samantha again, what happened?"

"Well, I telephoned, but Barbara answered. She said that Samantha was not feeling too well after the sudden change of climate, and that she had developed a chill."

"When was this?"

"The day after the party, of course. When else?"

Patrick was thoughtful. "I see. And have you called since?"

"Yes. Yesterday. I wanted her to come to this party we were going to last night, but this time Lady Davenport answered. She said that they would be leaving for Daven in a couple of days and that Samantha was too tied up with her mother's plans to see me."

Patrick rose to his feet. When he had seen Barbara, by accident yesterday, at a restaurant they both patronized, she had been gushingly effusive about Samantha. She had said that she was sorry she had not been able to see him, but with Samantha being here she was completely absorbed with being a mother. She had completely ignored the fact that Patrick had made no attempt to see her. Although Patrick did not mind her self-deception he was disturbed about Samantha's part in all this.

He wanted to see Samantha himself. He had something to ask her. But he did not see how he could possibly do so without her mother being present, or alternatively preventing such a meeting altogether. He had been foolish to show his feelings so plainly the night of the party. If he had acted as the dutiful suitor, none of this would have happened.

But his absolute astonishment at seeing the girl he had so strangely been drawn to on the plane had thrown his whole system into turmoil. To spend the rest of the evening alone with *her own mother* had been anathema to him. He had to have time to think. After all, the night of the party he had been told she was only 16.

Now he seemed to be no further forward. He had hoped that Andrew might have had access to Samantha, but it seemed that Barbara intended severing all connections her daughter might have with his family.

And, if she whisked Samantha away to Daven, it would be practically impossible for anyone to see her. Daven was a remote village to begin with. Apart from that, what excuse could he offer as to the reason he wanted to see Samantha?

"Look," he said, turning back to his nephew, "I've had a phone call from your mother this morning. She says that they are holding a barbecue this evening."

Andrew nodded. "I know. I saw Dad in town yesterday. Why?"

"Are you going?"

Andrew shrugged. "I wasn't. But I suppose you have some reason why I should."

Patrick half-smiled. "Well, I wondered whether Barbara might agree to attending such a thing. If so, I could invite both her and Samantha, explaining that you are going and would like Samantha to go, too.''

"And do you think Barbara will agree to that?''

Patrick shrugged. "Well, I like to think I have some influence with Barbara. . . . ''

"That's the understatement of the year!''

" . . . and if I should invite her to go, I doubt whether she would refuse.''

"Agreed.''

"So, if I invite Samantha to go with you, it might come off.''

"I don't understand all this,'' exclaimed Andrew. "I gather it's Samantha you really want to see.''

"Yes.''

"But why?''

Patrick shrugged his broad shoulders. "Are you seriously interested in her?''

"No more than usual. She's a decent kid. I won't hurt her. I'm not inhuman, you know. Who knows, it might come to something yet!''

"I doubt it,'' replied Patrick, frowning. "I . . . I might have other plans for Samantha.''

"But you said . . . I mean . . . she's only 16. . . . ''

"Is she?'' Patrick looked enigmatic. "We'll see. So, anyway, I can count on your assistance?''

"Of course. You could have called to tell me all this. At a more convenient hour.''

"I like to perform my duties early in the morning.'' remarked Patrick, smiling mockingly. "I'll go now, and you can return to your slumbers. I'll call you later in the day with the final arrangements.''

"Do that thing,'' said Andrew dryly, and Patrick finished his coffee and left.

Patrick drove back to his own house. As he had said it

was a beautiful September morning. Apart from the cool breeze it promised to be a really warm day. He left his car outside the front door and let himself into the building. Mrs. Chesterton emerged from the kitchen at his entrance and said hurriedly, "You have a visitor, Mr. Mallory."

For a moment, Patrick wondered whether it might be Samantha, but was swiftly disillusioned.

"It's Miss Harriet, sir. She has been waiting for half an hour."

Patrick raised his eyebrows. "Indeed!" He removed his overcoat. "All right, Mrs. Chesterton, I'll see her."

"Yes, sir." The housekeeper took his coat. "I put her in the morning room."

"Very good." Patrick ran a casual hand over his tie before walking across to the door of the morning room.

When he entered the room he found Barbara impatiently flicking over the pages of the *Tatler*. She looked up at his entrance. Upon seeing him she rose instantly to her feet.

"Darling! I've been waiting ages. Where on earth have you been?"

She crossed the room and bestowed a light, perfumed kiss on his hard cheek before allowing him to speak.

"I've been to see Andrew," replied Patrick, withdrawing himself from her, and walking lazily across to the window. "I'm sorry you've had such a wait. You should have called first to see if I was in."

"Yes, darling, I know," said Barbara, apparently unperturbed by his coolness of manner. "But I wanted to see you. I naturally thought you would scarcely be out of the house before ten. It's not your usual procedure."

Patrick turned and nodded in assent. His displeasure at seeing her had not changed, but if he wanted to get his own way he would have to appear more gracious than he was acting at present.

Smiling his disarming smile, he said, "Forgive me for my abrupt manner, Barbara. I'm absorbed by the new play at the present time. I'm afraid I tend to withdraw into myself for no apparent reason."

Immediately Barbara was all contrition.

"Oh, I'm the one who should apologize," she exclaimed warmly. "Coming here shamelessly like this without invitation, disturbing you."

"Nonsense," said Patrick smoothly. "I'm not working this morning, as you can see. Now. Would you like some coffee?"

"Well, Mrs. Chesterton did offer me some earlier on, and I refused. Yes, I think I would like some."

Patrick went to the door and issued instructions to his housekeeper. Then returning to Barbara he offered her a cigarette.

"Tell me, " he said without preamble, "why have you stopped Samantha from going out with Drew?"

Barbara was taken aback. She applied the tip of her cigarette to the flame of his lighter before replying. It gave her a moment to gather her thoughts.

"Well," she said slowly, "I can't really say that I've actually prevented her from going out with Drew. . . . "

"Haven't you? I understood from him that you told him Samantha had contracted a chill after her arrival in England. You never mentioned that to me when we discussed Samantha yesterday."

"No . . . well . . . actually, it was only a slight cold. I was worried about her, that was all."

"So then you've no actual objection to her friendship with Drew?"

Barbara bit her lip. "No . . . why should I have?"

Patrick half-smiled, rather sardonically. "Why indeed! The reason I am posing these questions is that my sister called me to tell me that she and her husband are having a barbecue this evening. They have invited us to go, you and I that is, and Drew of course. I thought Samantha would like to go as Drew's partner."

Barbara was clearly at a crossroads. Her own natural desire for his company was marred by the invitation to her daughter. She obviously did not like the idea of Samantha going with them. Patrick had a strong suspicion why.

"I . . . I think I ought to discuss this with Samantha," she said, slowly. "She . . . well . . . she may have other plans. She and Mother are leaving for Daven in the morning."

Patrick drew swiftly on his cigarette. He, too, was puzzled. He could not fully understand his own reasons for wanting to protect Samantha. Since he met her on the airplane he had felt a strange responsibility for her. He had known Barbara long enough to know that her acceptance of Samantha as her daughter was not altruistic.

But he could not understand why she had accepted the girl as her daughter at all in the circumstances. There had to be a reason, and he would not rest until he had found out that reason. Was it possibly anything to do with John Kingsley? After all, he had no reason to love Barbara after the way she had treated him.

He realized that she wanted to keep Samantha away from him for a more personal reason, but it was unlike Barbara to be jealous of anybody. Samantha was a lovely girl, of course. If she was already discontented before her daughter had been with her for any length of time, why did she not send her away again? Barbara was a rich woman. She could easily afford to send Samantha back to

Italy, or to some other place, where she need not interfere with her own life. The more he heard about the affair the more concerned he became.

Barbara was such a fiery-tempered creature and unpredictable when crossed. If Samantha was causing any great inconvenience to her mother, there might be drastic repercussions.

"Call her," he said coolly. "Or shall I?"

Barbara rose to her feet again. She had seated herself on a low lounger, but at his words she moved swiftly to the telephone.

"I . . . myself will call her," she said. "I expect she will be out, though. She and Mother were going shopping this morning."

Patrick did not offer any further comment and without looking at him again, Barbara lifted the receiver.

Patrick walked over to the telephone while she was making the call. He had no intention of allowing her to say that Samantha was not at home if she was.

Samantha herself was allowed to answer the phone. In the last few days, someone had always answered the telephone instead of her. As she had no reason to suppose they would lie, she thought that Andrew had not tried to get in touch with her.

Now, hearing her mother's voice, she said, "Yes, it's Samantha here. Do you want Grandmother?"

"No." Barbara ran a tongue over her lips. "Samantha, I'm with Patrick. He has asked me to ask you whether you would like to go to a barbecue tonight at his sister's house. She lives on the coast. Andrew is going and would like you to go as his partner."

Samantha gasped. Although hearing that her mother was with Patrick Mallory had slightly dulled the feeling of well-being it gave her, she nevertheless knew she would go anywhere if he was to be there.

"Thank you," she said formally. "I'd be delighted to accept."

"You have nothing planned with Mother?"

Samantha thought for a moment. "Oh no. She said she was going to have an early night, so that the journey to Daven tomorrow wouldn't tire her."

"I see." Barbara sighed. "Very well then, I'll relay your answer to Mr. Mallory."

"I gather she would like to come," said Patrick dryly, after Barbara had hung up.

"Yes. Thank you for asking us." Barbara resumed her position on the lounger. "Tell me, what do you think of my daughter?"

The question was not the simple one it appeared, but Patrick did not hesitate before answering. To do so would arouse Barbara's suspicions.

"I think she's a very attractive girl," he replied easily. "Not as beautiful as you, Barbara, because your slightness precludes any definite resemblance. I think she must be more like her father."

"Yes, she is. John was tall and well built, too.'

"John . . . Kingsley."

"Yes." Barbara looked swiftly at him, but Patrick looked relaxed and unconcerned. She returned her gaze to the coffee cup in her hand.

"Tell me about your late husband," continued Patrick, interestedly. "What did he do?"

Barbara replaced her cup on the tray and then said, "Well, he was a schoolmaster, actually. He taught here in London."

"I see." Patrick stretched his legs out in front of him, relaxed and lazy in a low chair.

Barbara got up and went over to him, perching on the arm of his chair. She ran a hand down his cheek and bending her head, put her lips to his ear.

"Darling, don't let's talk about John. Let's talk about us."

Patrick looked up at her. She was a very lovely woman. Dressed this morning in a light tweed suit edged with silver mink she was quite devastating. He wondered why her particular charm no longer seemed to work with him. He had known all along the kind of woman she was—self-centered and indulgent—but his own life had not been so blameless that he looked for perfection in others. Barbara had been a pleasure to take around and was quite a stimulating companion. Only now, whenever he was near her, the face of her daughter superimposed itself upon his mind. He found himself wishing it was Samantha who was trying to make love to him.

Not that Samantha had ever shown any tendencies in that direction. On the contrary, she seemed to resent his interference in her affairs and apparently found Andrew more to her liking.

He obviously struck her as being too old and experienced for her. He ought to feel that way himself. He had never been any woman's possession, and he did not want to start now.

Pulling Barbara onto his knee, he put his mouth to hers, allowing her arms to encircle his neck and press him closer. He despised himself for acting this way, but perhaps she might be able to lift the depression that was settling like a monkey on his back.

Barbara was excited and passionate. It was well over a month since Patrick had made love to her, and her senses were aroused to fever pitch.

"Darling," she whispered ecstatically, her lips caressing his ear. "You do care, don't you? I adore you so much. . . . "

Patrick's stomach tautened. He felt nauseated by his own behavior. With a wrench, he rose to his feet, depositing Barbara unceremoniously on the chair.

He ran a hand around the back of his neck and shrugged his shoulders almost imperceptibly. Sighing, he looked down at her flushed face.

"I'm sorry, honey," he muttered. "I know that's inadequate, but this isn't the right time or place . . . for . . . that!"

Barbara swung her legs to the ground and trying to contain her disappointment, rose slowly to her feet.

She looked at him curiously and then reached for her bag.

"What time do you intend picking us up tonight?"

Patrick straightened his back. "Let's see. Would six o'clock suit you? It's quite a run over to Sandwich."

"Yes, that's fine." She looked up at him archly. "We might find this evening is more convenient, mightn't we?"

Patrick allowed his lips to form a smile. "We might," he murmured softly and opened the door for her to leave.

CHAPTER FIVE

Samantha was in a panic. She alternately longed for, or
dreaded, the evening ahead. She and Barbara were barely
civil to one another now. An evening spent in each other's
company would be an ordeal for both of them. Since the
fateful cocktail party, Samantha had spent several hours
in her mother's presence. Barbara had been invited to
open a South London Women's Guild Flower Show and
Fete, which Samantha had had to attend. Similarly, they
had attended a luncheon given by the Theater Organiz-
ers' Association and also visited a hospital in Chelmsford.

Lady Davenport of course did not attend, and the time
they spent alone was a trial and a bore. Barbara had taken
an almost ridiculous dislike to her daughter. While
Samantha did not care much for her mother, she still felt
that she should make the effort. But all her overtures were
in vain. Only Clyde, who went everywhere with Barbara,
knew the real state of affairs.

Lady Davenport consoled her granddaughter as best
she could, and only the thought of Daven in the very near
future had sustained Samantha through the past few days.

The evenings were spent alone with Lady Davenport,
while Barbara went out. Samantha never knew who with.
She supposed it must be Patrick Mallory and tortured
herself with thoughts of them together.

She realized she was deteriorating into wretched misery, but the mental agony of the last few days could not be
denied.

Thus it was that she faced yet another period in Barbara's company. This time she would be forced to watch while Patrick Mallory and her mother behaved in the accepted way of lovers the world over. That night at the cocktail party he had been shocked and angry. Now there was nothing to interfere with his undivided interest in Barbara.

She dressed in slacks and a long red sweater. She rarely wore red, but tonight she felt like being reckless for a change. She no longer had any real desire to stay in London, so she might as well make her final evening memorable.

Lady Davenport was looking tired and wan when Samantha looked into her room to say goodby. Her grandmother had retired early and was in bed when Samantha entered the room.

"You look very young, my dear," she said warmly. "Surely Barbara can have no complaints tonight."

"I hope not." Samantha smiled gently. "Oh, Grandmother, what would I do without you? You make everything seem so much more normal."

"You would manage," replied Lady Davenport. "You're not without charm, you know. Everyone I've met who has spoken to you finds you utterly delightful, so I'm sure you would not have any difficulty."

Samantha chuckled. "I think you must be leaving Barbara out of that list. Anyway, darling, I must go. I have to collect my coat and it's almost six now."

"All right, my dear. Have a good time and don't let my daughter bully you."

"I won't." Samantha bent and kissed her cheek, then withdrew quietly from the room.

She slipped on her llama coat and was examining her face in the mirror when the door opened.

She swung around, surprised, and found herself face to face with Patrick Mallory. He was wearing close-fitting denim slacks, together with a thick green sweater. Over all he wore a short, thick, fur-lined coat. His hair was slightly tousled by the wind. His tawny eyes were lazily amused as he watched her. She felt her heart stand still for a moment, before continuing its mad racing.

"Hi!" he said softly. "Are you ready?"

Samantha pressed a hand to her stomach. "I . . . er . . . yes. Are you alone?"

"For the moment. Drew's waiting downstairs in the car. We have to pick Barbara up yet."

"I see. Well, shall we go?"

"Sure. That's why I'm here."

She flushed. He was mocking her again. Patrick, seeing the hot color stain her cheeks, moved toward her.

"Did you think I was amusing myself at your expense?"

He was close now, only a few inches away from her and doubly dangerous in this sweet and gentle mood.

She moved away quickly, and sweeping her hair back from her face, she said, "I don't care what you do, Mr. Mallory!"

Patrick watched her for a moment and then shrugged his shoulders.

"All right, let's go."

His voice was cool again. Samantha, attuned to his every nuance, felt herself grow cold. Why had she repulsed him like that? He had not tried to be rude to her. His words had been only gently jibing, with a world of warmth behind them. Now she had been rude. He sounded as though he had expected no better of her.

They walked along the corridor to the elevator and on

impulse she slid her arm through his. He looked down at her, his eyes unfathomable.

"I'm sorry," she murmured quietly. "I was bitchy, wasn't I?"

"Hm." His voice was soft again, and his fingers slid down her arm until they curved round hers. His hand was cool and hard. She felt her bones beginning to melt. He drew her close against him for a moment, and then he pushed her gently into the elevator.

Samantha did not know what it all meant. She had wanted to make friends with him. Now this had happened. It was entirely unexpected, and she supposed she was making more of it than necessary. After all, he was only holding her hand. As he thought she was a teenager, he probably saw himself as a father figure. Particularly with Barbara in the background.

When the elevator halted at the ground floor, Samantha released herself and preceded him out of the hotel. A low-slung sports car was waiting for them, and she looked around at Patrick.

"Is this yours?"

"Yes. It's an Aston Martin. Do you like it?"

"Mm, it's fabulous. Where do I sit?"

They had reached the car by this time, and Andrew slid out of the front seat beside the driver's.

"Where would you like to sit?" asked Patrick, smiling slightly. "Beside me?"

"If you want me to." Samantha was unconsciously alluring, and Patrick felt his senses beginning to swim a little.

"You . . . you'd better sit in the back with Drew," he murmured at last. "Barbara will expect to sit in front."

"All right." Samantha shrugged, but she cast a strange look a Patrick before stepping into the car.

When they reached Belgrave Square, Patrick went up to collect Barbara. Samantha and Andrew were left alone in the back of the car.

Andrew slid his arm around her and said, "This is cozy."

Samantha smiled, a little wearily. "Yes, isn't it? How long will they be?"

"Knowing Barbara, I really couldn't say," replied Andrew, grinning. "After all, she may not be ready."

"But Patrick said six o'clock, and it's after that now."

Andrew chuckled. "How refreshing to meet a woman who doesn't know that she should keep a man waiting!"

"But why?"

Andrew looked thoughtful. "Well, let me see . . . a man who has to wait for a woman is made more impatient. Consequently when he sees her, her absence has made his heart grow fonder."

"You're laughing at me!" Samantha was indignant.

"Not really, sweetheart. Anyway, I should think Pat will hurry her up tonight. He doesn't seem as enamored of Barbara as he used to be. He went to Italy for a holiday, but primarily I think to define his feelings for your mother. She's made no secret of her feelings for him; Pat isn't one to rush into anything like marriage without due thought." He laughed. "After all, he hasn't stayed a bachelor all these years and remained a celibate. He used to be quite wild in his youth. Now he doesn't have to make any effort at all. His success as a writer has opened all sorts of doors for him. He was always . . . well, quite wealthy, you understand. Before becoming known in the theater world, his friends were confined to the . . . er . . . upper bracket. You know what I mean?"

"Not really."

Andrew stared laughingly at her. "You mean you don't know?"

"Know what?"

"Well, I should have thought Barbara would have told you. His father was a peer." He shook his head disbelievingly. "Don't you know about Killaney?"

"What's Killaney?"

"It's in Ireland. His estate. He owns a large estate in County Galway. You've heard of Galway, I suppose?"

"Well, yes, vaguely." Samantha was amazed. "I didn't know."

Andrew shook his head. "If he knew I'd told you he would probably slay me. He hates any form of snobbery."

"And does he go to Ireland much?"

"Well, the estate has a manager by the name of Michael O'Hara: a good old Irish name that! And Mike sees to everything for him. Pat spends most of his time in London, although I think deep inside of him, he'd like to live in Killaney. It's a beautiful place. All green grass and rolling hills, with the sound of water in your ears when you go to sleep."

"You sound quite lyrical."

Killaney's like that. It's a poet's paradise. You must get Barbara to go there so that you can go with her."

"Hm. That's highly unlikely." She looked suddenly at him. "Why didn't you telephone?"

"But I did! Twice!"

Samantha looked puzzled. "But I don't understand. I didn't get your calls."

"No. Your mother and grandmother respectively advised me you were not available. I decided you were giving me the brush-off."

"Brush-off?"

"You know! Oh, telling me you didn't want to see me any more, in so many words."

"But that's not true! I was quite hurt when you had said you would phone and you didn't, or so I thought. There were so many places I wanted to visit. Now we're leaving for Daven in the morning, and I won't see them for goodness knows how long!"

"Well, I'm sorry, honey, but I did phone. Perhaps your relatives didn't like the idea of your going out with me."

"Apparently that's the case, but why?"

Andrew shrugged. Just then the car door opened, and Barbara stepped blithely into the seat beside the driver.

"Hello, you two," she said sweetly. "How nice for you, here in the gloom. Have you been behaving yourselves?"

As Patrick was getting in at the other side as she was speaking, Samantha felt her cheeks flame. She felt sure her mother was merely saying that to make it obvious to Patrick that they were two youngsters together.

Patrick himself barely glanced at them, before starting the powerful engine and putting the car in motion, but that did nothing to ease Samantha's annoyance.

Once out of London the car moved swiftly over the roads towards Sandwich. Barbara kept up a flow of conversation at the front, answered spasmodically by Patrick, who seemed to be concentrating on his driving. It was getting quite dark already, and the road ahead was brightly illuminated by the beam of the headlights.

Samantha, devoid of any desire to talk, found she was staring blindly along the stream of the lights and not seeing anything at all. Her only desire was to arrive at their destination and then make herself as inconspicuous as possible.

Patrick drove smoothly and expertly as Samantha had been sure he would. There was no harsh grinding of gears, no skidding on corners, just an easy rhythm that communicated itself to her. She felt she could have gone to sleep, so relaxing was the journey. Before her head dropped onto Andrew's shoulder, the car had turned between the wrought-iron gates that led up a drive to his sister's house.

The Frazers lived just outside Sandwich, and it was almost eight o'clock when the Aston Martin cruised to a stop outside the old, converted mansion that the Frazers occupied.

The house had been built in the days when money and land were no object, and it spread over a wide area. It was surrounded by a high wall, but, as it was perched on the cliffs, the back opened onto a private beach where the barbecue was to be held. There were several cars already parked in the drive. After Patrick had stopped the car, Samantha slid out willingly, glad to stretch her legs.

At their arrival, several children came darting out of the house towards them, flinging themselves ecstatically at Patrick, who produced candies and chocolates from the pockets of his coat, and swung the youngest, a girl, high onto his shoulders.

Barbara stood watching with some distaste, but Samantha moved forward eagerly. She had always loved children. Since her arrival in England she had met none at all.

Andrew grinned at her and said, "Those two urchins there are Debbie and Donald. They're the twins. Patrick has Jennifer, and this is Fran . . . short for Francesca, of course. The twins are eight, Fran's ten and Jennifer's five. The only one you haven't met is Steven. He's 14, but he's at boarding school at the moment, so I'm afraid you'll have to save that doubtful pleasure for later."

Samantha laughed. It was wonderful, she thought enviously, to have brothers and sisters like this. If only her family had been a normal happy one. If only she had had close contacts like these.

Patrick came over to them, still with Jennifer on his shoulders.

"Well!" he said. "What do you think of the rabble?"

"I think it's wonderful!" Samantha exclaimed warmly. "I was just envying them their complete lack of inhibitions. How wonderful to have a family like this!"

Patrick smiled, gently, at her. "Wait until you get married," he said, "and have a family of your own. Then the pleasure will be yours."

Samantha looked up at him, her tongue running lightly over her upper lip. "I know," she murmured softly. "I mean to have heaps of them."

"I'm sure you will," he said, so that only she could hear, and she turned away, unable to control her emotions.

The smell of the sea and seaweed was in her nostrils. She felt a wave of homesickness for Italy engulf her. It was all so familiar, but she no longer had a home there and no father to make her feel the security she now lacked.

The twins looked suspiciously at Barbara. They had met her before and were not impressed. She always wore too much perfume in their opinion. Tonight she was wearing a slim-fitting suit of heavy green silk to attend a party on the beach. It was stupid!

Fran attached herself to Samantha as they walked into the house to meet the children's parents and the other guests, who, Fran said, were having a pre-barbecue drink in the lounge.

"Are you Drew's girlfriend?" asked Fran, curiously, studying Samantha.

"Not really," replied Samantha, smiling. "I'm Miss Harriet's daughter."

"Barbara Harriet? You mean, Uncle Patrick's Barbara Harriet?" Fran was obviously astonished.

"Yes. Why?"

"Well, I didn't even know she was married."

"She's not now. Her husband's dead. At least I should say my father is dead. That sounds better."

"Oh! Then why does she call herself 'Miss' Harriet? Surely she should be 'Mrs.'"

"Well, yes. Actually she should be Mrs. Kingsley, but theater people always use their unmarried names. At least usually."

Fran grimaced. "You're not a bit like her."

"No. Well, I wouldn't be, would I? I'm much younger and more insignificant than she is."

"What does that mean?"

"Insignificant?"

"Yes."

Samantha smiled. It was unusual for her to have to explain the meaning of a word to anybody. It was usually the other way around. She looked around at Andrew who was just behind, and he grinned.

"Yes, I heard," he said. "Do you really know?"

Samantha raised her eyebrows indignantly and turning around she punched him playfully in the stomach, laughing. Andrew pretended to be mortally wounded. The twins, seeing the fun, came to assist. It was all uproarious and youthful. Barbara looked triumphantly at Patrick.

"You were right," she said silkily. "Samantha is enjoying herself. Children always seem to enjoy themselves, don't they?"

Patrick hoisted Jennifer to the floor, protesting that she was too heavy, and then looked at his companion.

"Do I take it that adults never enjoy themselves?" he asked sardonically.

"You're deliberately misunderstanding me," retorted Barbara and marched primly up the steps and into the house.

The Frazers were a couple in their forties. They had been married for nearly 20 years and were still very much in love with one another. Gina, Patrick's sister, was a tall slim woman, built very much on the same lines as Samantha. Her dark hair was still barely touched with gray. Giles, her husband, was a broad, fair-skinned, fair-haired man with the beginnings of a paunch, which the children and Gina teased him about unmercifully. He took it all in good fun and welcomed Samantha and her mother warmly.

The other guests turned out to be two couples who lived in the neighborhood, a lawyer and his wife and a retired Colonel and his unmarried daughter, Elizabeth, and several young people who were friends of Andrew and Francesca.

Everyone, with the exception of Barbara, was dressed in casual clothes, slacks mainly and bulky sweaters for the cool sea breezes on the beach. Barbara, who had brought a short fur jacket, donned that before descending to the sands. Samantha felt rather sorry for her. But it was not Barbara's nature to go anywhere without looking her dazzling best, and as slacks had never suited her short legs, she preferred to wear something more feminine.

The massive charcoal burner on the beach had been set up by the staff and tables had been set out plus wooden trestles with wooden forms for sitting on. There was every imaginable kind of food; from thick, juicy steaks to the lightest of meat patties, wrapped in lettuce with sliced tomato and tiny cucumber straws. A buffet table was loaded down with all the more accepted forms of food for a party, like jellies, ice cream (shivered at by everyone but the children), fruit salads, stuffed eggs, waffles, shrimps, prawns, toast spread with caviare and paté, and oysters served on their shells. There was also an assortment of cakes and pastries; mouth-watering in their richness.

Samantha, unused even yet to such abundance of everything, stared in amazement. Only when the children set the record player going did she rouse herself from her stupefaction and dance with Andrew.

For the kind of dances she had grown accustomed to the night she had spent in Andrew's company, the sand was an ideal surface. She soon began losing her inhibitions when she saw everyone else dancing as well.

Their parents were seated on low loungers set in a circle around the fire. More drinks were being dispensed by a white-coated waiter.

The roar of the sea was in their ears, and the smell of the surf was stimulating. Samantha wished it was warm enough to swim. She would have adored getting into a swimsuit and allowing the cold water to surge gently over her limbs.

More guests arrived before the steaks were ready, among them Ken Madison with some girls. Soom Samantha and Andrew were the center of a noisy crowd with the Frazer children milling around madly and trying to cause a rumpus.

The music was all very modern. The older members of the party sat around talking and smoking and drinking the delicious punch that Giles Frazer himself had made.

Samantha, escaping for a while from the throng, found herself beside Gina Frazer. Patrick's sister smiled encouragingly.

"Do you find us all completely mad?" she exclaimed,

laughing. "Most visitors wonder how I cope with such a bundle of livewires. My only consolation is that I can always tell if any of them are under the weather. They soon show up amongst the others. Ken, you know Ken?"

"Yes. He's Andrew's partner, isn't he?"

"That's right—well, Ken and his friends are as often here as away. My family table usually stretches to 12 or more every night. It's just as well Giles is so easy-going. Many men would find our life intolerable."

Samantha smiled. "Well, I think you have a marvelous family. I envy you. I've never known what it's like to have brothers and sisters."

Gina cast a strange glance in Barbara's direction. "No. You wouldn't have. Tell me, doesn't your mother like children?"

Samantha felt awkward, and immediately Gina was all contrition. "I'm sorry, dear, I shouldn't have said that. I'm always putting my foot in it, only whenever she comes here she seems to avoid contact with them. It's probably my imagination, but I can't help hoping she doesn't marry Patrick if that's the case. He adores our crowd. I'm sure he wants children of his own. My mother is always complaining about his staying a bachelor!" She laughed. "Poor Pat, he's such a nice person. I'm afraid we're apt to allow the children free license while he's here. They simply dote on him."

"Dote on who?" A husky voice was close to Samantha's ear, and she immediately recognized whose voice it was.

Gina smiled affectionately. "As if you didn't know! Are you enjoying yourself?"

"I guess so. Who on earth is that creature with Ken tonight? The one in the leopardskin tights and low-cut sweater?" He sounded amused.

"Oh, you mean Angela!" Gina giggled. Samantha, acutely conscious of Patrick's arm, casually across her shoulders, glanced around to see who he was talking about.

"Get the picture?" he asked, his warm breath fanning her cheek.

Samantha smiled, feeling achingly like leaning back against him. "Yes, I get the picture. What does she do, Mrs. Frazer?"

"Mrs.? Good heavens, my dear, call me Gina. Everyone does. As for Angela, I believe she's a dancer at some club in town. Ken has all sort of friends. They get successively worse."

Patrick grinned. "She's quite a dish," he murmured, his eyes following her progress as she moved sinuously to the beat music on the record player.

"Do you think so?" Samantha gazed at him.

"Sure. Don't you?" His grin grew wider and more amused.

"No, I do not." Samantha compressed her lips. "She looks . . . well. . . . "

"Don't bother to draw me a picture," said Patrick laughingly. "I can see for myself."

Gina had drifted off to speak to another of her guests. For the moment they were alone, just outside the ring of the firelight.

Samantha wriggled free of his arm and moved away walking slowly towards the sea.

"You were just baiting me, weren't you?" she accused him, as he fell into step beside her.

"Now, why should I do a thing like that?" he asked evasively.

"Well?" She thrust her hands into the pockets of her

slacks. "You couldn't possibly like a creature like that! Not . . . well . . . not to be with at all!"

"Why not?" He, too, had his hands in his pockets. He had discarded his coat and was just wearing his sweater and slacks.

Samantha looked away in annoyance. "Stop it," she said angrily. "I don't want to hear any more."

They were well out of hearing distance of the group around the fire now. Only their silhouettes could be seen against the pale moonlight.

Patrick halted at the shoreline and looked around at her.

"Well," he said softly, "and what would you like to hear?"

Samantha shrugged her shoulders. "Nothing. Everything."

"There's an answer," he remarked laughingly. "What am I supposed to say to that?"

"Oh, nothing." Samantha trudged her feet through the sand. "We go to Daven tomorrow."

"I know. Barbara told me."

"She would," muttered Samantha moodily.

"My, my, I have annoyed you haven't I? I'm sorry."

"Don't tease me," she exclaimed wearily. "I'm not a child!"

"I know," he said quietly. "You're 21."

Samantha stared at him. "How do you know that?"

Patrick shrugged his broad shoulders. "It's quite simple really. I paid a visit to Somerset House."

"Where's that?"

"In London. Oh, of course, you probably don't know about it. Well, it's the Registry of Births, among other things."

Samantha stared at him. "I see."

"You lied to me," he continued slowly. "You told me you were 16."

"I know. But how could I say I wasn't when Barbara. . . . Oh, what's the use?"

"I imagine Barbara didn't want to admit to having a daughter of that age."

"Yes, you're right, of course. Have you told her you know?"

"Of course not. Why should I?"

"Then why are you telling me?"

Patrick put out a hand and pulled her close to him. "So that when I kiss you, you won't think I'm doing it for kicks," he muttered softly, and encircling her throat with his fingers he forced her face up to his.

For a moment, Samantha resisted, but the urge to respond was too great for her. She slid her arms convulsively around him and pressed her body close to his. His mouth was warm and passionate, and there was nothing gentle in his touch. His fingers bruised the soft flesh of her shoulders, and his mouth forced her teeth apart almost savagely.

This was what it was like to be kissed by a man, thought Samantha, feeling the warmth of his body flooding hers. He smelled so warm and male. Just being close against his taut body gave her an aching feeling in the pit of her stomach. He was no longer mocking her, or teasing her. She could tell from the increased tenor of his breathing that he was wanting her as a man wants a woman, and he did not want to let her go.

At last he leaned his forehead against hers and said, "You wanted that just as much as I did, didn't you?"

She nodded, and he released her, reluctantly.

"Was I rough? Did I hurt you?"

Samantha pressed her hand to her stomach to quell its

nervous acrobatics and shook her head. She did not trust herself to speak. What a thing to have happened! What did he really think of her? Had she goaded him into it by tormenting him about that girl? She did not know, and her mind was in a turmoil.

Patrick was looking at her thoughtfully. He had not wanted to let her go, and his code had never covered this form of self-denial. What he wanted he had always taken. It was not pleasant to release her when his whole body wanted a closer contact with her.

Consequently, he was a little abrupt as he said, "We'd better go back."

Samantha hunched her shoulders. "Are you angry?"

"No. Why should I be angry?"

"You sound as though you are."

Patrick shrugged, and Samantha turned with a sigh and walked back towards the lights of the fire. She felt hurt and unsure of herself. She could not understand Patrick's attitude and decided he regretted kissing her at all. Really, she must be incredibly naïve! After all, he was a man of the world. He probably kissed dozens of women, just when it suited him.

When she reached the rest of the young group and found Patrick was no longer with her, she looked around disappointedly. Then she saw him. He was standing by Barbara's chair, talking to her. She was laughing animatedly up at him. What were they talking about? Had he told her what he had just done? If he had, Samantha felt as though she wanted to die.

She found Andrew at her side, and he was looking at her anxiously.

"Have you been walking with my dear uncle?"

Samantha flushed guiltily. "Well, yes. Why?"

"Oh, nothing." Andrew shook his head. He was

frankly puzzled. It was not like Pat to act in this way, and particularly not over a girl who was young enough to be his daughter!

"Come on," he said, sighing. "Let's dance. I've missed you."

Samantha smiled. "Have you? I'm glad somebody has."

The supper was served by more of the white-coated waiters, and Samantha found herself seated on a swing couch with another girl while Andrew stood nearby, talking and getting her anything else she wanted.

She ate very little. Her appetite was practically nonexistent. It was with great difficulty that she ate anything at all. If only Patrick had remained what he had been. Attractive, but distant. Now she could only assume she had in some way disappointed him, and it was terrible!

CHAPTER SIX

Patrick was dancing with Barbara. She had not wanted to dance on the sandy beach, but as it seemed the only way to be in Patrick's arms she had allowed herself to be persuaded.

Patrick found his eyes continually turning to where Samantha was dancing with one of the young members of Ken Madison's party. She had been instantly accepted by them. She was one of them. She was young, beautiful, and vivacious. Her hair hung loose and swung gently against her face; her eyes, veiled by the long lashes, darted mischievous glances at her partner; her slim legs moved rhythmically to the music. She seemed to be having a wonderful time.

Patrick looked away. She was *young*. However old she might be in reality, she was virtually untouched by life. What right had he to torment himself with thoughts about her? Surely, he told himself irritably, after knowing Barbara all this time, he could not have become infatuated by her own daughter? Yet he felt a protective instinct toward Samantha. Their meeting on the aircraft had seemed ordained somehow. After all, at that time she had been in limbo, so to speak. She had left her old life behind her and had yet to meet the new life ahead of her. He had been the intermediary. He was a link with both sections of her existence, and he felt responsible for her.

This in itself was ridiculous, he thought angrily. She

had now acquired a family of her own. She had a grandmother, and what was even more important, a mother.

Why was it he was so involved with her? She had never asked him for help or guidance. Their only contacts had been fiery ones. What was there about her that was causing him to feel so conscious of her all the time? She was attractive, there was no denying that, but Barbara was much more beautiful than her daughter if looks were the only consideration. Barbara was so much more delicately made for one thing, and there was a kind of agelessness about her.

The only solution to this was anathema to him. That he, Patrick Mallory, who for so many years had scorned anything but desire for a woman, should be feeling this way was ludicrous. He wanted no part of *love*. It was too tying. Too demanding. Love was for those who were statically minded. Like Gina and Giles, for instance. He supposed they were in love. They certainly acted that way. But to him, the idea of allowing any one person to hold your whole life in their hands was appalling. Besides, he was not built that way. At least he had never believed he was. He loved life, and he loved women. But only to a degree. Women were a necessary part of his life. Like writing, for example. But to marry a woman for any other reason than to acquire a mistress for his home and a hostess when necessary had never touched him before.

Before! His brain balked at the implied suggestion. He would not admit that he felt anything other than a temporary interest in Samantha.

He suddenly realized that Barbara was speaking to him and he looked down at her. She really did look wonderful tonight, and he knew he ought to be enjoying her company. For in reality, nothing had changed between them. He had always accepted Barbara for what she was. He was convinced that nothing she did could ever disturb him. She was vain, egotistical, at times slightly neurotic, but he had seriously considered her the most suitable applicant should the time ever come when he should decide to take a wife.

But Samantha had certainly changed all that. He had to admit he could never marry Barbara now and accept Samantha as his stepdaughter. Particularly as his feelings for her were anything but fatherly.

"It's eleven-thirty," Barbara remarked. "What time are we leaving?"

Patrick forced his mind into safer channels.

"When this shindig breaks up, I guess. Why?" His dark Irish eyes were lazy. "Are you tired?"

Barbara made a moue with her lips. "A little bored, perhaps."

"With me?" Patrick could have bitten off his tongue the minute the words left his lips. So long he had used his charm to fascinate people. It was second nature to react in like manner when something even vaguely questioning his authority was posed. Barbara reacted in the expected manner. She wound her arm closer about his neck and murmured;

"Darling, I'd never get bored with you."

Patrick felt stifled and disagreeable. This was not the way things should be. He wished desperately that the whole affair could wind up right then. He had had enough. After tonight he must find some reason to get away. His commitments might allow him a week, or ten days, out of London. He could go to Killaney. It was wonderful there at this time of year. There would be fishing, shooting, and perhaps some hunting.

Only in Ireland would he find the peace and tranquillity he needed to escape from the turmoil of his own thoughts. He already had the germ of a new play circling around in his head. It would give him an opportunity to get his thoughts down on paper. Away from Barbara, and Samantha, he would be able to see things in perspective again.

The music ended, and he extricated himself from Barbara's clinging arms just as Giles came striding towards them, a grim look on his face. He gave Barbara a strange glance and then said;

"Would you excuse us for a moment, Miss Harriet? I want to speak to Pat alone."

Barbara shrugged and turned away. Giles drew Patrick to one side.

Patrick frowned. "What's wrong, Giles? Is it the children?"

Giles shook his head agitatedly. "No, no, Pat, nothing like that. Look here, there's been a telephone message from London. It was someone called Emily. I believe she works for Miss Harriet's mother."

"That's right—a maid. Go on."

"Well, apparently Lady Davenport had a heart attack this evening—"

"What!"

"I'm afraid so. This ... er ... Emily thought it would be best if you broke the news to Miss Harriet."

"Then she's dead?"

"No. At least, I spoke to the doctor. He seemed to think she would be very lucky to last the night."

"Oh, God!" Patrick ran a hand over his hair and then hunched his shoulders. "So I guess we get back there as soon as we can, right?"

"Right. The doctor said she was asking for Samantha. That would be Miss Harriet's daughter, wouldn't it?"

"Yes. Samantha." Patrick looked grimly straight in

front of him. Then he seemed to pull himself together. "Look, I'll go tell Barbara. Then after we've gone you can explain to the rest of the party. Oh, and I'll tell Samantha too. She'll come with us, naturally. Tell Drew he'd better stay here tonight. I wouldn't think he'll want to come back with us anyway as things are."

"No, no. I'll speak to Drew. And I'll also explain to Gina. You just make yourselves scarce as soon as you can. Good luck, Pat."

"Thanks," Patrick nodded at his brother-in-law.

"And drive carefully."

"I will."

Patrick turned to look for Barbara. She was standing by the record player flicking over the records idly. He wondered momentarily how she would take the news he had to break to her. He had thought earlier on he had problems, but this created millions of complications whether he liked it or not. Just think, he pondered wryly, he had thought a trip to Ireland was the panacea for all his ills. How wrong he had been!

And Samantha. What about Samantha now? After all, she had been destined to live with her grandmother. They were to have left for Daven in the morning. What would happen to her now?

His stomach contracted. She had become so important to him. The most important thing in his life, and she didn't even know.

He walked slowly over to Barbara. Hearing his approach, she swung around.

"Well, well," she said. "Conference over already? Why so gloomy? What was it all about? I must admit I thought Giles looked green about the gills."

Patrick led her over to one of the benches beside the

now empty buffet tables. "Honey, I have something to tell you, so sit down. I want to be quick and get it over with."

Barbara's eyes danced. "Something to tell me? Why, Pat, how exciting!"

Patrick's eyes narrowed, but when she was seated he raised one foot on to the bench and leaned over her. She watched him avidly, her eyes sparkling like stars. She was sure it was something important he had to say. She was praying it was what she wanted to hear.

When the words came she was astounded as well as horrified. The genuine ageing she experienced showed in her face for a moment. She felt like a person who has been standing on two legs and has suddenly had them both swept from under her. She was glad she was sitting down. She was sure she would have collapsed. The disappointment and shock had been too great together.

"Is she dead, then?" she asked dully.

"No. But I understand the doctor thinks she may not last till morning."

"Oh no!" Barbara's face crumpled. "Oh, Patrick, why did this have to happen?" And then she burst into tears, sobbing loudly.

Patrick turned away. He found himself wondering whether the tears were gauged to extract some kind of sympathy from him, a kind he could not give. If she expected him to take her in his arms, he could not do it. He wanted to comfort her, but as a friend. Barbara would never accept him as a friend.

At last he turned around and said, "We'll have to go. Samantha has to be told, and we ought to get back to town as quickly as possible."

Barbara stared at him. It was a strange look, and he felt as though his emotions were blatant for all to see. She rose to her feet and slid a hand through his arm.

"What would I do without you?" she asked softly. "My righthand man!"

"I guess I'm not much good with crying women," he replied quietly. "I really am terribly sorry."

"I know." Barbara began to cry again, softly this time. "But if she should die, what will I do? I'll be completely alone. I can't live alone."

"But you don't live with your mother," pointed out Patrick bluntly.

"No. But she's always there if I need her."

How selfish can you get? thought Patrick disgustedly. Did Barbara ever think of anyone but herself?

"There's Samantha," he went on. "She's alone too."

Barbara looked speculatively at him. "Samantha is an independent sort of person, like her father. She doesn't need me."

"Doesn't she?" Patrick was enigmatic. "She needs someone."

Barbara half closed her eyes. "Do you have any suggestions?"

Patrick managed a tight smile. "Why should I have? Look, anyway, she's over there. We'd better let her know."

They walked across the sand to where the group of teenagers were dancing. Samantha, ever conscious of Patrick, turned to face them. Patrick felt painfully aware of his own feelings again. She was so tall, slim, and lovely standing there. The look in her eyes, a kind of hurt agony, tore him to pieces. In that moment he knew he loved her.

"Come here, Samantha," said Barbara abruptly. "We're leaving."

The drive back to London was the longest Samantha had ever known. She felt frozen with despair and anxiety, and although she had not shed any tears at the news of her grandmother's seizure, she knew they would come later. She felt numb and disbelieving. That the dear old lady who had made her feel so welcome and so needed here in England should be on the fringe of death was terrifying. Poor, darling Grandmother, to whom she had seemed to give so much pleasure.

Was it possible that her own arrival had precipitated this disaster? Had the over-taxation of her grandmother's health this past week been responsible for her heart giving out?

With thoughts like these for company Samantha was in no mood for Barbara's self-recriminations and spasmodic weeping. She felt sure her mother was simply "playing to the gallery" and trying to gain Patrick's sympathy.

Patrick had spoken little since their departure. He seemed wrapped in thoughts of his own, and Samantha wondered what he was thinking. After all, he had known Lady Davenport too. He must know how great a shock this had been.

At last they reached the town, and Patrick brought the big car to a smooth halt in front of the hotel.

He helped Barbara out, but Samantha forestalled him. Sliding out herself she walked briskly into the hall of the building.

Lady Davenport's doctor was waiting for them on their arrival at the suite. A dapper, little man in his late fifties, a moustache adorning his upper lip, he looked very perturbed and was pacing impatiently about the lounge.

One look at his expression confirmed Samantha's worst fears. Her body froze into immobility as Patrick closed the door, and they all looked at the physician.

"I very much regret to tell you," he began gravely, "That Lady Davenport died over half an hour ago."

"Oh, no!" Barbara brushed past him into her mother's

bedroom and rushing in fell on her knees beside the bed sobbing wildly. Emily came out of the room moments later and closed the door behind her impassively. Her face was pale as though she had been crying herself, but she was calm now, and composed.

The doctor rubbed his chin ruefully. Then he turned his gaze to Patrick.

"There was little I could do," he said slowly. "Her heart had been rapidly weakening over a period of years. Only two weeks ago when she advised me of her arrival in London, I advised her to take things very easily. She was an old lady. It did not take much. . . . "

"I understand," said Patrick, nodding. "And I'm sure Miss Harriet would like me to express her gratitude for all you tried to do. She's upset. She needs time to collect herself. To reconcile herself to the inevitable."

"Yes . . . well. . . . " The doctor turned to Emily. "Will you tell Miss Harriet I'll come around in the morning to see about the death certificate and clear up the details? There's nothing more to be done tonight."

"Yes sir." Emily moved forward. "Thank you for everything."

The doctor smiled, albeit a little sadly. "Thank you. You've been a tower of strength."

Emily looked pleased. Always in the background Emily's life had been an uneventful one, constantly in Lady Davenport's service. She had been grateful for the opportunity to try to save her mistress, even though it had been in vain.

After the doctor had left, Patrick loosened his coat and turned thoughtfully to Samantha. She still stood in the same spot as when she had first come in, as though she were rooted there. She looked stricken.

When Patrick addressed her she looked up at him with drowned, green eyes, and he moved closer to her.

"Samantha!" he muttered, uncaring of Emily behind them. "Samantha, please!"

"She's dead!" said Samantha, shaking her head. "Oh, Patrick, why do all the people I love die?"

Patrick's hard fingers closed on her shoulders, and he shook her gently. "Stop it," he said sternly. "Your grandmother was an old lady, very old as it happens. You heard what the doctor said. This could have happened at any time. Naturally she was excited about your arrival, but she fulfilled her wish to see you and have you here. That was enough." His eyes grew tender. "You have to believe that, Samantha. It's true."

Samantha sighed. "I know. And in a way I'm sure you're right, but it seems so unfair. She never had a chance. We were leaving for Daven tomorrow . . . . *today*! And now it's all over."

"What's all over?"

"This whole affair! This masquerade! I won't stay here now. Not with Barbara!"

Patrick's eyes hardened. "Oh yes, you will, Samantha. You belong here now. There'll be no running away."

"Running away? From what? Barbara never wanted me here."

"I wouldn't bank on that," remarked Patrick dryly. "I should imagine she had no choice in the matter. And if you leave now. . . . No, I think you'll be required to stay."

"And if I don't want to?"

"Barbara will find a way to make you, never fear."

At that moment Barbara emerged from her mother's bedroom. She had dried her tears and looked touchingly wan and defeated.

"Oh, Patrick," she exclaimed, "I'm so sorry. I completely forgot myself. Do forgive me. And Samantha! Darling child, can we bear this together?"

This was too much. Samantha felt nauseated, and she looked desperately from one to the other of them. Then, with a little muffled cry, she ran across to the door of her own room and opening it she went in. The door slammed behind her.

Barbara shrugged and looked, as though puzzled, at Patrick.

"Dear me! The child is upset." She sighed. "Things are going to be difficult."

"Why should they be?"

Barbara cupped her chin in one hand, her long nails curving lovingly about her creamy cheeks. "I'm not sure. I feel it somehow. Samantha is not an easy child to know."

"Child? She's not a child."

Barbara's eyes narrowed. "She's only 16," she said a little defiantly.

Patrick let the myth pass. This was not the time or the place for that particular argument. "I must go. I'll be around in the morning to see if there is anything I can do. By the way, the doctor said he, too, would be here in the morning. To clear up the details and so on. I expect the papers will have the story by then."

Barbara looked speculative. "Quite possibly. All right, Patrick. Thank you."

She leaned forward and kissed his cheek. "I seem to have to prompt you every time these days," she continued, a little coldly.

Patrick smiled mockingly. "So you do! I must try to be more aspiring. Goodnight, Barbara."

After he had closed the door, Barbara lit a cigarette with shaking fingers. She felt absolutely furious. Impotently furious. With Patrick she was so malleable, but he didn't even want to know. Why? Why? Why?

She paced the lounge angrily. Emily who had been silently tidying the room was ordered to bring her some coffee.

Emily, who had never had much time for her mistress's spoiled and wilful daughter, went away to get the coffee, muttering to herself. Barbara's contorted features did not deceive her, not for one moment. They were not due to grief at the death of her mother. Not she; she was only concerned about herself and Patrick Mallory. Not that he seemed particularly interested. Emily thought he seemed more than concerned about Miss Samantha. As she was only 16, why not? Barbara was too dramatic, too hysterical. Too egotistical too, by far. She forgot when she was acting, and when she was not.

Meanwhile, Barbara continued her pacing. Her mind was in a turmoil. There were so many things to be done. And undermining everything was the memory of Patrick standing close to Samantha, his eyes concerned and gentle. For Samantha! It was deplorable. He thought she was 16, too. If she was, he would be old enough to be her father. Had he no pride?

Why, oh, why were all her plans falling about her ears? First of all she had had to interrupt her own life and bring Samantha to London and acknowledge her as her daughter. Then she had had to suffer the fact of Samantha's youthful exuberance and disarming manner with people against her own more mature, sophisticated charms. Now her mother had died leaving the whole weight of responsibility on her shoulders. The responsibility of Samantha was the greatest of all.

It was cruel; too cruel to be fair. And on top of all this, had she now to stand by and watch the one man she could ever remain faithful to make a fool of himself with her own daughter? No! It couldn't happen. It could not be *allowed* to happen. Something would have to be done. Oh, how could he?

Emily brought the coffee and retired to her own bed without even saying goodnight. It would soon be light, Barbara thought wearily. The next day was already upon her.

Lady Davenport was to be buried at Daven. It had been her wish that she should be laid to rest in the family vault there, so Samantha saw her proposed home in very different circumstances to those she had expected.

Since that dreadful night when her grandmother died she had been living almost in a daze. She felt very much as she had done when her father died, for although she had known her grandmother such a short time, they had become so close. She had lived automatically, mechanically. Only when Patrick was there did she feel any of the security that had suddenly been taken away from her.

Barbara was cold and aloof. She acted warmly enough in front of the reporters who came to interview them and take pictures. As the papers gave the story plenty of publicity Samantha assumed that everyone would remark on her mother's bravery in the face of such a tragedy. But, alone with Samantha, she reverted to type and only her daughter bore the brunt of the bitter frustration she was feeling. Samantha did not realize that Lady Davenport's death was not the only thing troubling her mother and could not understand why she should be treated as though she were to blame. She never dreamed that Barbara might be concerned about Patrick Mallory and his concern for her daughter.

The publicity appalled Samantha in many ways. After

all, she had always thought that a death in the family was a family affair. To have every detail of her grandmother's condition broadcast for all to hear seemed almost crude. To see Barbara dressed all in black, a color that did the utmost for her fairness, playing the part of the desolate daughter clinging to Samantha for support through those terrible days was nauseating. Samantha did not doubt that Barbara mourned her mother's death, but her own position grew daily more intolerable.

Martin Pryor, the gossip-columnist, became a regular visitor. Although Samantha kept as much out of the lime-light as she could, Pryor did his best to include her in every article. He was still intrigued by her self-possession, that seemed out of place in a 16-year-old. Samantha, aware of this, wondered how long it would be before he too paid a visit to the registry as Patrick had done, and returned to confront Barbara with the facts. She dreaded to think what would happen when Barbara learned that Patrick, himself, knew the truth. Her thoughts turned to who it was had exposed her.

There were times when Samantha wished desperately that she had never come to England, even while she knew she could never have lived her whole life without meeting Patrick Mallory at some phase of it. The argument that she might never have known of his existence did not ring true any more, for surely they could have met in Italy. His mother's villa was not so far from Perruzio. It was not beyond the realms of coincidence that they might have met through her father. The way she felt about him proved that for her he was the only man she cared about. Although it was highly unlikely that anything more might come of it, she was still glad she had known him and loved him.

Daven was a beautiful old Elizabethan manor house.

Surrounded by tall trees, its brickwork mellowed and fes-
tooned with ivy, it looked sad to Samantha. The drawn
curtains at the windows showed blank faces to the world
outside. Its melancholy owed much to the fact that old
buildings seem to echo the feelings of those within their
walls, and the servants at Daven were very sad at the
death of their mistress.

Samantha drove down the day before the funeral, with
Barnes, in the Rolls. Barbara was already there, supervis-
ing the arrangements for the following day. She had little
time to spare for her daughter. Samantha was shown to
her room and then left to her own devices. After bathing
and changing into slacks and a sweater, she began a
lonely tour of inspection. No one had said she should not
look about if she wanted to do so, and she wanted to know
more about the house where Lady Davenport had spent
much of her married life.

She opened doors into rooms, long disused, even before
her grandmother's death. Most of the furniture, swathed
with ghostly white dust-sheets, eerily reminded her that
for a long time only one person had required
accommodation.

The furniture beneath the sheets proved to be very old.
Much of the damasks on chairs and sofas were faded and
smelled a little musty. She knew very little about antiques,
but she did not need to be an expert to realize that a great
many pieces were valuable. She recognized well-known
examples of Sheraton and Chippendale among the curved
legged chairs and drop-leaf tables, set with pieces of
china, glass, and procelain. Carved procelain figures that
she thought might be Meissen were jostling beside the
blue and white Wedgewood jugs and vases covered so
carelessly that she was almost afraid to lift the sheets for
fear of causing something to break.

In the huge library, books upon books lined the walls and, as they too were not set in any order, she thought it was likely that they had not been disturbed for years.

The bed she slept in that night, after consuming a lonely dinner alone in her room, was huge and would have accommodated at least half a dozen others. The mattress was a feather one. Samantha, unused to the rather suffocating warmth it provided, found it doubly difficult to sleep. It was a four-poster. The ornate ceiling of the bed was draped with heavy velvet curtains, that could be let down to seal the bed off from the rest of the room. Lying there, almost too warm already, Samantha hated the feeling of being closed in that they gave her and consequently at first light she was awake and out of bed before the cocks started to crow.

She swept back her curtains to let in the watery light from outside and looked out on a placid scene that calmed her disturbed mind.

The extensive grounds spread away to the distant hills. In the foreground she could discern well-laid-out flower beds and green lawns, surrounded by box hedges and statuary. There was a small pool, and she wondered if goldfish swam in its icy depths.

She dressed swiftly in the slacks and sweater she had worn the night before and sped down the staircase, reaching the cold air with an involuntary shiver.

She had not explored outside the previous day and spent an enchanted hour discovering her domain. There were stables, as her grandmother had said. The two hunters in the stalls delighted her, nuzzling her for sugar. The stable boy, who was all of 65, gave her some to feed them, and she won their friendship by helping him to groom them.

There was also a pony, a small black and brown thing,

that followed her around, and who she was sure she could grow to love. The stable boy told her it had not yet been named so she spent many minutes trying to choose one for her own amusement.

The funeral was to be at eleven o'clock, and when Samantha returned for breakfast she learned that all the staff were to attend, dressed soberly in somber blacks and browns.

Barbara drank only black coffee and smoked several cigarettes while Samantha ate some toast. Samantha was glad when it was time to go and get ready.

A visit to Hélène's before leaving London had provided her with a slim-fitting dark gray suit and a black and white Breton hat with a black band and black ribbons that hung over the brim at the back. Her hair curled out snugly from under the brim, framing her face, but her cheeks were pale and her eyes dark-rimmed and huge from weeping. Dressing for such an occasion had weakened her resolve not to cry.

Patrick arrived from London soon after ten. Although he must have arisen much earlier than was his wont he was as immaculately turned out as ever in a dark morning suit and a black tie. Over all he wore a fur-lined overcoat and he entered the hallway just as Samantha was descending the stairs.

Seeing him there, his hat in his hand, the fur collar of his coat turned up against the chilly elements, his dark hair ruffled from the breeze, almost turned Samantha's heart over. He had become so dear to her, dearer still now that she was virtually alone in the world again. She could not count on Barbara. She had shown only too clearly these past few days that whatever impulse had allowed her to admit Samantha to her charmed circle was fast waning. The sooner she returned to where she had come from the better she would like it.

"Hello," said Patrick softly. "Are you all right?"

Samantha descended the remainder of the stairs at a run and stood breathlessly staring at him.

"I . . . I am now," she murmured simply.

Patrick's fingers curved around the nape of her neck, and he drew her unresistingly toward him. His coat was rough and smelt of tobacco and was wonderfully reassuring against her cheek. For a moment they were alone in the hall, and Samantha trembled in the grip of emotions too strong for either of them.

His fingers caressed her neck persistently, arousing them, so that she looked up at him helplessly.

"We shouldn't—" she began, her cheeks burning.

"I know," he groaned, "but I need this," and he bent his mouth to hers.

It was a long, satisfying kiss, and Samantha clung to him shamelessly. She knew he was finding it just as difficult to release her. At last he had to push her gently away from him.

"Where is your mother?" he asked, forcing himself to act naturally.

Samantha ran a tongue over her upper lip. "I think she's in the drawing room. The caterers are preparing a lunch . . . for afterward."

Patrick nodded. "And what will you do . . . afterward?"

Samantha shrugged. "I don't know. I honestly don't know."

Patrick fastened his coat again. Samantha had loosened it, burrowing close against his warm body.

"What would you like to do?" he asked.

Samantha bent her head to hide confusion.

"I'm not sure."

Patrick moved closer to her again. "Aren't you? Do you want to come back to London with me?" His voice was barely audible.

She looked up, her eyes startled, into his face. At that moment Barbara emerged from the drawing room into the hall. She was wearing black. She had favored a slim-fitting black coat with a sable collar and cuffs. Her make-up was subdued but arresting, and the tiny black hat that was perched on her blonde curls drew attention to the delicate structure of her features.

Immediately Samantha drew away from Patrick, and there was no further opportunity for her to answer his question.

"Darling!" Barbara walked toward them. "So you're here! I thought I heard the car a few minutes ago."

"You did, Barbara. I've been ... talking to Samantha," replied Patrick easily. "Is everything under control? Is there anything I can do?"

They moved away together, talking, and Samantha had time to gather her scattered wits. What on earth had Patrick meant by that final remark? And what did it imply?

She was absolutely intrigued. This last encounter had confirmed one thing at least. He was attracted by her. But whether it was a lasting attraction, or just a transitory thing she had no way of knowing. After all, he was a so-phisticated man with sophisticated tastes. He might find it pleasant to dally with the wallflower in the garden, but surely when it came to picking he would choose the choic-est bloom. The ignorant, uncultured daughter of an old acquaintance (or old flame) could hardly be classed as that.

Why then had he invited her to go with him to Lon-don? Knowing she was 21 he would be quite aware that she was perfectly free to do as she chose, but, as it was so melodramatically put, what were his intentions? He had never mentioned love to her. Theirs had been a purely physical attraction so far. What did he intend she should do there?

She shivered. The idea that occurred to her could not be put aside. Did he intend that she should live with him?

She hugged herself, closing her eyes momentarily. Although she knew it was wrong, the thoughts that came uninvited to her head could not be denied.

Would it not be nice, a small voice taunted her, inside her brain, if he did want you in that way? To execute his every desire? To know the ecstasy of his possession if only for a short time at least? Was not half a loaf better than no bread? A short period of heaven!

"Excuse me, but aren't you Miss Kingsley?"

Samantha's eyes flew open, and she blushed, feeling foolishly as though her thoughts had been written on her face for everyone to read.

Before her stood an elderly man, dressed in a dark morning suit, his silvery head only slightly higher than her chin.

"Why yes," she replied awkwardly, "I'm Samantha Kingsley."

"I thought you were." His eyes twinkled a little. "I'm sorry I had to interrupt your dreaming."

Samantha's color deepened until she felt like a tomato. "Oh, please—" she began.

"No, don't apologize, my dear." He smiled. "I must introduce myself. My name is Bolam, Joseph Bolam. I was your grandmother's lawyer."

"Oh yes." Samantha smiled in return, and her color subsided. "How do you do? Are you looking for my mother?"

"Not especially. I wondered whether we might have a chat together. There's some time yet before we leave for the chapel, and I'd like to get to know you better. Your grandmother came to see me while she was in London and told me a great deal about you."

Samantha bent her head. "I only wished I had known her longer."

"Yes, I'm sure she wished that, too, my dear."

They walked together into the morning room. As in the other rooms much of the furniture was draped with sheets, but Samantha cleared a couple of armchairs and invited her guest to sit down.

"Tell me," said Mr. Bolam, when they were seated, "have you any plans for the future?"

Samantha sighed. "Not really. I . . . well . . . I don't want to impinge upon my mother's life. She is a very . . . busy woman."

"I'm sure. Barbara always was . . . busy." Mr. Bolam hesitated only a moment over the last word. "I understand she has a play coming up in December."

"Yes, that's right. I believe Mr. Mallory, Patrick Mallory that is, has written a play for her."

"Ah, yes, Patrick Mallory. I have met him. Is he here today?"

"Yes. Actually, he and Mother are together at the moment."

Mr. Bolam coughed rather awkwardly. "Is it possible that your mother might marry again?"

Samantha swallowed hard. "You mean Mr. Mallory, of course."

"Well, there has been some speculation, hasn't there? Your grandmother seemed to think it was likely."

"Yes." Samantha shrugged her slim shoulders. "I really couldn't say. I know nothing about it. Barbara hasn't discussed it with me.''

"And if they did, would you like to live with them?''

"Oh no!'' Samantha was vehement on that score. Live with Patrick and her mother! Knowing that they were man and wife! It would be tortuous and dangerous!

"That's interesting.'' Mr. Bolam nodded and patted her knee. "Don't worry, my dear. I'm sure you have no cause for alarm.''

"Alarm?''

"A figure of speech,'' replied Mr. Bolam easily. He glanced at his watch. "I think we ought to join the others now. Time is getting on.''

Apart from Barbara, Patrick, Mr. Bolam and Samantha there were several old friends of Lady Davenport who lived in the neighborhood who had been invited to join the family mourners. Emily, Lady Davenport's personal maid and companion, rode in Patrick's car with Patrick himself and Mr. Bolam, while other cars had been provided for the rest of the staff.

Samantha did not allow herself to cry in public, even though Barbara wept almost continuously. She found Patrick often by her side, and his nearness was a comfort to her.

The chapel stood in the grounds of the estate. After the short service, it was there, in the family vault, that Lady Davenport's remains were laid to rest.

Barbara's agent, Charles Barratt, had arrived from London also, and he escorted Barbara back to the house in his car. Thus it was that Patrick offered Samantha a seat in his car for the return journey, and she accepted. No one else joined them, and they drove back alone.

Patrick glanced at her as she slid into the car, his eyes warm and gentle. Samantha had to force herself not to touch him, or to ask for his protection. When he joined her in the car, his thigh was close to hers. She felt the palpitations of her heart.

She purposely avoided looking at him after that and stared unseeingly out of the car window instead.

"You're quite safe with me, you know," Patrick remarked, as he swung the car around and drove back to the house.

"Safe?" Samantha twisted her gloves together in her lap. "I don't understand you?"

"Don't you? Well, my dear, you're acting as though I was the villain of the piece about to seduce you," he said with a twisted grin.

"Don't be crude!"

"That's not crude. It's true. What did you think I meant by our brief conversation in the hall?"

"I . . . I can't imagine."

"Judging from your expression, I would say you had a very vivid imagination," he said bluntly. "Good God, Samantha, what do you take me for?"

Samantha compressed her lips for a moment. "I . . . I don't see that it matters what I think," she replied. "But I would like to know what you meant by that remark about my coming to London with you."

Patrick's fingers tightened on the wheel.

"*You* ask me that!"

"Why not? How am I to know what goes on in your head?"

Patrick looked absolutely furious, and Samantha felt herself begin to tremble. He halted the car at the front door and looked at her with angry sparks darting in the tawny depths of his eyes.

"Get out," he said coldly.

Samantha complied and glanced back at him. He remained where he was in the car, and with shaking legs she mounted the steps to the door. What had she done now? Where was it all going to end?

CHAPTER SEVEN

The lunch was over, and Mr. Bolam requested that Barbara, Samantha, and Emily should accompany him to the library. Samantha, unused to the fact that wills were often read after funerals, asked why she should be invited. She could not, in all honesty, see what Mr. Bolam had to say to her now that he could not have said when they were talking together this morning.

"Your mother, yourself, and Emily are the three chief beneficiaries under your grandmother's will," said Mr. Bolam solemnly. "Have you never been present at the reading of a will before?"

Samantha shook her head.

"Come along then. Let's waste no time. Miss Harriet!"

The preliminaries were brief and to the point. All Lady Davenport's staff were provided with small bequests of 100 pounds, and, as there were quite a number of staff at Daven, Samantha was amazed. She remembered her grandmother's words when she first arrived in England. Lady Davenport had said that she had only been provided with an adequate income by her late husband, and that Barbara controlled the remainder. How then could she afford to be so generous and provide such legacies for these people?

Emily was the first of the three of them to be mentioned. She was provided with 1000 pounds, plus an income of 500 pounds a year until she died.

"To make her independent," were Lady Davenport's

exact words, and Emily was overcome by emotion and sought about blindly in her purse. She was deeply moved by this expression of thanks for her faithful service. Samantha, who had also a growing affection for the elderly woman, smiled warmly at her. Barbara gave no indication of her feelings in the matter, apart from a rather patronizing glance in Emily's direction.

To Barbara's astonishment, she was next on the list. She leaned forward in her seat, her eyes narrowed, and Samantha wondered what Mr. Bolam thought of her avid curiosity.

"To my daughter, Barbara, who already has so much, I bequeath a legacy of 10,000 pounds, most of it already vested in shares. . . . " Barbara gave a shocked gasp, and Mr. Bolam went on " . . . and the family jewelry, which will realize a quite considerable amount should she ever have need to sell any of it. My only withdrawal from this is that Samantha should have the pearls that were my mother's, on her wedding day."

Barbara had risen from her seat now and stared disbelievingly at the lawyer.

"Is that all?" she exclaimed angrily.

"I believe so." Mr. Bolam scanned the will. "Yes, Miss Harriet. That is all, so far as you are concerned."

"But this is ludicrous," she cried impotently. "It can't be right. What about Daven? . . . the estate? . . . this house?"

"If you care to wait a few moments longer I will continue," said Mr. Bolam, eyeing her sternly. "May I go on?"

Barbara nodded her head violently and slumped back in her seat. She lit a cigarette with fingers that were not quite steady and then waited for the next pronouncement.

Samantha herself was trembling. What did this all

mean? It was all Greek to her. After all her grandmother had said, could Barbara not hold the purse strings?

Mr. Bolam gave Barbara a further cold, disapproving glance, and then resumed his reading of the document.

"And finally, to my granddaughter, Samantha, I bequeath the remainder of my estate, including Daven House and its adjoining properties."

Now Samantha gasped. Surely she must be dreaming! It just was not possible! Daven was hers!

Mr. Bolam's voice went on, "I have left Samantha the house and the income with which to maintain it because she has no other home now that her father is dead. Should Barbara marry again I am sure she will prefer to have her daughter independent of her."

"She must have been mad!" exclaimed Barbara savagely, rising to her feet again. "It can't be true! Why, she didn't even know Samantha was coming until a few weeks ago."

"No, I agree," replied Mr. Bolam. "At least in part. She did not know Samantha was to be here, but when she did she came to see me. While she was in London in fact. Only a few days before she died she altered her will in Miss Kingsley's favor."

Barbara crushed out her cigarette with brittle movements. She was clearly fighting a losing battle with her temper. Samantha, too astounded to speak, was unable to take any part in the conversation.

It was all so fantastic that as Barbara said it could not be true. That she should own a place as large and imposing as Daven was utterly incredible.

Mr. Bolam looked at Samantha, ignoring Barbara's outburst for a moment. "There is also a letter for you, my dear," he said, kindly, taking an envelope from his brief case. "Your grandmother asked me to give it to you on her death. I believe there is some sort of explanation inside."

"What does she need explaining?" ground out Barbara, rudely. "It's I who deserve an explanation for all this. Of all the underhand things to happen, this is absolutely unique!"

"Unfortunately I have no letter to give you," said Mr. Bolam, smoothly. "And besides, Miss Harriet, if you don't mind my saying so, you have been very adequately provided for. You never did like Daven. Your mother told me so many times."

"I do mind your saying so," retorted Barbara, all thoughts of ladylike behavior blowing out of the window. "I think it's absolutely appalling. That that creature . . . " she pointed at Samantha " . . . should walk in here and take over. . . . "

"That 'creature,' as you so impolitely put it, is your own daughter," exclaimed Emily, speaking for the first time.

"You keep out of this, you old harridan!" exclaimed Barbara, venting her wrath on Emily now. "Creeping around Mother, trying to ingratiate yourself with her, making her rely on you utterly. Don't think I don't know what you've been doing. . . . "

"Enough!" Mr. Bolam rose to his feet holding up his hand. "Miss Harriet, you forget yourself. Your words are slanderous, I hope you are aware. If Miss Lawson wishes to. . . . "

"Oh, shut up! All of you!" Barbara's face was ugly. "I intend to contest this. Don't think I'll let it end here!"

"If you do you'll be stirring up a pretty mess of publicity for yourself," said Mr. Bolam, angry himself now. "The papers will make a field day out of it. 'Mother contests will because daughter is chief beneficiary.' "

Barbara was shaking with fury, impotent fury. "You make me sick! The lot of you!"

"Please be quiet!" Mr. Bolam controlled his own anger. "Samantha, my dear, here is your letter."

"Thank you." Samantha managed to articulate the word, and took the letter from him. She opened it with trembling fingers, watched by her mother who looked as though she was about to wrench it from her hand by force and so learn its contents.

The letter began:

"My dear Samantha,

I must first of all ask you to forgive me for the rank untruths I told you on your arrival in this country. It was imperative that you remain here, on Barbara's terms, and there was no other way that I could see to persuade you, except by placing my future in your hands.

You proved to be your father's daughter in this, and I loved you for it. But as things are now I can provide you with a home you never expected, and I hope it will make up to you in some part for the terrible way you have been treated by this family.

Don't let Barbara intimidate you. I am sure she will do so when she learns the contents of this will, for although she never desired to live at Daven, she knew its worth in a monetary way.

Now, you hold the cards. Daven is yours. No one can take it away from you. You can live there, or use it whenever you wish. You are virtually an heiress and need never scrimp and save again. You can visit your beloved Italy whenever you wish and always have a home in this country to come back to.

Maybe one day, you will meet someone with

whom you can share your life, and maybe you will live at least part of the year at Daven. It would be good to think the old house will ring again with the sound of children's voices, and all the rooms be opened up instead of sleeping away the years like museum pieces.''

Samantha turned to the second page, and Barbara strode back and forth across the room.

"Well!" she said. "What does it say? Some sentimental drivel, I've no doubt."

Samantha looked up at her, for once immune from her jibes. "Yes, it is sentimental," she said. "But it's not drivel. It's wonderful. I'll treasure this all my life."

"Rubbish!" Barbara picked up her purse. She turned to Mr. Bolam. "I presume I'm free to go."

"I don't see why not." In truth Mr. Bolam wished she would.

"Good." Barbara walked to the door. She looked back at the three of them malevolently. "You make me sick!" she said again and went out, closing the door with a bang.

Mr. Bolam cleared his throat after she had left, and Emily stood up nervously.

"I'd better go, too," she said. "I have to organize the clearing up, you understand?"

"Of course." Samantha rose also and went over to Emily. "Don't take any notice of anything my mother said, Emily. She was tired and overwrought, and disappointed, too," she added ruefully.

"That's all right, Miss Samantha," said Emily, smiling. "It's you I feel sorry for."

"Don't feel sorry for me. I can take care of myself," replied Samantha, with more confidence than she was feeling.

"Very well, miss. I'll see you later then."

When Emily had gone, and Mr. Bolam was gathering his papers together, Samantha returned to her grandmother's letter. Her mother's words had really not surprised her as much as her grandmother's legacy. Barbara no longer shocked her that way, although the malicious anger she had seen in Barbara's face almost frightened her at times. Lady Davenport had been right. When Barbara was crossed she was terrible, indeed.

The letter continued:

> "Mr. Bolam is my trusted friend as well as my lawyer, and should you need any guidance in business matters he is the one to whom you should turn. Daven has been run by a competent manager these past 25 years or so. The manager, Jim Edwards, will give you any help you need in this direction.
>
> I do hope you find life a little easier than I have done. You were right about my loving Barbara in spite of everything. She is avaricious and egotistical, I know, but she is my daughter and I am to blame.
>
> Forgive me again, my dear, for deceiving you. At least it proved that you stayed for my sake and for no other. I was grateful for the time we have had together.
>
> Your loving grandmother,
> Lucia Davenport."

Samantha felt tears pricking at her eyes again and blinked them back. Mr. Bolam was watching her, and he said, "Well! I told you you had no reason to worry."

Samantha smiled. "Yes, you did, didn't you? Does this really mean I can stay here as long as I like?"

"Of course. This house and its grounds, the estate, it's all yours now. No one can take it away from you. You need not worry, you know. Your mother would not dare to risk the publicity of a court case contesting the will."

"I think she's a very frustrated woman."

"So do I! Mentally frustrated." Mr. Bolam bit his lip. "Well, I suppose I will have to be getting back to town."

"Yes. Do you mind if I stay here for a while? I have so much to think about."

"Of course. I'll contact you within the next few days to explain the details."

"Thank you, Mr. Bolam, you've been very kind."

"Not at all. It's my job."

Samantha smiled and shook hands with him. "All right, you have it your way. Thank you, anyway."

Mr. Bolam went out closing the door. Samantha, feeling weighted down by new responsibilities, re-read her letter, trying to absorb all the things that had happened to her during the last hour. It still wouldn't sink in. It was entirely too overpowering for a girl who had never known what it was like to have more money than she knew what to do with.

She wondered what Patrick would say; what he would think. Had he yet realized she had not been discourteous to him, but that in her unsophisticated way she was trying to understand an enigma?

She prayed he would stay for dinner. Barbara was sure to invite him. Perhaps afterward she might have an opportunity to speak alone with him. She wondered when Barbara would return to town. Would she stay on for a few days? Or would she want to get back to the social rounds.

As for herself, she had decided she would stay on here, at least for a while. It would give her the chance to relax, as she had not done since she arrived in London, and be herself again.

She emerged from the library to find the place almost deserted. Colonel Winch, an old friend of Lady Davenport's, was drinking sherry in the drawing room, but otherwise it was empty.

"Where is everyone?" she asked, in surprise.

Colonel Winch rose quickly to his feet. His booming voice was considerate.

"Well, my dear, most of the staff have returned to their duties. Your dear mother is upstairs, I believe, and Mr. Mallory left for London about 15 minutes ago. The . . . er . . . lawyer, Bolam, he went with him."

Samantha felt as though the bottom had dropped out of her world.

"Mr. Mallory has left?" she echoed stupidly.

"Yes, miss. He had a few words with your mother, and then he went straight off. She couldn't persuade him to stay."

"Oh lord!" Samantha sighed heavily.

"Is something wrong?" The Colonel looked kindly at her. "I expect this has been rather an exhausting day for you."

"Yes. Yes, it has." Samantha twisted the letter in her hands. "Thank you, Colonel Winch. I . . . I think I'll go and change."

"Quite so. And I must be off. Give my *adieu* to your mother, won't you?"

"Of course." Samantha saw the Colonel to the door and then turned back into the hall. She felt utterly alone and unable to face the thought of meeting her mother.

She went up to her room and changed from the gray suit into a pair of cotton slacks and a printed, silk overblouse.

She combed her hair, rinsed her face, and applied a little lipstick to her mouth.

She did not know what to do now. It was not yet late in the afternoon, and as she did not know her mother's movements she could not plan ahead. Why had not Barbara returned to town with Patrick? Surely if he was leaving she would want to leave too.

She lit a cigarette and seated herself on the window seat. A pale sun was painting the fields a golden color and lifting the twirls of mist from the hills. Had she felt in a more relaxed frame of mind she might have gone down to the stables again and taken out one of the horses, but, feeling as she did, she could not sum up enough energy to take her there.

She pondered on what to do next. She could call Patrick of course, this evening perhaps. But if she did so, what could she say? Without being able to see him and gauge his mood from his expression, she felt helpless to exonerate herself. And besides, she might be on the wrong track even now. He might have been angry with her for some other reason.

There was a tap at the door, and Emily entered at her bidding. She smiled kindly at the girl and said in a gentle tone, "Now then, Miss Samantha, why are you sitting about up here all by yourself moping? What on earth is wrong?"

"Oh, Emily!" Samantha sighed. "Everything seems to have fallen apart."

"I know. But you'll get over it, miss. Your grandmother was an old lady, and she was very tired."

"Yes, I suppose so. It's just that I don't know where to turn next. What would you do? Here I am, surrounded by my own belongings, and I have no idea where to begin to take up a life of my own. My life has always been run for me, first by my father, and then by Grandmother. I'm afraid I'm rather an aimless creature at the moment."

Emily smiled. "That will pass. It's natural enough. Don't try to rush things. You've plenty of time. Years, in fact. Good heavens, you can't be expected to take up the reins exactly where your grandmother left off. Mind you, there's talk in the kitchen about what you intend doing with this house, and the staff. You see, it was always expected that Miss Barbara would take over if anything happened to Lady Davenport. As everyone knows she has no liking for this place, they all expected to get their marching orders. Now they're not so sure. . . . "

"Of course they must stay," exclaimed Samantha at once. "Goodness, I don't want to turn anyone out of their homes. Besides, if I'm to stay here I shall need help to run this place. It's so enormous. Please assure them on that score. They have no need to fear. I won't be selling Daven."

"Now I'm really glad to hear you say that, miss," said Emily, with a satisfied expression. "It's what your grandmother hoped you would say, that I know. She discussed this with me, you know. About leaving the house to you. She was sure you would love it, just as she had done."

"Oh, I do. At least, I'm learning to. There's so much to be done, though. It's practically falling apart at the seams."

"I know. But Lady Davenport was too old to worry about repairs, and Barbara could not have cared less what happened to it. You see, the estate is worth much more than this old building. As land is becoming so expensive these days, the mistress expected that her daughter would sell the whole place to the highest bidder. The house was not important. But you, you have the chance to renovate it if you want to. It could be made so beautiful."

Samantha smiled. "Oh, Emily, you've made me feel loads better. With all the things I want to do here, I can busy myself for years ahead."

"And why should you want to busy yourself for years ahead?" exclaimed Emily, astutely. "You'll be marrying soon and producing children of your own. You'll have no need for other occupations. Don't I know that you're more than any 16? Wasn't I there when you were brought to Daven as a baby?"

"Were you, Emily? Really?"

"Oh yes, I was there. Lady Davenport made such a fuss of you, too. She was really upset when Mr. John came and took you away."

Samantha sighed again. "That was a long time ago."

"Yes, but you're a grown woman now. You can do as you wish. You're answerable to no one."

"Isn't she?"

The cold, sardonic voice from the doorway caused them both to swing around in astonishment. Barbara stood there, dressed in a heavy silk housecoat, smoking a cigarette. How long had she been there? How much of their conversation had she heard?

"I thought you'd be here," she said, addressing herself to Emily. "Filling the girl's head with your own foolish fantasies. I told you before, you're through. Encouraging my mother in her foolishness. Just because we were forced to bring this brat here and acknowledge her, you had no need to be underhand about wheedling her into my mother's affections. I might have known you were at the bottom of all this. You've always hated me. . . . "

Emily's face was cold and frozen with emotion. But she managed to speak. "I never hated you, Barbara. But you were jealous of me. Just as you are of anyone who might conceivably steal the limelight from you. You never wanted your child, but why? Was it that you were such an unnatural mother, or was it that you were afraid she might grow too attractive and take some of the attention from yourself?''

"Be quiet!"

"I won't. I've been quiet too long already. If your mother knew some of the things you have done she would turn in her grave, God rest her soul."

Barbara strode across the room and slapped Emily viciously across the face. Samantha sprang to her feet.

"Oh, Emily," she began. "Mother . . . !"

Emily shook her head. "Don't worry, miss, I'm going. But I'll come and see you again, when you're not so distraught. Don't give in, love. You'll be all right."

"Get out!" screamed Barbara furiously, and Samantha, afraid that her mother might attack Emily again, hurried her from the room. Then she turned back to face her mother.

"Well!" said Barbara. "And what do you think you're going to do now?"

Samantha shrugged. "I'm not sure yet. I need time to think . . . to gather my thoughts. . . . "

"And you expect to do that here?"

"Of course. It's my decision after all."

"You seem to be making all the decisions, don't you?"

"I don't understand you, Barbara."

"No. And I don't suppose you ever will," remarked Barbara, lounging on a chaise longue, her expression malicious.

"Will you please go?" said Samantha, trying to keep calm.

"Why should I? You are my daughter, after all."

"In name only," retorted Samantha hotly.

"Oh, really, we are getting spiteful!"

Samantha ran her tongue over dry lips. "Please, don't let's have a scene."

"Why not? I feel like a scene. I think I've had a raw deal all around."

"I don't know what you mean."

"Patrick Mallory. As if you didn't know!"

Samantha flushed, unable to control her color and Barbara nodded angrily.

"You see, I can't even mention his name without you blushing. It's ludicrous. Good heavens, what on earth do you think you mean to him?"

"If you don't think I mean anything to him, why are you saying you've had a raw deal?" asked Samantha bravely.

"A good question. Well, my dear little viper at my bosom, when our mutual friend left this afternoon, he made it quite clear that he wanted nothing more to do with any member of this family."

"What!" Samantha was flabbergasted. "Why?"

"Well, he tells me he knows your right and proper age, and that I ought to be flogged for deceiving everyone. Particularly as I was ruining your chances of happiness in the process. Now what do you suppose he meant by that remark?"

"I can't imagine." Samantha felt near to tears.

"Nor can I, for once. But something you said must have upset him. He also told me he has had an offer from an American film company for the rights of his last play. They want him to go to California soon to clinch the deal, if he's willing. I would say from his expression when he left here, he was all too willing, so I think we've both lost, don't you?"

Samantha felt numb. "I . . . I can't believe it."

"Really? Then that proves my suspicions. I can't understand how a man of Patrick's intelligence could allow himself to become involved even temporarily with you.''

Samantha collapsed onto the window seat. What price now her plans for the renovation of Daven? Hadn't it been in the back of her mind that she would do it, not only for herself, but for Patrick?

"I thought that would shock you out of your cloud world,'' remarked Barbara smugly. "And it's not all. Not by a long chalk.''

"What else could there be?'' asked Samantha, uncaring of herself. Surely Barbara could hurt her no more. If everything was over with Patrick, nothing else could hurt her now.

"Just what did Mother confess to you in her charming letter of explanation?''

"That's my affair.''

"Partly, I admit, but I bet she didn't give you the reason why you were brought here.''

"Why I was brought here!'' echoed Samantha stupidly. "Why, when Grandmother was informed of my father's death she immediately made arrangements for me to come.''

Barbara smiled cruelly. "Yes, she did that all right.'' She laughed mirthlessly. "Oh, my, Samantha, what a little innocent you are.'' She rose to her feet and strolled across to the window. "Your charming grandmother brought you here because she had no choice in the matter.''

Samantha stiffened. "Stop talking in riddles and explain yourself. What do you mean, she had no choice?''

Barbara turned back and leaned against the window. "Your father made a stipulation in his will to the effect that on his death you should be informed of my existence, brought to England, and acknowledged as my daughter.''

"What!'' Samantha felt sick.

"Yes, darling. I thought you didn't know that little titbit."

Samantha pressed a hand to her churning stomach. "But . . . but how could he do that? He had no guarantee that you would accept me."

Barbara stared scornfully at her. "Hadn't he? Only the best guarantee in the world in my circumstances."

"Oh, go on," cried Samantha, almost in tears. "What guarantee?"

"He wrote a letter, describing the circumstances of our marriage and subsequent divorce . . . dates, names, everything. You must have realized since you arrived here what onus is placed on the press in my circle. That particular . . . shall we say unsavory scandal . . . would have finished me. He knew that. The letter was to be delivered into the right hands should I refuse to acknowledge you."

Samantha closed her eyes in despair. She had never known one person could be so humiliated.

"Unfortunately," continued Barbara, "John forgot one small detail. Your age. There was nothing to say how old you were. I took advantage and was grateful for small mercies. What do you think of your darling grandmother now?"

Samantha felt the tears beginning to trickle down her cheeks.

"I feel just the same," she whispered. "I don't care what you say, Grandmother did care for me."

"She also acted upon my instructions. Had you refused to stay in England the story would most probably have come out anyway. It was imperative that you should stay. I told her to use any means in her power to prevent you leaving. She obviously succeeded."

"I think you're the most hateful person I've ever known," whispered Samantha weakly. "You're not content until you have everyone groveling at your feet, are you? How could you tell me this? How could you?''

Barbara's face darkened. "Because you've caused nothing but trouble for me, ever since your arrival."

"Not least of these troubles being Patrick," murmured Samantha shrewdly.

"Exactly. Well, now you have your house, your estate, and your wealth, but much happiness may you get from it."

"Thank you . . . for nothing!"

Barbara shrugged eloquently. "Poor empty-headed creature," she said sneeringly. "What do you really have? Nothing."

Samantha wiped her eyes. "And what about you?"

"Me?" Barbara smiled smugly. "I have my work . . . and my home in London amongst my friends. And even Patrick will return from California eventually. He'll forget. Men always do. You may have a step-papa yet."

Samantha looked up. "And what if I decided to tell the press of my own accord?"

Barbara shook her head confidently. "You won't, darling. You haven't it in you to be cruel. That's why you'll never get anywhere, be anyone. Besides, think of the memory of Mother. You wouldn't like all her efforts to have been in vain, now would you?"

Samantha was defeated. As Barbara had said, she would not denounce her. Not now.

Barbara walked lazily to the door. "I'm going to dress now," she said. "I think I will go back to town after all. I've . . . er . . . done everything I came to do, I think."

Samantha watched her close the door, and then flung herself on the bed in a paroxysm of weeping. She had been unhappy before, but this was torment. All her hopes and dreams were shattered. Even the gentle love she had had for her grandmother seemed besmirched now by her mother's ugly words and accusations. Even this house held no joy any longer. It merely seemed another effort to keep her out of Barbara's life, and silence her forever.

After a while she sat up and dried her face. Tears were for the weak, and she would be weak no longer. There was nothing she could do tonight, but tomorrow . . . tomorrow she would go away.

The decision made, she felt better. She had a little money that her grandmother had given her for her personal use. It would be sufficient to take her wherever she decided to go. Once there, she would find work, get a job, forget she had ever known her mother or her grandmother . . . or Patrick Mallory.

But where could she go? She knew very little about England and had no friends here. In Italy there was Benito, but that was no good either.

Then she remembered Matilde. She had said that should she ever need help she could be contacted at her sister's in Ravenna. Surely if she went there she could find lodgings for a while until she could get a job and rooms of her own. After all, she spoke Italian like a native. There was nothing to stop her from going there.

She twisted her handkerchief between her fingers. She had to think. She would call up the airport later and see if there was a flight tomorrow. Her passport was in order. Soon she would be away from her. All the deceit and hatred she had known would be in the past. What did it matter that no one knew of her departure? No one cared anyway, except perhaps Emily, and she was gone now. Barbara would be glad to see the back of her and Patrick . . . . Well, he had made it plain what he thought of her.

Barbara left without seeing her daughter again, and Samantha was glad. She could not have borne another argument. She felt too strung up and scared to think straight. For once, she was acting impulsively. All her life she had thought before doing. Now she was going, and she did not intend to think about it until afterward. She would have plenty of time for thought in years to come.

CHAPTER EIGHT

It was almost a week later when Patrick turned his Aston Martin between the drive gates of Daven and drove smoothly up to the house. The house looked much the same as it had done the last time he was here, and he was surprised. He had thought that Samantha would have begun clearing out the rooms, drawing back the curtains, and banishing the gloom. Instead the house looked deserted. The only smoke curling from the chimneys seemed to be coming from the kitchen quarters.

He had had plenty of time for thought during the past few days and he knew now what he had to do. Whatever Samantha's feelings in the matter they had to have a talk, a serious talk. He wanted to know once and for all where he stood.

He had told himself frequently that she was too young for him, not only in her age but in her awareness of life. But his emotions had never been aroused like this before, and he had found he could not sleep nights worrying about her.

He had left in a temper the day of the funeral, partly due to his conversation with Samantha and her implied suggestion of what his invitation had meant, and partly because of the row he had had with Barbara. He had not meant to tell her he knew about Samantha's age, but when Barbara began talking about her frustration over the estate his temper had got the better of him. There had been some harsh words. He had left knowing he would not be allowed to see Samantha alone while her mother was there.

During this week he had wanted to drive here many times, but he thought it would be best to give her a little time to recover from the shock of her grandmother's death. Today he had decided he could wait no longer and directly after breakfast he had driven down.

Now, seeing the house in this desolate state, he felt a sixth sense warning him that all was not well. His stomach was churning, and he felt his senses tingling with an unknown awareness of disaster.

He slid out of the car and stood for a moment, hands in the pockets of his overcoat, looking up at the house. Then he mounted the steps and rang the bell.

It tolled mournfully around the house, and he hunched his shoulders impatiently.

He did not have very long to wait before an elderly man servant opened the door.

"Oh, Mr. Mallory!" he exclaimed in surprise. "What can I do for you?"

Patrick frowned. "I'd like to see Miss Samantha, if I may."

"Miss Samantha?" The old man's eyes grew puzzled. "But she's not here. . . . "

Patrick clenched his fists in the pockets of his coat. "What do you mean, she's not here?"

"What I say, sir. She left the day after the funeral. I thought you would have known that."

Patrick felt an acute sense of anxiety. "No. Why should I?"

The old man shrugged. "Well, sir, Miss Samantha said she was leaving for London, and I presumed she would be staying with her mother there. As you know Miss Harriet so well, I naturally thought. . . . "

"I see." Patrick swung backward and forward on the heel and sole of his shoes. "And have you heard nothing since she left?"

"No, sir. Oh, forgive me, will you come in?"

Patrick hesitated. "No, I think not. There's nothing for me here." He felt disturbed. Barbara and Samantha would hardly be living together in the circumstances, but this old man was not to know that.

"All right," he said at last. "Thank you."

The man smiled, and Patrick walked slowly down the steps and slid into the driving seat of his car. Setting the car in motion, he cruised slowly down the drive and out onto the road again. All the while, his mind was actively working, puzzling on this turn of events. There was something about it that was not quite right. Why would Samantha return to London? Where would she go?

He drove through the village. It was a small, country village with a general store-cum-post office comprising its whole commercial trade. There was a small hotel, the Queen's Head, and a small church.

Patrick called in at the hotel for a drink, before driving back to London. It was full of locals, and he did not stay long. He slid back behind the wheel of the car and drove back to town. He felt perturbed, and there seemed little he could do about it. Where was he to find Samantha? Could he ask Barbara if she knew where she was? It was not a palatable thought, but at present it was his only one.

He drove to his house. Going in he called Mrs. Chesterton. She came hurrying out of the kitchen quarters, a surprised expression on her face.

"Why, you're back, sir!" she exclaimed. "I thought you would be late."

"So did I," remarked Patrick moodily. "Tell me, have there been any calls while I've been out?"

"No, sir. Were you expecting one?"

Patrick shook his head. "Not really." He sighed. "All right, Mrs. Chesterton, thank you."

"Have you had anything to eat, sir?"

"No. But don't worry, I'm not hungry."

"Nonsense." Mrs. Chesterton tutted angrily. "I'll fix you a snack and bring it to your study."

"No, I'll be in the lounge. I want to make a phone call."

"Very good, sir."

Patrick removed his sheepskin overcoat, and, throwing it over a chair, he walked into the lounge. He lit a cigarette and drew on it deeply before lifting the receiver and dialing Barbara's apartment number.

The purr on the other end of the line seemed to go on for ages, although it was actually only a few moments before Clyde's voice answered.

"Miss Harriet's apartment. Who is calling, please?"

Patrick stubbed out his cigarette abruptly. "Mallory," he said shortly. "Is Barbara there?"

Clyde's voice changed noticeably. "Oh, Mr. Mallory. Well, she's just getting up, I'm afraid, but I think she'll speak to you."

"Thank you." Patrick was impatient.

A few minutes later Barbara's voice came silkily down the line.

"Darling," she exclaimed warmly. "How wonderful of you to call. Have you forgotten our little argument? I hope so. I have . . . it was all my fault. . . . "

"I agree," replied Patrick grimly. "Barbara, is Samantha staying with you?"

"Samantha!" Patrick could tell from the tone of her voice she was floored by his abrupt question.

"Don't bother," said Patrick. "I can tell from your tone that she's not."

"But, darling, why should she be? After all, she has Daven now. Why should she want to stay in a stuffy, old apartment in town?"

"Yes. Okay, Barbara. Thanks."

"Is that the only reason you phoned?" Barbara's voice had hardened.

"Yes, I think so. Thank you for your trouble."

"Oh, but Pat. . . . "

But Patrick had hung up on her. It was obvious Barbara had no idea where Samantha might be. It was infuriating. And worrying. If she was not with Barbara, where could she be in this great city? She knew nothing of London, of Londoners. The prospect of Samantha trying to make her way in this huge and sometimes frightening metropolis was disturbing. She was so innocent, so untouched. How could she look after herself here, among people she did not even know?

But why, why was she here? Why was not she still at Daven? Was it possible that something had happened that he knew nothing about? Something that might have caused her to leave her new home? But what?

He paced about the room restlessly, trying to find a solution. Mrs. Chesterton brought him some cold chicken on a tray, but he barely touched it. He was too tense, too involved with his own thoughts.

It was possible that Barbara did know more than she had said. For all her innocent tone she was not reliable, and it was quite possible that she might have some reason for pretending that Samantha was still at Daven when in reality she knew she was not.

That brought him back to the reason for Samantha's departure. Of course, Barbara *had* remained at Daven on the day of the funeral, after he had left with Mr. Bolam. Could she have said something to cause Samantha to think twice about her inheritance? She had been furious because Samantha had been willed Daven by Lady Davenport. When Barbara was angry she did not care who she hurt.

He lit another cigarette and stared moodily out of the window. There seemed little he could do. There was no one apart from Barbara to whom he could turn.

And then he remembered Emily. He had always liked Emily. She was a staunch sort of person and seemed to have taken a liking to Samantha, whereas she had always seemed rather antipathetic toward Barbara. She had, after all, known Barbara since she was quite young herself. She was not blinded by the aura of success that emanated from her employer's daughter these days. She might credibly know something of Samantha's movements. If he could get in touch with her. . . .

But again, he was brought up short by the knowledge that he knew no more how to find Emily than he did to find Samantha.

Unless. . . . Emily had lived most of her life at Daven. It was possible that someone in the village might know her intimately, and maybe even know her whereabouts. That was the answer. Daven. And Emily.

He arrived back in the village of Daven at eight o'clock that evening. He drove straight to the Queen's Head. Of all places in a village of this size, the local public house was the most likely to have the information he needed. Daven House, as the local manor, and Emily, coming from there, was bound to be an object of interest. People always wanted information about the gentry, and Emily would be a prime observer.

The bar was much fuller now, with plenty of evening visitors swelling the local population. He ordered a

Scotch, and then, leaning on the bar, he asked the barman whether he was acquainted with Emily Lawson.

The barman eyed him strangely. "And what would you be wanting with Miss Lawson?" he asked. "You're a city chap, aren't you? Are you some relative or something?"

Patrick shook his head. "No, not a relative. I want to speak to Emily on a personal matter. Do you know where I can find her?"

"Miss Lawson sometimes visited Mrs. Peel at Stone Cottage," said the barman. "Likely she might know where you can find her."

"Thank you." Patrick swallowed his whisky, and, conscious that he himself would become a subject for discussion as soon as he had left, made for the door.

He did not bother inquiring where Stone Cottage was. In a village of this size, surely he could find one cottage.

He left the car on the parking lot beside the hotel and, hands in pockets, began to walk along the main street. He passed the shop, the doctor's house, the churchyard (he smiled at this), and finally a house with a "Police" sign outside. There was no Stone Cottage on this side of the road.

The other side of the street proved just as disappointing, and he sighed in annoyance. He had no wish to go back into the bar and ask for more information.

He was standing on the edge of the sidewalk pondering his next move when a voice said,

"Why, it's Mr. Mallory, isn't it?"

Patrick swung around. "Emily! Hell, am I glad to see you!"

Emily frowned. "Are you looking for me, then?"

Patrick nodded. "Are you living in the village?"

"Yes, I'm staying with my friend Mrs. Peel at the moment. I don't know what I'm going to do yet. I haven't really had time to gather my thoughts together. I was just on my way over to the house to see Miss Samantha. Have you been there, too?''

"Samantha's not at the house," said Patrick, shrugging wearily. "I thought you might know where she was,"

"Not at the house!" Emily was taken aback. "But then where is she?"

"If I knew that, I wouldn't be here," exclaimed Patrick, rather abruptly, and then he sighed. "I'm sorry, that was rude. It's just that I'm half off my head, looking for her. I've called Barbara, and she doesn't seem to know where she might be. At least, well, she said that Samantha was at Daven."

"Oh!" Emily frowned deeper. "That is worrying." She looked up at Patrick. "Have you no idea where she might be? Has she just disappeared?"

"Oh, no, not exactly. I asked an old chap up at the house where she was, and he said that she had said she was going to London. They naturally assumed she was staying with her mother."

"I should think nothing was further from the truth," said Emily dryly.

"I thought that myself," Patrick nodded glumly.

"Particularly after the row they had the day of the funeral. . . . "

"Row! Did they have a row?"

Emily put a hand to her throat. "Well, sir, I don't like talking about things like this."

"Oh, come on, Emily, this is important. What was it all about?"

Emily bit her lip. "Well, sir, I was talking to Miss Samantha, after you had gone, of course. We were talking about Daven, and Miss Samantha said she would like to do the whole place over . . . make it a proper home again.

I said that that was what her grandmother would have wished when who should come bursting in on us but Miss Harriet. She was rude . . . very rude . . . to me, really, and Miss Samantha became upset. I was practically ordered out of the house, and after I'd gone, heaven knows what took place. I only hope Miss Harriet didn't tell Miss Samantha about her father's last instructions. . . . ''

"What instructions? Has this something to do with Samantha's arrival here?''

"Yes, sir.''

Patrick groaned. "I guessed as much. Come on, Emily, let's go and sit in the car. This is not the place for a discussion of this sort.''

In the car, Emily told Patrick the whole story. Lady Davenport had had no secrets from her companion, and Emily related everything. Patrick, who had always thought Barbara's actions were not in character, now understood a lot of things. He could also see that if Samantha had been told this story, she would feel as though she had been betrayed. Particularly, in her weakened state. On top of everything, this would have seemed the last straw.

"And do you think it's likely that Barbara told Samantha this?'' he asked when Emily had finished.

"Well, sir, judging from her expression, I should think it was very likely.''

"Oh, God!'' Patrick rested his chin on his hands on the steering wheel. Poor, unhappy Samantha. She must have thought nobody cared a thing about her. He had only made matters worse, treating her as he had done. He could not free himself from the blame he felt in all this.

Emily sighed heavily. "So she's gone.''

"Well, if she was told that, she would feel like running away. I think I would, too, in her position.''

"Yes, sir." Emily bent her head. "And to think I didn't even know she wasn't at the house!"

Patrick sighed. "And when you would eventually have found out, what would you have done? You would surely realize that Samantha couldn't be with her mother?"

"Yes, I suppose I would. I'd have been very worried, sir. Just as I am now. I can't think where she might be. She knew no one in London. She wasn't the sort of girl to enjoy managing alone."

"I know." Patrick shook his head. "I think for a while here she found security, but now, with her grandmother dead . . . and possibly with the germ of that story you have just told in her mind, she feels completely alone. But where would she go? Where?"

Emily desperately tried to think. Was there anyone else Samantha had known?

Suddenly she said, "I suppose it's possible that she's gone back to Italy, sir."

"Italy!" Patrick smote a fist against the palm of his hand. "Of course, Emily. I should have thought of that. She had friends there. She may have gone back to see them."

"It may be only temporary," murmured Emily doubtfully, "but if so, why didn't she tell anyone where she was going?"

"That's interesting. Anyway, I now have a lead. I'll contact the airport when I return to London and let you know what happens. Is your friend on the telephone?"

"Mrs. Peel? No, sir. But a message left at the Queen's Head will reach me."

"Right, thank you, Emily." Patrick smiled. "I'll find her, don't worry."

Emily smiled gently in return. "I always thought it was

Miss Samantha who took your eye,'' she murmured in a satisfied way.

Patrick grinned. "Emily! Those are private thoughts. You shouldn't broadcast them."

"I know, sir, but Miss Samantha was so upset, and I'm sure you're the only person who can change all that."

"I hope you're right." remarked Patrick dryly. "I'll have a damn good try."

Samantha entered Sophia da Silva's house in the Via Algante in Ravenna. Outside it was pouring with rain, and Samantha was wearing a white raincoat that she had bought in Milan on her arrival back in Italy. Since she returned, over a week ago, it had rained almost every day. It was quite cold too, for the time of the year.

But the weather, if anything, only reflected Samantha's mood. She did not care what it was like really. She was sick at heart and miserable. After all, Ravenna was not like Perruzio, where she had known everyone. Ravenna was a strange place, much as London had been, and old Matilde and her sister Sophia were the only people she knew. She had paid a visit to Perruzio, of course, to see her father's grave. It seemed strange that it was such a short while ago he had been buried. So much had happened that it seemed like a lifetime now.

She had been returning to the square to catch the bus back to Ravenna when a voice had hailed her. Swinging around, she had found Benito standing behind her.

"Samantha?" he asked incredulously.

Rain-washed and windswept as she was, she could understand his rather doubtful question. Her hair was dressed differently, and in the cheap but smart raincoat and high heels, she looked much different from the badly dressed girl who had left.

"Hello, Benito," she said, managing a smile. "How nice to see you again."

Benito could only stare at her. "But . . . but . . . " he began, in Italian, and Samantha reverted to his language to speak to him.

"Don't look so astonished," she said easily. "I'm not a ghost. I'm living in Ravenna with Matilde and her sister at the moment. I'm going to get a job. Sophia, Matilde's sister, knows of someone who has a young child and who is wanting a nurse-cum-housemaid. I'm thinking of taking the position."

Benito looked flabbergasted. "But you can't," he cried, in amazement. "Samantha, you know how I have always felt about you. I thought when I saw you that you were coming to see me."

Samantha's face colored. "Benito, Benito, I'm sorry if you thought that, but I'm afraid I only came to see my father's grave. . . . "

"And your trip to England? Was it not a success?"

"No." Samantha spoke shortly.

"Then what do you intend to do?"

"I've just told you."

Benito moved his shoulders exasperatedly. "That's ridiculous," he said angrily. "Samantha, please. . . . "

"Benito, before I left, your mother and I had a talk. She doesn't really want me as a daughter-in-law anymore. I realize myself now that what was between us was simply not the real thing."

Benito's face grew red. "How can you know that? Have you met someone else in England?"

Samantha bent her head. "Yes."

"Then why are you here?" In Benito's simple mind there were only blacks and whites, with no shades of gray.

"It's a long story," replied Samantha, looking up the

road for the bus, wishing desperately that it would come. She had no desire to have another argument with Benito.

"Are you going to marry this man?"

Samantha shook her head.

Benito moved restlessly. "But why?"

Samantha compressed her lips. She felt the tears pricking at her eyes, and she angrily blinked them back.

"Because he doesn't want me," she cried. "Now leave me alone. Please."

Benito ran a hand through his hair. "I'm sorry, Samantha."

Samantha moved her shoulders helplessly. "Oh, Benito, what can I say?" She ran her tongue over her upper lip. "How have you been?"

"Oh, I'm all right. Silvana had another boy." Silvana was Benito's sister. She already had three boys.

Samantha smiled. A couple of months ago this conversation would have been her whole world.

"Was she disappointed?"

"No. Mario wants plenty of good sons to follow him."

Samantha turned and looked up the road again. If only the bus would come!

Benito, sensing her distress, thrust his hands into his pockets.

"Well," he said, "I'll go. Mama is expecting me back."

Samantha sighed. "All right, Benito. It was nice seeing you again." It was inadequate, but there was nothing else she could say.

Benito nodded and then ambled off down the street, glancing back occasionally at her. Samantha waved and wished again that the bus would come. Suddenly it did. She was so thankful. Nothing was the same any more. She realized that with a sharp sense of loss. Even Perruzio, her home for so many years, had become alien to her.

But that was four days ago now, and today she had been to see Signora Marcasi. The stout, fulsome Italian woman had not impressed Samantha, any more than her pudgy, spoiled little boy had done. Young Vittorio was certainly a handful, and his persistent attempts to annoy Samantha had eventually succeeded. She had wanted to rush out of the house in the rather select area of the town and never see either of them again.

But she had apparently impressed Signora Marcasi. As her husband, an industrialist, was taken with the idea of having an English nanny for his child, Samantha had been offered the position.

Strangely reluctant to commit herself, Samantha had asked if she might have a day to think it over. Signora Marcasi had obviously thought her rather impolite to suggest such a thing, but she had had no choice but to agree. It was with these thoughts in her mind that Samantha entered the house in the Via Algante.

Matilde came to greet her as she was removing her raincoat.

"Well!" she said eagerly. "Was the interview a success?"

Samantha sighed and ran a hand over her damp hair. "I suppose so," she said wearily. "Signora Marcasi was pleased anyway. Oh, Matilde, I just can't see myself getting along with the family, that's all. I've asked for a while to think it over. Signora Marcasi wasn't pleased, but I have to have time."

"Of course." Matilde nodded understandingly. "But Sophia may be disappointed you did not accept at once. She thought it was a wonderful oportunity. The Marcasis are rich people here. They are respected and liked."

Samantha walked down the stone-floored hallway to the kitchen where they spent most of their time. The house was not large; only two rooms up and two down. There was no bathroom, and no privacy from the other occupants of the house. It suited Matilde and Sophia, but Samantha knew she would have to find somewhere of her own soon.

Sophia was out shopping, and Samantha gratefully accepted the cup of coffee Matilde thrust into her hand.

"If you do not take this position, little one, you may find the next one even more objectionable," said Matilde shrewdly.

Samantha smiled affectionately at her. "Dear Matilde. I know. And of course I will take the job, I suppose; it's just that I feel so unsettled."

Matilde nodded. Samantha had told her the whole story when she arrived. She had not made any comments, neither for nor against Samantha's actions. Samantha herself did not even know whether she was doing the right thing, as yet, and she wondered if she had been foolish to flee from a life of luxury to comparative penury.

But even as these thoughts crossed her mind, she thrust them back. She could not stay in England, risking the chance of meeting Patrick and her mother together. Possibly even witnessing their eventual marriage. She wanted to know nothing more about them, so that her thoughts could stay as they were now. At least, without knowledge she could not torture herself with thoughts of them together.

Sophia returned, and they ate their evening meal in silence. Sophia was younger than Matilde and a widow. She seemed surprised when Matilde told her of Samantha's interview and her subsequent request for time to think about the proposition. Fortunately she sensed that Samantha was in no state to be lectured to and kept her own counsel.

After supper, Samantha put on her coat again and went for a walk. It was a fine evening, after the terrible day, and she enjoyed the fresh, clean air, blowing in her face. She wished Ravenna was a coastal town, so that she could walk by the sea. She loved the sea, and she had seen little of it since she left Perruzio about six weeks ago.

Six weeks! What a multitude of things could happen in so short a time!

The next morning she woke early, to find the sun was shining for the first time since her arrival. She opened her window wide and leaned out. The air was warm. She sighed, feeling more relaxed. It was wonderful how the sight of the sun could make you feel better inside.

She had told Signora Marcasi she would go and see her at three o'clock that afternoon, so she had the morning free, to do as she pleased.

After some rolls and coffee, dressed in slacks and a light wool jacket she left the house to do some shopping. Sophia had given her a list and, as she liked to bargain with the store keepers, Samantha was feeling more herself. Time would heal everything, she told herself, confidently, ignoring the empty ache she felt inside.

It was afternoon before she returned to the Via Algante. She turned into the road, walking easily, the basket swinging on her arm.

Then she felt her stomach plunge sickeningly. A large continental convertible was parked outside Sophia's small house, looking incongruous in the narrow street, its sleek lines signifying its exclusiveness.

Whose could it be? Surely Sophia and Matilde knew no one with a car like that! Unless of course it belonged to the Marcasis. She relaxed, albeit a little despairingly. It must belong to the Marcasis. No one knew she was here. Not Patrick, or Barbara or Mr. Bolam.

She walked on up the road and entered the house feeling her nerves grow taut like violin strings. She was trembling, and yet there was no reason for all this.

Calm down, she thought, trying to do just that. Stop tormenting yourself with stupid dreams and fantasies.

She walked down the passage to the kitchen. Sophia was stirring some soup on the stove as though nothing momentous had happened. She smiled as Samantha came in.

"Did you get everything?" she asked.

Samantha's heart subsided abruptly. "Yes, I think so. When is lunch ready?"

"In about 15 minutes." Sophia returned to the soup.

Samantha sighed heavily. "Where's Matilde?"

"Oh, she's in the other room. Someone came to see her. Go in and tell her lunch is nearly ready. Ask her guest if he wants to stay and have some. We haven't much, but what we have is good."

"All right." Samantha left the basket on the table and crossed the passage to the room that was only used on special occasions. Knocking lightly, she opened the door and stepped inside.

Then she really felt as though her heart had stopped beating completely. Standing on the hearth, his back to the empty fireplace, stood Patrick, looking as attractive as ever in a lightweight suit of dark blue, and a loose mohair coat.

"Patrick!" she exclaimed, her voice almost breaking in her emotional state.

"Hello, Samantha," he said lazily, as though it was the most natural thing in the world that he should be there.

Matilde rose from her seat on the couch. "This . . . gentleman has been waiting for you, Samantha," she said. "Are you feeling all right, dear? You look quite pale."

Samantha shook her head. "I'm . . . I'm fine," she stammered.

Then she gathered her scattered wits and tried to take the consternation out of her voice. "What are you doing here, Patrick? Did Barbara send you?"

"Nobody sent me," he said, his voice serious now. "I came to find you and take you back."

Samantha stiffened her shoulders. "Thank you for your trouble. But I don't want to go back."

Patrick glanced at Matilde and with an imperceptible shrug of her shoulders, she made for the door.

"I'll leave you two alone," she said quietly. "I'm sure you have a lot to say to one another."

Samantha caught Matilde's arm. Suddenly she felt afraid of this arrogant stranger who stood staring at her with unfathomable depths to his tawny eyes.

"No, Matilde, don't leave. There's nothing to be said that you can't hear."

Matilde freed herself firmly. "Samantha, darling, you must face this alone. I cannot help you," and she went out, closing the door behind her.

After Matilde's departure, Samantha leaned against the door, one hand on the handle to make her escape should the need arise. Her color was high, and she felt totally unable to cope with Patrick in this mood.

Patrick shrugged his broad shoulders. With deliberate movements, he removed his overcoat, and loosened his jacket. It was much warmer here than in England, and he had not had time to change.

"I don't know what you expect me to say," said Samantha desperately. "I left England for good. I don't want to return. I don't like the people, and I don't know anyone any more."

"You know me," remarked Patrick, dryly.

Samantha sighed. "I understand you have had an offer to go to the United States to make a film of your last play."

"That's right. I leave in two weeks time. The play in London has been left in the hands of my agent. If my presence is required I can easily fly back."

"I see." Samantha bent her head. "I'm pleased for you. You'll really be famous after this."

Patrick smiled tightly. "Do you think that's important? Being famous, I mean."

"I don't know. It depends who you are. Barbara will love it."

"What does Barbara have to do with it?" Patrick's voice was cold.

"I don't know that either. But I expect you'll work something out. It's a pity she has this play coming up. She could have gone with you."

Patrick frowned. "Stop talking in riddles. Barbara and I are nothing to each other. We were . . . well, friendly . . . once, but that was all over long ago. She knew it, too. She still does, but she won't admit it."

Samantha twisted her hands together, releasing the door knob.

"Then why have you come here? I don't understand."

"Why do you think I've come, you little idiot?"

Patrick crossed the room forcefully, pulling her into his arms. Grasping a handful of her hair, he forced her head back and pressed his mouth against her throat, his lips warm and insistent.

"Go on," he groaned, as his mouth sought the nape of her neck, "tell me why I've come."

Samantha forced herself not to respond and cling to him. It was a torment and an ecstasy to be so close to him.

His body was so demanding and passionate. His touch left her weak and unable to think coherently.

With a little cry, she wound her arms around his neck, uncaring any longer what he meant by his caresses. She adored him and could not repulse him. She might be emotional and stupid, but she could not help herself.

"Oh, God!" he muttered as his mouth found hers. For a long minute there was silence in the small room that had so suddenly become a paradise to Samantha.

It was with difficulty that he at last allowed her to be free, and his hands gripping her shoulders he said,

"Samantha, have you any idea of what you've done to me?" He shook his head. "Hell, and I thought I was long past the age to fall in love."

Samantha traced the curve of his jaw with her fingers.

"Oh, Patrick, why didn't you tell me?"

Patrick's fingers tightened so that they hurt, but Samantha loved it. "I tried to tell you, the day of the funeral. But I guess, as usual, I made a mess of it. Even now, you're probably speculating in your mind as to my intentions. . . . "

Samantha blushed, revealing her innocence.

"You see!" Patrick grimaced. "What am I? Some evil demon or something! Did you honestly think I might suggest we have an affair?"

Samantha shook her head. "I didn't know," she confessed. "Patrick, tell me properly, please."

Patrick smiled. "I love you. I want to marry you. Will you have me?"

Samantha closed her eyes for a moment. This must be a dream.

"You know I will," she whispered achingly. "But can we? I mean, you're going abroad, and then there's Barbara. . . . "

We both have a lot of talking to do," he agreed. "To begin with, the trip to America might do nicely as the start of our honeymoon. Would you like that?"

Samantha gazed at him. "Oh, Patrick, you know that would be marvelous!"

"Good. Then that solves that problem. Now, after our honeymoon, we'll return to England. We might even stay at Daven, if that's what you'd like to do. . . . "

"Oh, I would!"

"Good." He smiled mischievously. "And as for Barbara—well, I don't think we need to concern ourselves too much with her. If the story of your background ever comes out, that's her affair, but I don't think we need be unnecessarily unpleasant about it. . . . "

"Oh, I'm glad you said that," said Samantha quickly. "I don't want to cause her any more trouble. . . . "

" . . . and that still leaves Killaney. Would you like to spend some of the year there?"

"Will we have time?" Samantha laughed, feeling light-hearted for the first time in weeks. "Patrick, darling Patrick; it's like a dream come true."

Patrick pulled her back into his arms. "Don't look at me like that, honey," he murmured, his mouth against hers. "I'm wanting you so badly, and I know I'm not going to take you . . . not yet."

Samantha hugged him close. "But how did you find me? How did you know where to begin?"

Patrick sighed. "It's a long story. I went down to Daven and you weren't there, so I found Emily. She told me about the row with Barbara the day of the funeral. After we realized you couldn't still be in London, Emily suggested here, and I contacted the airport and sure enough you were booked on a flight to Milan a week before. So I settled my affairs and took a flight to Milan myself." He

laughed. "Am I boring you?" and when she shook her
head, he continued, "I hired the car and drove to Perruzio. Everyone there knew your name, but no one could tell
me where you might be, until I ran into a chap called
Benito Angeli. . . . "

"Benito!"

"Yes. A chap in the village said he was the only person
likely to know. He said he had seen you a few days ago,
and that you had said you were staying with Matilde's
sister in Ravenna, and here I am. Does that satisfy you?"

"Perfectly." Samantha drew away from him. "I still
can't quite believe it. It's all so wonderful."

Patrick drew her back against him. "But it is what you
want, isn't it? You're not in any doubt?"

Samantha slid around in his arms. "In any doubt?" she
echoed, shaking her head. "Patrick, I was never in any
doubt. I think I knew, right from that moment on the
plane."

Patrick pressed her closer against him. "I think this is
getting too intense," he muttered softly. "Do you know
where we're going now?"

Samantha looked up at him. "No. Where?"

"To a villa on the shores of Lake Como, to see a certain
Signora Mallory. . . . "

"Your mother!"

"Yes, my mother. I think it's about time she met you,
don't you? After all, you'll be related in a week's time."

"All right, darling. I don't care where we go, as long as
we're together."

"My sentiments exactly," murmured Patrick, his lips
against her hair.

RATA FLOWERS ARE RED

Rata Flowers Are Red

Mary Moore

Misjudging Bruce and breaking her engagement was upsetting enough; meeting Mark Palmer only added to Judy's confusion.

Judy had gone to work on his farm hoping to sort out her problems. Instead, she'd fallen in love with a selfish, calculating, greedy man who would marry a woman for her money. At least he'd been honest with her.

"The setup here is difficult," Mark said. "My uncle left me the farm provided I could double production in five years. But he added a few strings. If I marry Zelda before March, I'll get $10,000."

What was wrong with her, Judy wondered. How could she love a man like that!

CHAPTER ONE

Judy walked quickly down Oxford Terrace, her heels beating out a rapid tattoo on the pavement. There was really no need to hurry, but the anger inside her had built up a sense of urgency. Now that she had made up her mind to break her engagement, she wanted it finished quickly. She was quite unaware of the admiring glances she drew from the people who were sitting on the seats along the banks of the Avon river, enjoying the warm spring sunshine. She was dressed in a leaf-green suit, and the sun picked out the copper tints of her shining cap of hair. Her tall slim figure and long-legged stride seemed to emphasize that spring had really arrived.

Thoughts chased each other chaotically through her mind. How gloriously happy she had been when she left England two months ago to fly to New Zealand. To fly to Bruce. Even the fact that she had finished her nursing training and had passed her finals with honors had been of little significance compared to the fact that she was at last on her way to be with Bruce again after a six-month separation.

Their reunion had been all she had hoped for. The parting had, if anything, strengthened their love for each other. His family had welcomed her with open arms. Judy had been delighted. She had expected a certain amount of restraint, perhaps even resentment, because Bruce had met and planned to marry an unknown English girl. But Mrs. Clarkson had received her with enthusiasm and had insisted that Judy stay with them until the wedding. Judy had been thrilled at the warmth of her reception and delighted to have the chance to get to know the members of the family intimately. Perhaps that was where she had made her fatal mistake. Perhaps she would have shown more wisdom if she had taken a temporary nursing position while the wedding arrangements were made.

Of course she and Bruce had planned to marry soon after her arrival. Mrs. Clarkson had talked them into waiting for three months to give her time to arrange a proper wedding, as she called it. She had said it would hardly further Bruce's career to have a small, quiet, hole-and-corner wedding. Well, Mrs. Clarkson had had her way. But then, thought Judy bitterly, didn't Mrs. Clarkson always get her own way?

Oh, what was the use of going back over the misery and frustration of the past month? She was meeting Bruce now to hand back his ring. It was over. Finished.

The car was parked in the usual place. How often in the past few weeks had she been sitting in the car waiting for Bruce to finish work! It had been one part of the day when she could have him to herself. Her eyes blurred with tears as she blindly groped for the door handle. She climbed in and slammed the door viciously. She had reached the end of the road. No one could say she hadn't tried to please his mother. At first she had given in because she did not want to start off on the wrong foot. But as time went on Judy discovered that she was always giving in. The only way to satisfy Mrs. Clarkson was to surrender completely to her wishes. To do this, Judy had found, was very difficult. Her normally lighthearted, impulsive, independent spirit had been slowly suffocated.

The episode this afternoon had shown her quite clearly that Mrs. Clarkson had every intention of managing and controlling their lives after they had married. She made that abundantly clear. This morning Mrs. Clarkson had been terribly excited when she had discovered the house next door was up for sale. Judy had thought it was only natural for her to be interested as she would have to live next to the new people. When Mrs. Clarkson had rushed off to town to keep an unexpected business appointment, Judy hadn't given it a thought.

Judy still felt numb from the shock of Mrs. Clarkson's surprise announcement when she returned home, that she and Bruce had gone to the real estate agents at lunchtime and paid a deposit on the house next door. Judy had sat in horrified silence while Mrs. Clarkson had burbled on about how wonderful it would be to have them so near. How she would be able to help Judy with the housekeeping, and when the children came she would be able to advise Judy and teach her how to bring them up. Judy had shivered. Without excusing herself she had gone upstairs and packed her bags. She had called a taxi, booked a room at Coker's Hotel and left. She had been lucky to leave without Mrs. Clarkson's knowledge. She had felt that the least Bruce was entitled to was being told first that she was breaking her engagement. If she had said goodbye to Mrs. Clarkson she knew that she would not have been able to control herself. She knew also that his mother would have called Bruce straight away. That woman . . . ! Angrily she pulled off her engagement ring when she heard Bruce approaching the car. She put it on the seat, then turned to stare out on the window side, while she fought desperately to control her emotions.

Judy heard the door open and felt rather than saw Bruce slide into his seat. She noticed his momentary hesitation before he got in, so he must have seen the ring. She must be quick before he started to plead or argue. She continued to gaze out the window. It was easier than facing him and seeing the hurt look on his face.

"I'm giving you back your ring, Bruce. I'm not going to wear it. I am not going to marry you, next month or any other month. We're finished, all washed up. You're not a man, you're a mouse. You're completely spineless, a jellyfish. Your mother has you tied to her apron strings, and she'll never let you go. She may be able to direct you, control your every thought, but I'm damned if she's going to boss me!

"What she did this morning was unforgivable. She went downtown and without mentioning a word to me, had you pay a deposit on that house. What were you thinking of? You could have called me and asked what I thought of the idea before you paid over the money. But I can bet it was all your mother's idea to give me a lovely surprise. You spineless idiot, she knew I would stop you. She knew, and you did too, that our plan was to buy a new ranch-style home out at New Brighton where we would have young married couples for our neighbors.

"When she told me about it I couldn't believe it. She's a Dracula, a vampire, a—a parasite living on other people's lives!" Judy choked, her eyes were full of tears. "I've packed my bags and moved to a hotel. I'm leaving Christchurch tomorrow, and I won't tell you where I'm going. I can't—I don't even know myself yet. But I'll get a job somewhere. I'll never see you again, I hope. Oh, Bruce, how could you let her do this to us? I'm ashamed of you. I've begged and pleaded for you to make a stand, but you have got no backbone. Well, haven't you anything to say?"

"No, nothing really, except that you look quite magnificent when you're in a temper."

Judy swung around, her startled eyes meeting the amused gaze of a complete stranger.

"Who are you?" she demanded furiously.

"Well, thank God, I'm not that poor jellyfish, Bruce. My name is Mark Palmer. What's yours?"

Ignoring his question, she stuttered, "Wwh-what are you doing in this car? Get out at once!"

Mark laughed, "For someone who doesn't like being bossed, you're pretty good at giving orders! And I'm not going to get out. I'm perfectly entitled to be here. This is my car."

"It is not. It belongs to Bruce Clarkson. I'm his fiancée."

"From what I heard it doesn't sound like a very permanent position." The wretched man grinned. "About the car—I'm afraid you must have been in such a filthy temper that you didn't check very carefully. The car directly behind us is the same color and make; perhaps that one belongs to Bruce."

Judy twisted about in her seat, and to her horror realized that the man had spoken the truth. His remark about her temper had not endeared him to her. She had made a complete fool of herself, and the beast looked as if he was enjoying every minute of it. Judy shrugged her shoulders. There was nothing to do but apologize and make as dignified an exit as possible under the circumstances.

"I'm terribly sorry, Mr. . . . Mr . . . ?"

"Mark," he offered helpfully.

Judy glared at him, "I'm sorry if I've caused you any inconvenience." Her voice was coldly polite.

"Oh, don't apologize. I found your performance vastly entertaining. I wouldn't have missed it for worlds. It's not every day I find a long-legged beauty waiting in my car for me. This has really made my day."

"You're insufferable!" said Judy as she vainly tugged at the hem of her skirt. "And leave my legs out of the conversation!"

Mark looked in the rear vision mirror. "Say, would that be your unbeloved Bruce getting into the car now? Poor fellow, he's in for it. After practising on me you should be able to give the second performance with even more vim and vigor."

Judy panicked. She couldn't face Bruce at this moment when she was completely demoralized. It had been bad enough saying all those things when she had been in a white-hot rage, but she simply couldn't do it in cold blood.

"Oh, take me out of here," she implored Mark. "Drive around the corner and let me out. Please. I can't face him now."

"I will if you tell me your name," Mark offered.

"Judy Somers, as if it matters. Oh, please hurry!"

"Right, Judy, crouch down under the dashboard, so that he won't recognize you." He started the car and pulled out into the traffic. He drove through the square and down Colombo Street toward the station until he found a place to park near a well lighted grill-room.

"You can come up for air now," he told Judy. The only answer he received was a muffled sob. He lit a cigarette and smoked it in silence. When it was finished he spoke to Judy.

"Would you like a loan of my handkerchief?"

"No."

"You disappoint me. All the best films have the hero offering the damsel in distress a nice clean handerchief. Sure you won't change your mind?"

He received no reply, but he knew she had stopped crying.

"That chap Bruce must have been a real idiot not to hang onto a girl like you. Fancy letting his mother get in the way. Me, I'd have traded my mother and a couple of aunts as well, to get hold of a girl as pretty as you."

That brought Judy upright with a jerk. "You had no right to listen! It was a sneaky thing to do. Why didn't you say something?" Her green eyes flashed fire.

"Here, be fair," Mark protested. "I didn't have a chance to get a word in edgeways. Naturally I was surprised to find you here. Before I had time to say a word you blew your top. I took note of your red hair and decided that it was a lot safer to sit out the storm."

"I don't have red hair!" Judy shouted.

"Well, let's say reddish brown," said Mark soothingly. Then he spoiled everything by adding, "And green eyes. Wow, what a combination!"

"I have brown hair and hazel eyes." Judy glared at him, then looked around her. "Where are we?"

"In Colombo Street down near the station."

"Good, I know how to find my way to the hotel from here."

"I'll drive you wherever you want to go. Which hotel are you staying at?"

"Coker's. But there's no need to drive me there. It's just along here. I can walk," and then she added belatedly, "Thanks."

"Would you like a cigarette?" Mark suggested.

"No, thanks, Mr. . . . er Mr . . . ?"

"Mark. Really, Judy, after all we've been through together you can hardly insist on formality," he laughed.

Suddenly the humor of the situation struck her. It was quite crazy. Like a Mad Hatter's tea party. Judy's lips trembled, a dimple quirked, and then she smiled. She looked at Mark, and then they both broke into peals of laughter.

Oh, the blessed healing relief of shared laughter! Judy felt that she had shed a straitjacket she'd worn for weeks. Slowly she sobered up.

"I really am most awfully sorry to have been such a nuisance to you, M-Mark," she said shyly. "This has been a terrible day for me, as you may have guessed. Then I had to make matters worse by climbing into the wrong car and breaking my engagement with the wrong man. I think you took my whole performance remarkably well." She gave him her normal, wide smile. It was amazing how much at ease she felt with him. She should have felt small and humiliated but there was something about him that gave her confidence.

"Why, thank you, ma'am, for them kind words. I gather you've had a fairly bad time lately. Now to show that I really am forgiven, will you come and have a bite to eat with me?"

"No, thank you," replied Judy quickly.

"I have a lot to do."

"I'll say you have," said Mark blandly.

"You've to see Bruce and break off your engagement. That won't be easy. He'll have probably traced you to the hotel by now and be waiting for you. I think you'd be better able to face the difficulties if you had a good meal first. What do you say?"

Judy still hesitated. He was probably right about Bruce. By now they would have discovered her missing. It was an easy task to call around the hotels to see if she had registered. She needed more time.

"Another thing," Mark grinned at her. "Just a small point, of course, but the next show is going to lack fire if you haven't your ring to throw back at him. I'll keep it safely for you until we've had something to eat."

Judy was appalled. She had completely forgotten about the ring. Wouldn't she have felt terrible if she had jumped out of the car earlier and left the ring with Mark? How would she have traced him? How would she have explained to Bruce?

"Goodness me, you wouldn't resort to blackmail to get your own way? Or would you?"

"I wouldn't hesitate. I'm a desperate character. I would even consider kidnapping if all else failed."

"Then it looks as if I have no option. I'm only a poor defenseless female, entirely at your mercy. I will accept your gracious invitation."

"That's my girl! But I'm not sure about the defenseless-female bit. Sorry I can't take you to dinner, but I haven't much time. I have to get on the road home. I have a 200-mile drive in front of me tonight, so let's nip into this grill-room and see what they have to offer."

He walked around and opened the door for her. Taking her arm, he led her into the pleasant warmth of the grill-room. She was surprised to find that she only came up to his shoulder. She was quite tall herself, so he must be about six feet or a bit over. Idly she wondered what he did for a living. She guessed he would be a professional man, or perhaps an up-and-coming business executive.

They found a table and gave their order, Mark leaned forward and regarded her speculatively. "Pardon me for referring to the earlier part of our meeting, but it's of great importance to me—at least one thing you said is. You said that you were going to leave Christchurch and also that you were going to have to find a job. Did you mean that, or were you just saying it to bring Bruce to heel?"

"I meant every word I said."

"What sort of work did you have in mind?"

"I'm a trained nurse. I don't suppose it would be hard to get a position. I would like to go to some small country district, if possible."

"It's fate, that's what it is! But I'd better start at the beginning. I'm a farmer. What are you looking so startled for?"

"You don't look like a farmer," Judy stated positively.

Mark shook his head sadly. "You townies are all the same. Just because a fellow doesn't wear rubber boots and chew straw all the time, he doesn't look like a farmer! For your information, I don't wear this suit when I'm milking the cows. Okay, where was I? Oh yes. I have a farm on the West Coast."

"What sort of farm? How big is it?"

"Eight hundred acres. It's a mixed farm. Mainly devoted to town-supply milking, but I do have a few hundred ewes and have some run cattle. I came over today to give a paper at Lincoln College."

"What was the subject of the paper?" interrupted Judy.

"Budgeting. How to increase production with only limited capital."

"I thought all New Zealand farmers were rich."

"A few of them are very rich; a lot of them are comfortably off, but the majority of them are like me, scratching for a living. Farming on a shoestring and hoping they don't slip and hang themselves with it. Now don't interrupt. I lose the thread of my discourse. I have a pair of ten-year old twins at home, and until six weeks ago my mother stayed to look after them. She has had a lot of worry that I won't go into just now, but the result was that she suffered a slight heart attack. She has been in hospital ever since.

"The doctor said that if I could get someone to help, I could bring her home. She doesn't need nursing, only someone to keep an eye on her, and see that she doesn't overdo things for a start. I had one housekeeper a couple of weeks ago, but she turned out to be an alcoholic. I came in one afternoon to discover her rolling drunk with the twins as interested spectators, so she had to go. This is the busiest time of the year on the farm. I simply can't stay in with the kids when they come home from school, and though they're out with me a lot, I can't take them with me in all weathers.

"I put an ad in the newspaper saying I would be in Christchurch today and would interview any applicants for the job. Two applied, and both were hopeless."

"In what way were they hopeless?" asked Judy.

Mark waited until the waiter had served their meal and left. He looked slightly embarrassed. "One of them wanted an astronomical wage, that I can't afford. The other one intimated that she was quite prepared to offer me all the home comforts, and I mean all. She said quite frankly that she would be quite happy to accommodate me if I didn't like sleeping alone." He shuddered.

"I don't believe you!" Judy's gay laugh rang out.

"It wasn't funny," Mark glowered. "After that I tried all the employment agencies and the Labor Exchange. Nothing. No one wants to go out in the country. Now, I know I have a colossal nerve, but I have to ask. Would you be interested in a position like that? You did say you preferred the country. I don't want to pressure you, but even if you could come for two or three weeks it would be wonderful. What do you say?"

Judy gave him a long, steady look. Of course she knew that she could not judge a man's character at one glance, but his clean cut features made a favorable first impression. He had a strong, deeply tanned face, a firm mouth and determined chin. There were laughter lines around his eyes—blue eyes that held a glimmer of amusement.

"I won't press you for an answer. Eat up, or your meal will go cold. I don't expect you to take me at face value, you know. I'll give you the names of several folk here in Christchurch who will vouch for my character. This steak is really good. I was starving!"

As Judy ate her steak, eggs, and french fries she was surprised to find how hungry she was. She had been so much on edge lately that she had not felt like eating much. She much be mad to think of going off with a man she hardly knew. But it was a job. And what was the alternative? Leaving Christchurch tomorrow for an unknown destination and then applying for a position. She was seriously tempted. After all, he did offer references, and there was his mother and children there. And he did have a sense of humor; that was most important.

"How do you know I'll be suitable?" she asked curiously. "I haven't any references, and I hardly think Mrs. Clarkson would give me one."

"You'll be just right. You're strong and healthy, and you'll need to be to keep up with the twins. You can laugh at yourself: this I consider a most necessary virtue. You've shown that you have a fine independent spirit. You'll fit in just perfectly."

"You don't even know if I can cook," Judy protested.

Mark laughed, "Even if you can't boil water, I would still want you. To have someone as pretty as you about the place would make everyone feel so good, it wouldn't matter what we ate."

"Flattery will get you nowhere," Judy told him firmly. She couldn't help feeling pleased all the same. Mark had shown quite obviously that he like and admired her. After weeks of trying to walk a narrow tightrope of behavior to gain Mrs. Clarkson's approval, she suddenly felt free.

"Tell me about your children. What are their names.?"

"They aren't my children," Mark looked horrified, "they're my brother's kids. You must have misunderstood me. Peter and Vicki are living with me while their parents are overseas. I'm not married."

Not married, thought Judy, and was ashamed of the thrill of pleasure she felt.

Mark took a piece of paper from his pocket, and a pen, and wrote down three addresses.

"Here are the names, addresses, and phone numbers of three people who will speak for me. The first one is Basil Watson, of Watson, Watson and Taylor, lawyers. I was at school with him. The next one is the Vicar of All Saints Church. And the last is my aunt, Mrs. Morris. She's rather a pet. Go out and see her. She would come and help me herself, only her husband is an invalid. Well, what's the verdict?"

"I'll come." Judy's face lit up with delight as she imagined what Mrs. Clarkson's reaction to her impulsive decision would be. Her slightly slanted, witch-green eyes sparkled wickedly. "I've decided the devil you know is better than the devil you don't know."

Mark pretended to be hurt. "I don't care for your reasoning, my dear girl. I find your allusion to my character extremely painful." Then he smiled, "But I'm very relieved that you've decided to take us on. You've taken a tremendous load off my shoulders. You're definitely not the mercenary type. You haven't even asked what I'm going to pay you." He named a figure far in excess of what Judy expected.

"Certainly not. I wouldn't get as much as that at the hospital. I think ten pounds a week—sorry, I mean 20 dollars—would be generous. It's hard to get used to thinking in dollars and cents. And I'll come for two weeks' trial. If I don't like it, or if you don't find me suitable, we can stop there with no hard feelings. Agreed?"

"I think two weeks' trial is a good idea, but I'm not having you working for a pittance. I'm not a pauper. Say I pay you the same wage you would get from the hospital. Will that suit you?"

"Yes," agreed Judy thankfully. "When do I start?"

"I'd like to take you with me tonight, but I can hardly expect you to set off into the night with a complete stranger. There's a train that leaves Christchurch at ten-twenty every day. Give me that envelope, and I'll write my address and phone number on it. You can check up on me tomorrow. If you haven't changed your mind, send me a telegram saying which day you're traveling. You buy a ticket to Stillwater, and I'll meet you there. The train gets in about two-thirty, I think."

Mark sat back and lit a cigarette. "Well, that's all the details taken care of. I'll run you back to the hotel and get on my way." He picked up the tab, then took her ring from his pocket, and put it in front of her. "That young chap of yours must be very unimaginative. Fancy choosing an ordinary diamond ring for a girl like you. If I bought you an engagement ring it would be a large square emerald."

"It's a very valuable ring," Judy's eyes flashed. "And you never will have to worry about buying me an engagement ring. If I ever get married, and I don't think I will, I'll take good care to choose an orphan. There'll be no mother messing up my wedding plans another time!"

"But you haven't met my mother yet. She's really something. Plenty of girls have wanted to marry me just to get her for their mother-in-law."

Judy giggled, her anger forgotten. He really was ridiculous! She placed the ring in her purse and went out to the car.

Mark drove the short distance to the hotel and parked the car. He turned to Judy, his voice serious for once. "Judy, just a minute before you get out. I have something to say to you. You're only a young girl, and your family are a long way away. You're making a big decision when you hand back that ring. Take my advice, don't be hasty. This afternoon you are very upset. Perhaps you said things you didn't really mean. You've had time to cool down. Think carefully before you act. I suggest that you call his home to let them know where you are, then tell him you'll see him in the morning. I think it's always best to have a good sleep before deciding anything important. You know the old adage 'sleep on it.' "

"No, I wouldn't sleep. This decision isn't as sudden as you think. I've been worried for the last month. I've given it plenty of serious thought. I won't change my mind," Judy said stubbornly.

"Bruce is still in love with you, I presume?" Mark made it a question.

"Yes."

"And you must have loved him, or you wouldn't have promised to marry him. Don't you love him now?"

"Yes—no. Oh, don't keep at me! I don't know what I feel for him. I did love him very much when we met in England, but he seems a different person in his own country. I still like him, but I feel sorry for him now. He's clever and intelligent, and is highly respected in the firm where he works. It's just his private life that's such a mess. He never makes a move without his mother's approval. I thought if he would transfer to another town our marriage would have a chance. I nearly had him persuaded, but he talked it over with his mother. She became so upset that he dropped the whole idea." Judy's voice was bitter.

"Perhaps you overestimate his mother's control. Once you're his wife you will have a lot more influence with him."

"Not if she's living next door. Anyway, whose side are you on?" Judy cried accusingly.

"I'm not on either side. Personally, I hope you get rid of him and come over to the Coast, but I don't want you to make any mistakes that you may be sorry for afterward."

"I'm sorry," muttered Judy contritely. "I know I'm a bit touchy on this subject. And it's good of you to bother with me, especially when you have a long drive in front of you. But I'm not a child. I'm old enough to know my own mind. I know now that I couldn't marry Bruce. I couldn't be happy with a man I didn't respect.

"Mrs. Clarkson says she only wants the best for us, and I'm sure that's the truth. She refers to her interference as, quote, a gentle guiding hand, unquote. I know that she had many good points; she is an excellent housekeeper, a marvellous cook, better than I will ever be. She's on all sorts of committees and works hard. She has the best garden in the street. Perhaps she does always know best, but I want to be free to make my own mistakes. Oh, you don't want to hear all this."

Mark encouraged her. "Tell me. I'm interested, and it may help you if you get it off your chest."

Judy continued, "You would think being so busy, she would be happy to let us go our own way, but no, she takes an interest in every move we make. For instance, Bruce and I planned to have a small, quiet wedding shortly after I arrived. His mother said it wouldn't help his career to have a rushed, hole-and-corner wedding. She said it would take her three months to prepare for the type of wedding she wished us to have. So we waited. I wanted to have Bruce's two little nieces as my attendants, but she thought it more fitting to have three girls of my own age. I gave in. Honestly I don't want to bore you with all these petty details, but you must understand that there's no satisfying Mrs. Clarkson. No arrangement is too small to escape her notice. If Bruce and I plan to dine out, she says she has people coming for dinner especially to meet me. So we stay in. When we discuss buying furniture, whatever I choose, she has some good reason why it's not suitable. Every time she talks Bruce around to her way of thinking. He's like putty in her hands. I could go on and on, but I won't. This afternoon when she told me we were going to live next door, I could see the writing on the wall. I need to get out and quickly."

"I'm sorry you've had such a rough time, Judy," Mark said sympathetically. "Bruce, sounds to me as if he's sadly lacking in intestinal fortitude. He deserves to lose you. And as for his mother, she sounds a real beaut." He got out of the car and went around to open the door for Judy, then escorted her to the hotel.

Taking her cold hand in his large, warm one, he said goodbye. "I'm glad we met, Judy. Remember if you change your mind, you have my best wishes. If you decide to come over to the Coast we'll do our best to see you enjoy yourself. Send a telegram, and I'll be waiting for you." He gave her hand a comforting squeeze and walked away to his car.

CHAPTER TWO

Judy caught the train with only minutes to spare. Her face was flushed as she sank thankfully into her seat. What a rush! She felt quite jubilant. Last night, when Mark had driven off, she had promised herself that she would be on the train the next morning come what may. And here she was. She did not know why the thought of catching the train had become so important, but she had used it as a crutch to support her through the painful meeting with Bruce last night.

He had been waiting for her when she returned to the hotel. He had been worried and upset about her disappearance. Poor Bruce, she had felt a swift rush of pity as she saw his anxious face.

They had gone for a drive. The name of the place she did not remember, but it had been a beautiful spot. The sky had been alive with brilliant stars and the light of the full moon shone on the sea. The sound of the waves crashing on the shore had seemed but an echo of her own smashed hopes and dreams.

There she had told Bruce she would not marry him. He had been quite marvelous, she had to admit that. He had listened to what she had to say, without interrupting or arguing. Bruce had agreed that his mother was too possessive and that he had been unfair to Judy. He had been quiet and controlled, but had not attempted to hide how deeply hurt he was. He begged for another chance.

Judy had found herself weakening. She had loved him

very much, but she knew deep in her heart that their marriage would not work out. She was sorry for him, but pity was no foundation on which to base a happy marriage.

Bruce had promised to see the real estate agent first thing in the morning and cancel the deal even if it cost him money. He promised to apply for a transfer to Wellington and was reasonably certain it could be arranged within two months. He promised to agree to anything Judy wanted, if only she would marry him. He had been quietly determined and sure of himself, adamant that he would not accept her decision as final. Judy had never admired him more. If only he had shown that firmness with his mother a month ago there would have been no broken engagement now. Even so Judy had held to her purpose. She was scared to trust him. She had been hurt too often. The magic had gone from their romance.

Finally he realized that she was determined to give his ring back. "Very well, Judy, I'll take the ring and keep it in the hope that one day you'll let me put it back on your finger where it belongs. I love you so much. I know that I've been a fool. If you give me another chance I'll make amends. Perhaps it's a good idea for you to go away, but you must let me know where you will be. Let me write to you." His voice was desperate. "Let me see you once again. Take all the time you want to reconsider your decision. One month, two months, I don't care how long, but you have to let me see you once more."

Judy had not the heart to refuse to see him again, although she told him it would be useless. She would not change her mind. She advised him to get away from his mother and start living his own life, not for her sake, but for his own.

They had parted friends, but Judy knew that they had lost something very precious. It would never be the same between them. She had gone to bed shaken and miserable, and had cried herself to sleep.

The clickety-clack of the wheels, and the rocking motion of the train were soothing. Her thoughts turned to what lay ahead. She began to feel a bit apprehensive. Perhaps she had been too impulsive jumping at the first offer of a job.

What did she know about Mark Palmer? Nothing. This morning she had decided that since Mark had given her the position on face value, it would be mean of her to check up on his credentials. Now she was not so sure. She might be heading into a very difficult situation. Then and only then did she remember that she had not sent the telegram to say she would be arriving today. What an idiot she was!

"Good morning. Mind if I sit here?"

Judy looked up startled to find an elderly man putting his case in the luggage rack above her head. She smiled and moved over nearer the window.

The man sat down and gave Judy a friendly smile. "Cass Davis is the name. My daughter doesn't approve of me smoking, and so she booked me into a non-smoking compartment. I've just had the guard change me through here." He lit a cigarette with obvious satisfaction and winked at her. "What the eye doesn't see the heart doesn't grieve over!"

Judy had to laugh.

Mr. Davis settled down to read his paper, and Judy stared blankly out of the window. Her mind was filled with unhappy thoughts. She would have to send a cable to her parents to let them know the wedding was off. Not that the news would affect them much. They had let Judy go her own way for a long time. She had been 12 when they had been divorced. They had been pleased that Judy had accepted the breaking up of their home with apparent indifference. But that indifference had only been on the surface. The hurt had gone deep, and the feeling of insecurity had taken years to conquer. She had been sent to boarding school and had spent the vacations being shared equally between them. They had both remarried and had young families. Judy knew they still loved her, but the feeling of being a visitor persisted whenever she visited either household.

From this experience she had become determined to make sure that if she ever married it would be for life. She would not be guilty of giving any child of hers that lost, lonely feeling that she had suffered when her parents split up. But how could you be sure that love would last? She had believed that Bruce was the right man for her. She was shaken with doubts. She had read somewhere that children from broken homes had less chance of making a successful marriage than those from happy, secure homes. Well, if that was the case she would never marry.

"Have you ever been to the Coast before?"

Judy suddenly realized that her seat companion was speaking to her.

"No, this is my first visit," she replied, only too happy to have someone to talk to. Anything was better than sitting brooding.

"Great place. I've just been on a visit to my daughter in Christchurch, and I'm real glad to be heading home. My son has a farm in Totara Flat, and I live with him and his family. His wife is a great girl. I potter about the place and do odd jobs for them. I'm real lucky I have such a good home. You know, I went out to an old people's home when I was in Christchurch, to see a friend of mine. It would fair break your hear to see those old folk. I reckon it would be a living death to be shut in one of these places.

Mind you, I'm not saying they're not well cared for, but after a life of hard work, to be shoved in there by your kids as if you were a nuisance! It must be hell.''

"It doesn't sound as if you have to worry, Mr. David," Judy consoled him.

"No, I'm one of the lucky ones. I went over to live with June, she's my daughter in Christchurch, when Mother died. She made me real welcome, you know, but I couldn't take city life. Not after living on the Coast all my life. Where are you from? You're not a New Zealander—I can tell by your accent.''

"I'm English. I've been in New Zealand nearly two months. If you've lived on the West Coast all your life you must know a great deal about it.''

"Wonderful people on the Coast. They're different to the rest of the New Zealanders, I reckon, more open, more friendly, more hospitable. They're not very partial to law and order. I don't mean they're lawless, just a bit touchy about too many rules and regulations. They obey the laws they find reasonable. The others they just ignore. They're basically very honest people, so there's very little crime over there. No, it's just the petty, little laws they get into bother with, like the one about closing pubs at six. It never worked on the Coast. Damn silly law anyway. I could tell you some real funny things about the Coast if I had a mind to.''

"Oh, do tell me," Judy encouraged eagerly.

That was all Cass Davis needed. For an hour he talked, and Judy listened, entranced. He told her of people and places up and down the Coast—stories about the early pioneers, and the hardships they faced. Some of the tales were sad, stark tragedy, and others were hilariously funny. It soon became clear to Judy that this man knew and loved the open, outdoor life; that he loved the bush, the mountains and the birds, and even the wild treacherous rivers. No wonder he couldn't settle dwn to city life. He talked interestingly and well.

"Mustn't bore you too much, miss," he said eventually, "but now you have some idea of what makes a West-Coaster. Other people call them rugged individualists, but they're good-hearted folk, and I knew you'll be glad you came. I'm going to have a bit of a snooze now. Wake me up when we get to Otira for lunch."

After listening to the old man Judy found herself looking at the bush and mountains with different eyes. The scenery was magnificent. The train was now traveling an hour late because of the washouts after the flood last week.

They stopped at Otira, and when Mr. Davis returned he had two friends with him. He introduced them to Judy as Sam and Bill Gray. They tipped the next seat over so they could sit facing Judy and Mr. Davis.

The short, fat, jolly-looking one, named Sam, laughed as he sat down, "Trust old Casanova Davis to choose a seat beside the prettiest girl on the train."

Judy had to smile when she heard the nickname. She guessed it had been well earned. Anyone as handsome and charming as he was at 70 must have been a great man with the ladies in his youth. She enjoyed listening to their conversation, but when she heard Mark Palmer's name mentioned she really became interested. The two men were farmers and had been at Lincoln College when Mark had given his paper.

"Clever young feller," Sam Gray said. "Tough too. When he first took on that farm none of us thought he'd make a go of it, but he sure is holding his own."

"Don't think I know him at all," admitted Cass. "He's not the Palmer that plays fullback for the Coast team, is he?"

"Yeah, that's him. Plays a good game, too. He was picked for the Island trials, but he told the Rugby Union he wasn't available. Pity too, I reckon he had a fair chance of making the All Blacks. Great boot on him, and he's not scared to tackle."

Judy was really alert and listening intently.

Bill Gray laughed." He looks such an easygoing chap, but you don't want to be fooled by that smile of his. No, sir. He can look after himself—remember that time he gave those Walters boys a thrashing? They thoroughly deserved it. Remember that, Sam?"

"Yeah, I won't forget that in a hurry," Sam chuckled. "It was like this, Cass. The boy inherited the farm from his uncle. Before he had time to get to know his own cattle there was a sale at Ngahere. Old Walters had a mob in, and the boy sat up on the rail watching them being sold. He didn't realize that half them were his own cattle." The men all laughed.

Judy was horrified, before she could stop herself she burst out, "Why didn't someone tell him?"

"Listen, miss, if he was too silly to know his own cattle he deserved to lose them. I didn't know they weren't old Walters's cattle, and even if I had known, I wouldn't have poked my nose into something that didn't concern me. Get yourself into a lot of bother that way. Anyway, when young Palmer mustered his cattle he found out he was short and went looking for them. Someone must have told him what was what, so he kept his eyes open. A couple of months later he missed about 70 ewes. He trailed them up the riverbed and could see that they'd been driven. He found them inside Walters's boundary fence. He opened the gate to drive them back when the two Walters boys came on the scene and there was hell to pay."

Bill chipped in, "It must have been a beaut fight. I

called in to see Palmer that night, and he was a real mess. He was smiling even though it must have hurt him. He said that the other two looked worse than he did.He bet me it would be a long time before they pinched any more stock from him."

Judy was disgusted. "What an uncivilized way to behave!"

"Uncivilized it might be, young lady," Bill said, "but sometimes it's the only way a man can make his point. Those two boys were spoiling for a fight, and they had more than they bargained for. What did you expect Palmer to do? Walk away and leave his sheep?"

Judy protested, "Surely you have a police force? He could have gone home and called them."

"You don't know what you're talking about, if you'll pardon me for saying so. If he'd left the sheep he would have never seen them again. By the time the police came into action they would have been miles away. The police are willing to help, but cases like that are well-nigh impossible to prove."

Judy protested, "What about earmarks and brands? Don't they prove who owns the sheep?"

"Up to a point they're satisfactory. Well, farmers aren't allowed to use branding fluid any more, as a means of identification, because it spoils the wool," Cass pointed out. "And earmarks are chancy. Anyone can go to Addington sale and buy sheep with his neighbour's earmark on. There are sheep there from three or four different provinces, and earmarks can't help being duplicated. A dishonest man has plenty of ways of covering his tracks, believe me. The police move too slowly. By the time you notify them, and they come out to investigate, the stolen stuff is hanging up in a butcher's yard, nine times out of ten. No, the boy did the only thing he could."

"You all seem to accept it so calmly. Is there much stock stolen?"

"Course there is. Anyone who has sheep expects to lose a few lambs over the Christmas period. Fellers come out from town and nip off one for their dinner. Nobody really minds, even if you did you have a fat chance of stopping them," Bill explained. "No, the real trouble starts if you get a crook for a neighbor. Most farmers are honest enough, but occasionally you get one like old Walters in the district; then you must watch him like a hawk. Cunning old devil, he is. I'm glad he's not a neighbor of mine."

"You bet," agreed Sam, "and Palmer has enough on his plate without any extra. Do you remember old Jack Palmer, Cass?"

"Yes, I met him once or twice. Seemed a nice bloke."

"Well, Mark is his nephew. Jack died four years ago, and the boy inherited the farm with a few strings attached. Rumor has it that he and the old boy didn't see eye to eye. Mark went to Lincoln College and came back with a lot of high-falutin' ideas. They used to argue like mad. Mark became a farm advisory officer after he had his degree. The story is that Jack left the farm to Mark in his will provided he can double the production in five years. He made him pay a pretty steep lease for it during those five years too, so the boy hasn't much money to prove his fancy theories. But I'll say this for him, he works like a man possessed. We all thought he wouldn't have a hope, but we could be wrong, I reckon."

Bill said, "Poor beggar, he lost a lot of stock in a big flood the first year he was there. Knocked him for a six, it did, but it didn't knock that smile off his face. I like him. He's a decent chap. Never too busy to give a neighbor a helping hand. He was coming past my place one day just as my trailer broke, and five wool bales came off on the ground. First time I met him really. He came straight in and gave me a hand to get them on the truck. They were heavy brutes of things to lift, but it didn't seem to bother him at all. I hope he makes the grade.''

The train had stopped again. It was going to be quite late by the time they reached Stillwater. The men were talking about someone Judy didn't know, so she sat quiet, and thoughtful. There was more to Mark Palmer than she had first thought. It was hard to reconcile the pleasant, debonair young man she had met last night with the determined fighter these men had talked about.

She felt embarrassed that she had not mentioned that she was going to stay at his farm—almost as if she had been eavesdropping on a conversation. However, there really had not been an opening to say anything, and now the subject had changed. What had that man said? Something about not being fooled by his smile. Judy thought ruefully that the warning had come a bit late for her.

CHAPTER THREE

On arrival at the Stillwater Station, Judy collected her cases and put them in the waiting room where there was a lovely, big, coal fire burning. She found a public telephone box and tried the number Mark had given her. There was no answer. She went to the cafeteria and ordered a cup of tea. It was steaming hot, and she felt much more cheerful when she had finished it. Once again she tried the telephone, and this time a little girl's voice answered her.

"Could I speak to Mark Palmer, please?" Judy asked.

"Uncle Mark is still at the shed. I'm Vicki. Can I take a message?"

"Hullo, Vicki. Could you tell me when your uncle will be home?"

"I don't know. He's nearly finished."

"Would you tell him that Judy Somers is at Stillwater Station, and ask him to come and get me, please."

"Who?"

"Judy Somers. He'll know who I am. You won't forget, will you?"

"No. Goodbye." Judy heard the receiver click down. She felt annoyed with herself as she returned to the wating room. If she had remembered to send the telegram she wouldn't have to sit here waiting. She was very tired after her sleepless night last night, and the long train journey. Time passed so slowly, and her head began to nod.

She woke with a start. How long had she been asleep? She looked at her watch. It was six o'clock. Surely Mark must have finished his work now? It was dark outside. Perhaps the little girl had forgotten to give him the message. More frightening still was the thought that maybe he did not want her. He would not just leave her here. Or would he?

Then she saw his tall, rangy figure come through the door. He walked over to her, bent, and kissed her quickly on the cheek. "These your cases? Right, come on, follow me. I'm late."

Judy was furious, but he had disappeared through the doorway before she had time to recover. She grabbed her bag and small case and hurried after him. She followed him down the platform and across the railway tracks to his car. He had put her cases in by the time she approached and was holding the door open for her.

"What do you mean by kissing me? You have a nerve! I've a good mind not to go with you."

"Oh, come on, now. Hop in. The kids are waiting. Imagine how my stock has shot up with the locals after them seeing me kiss such a pretty girl. Now jump in and stop making a fuss. I'm in a hurry."

Judy got in. Put his stock up, had she? Well, if he ever tried that again, she would give the locals something to talk about! She waited for him to get in and drive off before she really gave him a piece of her mind, but he didn't give her a chance.

"Wonderful to have you here, Judy. You don't know how wonderful. I really didn't think you would come. Now, I have to go in here for a minute and see a chap. I won't take you as we must get back to the kids before they murder each other."

He was back very quickly and drove rapidly back down the road they had come and out onto the main road. "That was the local schoolteacher's house. I had to see him to ask for a loan of his wife." Mark grinned wickedly at her surprised face. "These West-Coasters are very generous. They'll give you anything, if you ask them nicely."

"So it seems. Surely lending his wife is carrying generosity a bit far."

"Oh, but he realized that my need was great."

Judy knew he was laughing at her, so she kept quiet.

"I'd better explain. I went in to ask him if his wife would come and be chaperon tonight. Nan will be home tomorrow, but tonight it's a bit awkward. In a small country place like this you can't be too careful. If you stayed at home with just me and the twins, I'd probably have to marry you to keep your good name."

Judy appreciated his care of her. "Thank you very much, but I can assure you that I wouldn't be asking you to make an honest woman out of me. You're quite safe. I hope I haven't been a nuisance arriving without warning, but I forgot to send a telegram this morning. Wouldn't it be better for me to stay at a hotel instead of bothering the school teacher's wife?"

"Oh, it won't bother Claire MacLean. She's a real poppet. She said it will make Steve appreciate her more if he has to look after the kids tonight. Here we are."

They turned off the main road, crossed the railway tracks and drove down a steep hill. When they stopped Mark carried her case, and she followed him along a cement path and into a warm kitchen. As they entered Judy could hear children screaming. Mark dropped her case and ran.

He came back pushing two children in front of him.

"Do let me introduce you to your charges. This repulsive creature is Vicki, and this equally repulsive little boy is Peter. They're ten years old. I told them to tidy up to meet you—and just look at them!"

Judy looked at the two bedraggled children and thought it better not to smile. But it was very hard to keep a straight face. They were both soaked to the skin and had some yellow gooey substance plastered on them. It was all through the little girl's long wet hair, while the little boy had a pair of scissors clutched in his hand. Both glared defiantly at her.

Mark gave them another shake. "Well, explain yourselves. I told you to change and wash, and then I come back to find you like this. Peter, what were you doing with those scissors?"

"I was going to cut Vicki's hair," Peter said flatly.

"He was too!" shrieked Vicki, twisting around, trying to aim a kick at Peter. "He was going to cut all my hair off and make me bald!"

Mark looked exasperated. "What in the world did you want to cut her hair for?"

"Because she broke my bantam's eggs."

"This is becoming like a Mad Hatter's Tea Party," said Mark grimly. "Why did you break his bantam's eggs, Vicki?"

Vicki started to sob. "B-because it said in a book that egg shampoo was good for washing hair, and I wanted to look nice for the new lady." She gave a hiccup. "I only wanted two of them, and he bit me and I scratched him and he threw water over me and I threw the rest of the eggs at him and he tried to cut my hair off and I threw water at him and—"

"That's enough," roared Mark, "That's more than enough! I don't know what I'll do with you. I'll let Judy deal with you."

Judy risked a smile. "Vicki is quite right, eggs are very good for hair, but not applied the way she's done it. Of course she should have asked Peter before taking them.

Come and show me where the bathroom is, and I'll help you both clean up."

Mark loosed his grip on the children. "Now you know, Judy, why I mentioned you would have to have your health and strength unimpaired to deal with these two. I hope first impressions aren't lasting, because they really aren't bad little monsters usually."

Judy hustled the children through the door to the bathroom. When she saw the mess they had made, she gasped.

"Well, you don't believe in doing things by halves, do you? We'll leave the bathroom till later. Which of you do I start on first?"

"I'll do myself," announced Peter with great dignity. "I'll go and have a shower in the wash-house while you do Vicki. Gee, isn't she a beaut mess?" He started to giggle.

"Take a look at yourself," said Vicki indignantly. Then she started to laugh, and Judy joined in. The three of them laughed until the tears ran down their faces. The ice was broken.

Judy recovered first. "Peter, will you bring my case through from the kitchen? I'd better change."

Vicki showed her to her room. She quickly slipped into a pair of jeans and a sweater and hurried back to the bathroom with a bottle of egg-creme shampoo.

As she soaped and washed Vicki's hair, the little girl chatted nonstop. Judy cleaned the walls, while Vicki had a bath.

Judy followed Vicki back to the kitchen. It was a large, comfortable, but very untidy room. A cheerful fire was burning in the open fireplace. Mark was serving supper while Peter finished setting the table.

"Can I do anything to help?" Judy offered.

"No, certainly not," replied Mark. "You can be a guest tonight, but tomorrow I'll thankfully give up the role of chief cook and bottle-washer. Come on and sit up to the table."

"Not stew again, Uncle Mark!" wailed Vicki.

"Stew again, yes. You know I can only cook stew and potatoes." Then his blue eyes took on a mischievous twinkle. "Actually, I was thinking of having scrambled eggs for a change."

"Oh, that's not fair!" protested Peter, but he joined in the general laughter.

Judy enjoyed her supper very much, finding to her surprise that she was very hungry. She was quiet, but enjoyed listening to the conversation and laughter of the others.

It was easy to see that there was a real bond of affection between the twins and their uncle. Also they shared a strong family resemblance. The three of them had the same startling blue eyes and dark good looks.

As they finished the meal a telephone rang somewhere in the house.

"Excuse me," said Mark to Judy. "You twins off to bed. There's school in the morning. Look sharp now," and he went through to answer the telephone.

Judy started to clear the plates away to the sink.

"We'll help you do the dishes, Judy," offered Vicki happily.

"No, we won't," said Peter. "Uncle Mark said we were to go to bed, and he meant it. Goodnight, Judy. I'm glad we have someone nice like you."

"Oh, so am I. I love having someone pretty and young. You ought to have seen the last one. A proper old bag, she was." Vicki giggled at Judy's shocked face. "Goodnight, Judy," and she danced and swirled out through the door before Judy could think of admonishing her.

Judy cleared the table, then found some detergent. She had half finished the dishes by the time Mark came back.

He stood looking at her with a thoughtful expression on his face.

Judy became restless under his penetrating gaze. She felt her face flush. "What's the matter with me? Have I a smudge on my face?"

"Oh, no, your face is quite beautiful," answered Mark, reaching for a tea towel. "Just thinking what a lovely sight it is to see someone else washing the dishes."

"Have you been without a housekeeper long?" asked Judy.

"Long enough. In fact, I'm sure I'm developing all the symptoms of housemaid's knee."

Judy laughed. "I'm sure you'll recover. Where do you keep the broom?"

"Leave the rest until the morning. Come and sit down by the fire. You've had a long trip. I meant to give the house a blitz before you arrived—however, you've seen us at our worst now. Are you still prepared to stay?"

"Yes, at least for the trial two weeks."

"Good. That phone call was from Mother. I saw her this afternoon. I hope you don't mind that I told her all about you. She's looking forward to meeting you very much. She was so excited about coming home. I was worried in case you changed your mind. I told her I would pick her up at four o'clock tomorrow afternoon. She has to wait until the doctor does his rounds after lunch, or she would have insisted on me being there first thing in the morning."

Mark stood up to get his cigarettes from the mantelpiece. "I'll go through and see if the twins are asleep. I want to tell you about them."

When he returned he sat down; his face was serious. "I want to tell you this before Claire comes. I told you that Peter and Vicki are my brother Paul's children. Paul is a doctor. He specialized in tropical diseases. Early this year he had the most wonderful opportunity to go to South America to further his studies, and he took Betsy, his wife, with him. They left the twins here with me. Mother came with them to look after us all. Everyone knows that, but what I'm going to tell you now is only known to Mother and me. Whether you think we're right or wrong I want your word that you won't mention it to anyone, especially the twins."

"You have my promise," Judy said readily. Mark nodded as if satisfied. "They've been away eight months. Three months ago we had word from the leader of the party that Paul and Betsy had gone farther into the interior with four native helpers, and that they had lost contact with the main camp."

"Have you heard any further news since then?" asked Judy anxiously.

"Yes, but not good news." Mark sighed. "Six weeks ago we learned that the native helpers had returned to the main camp. They said that Paul and Betsy had been in a canoe that had capsized. They were swept over a waterfall. The guides had searched the area, but could find no trace of them. The man who wrote told us there was very little hope of them turning up alive after all this time. The country they were in was particularly wild and rugged. Even if they had got ashore, they would have been without guides, and without their equipment. There are mosquitoes, snakes, dangerous swamps, not to mention hostile natives."

Judy was appalled. How petty her worries were compared to what this family was facing! "What a terrible time for you. No wonder your mother was under a strain," she said sympathetically.

"Yes, it's been pretty rough on her," Mark agreed.

"We decided in the beginning to keep it from the twins. Why worry them when there may be no need? Then when we received the next letter we did not know what to for the best. I just can't believe that Paul and Betsy are dead, and Mother feels the same way. After all, their bodies weren't found, even by the party that went out from the main camp. Somehow I feel that they'll turn up. The leader of the expedition said he'll come and see us when they return to New Zealand at Christmas. So until then Mother and I have decided to say nothing to the twins. Perhaps it's just cowardice, that I can't bear to tell them, but I don't think so. Paul and Betsy were capable, physically and mentally, of dealing with any emergency. I won't give up hope yet."

Judy did not know what to say to comfort him. "I'm inclined to believe that they're safe," she said slowly. "Especially as your mother feels the same way as you do. Mothers seem to have a sixth sense as far as their children are concerned. There were so many stories during the war proving that they do. I've heard of mothers knowing the hour their sons died, days before the War Office notified them. If your mother feels that Paul is still alive, then I think you were right not to tell Pete and Vicki."

"Thanks, Judy. Your sympathy has helped. Of course the twins are disappointed that they haven't had any letters for so long, but they think it's because of the trip. We try to act as natural as possible, otherwise they would be quick to notice we were worried. It hasn't been easy, I can tell you."

They heard a car stop at the gate. Mark stood up. "That will be Claire, I'll go and bring her in."

Judy liked Claire as soon as she met her. Claire was small and fair with lovely, brown eyes that danced with fun.

"I think I must really be on the scrap heap when I get

asked to play chaperon! Steve says I'm too flighty for the job, but he's only worried that if the kids cry he'll have to get up for them."

Judy laughed and asked, "How many children do you have?"

"Two little darlings, Jane is three, and Robin is two. You tell her, Mark, aren't they wonderful children?"

"Oh, quite wonderful," Mark agreed with a smile. "Exceptional children, Judy, they really are. They never cry, never get cross, never fight, always go to sleep when they're told. . . . "

"Stop it! You're not fair," Claire cried. "They're not angels, I admit that, but they're nicer than anyone else's kids, so there!"

"And there you have a completely genuine, unbiased opinion," teased Mark.

Judy laughed; she could see these two were very good friends. It amazed her to see Mark smiling and happy as if he didn't have a care in the world. Only minutes before he had been so serious, so genuinely concerned about his brother. She realized how much easier it would have been for him and his mother if their friends knew the trouble they were in. They would be offered plenty of sympathy, she was sure, but if too many people knew there was always the chance that someone would speak out of turn in front of the twins. She admired their courage.

Judy, Claire, and Mark had coffee, and were all happy to retire early.

Although Judy was very tired, she found it hard to get to sleep. She kept thinking of the twins. Poor little children, waiting every day to hear from their parents, quite unaware that they might never see them again. What a nice person Claire was. She looked far too young to be married with two children. She thought of Mark. Which was his true character? One side was lighthearted, teasing and acting like the charming idiot, and the other was serious, sensitive, and compassionate.

CHAPTER FOUR

The next two weeks passed as if on wings. Judy decided to spring-clean the house. The weather was beautifully fine. She washed, scrubbed, and polished. The house had been remodelled inside and out just before Mark had taken over. By the time Judy finished turning out the cupboards and drawers of each room, and washing the covers and curtains, the whole house sparkled.

Judy loved Mrs. Palmer. As she worked from room to room they talked and discussed every subject under the sun. Judy had known at the first meeting that she was going to like her. As each day passed the bond of friendship strengthened. Mrs. Palmer's wise, kindly eyes followed the trim, energetic figure as she moved deftly from one task to another. She understood from listening to Judy more than the girl realized of the loneliness of her adolescent years, and of her longing to find a place of her own.

Judy accepted joyfully the warmth, love, and understanding that Mrs. Palmer offered her.

One evening after Judy had supervised the twins going to bed, she put the ironing blanket on the table and switched on the iron.

"Judy dear, leave that until tomorrow. You're doing far too much," Mrs. Palmer protested.

Judy laughed gaily. "I'm not; I'm just loving it here. When I do this ironing and put it away we'll have finished the spring-cleaning."

"We will have finished," replied Mrs. Palmer. "Very nice of you to include me when you wouldn't let me do a hand's turn. You've worked like a Trojan. The whole house looks lovely, fresh, clean, and sweet. It was a lucky day for this family, the day Mark met you."

"Lucky for me, you mean," Judy said. "Do you know, I've hardly ever lived in a house—I mean, been part of a household. And you've let me do just what I liked. After years of boarding schools and living in hospital nursing homes this has been a wonderful experience."

Mrs. Palmer smiled at Judy's bright, flushed face. This gay, lively, young girl had lifted such a load off her shoulders. The twins adored her, and no wonder. She was marvelous with them.

"Did Mark say what time he would be home?"

Judy paused in her work and looked at the clock, "Oh, he shouldn't be long. He said the meeting would finish about ten. Would you like to go to bed now?"

"No, I had a rest this afternoon. I'll stay up and have supper with you when he comes in. Have you much more to do?"

"I've nearly finished," Judy answered, switching off the iron. "Tomorrow I'm going to start on the garden."

"You'll do nothing of the sort, Judy. You've worked so hard since you arrived, you'll have to take a day off for a rest. Now I insist. The garden can wait, I feel so ashamed just sitting around doing nothing. Tomorrow I'm going to do the cooking while you have one complete day free."

"We'll see," Judy said soothingly.

"There's the car. That will be Mark home." Mrs. Palmer put the kettle on. "I'm making supper to show my independence. Don't you 'we'll see' me, madam. You'll make me think I'm back in the hospital!"

They were still laughing when Mark came in. Judy

picked up the pile of freshly ironed clothes and put them in the cupboard.

"How did the meeting go, Mark?" his mother asked.

"Okay. Much the same as usual. They need some younger men in the executive positions. I think there'll be a shake-up at the next annual meeting. What were you two laughing about?"

"Judy has been bullying me, Mark," complained his mother, handing him a cup of tea. "Now sit down, Judy, here's your tea."

"You can see who's doing the bullying, can't you, Mark?" Judy said as she meekly accepted her tea.

"Don't let her get the upper hand, Judy. She's a very wicked old lady. Too fond of getting her own way altogether, aren't you, Nan?"

"Wait until you hear what I'm arguing about before you take sides, Mark," said his mother firmly as she joined them by the fire. "Judy has been working hard ever since she arrived. I want her to take the day off tomorrow. She wants to do the garden."

"Your mother wants to take over the cooking, and you asked me here to see she didn't work too hard, so you can decide."

"Not me. You can fight it out between you. My money will be on Nan. She's had years of experience and is very skilled at defeating her opponents in the most devious ways. Aren't you, pet?"

"Yes," admitted Mrs. Palmer complacently, and they all laughed together.

As Judy prepared for bed that night she thought how wonderful it was that she fitted into the household so easily. Mrs. Palmer was a dear. The twins were mischievous, but lovable. And Mark—Judy shied away from investigating her thoughts on Mark.

Bruce had written three letters. She must answer him. But what could she say? She had been so busy it had been relatively easy to push the problem of their relationship away to the back of her mind. She sat in bed with a pen in her hand staring at a blank page. Finally she wrote a newsy letter of all her doings over the last two weeks, signed it and sealed the envelope.

Poor Bruce, he would search the letter for some personal message, but he would look in vain. She was not ready to come to any decision. Life was so free and uncomplicated in this warm, friendly household. She had no desire to pitchfork herself back into the strained battle of trying to reach a decision.

Some day soon she would discuss her problem with Mrs. Palmer. Strange how neither Mark nor his mother had questioned her as to the outcome of her meeting with Bruce. She appreciated their attitude of waiting until she was willing to talk. The friendliness of their welcome, the approval they showed of the work she did, and the genuine pleasure they took from her company soothed her after the buffeting she had received from Bruce's mother.

She snuggled down in her comfortable bed, content and relaxed.

The next morning she found that Mrs. Palmer was in control of the kitchen and had no intention of being displaced.

"It won't hurt me to do the cooking, Judy. Go over to the shed and watch Mark milking the cows."

Judy wandered out into the bright sunshine. It was a beautufil morning. How close the snow-capped mountains looked. The Southern Alps dominated the whole scene. She walked down the lawn to the little creek and gazed into the water.

The children had some pet eels and were always begging the scraps to feed them on. The twins were very proud of them, but Judy thought they were horrible. As she watched, a huge eel slid through the water and nosed against the bank expectantly. Judy shuddered. There was something repulsive about the long, snake-like body. How the children could like them she would never know. They even named the wretched things, and they laughed at Judy for being scared of them.

"Come on, Judy, we're going to feed the calves. Come and help us," called Vicki.

"She's not to help, Vicki—just watch. You know Nan said she was on holiday today," Peter said.

"I'd love to watch," answered Judy, catching up with them. "I wouldn't be much help anyway, Vicki. I've never been on a farm before."

"Oh, I'll show you what to do. It's easy," replied Vicki importantly.

Judy followed them across the yard to the cowshed. Her interested eyes took in the big, concrete yard, the pipe rail fence, the white-painted walls, and the gleaming, stainless steel pipes. Everything was spotlessly clean. Mark did not notice her by the wall. A radio was playing the latest rock music, and the twins were busy collecting some small buckets.

Judy watched Mark move from one bail to the next. The cows were black and white. They looked enormous to Judy. Mark moved swiftly yet quietly amongst them. She saw the pattern of work emerging. Let one cow go, put the machines on the next, wash the cow that had walked into the empty bail and take a few squirts of milk from it, move on to another bail, let the cow go, back and put the machines on the washed cow. Judy was fascinated. It looked so easy, so effortless, but Judy was not deceived. Mark looked up and smiled, "Hello, what do you think of my cows? Beauties, aren't they?" He patted one cow that was standing ready for a bail. "This is Lucy, my pride and joy. Wait until the herd-tester comes. You're going to be the best cow in the district this years, aren't you, my pet?"

He changed several more machines and then came through to the small room beside Judy. He pulled a full can of milk away against the wall and put a new one under the cooler. The children came in. "The calves are ready, Uncle Mark," Vicki yelled above the noise of the machines and music.

"Right, go on with the shed. I'll be a few minutes before I can carry the milk out."

Judy was astonished as the twins went into the main yard and carried on with the work. The children were so quick, so capable, and yet so small.

"Want to have a go?" Judy jumped; she had not heard Mark walk up beside her. "No, thanks, I couldn't do that—I'd be too scared. Do the cows like the latest songs?"

"Of course they do. Actually it makes them much quieter; they don't jump at every sound—and strange voices don't affect them."

Judy followed the twins out to the calf pens. She watched the children get the buckets of milk ready and then bring in the smallest calves first.

"These are the youngest," explained Peter. "They're still on fresh milk. The next lot are on half and half, half fresh milk and half skim milk, that is, with a little oil, and the bigger ones have skim milk, oil and mash."

The calves were quickly fed and put back in their paddock. The twins scrubbed the buckets and put them in a rack.

"Come on, Judy, we're going home now, or we'll miss the school bus," Vicki told Judy.

"She's staying with me," said Mark. "Now off you go. Thanks for the help."

"Judy's our friend," Vicki protested. "Me and Peter brought her over. You're not fair!"

"No, I'm not fair, I'm very dark," laughed Mark. "Now scat. Quick!" As the children ran off he said, "Come and sit in the sun by the water trough while I finish up."

Mark milked the last of the cows and put them out, then hosed down the yard and rails. He washed and sterilized the machines, then went into the side-room to put the milk cans in the huge wall-length refrigerator. Judy was content to sit in the warm sun and listen to the pleasant music while she watched his quick, energetic, methodical movements. In an astonishingly short time the cleaning up was done.

Mark grinned down at her. "I'm sure you've enjoyed watching me work and are full of admiration for my supremely efficient methods."

Judy, who had been doing just that, said primly, "Oh, I'd heard the colonials had no little conceit of themselves."

"Oh, had you? Did you also hear that we don't like being called colonials and that we're wild and reckless, especially when insulted before breakfast?" Without effort he scooped her into his arms and held her poised over the water trough. "Apologize or I'll drop you in!"

Judy struggled wildly. "Let me down! You wouldn't dare!"

"Oh, wouldn't I?" His blue eyes were full of mischief. He lowered her feet into the water. "Say sorry like a lady for calling me a big skite. One, two, three!"

"I'm sorry!" Judy yelled.

Mark set her carefully on her feet. "Thank you for your most abject apology."

"You're no gentleman," stormed Judy. "You hurt me."

"I did not," replied Mark, smiling, and held the gate open with exaggerated courtesy. "Let's go home and get some breakfast. Come on, Judy love, I don't like fighting on an empty stomach. Don't sulk."

"Oh, you're impossible," replied Judy, but she smiled as she went through the gate beside him. It was extraordinary. If any other man had treated her like that she would have marched off in high dudgeon. But Mark seemed to be able to tease her, make her fighting mad, then disarm her completely with that wonderful smile of his.

After breakfast Judy tidied and cleaned the bedrooms. As Nan still would not let her into the kitchen, she wandered out into the garden. How lovely it was! The huge lawn, swept down to the creek that was bordered by a mass of golden daffodils. Two huge rhododendron trees were just coming into bud. Some forsythia trees were in bloom with their shower of golden bells; and the heavenly scent of a heavily laden daphne tree filled the air.

Nan joined her. "There's just a small patch of garden to weed, Judy. Here along the cement path. Mac does the lawns and shrubs, also the vegetable garden."

"Who is Mac?"

"He's an old man who lives across the road. He's a grand old chap, Mr. McTaggart, but he takes a lot of knowing. He keeps the place looking lovely."

"Yes, it really is beautiful. I wondered how Mark found time to do the lawns."

"Oh, Mark!" laughed Nan. "He would rather plough and sow 100 acres than do a small vegetable garden. Mac has been here as long as I can remember. He taught both

Mark and Paul to fish, and last year he taught Peter. They're both eagerly looking forward to the fishing season that starts in October."

While Nan went inside, Judy became busy with her gardening fork. It took her about an hour to weed and dig the small garden. She was busy admiring her work when around the corner came an old man. He was tall, straight, and almost gaunt. His hair was snow-white. He eyed Judy up and down, then looked at the garden.

"You've no done a bad job there, lassie."

"Thank you." Judy brushed her hair back from her forehead. "Are you Mr. McTaggart?"

The old man nodded. "And you'll be Judy. The children have been telling me of you."

"You like gardening, Mr. McTaggart?"

"Yes." The soft Scottish burr was most apparent.

"How long have you been in New Zealand? You haven't lost your accent."

"I have no kept track of the years. I came here as a young lad of 18 to seek my fortune."

"And did you find it?"

"No, but I found something a lot better—contentment."

"What part of Scotland do you come from?"

"I was born in Skye. The Isle of Skye."

"Why, isn't that strange! I was on Skye last year. I went with a friend on a trip to Scotland last year and went to several of the islands."

The old man's keen eyes brightened, and he questioned Judy eagerly on the changes that had come to the Island since he was there last.

"Have you ever been back, Mr. McTaggart?"

"Oh yes, I went back. I had no been in New Zealand only but a few years when the war broke out, and I went to

France. Spent four years in the trenches there. I went to Skye on leave, and a great fuss of me they made.''

Nan came to the door. "Cup of tea, Judy. Oh, good morning, Mac. Come and have a cup of tea with us?''

"No, thank you, missus. I'll be away to my work,'' and he walked briskly away.

As Judy and Mrs. Palmer sat down for their tea Mark walked in.

"My word, you ladies do yourselves proud. Every time I come in you're sitting gossiping over a cup of tea,'' he teased.

"For that you can get your own cup of tea,'' said Nan firmly. "Judy has been working hard in the garden this morning.''

"I met Mr. McTaggart,'' Judy offered.

"I'll bet that didn't take long. Mac would say Good morning and that would be that. He's one of the strong silent types like myself.''

"Oh, I wouldn't say that. He talked to me for ages. I think he's a real poppet.''

"Ye gods!'' cried Mark. "If he hears you calling him a poppet you'd better look out.''

"It's true, Mark,' said Nan. "She had old Mac eating out of her hand. I looked out and saw them going hammer and tongs, so I waited a while before I called them.''

"Our Judy is quite a girl. One look from her, and we men are down on our knees.''

It wasn't so much what he said, but the look in his eyes that made Judy blush.

"Now, Mark, you just stop teasing Judy,'' said Nan sternly. "Have another scone, Judy, you earned it.''

"What are you doing with yourself after lunch, Judy? Would you like to come for a walk around the farm with me?''

"Why, I'd love to." Judy's face lit up with pleasure. "But what about you, Nan?"

"Now stop worrying, I'm fine. I'll go to bed for a rest after lunch—that's a promise. You go with Mark. The walk will do you good. You've been tied to the house ever since you arrived." Nan patted Judy's hand affectionately.

"Watch her, Judy. She's a very cunning old lady. She knows you've been here two weeks, and she's worked you like a slave. Now she's trying to sweeten you up in case you've decided to up stakes and leave us to it."

"Oh, I wouldn't do that. I love it here. I mean—that is," Judy blushed and stammered, "if you want me to stay."

"Want you to stay?" Mark grinned. "Nan and I were discussing the purchase of a ball and chain—"

"Shh, don't be ridiculous, Mark. Judy my dear, of course we want you to stay. I can't tell you the difference it's made to the whole family having you here. We were at our lowest ebb. I was becoming so depressed, lying in hospital, worrying about Mark and the children, about Paul and Betsy, and then Mark brought you home."

"Not bad for a pick-up, is she, Nan?" Mark's smile was wicked.

'Out of here, Mark! Out you go! I'm ashamed of you." Nan chased him out the door and shut it firmly behind him. "I'm sorry, Judy. Mark shouldn't tease like that."

"Don't worry, I'm not offended." Judy giggled. "I think he's a proper nut."

After lunch she walked down the farm road with Mark. The sun was shining, the gorse was in bloom, the grass green—it was glorious.

Mark explained, "This road we're on was originally the main road. When the railway came through they built the main road on a higher level. Suits me fine having a good road from one end of the farm to the other; the bridges thrown in too. I don't know where I'd be without it when the farm floods. I have to bring all the stock up here."

Judy, who had been looking with interest at the green fields sloping gently down to a river in the distance, turned incredulously. "You mean a flood could cover all your farm?"

"It has many times," Mark answered.

"You're joking again."

"I'm telling the truth, Judy love, and it's no joke. You remember the name of the station the night you arrived?"

Judy nodded. "Stillwater."

"Yes, Stillwater. Well, below Stillwater, on the way to Greymouth, there's a gorge—very narrow—with sheer, rock walls. When it rains for two or three days—heavy rain, I mean—the water from back country creeks and rivers comes roaring down the Grey. It can't get through the gorge quickly enough, so it backs up and up. This farm, except for this road and the house, goes completely under water. Not a raging flood water, still and quiet, but just as deadly."

"It must be horrible," Judy shuddered, feeling cold in spite of the sun.

"It's not that bad really," replied Mark. "I have friends who live up country. When the river there bursts the banks in a big flood they call me, and I know I've got about four hours to clear the stock. I was caught badly the first year I was here, but I'm a bit more careful now. You'll probably see a flood one of these days."

"I don't want to," Judy answered hurriedly.

"Neither do I want one, but we usually get a good flood in September or October. Of course, plenty of times I move the stock and it's only a false alarm. If I don't move quickly at the first sign then they're cut off. See how those deep gullies run through the farm. The water fills those first then gardually covers the farm. When I own it, I'm going to bridge those gullies, and I won't be forced to clear the stock every small flood.''

"When will you own the farm?'' asked Judy.

"The beginning of March is D-Day. At the moment I lease it from my uncle's estate, but in five months' time it should be mine, God willing.''

"I wouldn't want to own it if half the time it's under water.''

"How you women love to exaggerate—half the time! Sometimes there isn't a big flood in two or three years. Sometimes it can go under water three times in one week, but the point is all the best land on the Coast is near the river. Anyway, the water only stays about 12 hours at the outside.''

They walked down off the road and crossed a little bridge. The scent of the blue gums was strong and tangy. Judy crushed the leaves in her fingers.

"See those big pines there on the hill? They're more than 100 years old. The first settler on this farm planted them.''

Judy loved her walk around the farm and noticed the pride in Mark's voice as he showed her his stock—the sheep, the calves, the yearlings, the two-year-old steers, and, as they came in a full circle back to the house, the black and white dairy cows, sleek and healthy.

"I've been all over the farm,'' she boasted to Nan and the twins at afternoon tea.

"That you haven't,'' interrupted Mark. "You've seen about half of it. I've 300 acres across the creek to the north. It's pretty rough up there. A lot of it's swamp, flax, and bush. I'll take you that way next time.''

"Hurry up and finish your tea," begged Peter. "Then you can come and get the cows with us."

"No, Judy has done enough walking today. She's too tired to go for the cows with you—another time perhaps," Mark said firmly.

Judy, who had been feeling tired after walking for hours, could not bear to see the disappointment on the twins' faces.

Vicki, always the most aggressive, was arguing. "You had her all day, Uncle Mark. You showed her all your moldy, old farm, and when we want to show her our things you say she's too tired. You're mean. You said Judy came to look after us, and now you're keeping her for yourself."

Judy laughed and felt a warm glow of happiness at being wanted. It wiped away her fatigue. "I'm not a bit tired. Get Nan's rubber boots out again. I'll be there in a minute."

The twins showed her all their favorite places on the way down for the cows—the pond where they caught tadpoles, a tree hut they had built last summer, a wild duck's nest. When they returned to the shed Mark had the motor going, and the twins wanted to teach Judy how to milk the cows.

"No!" Mark was firm. "Judy is tired, she's going to sit by the water trough and look delectable, while you two show her what good workers you are."

"Why can't I learn?" questioned Judy.

"Because I'm not having you getting hurt while you're here. It's not as easy as it looks. Now go and sit down out of the way."

"If a little girl of ten can do it, I don't see why I can't."

"*Go and sit down!*"

Judy was really rather relieved and did what she was

told. Later, during a pause in the milking, Peter sidled up to her and whispered, "Uncle Mark's just being stuffy. Me and Vicki will show you how to milk on the weekend. We won't let him know until you can do it real good."

Judy, who had only argued with Mark because she was tired and feeling contrary, rather than because she had real desire to learn how to milk, wondered what she had let herself in for. She was thankful that the twins had confidence in her ability, but realized that she would have to do the work, or they would think she was letting the side down.

Later on that evening after the twins were in bed, Mark realized that he had left the gate behind the orchard open. He went out to the back door, then returned. "Come for a walk down to the orchard with me, Judy. There's a beautiful, full moon. I'll bet you've never seen anything like it."

"I'm comfortable here, thanks," Judy replied.

"Look, Mark, you've walked the poor girl off her feet today. Leave her in peace."

"She's just lazy," Mark coaxed. "Come on, Judy. It's such a beautiful night I want to share it with someone."

Judy went through to her room and put on a jacket and shoes. They walked in silence down to the orchard. Mark closed the gate, and they leaned on it as they looked at the sky.

"Thank you for making me come, Mark," Judy said softly. "I've never seen the moon so big. It's magnificent: the snow on the mountains shining in the moonlight, and the scent of the blossoms. I can't find the words to describe it. Those mountains seem to call me. One day I'd like to try climbing them."

Suddenly from the tree above her came the most horrible chuckling—like the laugh of a madman.

"Mark!" screamed Judy and threw herself into his

arms, terrified. Mark's arms closed around her as he roared with laughter.

"What are you laughing at? What was that horrible noise?" demanded Judy indignantly, trying to release herself.

"That was only an opposum up the plum tree, Judy. Now stand still and tell me, did you mean what you said to Nan this morning about wanting to stay here?"

"Yes. Let me go."

"What about Bruce? Are you still going to marry him?"

"I don't know. I told him I'd think it over and that's what I'm doing. There's no hurry. Let me go."

"One more question. At this moment, then, you're not engaged to Bruce?"

"No." The sensation of being held in Mark's strong arms was making Judy feel very peculiar.

"Good," replied Mark and bent and kissed her competently and enthusiastically, then quietly released her.

"How dare you kiss me?" demanded Judy angrily.

"No trouble. You launched youself into my arms—I'd be a fool not to avail myself of the opportunity. At least I checked to see if you were free first. I think I was very helpful."

"Helpful?" sputtered Judy indignantly.

"Yes, helpful. You said you were trying to make up your mind whether to marry Bruce or not. Well, now you know what it might be like if you don't marry him."

"You haven't helped at all—you've made me more confused."

"In what way?" asked Mark innocently.

"Never mind. I'm going home."

"Don't be mad, Judy love, I'll behave myself. Come and see the little chap who frightened you."

Judy let him lead her forward to see the furry, little opossum. It peered down at her with bright, inquisitive eyes. "Oh, isn't he a darling? I'd love to cuddle him."

"Well, don't," advised Mark. "They have very strong, sharp claws." Taking her hand in his warm comforing clasp, he walked slowly home. "Have you enjoyed your day off, Judy?"

"Very much, but I'm tired."

"You'll sleep well tonight. I want to add my thanks to Nan's—it's been wonderful having you here. Bless your generous heart for coming. It's not only the work you've done, but you've brought laughter and light—the whole atmosphere has changed. I can now concentrate on the farm without worrying about Nan and the kids."

At the steps he released her hand and turned to face her. He looked at her steadily for a few moments, and Judy felt oddly breathless. His hand came up and gently traced the outline of her face.

"You're very beautiful, Judy. You have much to offer a man. Take your time deciding your future. Don't waste yourself on a man who's not worthy of your love." Then he smiled. "Sermon over for tonight, off you go to bed. I'll sit here and have a smoke before I go in. Goodnight."

"Goodnight, Mark." Judy hurried inside.

She could not get away from him quickly enough. He disturbed her. Nan had gone to bed. Judy quickly washed and undressed. Before she got into bed she looked in the mirror. . . . Beautiful? No, she wasn't beautiful, but her face was flushed and her eyes were shining like a child who had just seen a Christmas tree.

Angrily she switched off the light. Darn it all, what was the matter with her? Two weeks ago she was breaking her heart over Bruce, and now she was all of a quiver because

Mark had told her she was beautiful. Her heart couldn't be trusted—she must be a very fickle, shallow-minded girl.

She tried to think of Bruce, but before her was the image of Mark's deep, blue eyes, and his teasing, tantalizing smile. All right then, admit it. He was an exciting person to be with—she couldn't ignore him—he was so vital, so attractive so—so—so comforting somehow. That slow, sweet, smile would be her undoing if she wasn't careful. He was only her employer—he meant nothing to her, just her boss—she meant nothing to him. She must keep it that way. Her life had enough complications without adding any more.

CHAPTER FIVE

"Are you going to see Uncle Mark play football, Judy?" asked Peter on Saturday morning. "It's the last game of the season. If his team wins this one, they'll win the competition. It will be a great game."

"I don't know a thing about soccer, Peter."

"I'll go with you, Judy, and tell you what's going on. Uncle Mark is a beaut player," Peter told her earnestly.

"He's the best in the world," cried Vicki with her usual enthusiasm.

"No, Vicki, that's not true—the All Blacks are the best in the world. Don Clark—"

"Blow Don Clark. Uncle Mark is the best."

Peter, who took his soccer seriously, was annoyed. "Oh girls! They don't know anything," and he ran off.

"I do! I do! I know everything," screamed Vicki, racing after him.

Judy smiled. It was amazing what different natures they had considering they were twins. Vicki was volatile, excitable, and imaginative while Peter was steady, responsible, and thoughtful, but both possessed a lively sense of fun.

After lunch Mark said to Judy with a quizzical expression on his face, "I hear you won't want to live if you can't come and see me play soccer.

Judy was stopped from a hasty denial by the anxious, pleading look on Peter's face. So that was it! Peter was using her to get to the game.

"Well, I don't think I put it quite as strongly as that, but yes, I would like to see you play."

"Do you know anything about soccer?" Mark asked.

"Just that the All Blacks are the best in the world. Peter has promised to come and explain the game to me."

"That's a good boy, Peter," teased Mark. "Giving up a whole Saturday afternoon to teach Judy the rudiments of the game."

Peter's honest face flushed. "I wanted to go too, Uncle Mark."

"Well, so you shall. Do you want to go too, Nan? Vicki?"

"Not me," replied Nan flatly. "I hate soccer. Great big men chasing a little ball and getting their clothes in such a mess."

"Nan, you're a shocker, a disgrace to New Zealand. However, we'll see if we can make a convert out of Judy."

"I'm going too," shouted Vicki. "I'm going to see Uncle Mark play. He's the best in the world, aren't you, Uncle Mark?"

"Oh, without doubt," Mark laughed, picking the little girl up and tossing her in the air, to her wild delight.

Peter took his task seriously, and while they waited in the grandstand for the game to start, he carefully explained the rules to Judy.

"Here they are now, Judy," he said. "Uncle Mark is the one out in front. He's the Captain. See, his team wears red sweaters. The others wear green."

Once the game started Judy felt herself caught up in the excitement. The supporters of both teams were extremely vocal, and the candid comments would have made some of the players' ears burn if they could have heard.

At half time the score was even; eight all. The air was

tense. Then the green team scored a try but failed to convert it, making the score eight. Peter's face was grim.

"You wait, Uncle Mark's team will win."

Personally Judy though it doubtful. Time and time again Mark's team were pressing on the goal line, but each time the green team's defense was too good. Then, just in the closing seconds of the game, Mark took the ball on his own 25 and started to run. He raced down the field, over halfway, side-stepped two men and was still going. He was over the 25 and stepped out of a tackle. The crowd were on their feet yelling. He had only one man to beat. He ran straight at him, then swerved at the last minute. Judy found herself on her feet screaming "Mark, Mark! with Peter and Vicki as he touched down for a try.

The crowd cheered and cheered. It had been a magificent run. Then they hushed as he went back to take the kick.

"I don't know if he can do it," Peter muttered anxiously. "It's not an easy kick. Oh, I hope he does."

Mark stood up from placing the ball, then stepped back several paces and ran in and kicked. It soared up beautifully high and straight, directly between the posts.

His supporters went wild. As the referee's whistle went for full time they poured out on the field.

"Oh, boy, oh boy! Isn't he beaut, Judy?" cried Peter.

"See, I told you Uncle Mark was the best," Vicki spoke with smug satisfaction. "The best in the world. Wasn't he wonderful?"

"He certainly was," agreed Judy, smiling. The twins were apparently among Mark's most ardent admirers.

They made their way out to the car to wait for Mark.

"He won't be long, Judy. He has to shower and change. Oh, that was a really good game. Are you glad you came?" Peter asked.

"Very glad."

When Mark arrived the twins were all over him. He started the car and pulled out into the traffic. "Well, Judy, What did you think of your first game?"

"I really enjoyed it. It was tremendously exciting, especially your try. I'm sorry I won't be able to see any more games."

"Well, not this season. It's all finished for this year. The boys are throwing a party tonight. Would you like to go along with me? It will be a good show."

"I'd love—" Judy stopped suddenly, remembering her resolution not to get involved. "Sorry, Mark, I don't think I should." It was hard to say.

"Second thoughts aren't always the best, Judy."

"Perhaps not, but—"

Vicki burst in indignantly, "I think you're mean, not going to the party with Uncle Mark."

"That will do, Vicki," Mark said firmly. "Judy has a friend in Christchurch. He might be very angry if she went out with me."

"I bet he's not as nice as Uncle Mark." Vicki was not pacified.

"Now, now, Vicki, don't be rude," said Mark.

Peter suddenly joined in, "If Zelda doesn't mind you going out with Judy, Uncle Mark, why should her friend mind?"

"That will do, you two—shut up and sit quiet. See, down there, Judy, that's the gorge I was telling you about. Remember, the one that causes the flooding."

That evening when Mark went out Judy regretted that she had refused to go with him. The house suddenly seemed quiet and dull. Who was Zelda? She would have liked to ask Nan, but did not want to appear interested. He must have a girl then. Zelda—what an interesting name. Of course someone as attractive as Mark wouldn't be unattached at his age. She tried to ignore the flat feeling of disappointment. Why should she care?

"Come on, twins—I'll give you a game of checkers. I'm feeling lucky tonight. Last time we played you both beat me. Tonight it will be different."

The twins were enjoying coaching Judy in the milking shed. Whenever Mark left them alone in the shed, Peter made Judy bail up to the cows. Then gradually she learned to wash them, use the strip cup, and finally to change the machines.

The first time she put on the machines she did it perfectly. The next time it was a disaster. She fumbled about until she lost all the vacuum, and all the machines in the shed fell off. Vicki, who was on guard watching for Mark, raced in and hissed, "Get back by the trough—here's Uncle Mark. We'll take the blame."

Mark scolded them for being so careless and helped them put the machines back on. The twins giggled conspiratorially. Judy did not want to try again, but they bullied her into it. Soon she was almost as proficient as they were in the shed.

Each day after they went to school Judy helped Mark scrub up the shed.

One evening when Mark failed to return at milking time the twins and Judy brought the cows in, set up the shed and started the milking. By the time Mark arrived hot and bothered just at dark they were finishing off.

As it happened, the twins were out feeding the calves, and Judy was coping single-handed, with the shed. She already had the separator turned on for the excess milk.

Mark stared in astonishment. "Where did you learn to milk?"

Judy grinned at him impishly. "Ask the twins! They thought I was upset because you wouldn't let me learn to milk, so they decided to teach me on the side."

"Wow, what a surprise! You're really one in a million, Judy. Where are those kids anyway?"

"Out feeding the calves. Here they are now. Look, if you aren't going to help, get out of the way so we can finish off. Go and sit on the water trough so you don't get hurt."

The twins laughed uproariously. "Serves you right, Uncle Mark," jeered Peter. "We knew she could do it."

Judy let the last line of cows go and started hosing down the shed, while the twins pumped the water through. Mark took charge of the separator room.

"I'm amazed, downright amazed. How did you learn to set up the machine—the separator?"

Judy was quite nonchalant. "You don't think I've been sitting here with my eyes shut for the last six weeks, do you? I've helped you dismantle the darned thing every morning, so I just reversed the order. Easy!"

Well, I'll be damned. What a great bunch of kids you are! I came home really thinking I'd be all hours getting finished, and here I find you've done all the work. You are proper marvels."

The twins reveled in his praise. At dinner time they shared the joke with Nan and became overexcited, but one one wanted to spoil their fun. The twins delayed going to bed trying to extend the happiness of the evening.

"Wait until I go home to England and tell my friends I milked a whole herd of cows. They'll never believe me," said Judy.

"You're not going home, are you?" asked Vicki anxiously.

"Not yet, not for a long time," Judy soothed.

"Why don't you stay here—I mean for always?" Peter suggested.

"Oh, I couldn't do that. Some day I'll have to leave, but I'll always remember this farm and the happy times I've had here."

Peter persisted, "You mean when Mom and Dad come home, and Nan and Vicki and me go back to Dunedin."

"Yes, I'll have to leave then," replied Judy, smiling at their eager faces.

"Why don't you marry Uncle Mark? Then you could stay," Peter wanted to know.

"Now that is an idea, Peter," Mark laughed. "I wonder I didn't think of it myself. She can cook—she's not bad-looking. Now you've taught her to milk she'd be invaluable. Yes, I must consider it."

Vicki danced up and down, "Yes, do, Uncle Mark, then we can keep her." Then her face fell. "Oh no, you can't. You've got to marry Zelda, so you can get all that money."

There was a sudden shocked silence. Judy did not know where to look—Vicki, now aware that something was wrong, started to cry.

"Where did you hear that bit of news, Vicki? Have you been listening at the door when Nan and I were talking? You're a very naughty little girl—you need a good thrashing!" Judy had never seen him so angry.

Vicki, now thoroughly upset, screamed, "I didn't listen at the door. I hate you! I hate you!" and she ran from the room sobbing bitterly.

"Do you know what she was talking about, Peter?" Mark demanded.

"Yes, I do," shouted Peter fiercely, "and I think you're rotten. Vicki came out one night for a drink ages ago, and you and Nan were talking. The door was open. She came and told me, something about a will. If you'd shut the door she wouldn't have heard. I wish—I wish Mom and Dad would come home. I hate it here!'' He burst into tears and ran out, slamming the door behind him.

Judy was shocked that Peter should cry. He was such a tough, hard, little boy. She had seen him get some really sore hurts without making a fuss. Poor little fellow, he must be very upset.

Nan stood up, obviously very distressed. ''The poor little things! What a pity when they were so pleased with themselves. I must go and comfort them.''

''Nan, do you think they could have heard us discussing Paul and Betsy? How could we have been so damned careless? I feel sick at the thought.''

''Now, Mark, don't worry. I'm sure they wouldn't have kept it to themselves if they'd heard us discussing Paul and Betsy. They would have asked questions.''

''Then go through and talk to them, Nan—I'll come and make my peace later. Poor little brats. I shouldn't have jumped at Vicki like that, but I was upset about what they might have heard.'' He turned abruptly and walked quickly out of the kitchen.

''Can I do anything, Nan?'' Judy asked.

''Yes, dear. In about ten minutes bring them through a cup of hot chocolate and a cookie. Yes—and an aspirin for Vicki. She's a very highly strung little girl, and she adores Mark really. It's such a shame.''

Judy thoughtfully tidied the kitchen and did the dishes. What an extraordinary statement to make! She tried to remember Vicki's words. Something about he had to marry Zelda, or he would lose all the money. Then Peter mentioned a will. Neither Mark nor Nan had denied that the statement was true. They were both more upset by their own carelessness in leaving the door open. It was easy to understand their dismay at the thought that the children might have learned of the news that their parents were believed dead. And to learn of it in such a manner would have been much worse than if they had been told in a straightforward way. But "marry Zelda or lose the money" sounded so extraordinary. Well, it was none of her business.

Judy made up the three chocolate drinks, placed some of the twins' favorite cookies on a tray, and an aspirin, then carried it through. Nan was sitting on Vicki's bed with her arm around the little girl. Peter was lying on the end of the bed. They were talking quite happily, but Judy noticed that Vicki was still giving an occasional hiccup, and that she had her mother's picture clutched in her hands.

"Oh, how nice, Judy. Come on in. We were just talking about the twins' mother, Betsy. Let Judy have the photograph while you drink your chocolate Vicki. Be careful you don't spill it. Chocolate stains are so hard to get out. I am glad you brought me a cup too, Judy."

Judy looked at the photograph. What a happy family group—Peter and Vicki standing with their parents on the steps of a lovely, modern home. The father was tall and dark with a fine intelligent face. The mother had an arm around each twin and was laughing. Judy was surprised to see that their mother was not much taller than the twins.

"Why, you two are nearly as big as your mother," she commented.

Peter, scenting criticism, said, "She's little, but she's tough. Dad wouldn't have taken her with him if she hadn't been strong. She can ride, shoot, ski and swim. She used to go mountaineering before she had us. Dad says he would rather have her with him, if he was in a tight corner, than any man he knows."

"Oh, I'm sure he would," Judy agreed hastily. "I think she looks quite lovely. I didn't mean anything derogatory by saying she was tiny. I'm so tall myself that I envy small dainty girls. They look so much more feminine."

"You're okay," Peter said gruffly.

"You should see Mommy when she's going out with Daddy at night," Vicki put in eagerly. "She has beautiful dresses, really gorgeous, and wears earrings and everything. Daddy says she looks like a princess. She smells lovely too."

Judy felt a sudden surge of anger at the missing Paul and Betsy. How could they go off and leave their children? They must have known the risks involved. When you have children, you should stay and look after them, not go gallivanting all over the place. She knew that Mark and Nan loved them and cared for them, but children need their parents.

"When do you think we'll hear from them Nan? It's ages since we had a letter."

Judy could see Nan looked strained. "You've finished your hot chocolate. Nan, you're looking tired. Why don't you go to bed? I'll read a little to the twins. We have only one chapter left to read."

Nan kissed each child and giving Judy a grateful glance left the room.

"Promise you'll go to your room, Peter, and you'll settle down as soon as I finish, Vicki?" asked Judy as she found the place in the book.

"Yes," chorused the twins. As Judy's pleasant voice read on they relaxed, became interested in the story, and forgot their worries. When she finished she settled them for the night and went along to see Nan.

"Are they better now?" Nan asked anxiously.

"Yes, right as rain. Don't worry, Nan. You know how

children say things they don't mean when they're upset, but they forget quickly. How are you feeling?"

"Better now, thanks. It's so silly to get upset, I know, but when you're under a strain it isn't easy to remain calm. I've taken one of my pills, so I should have a good night."

"Is there anything I can get you before I go to bed?"

"No, nothing, thanks, dear," answered Nan. "Goodnight, Judy, and thanks."

Judy went out to the kitchen to make sure the fireguard was up and then went to bed. There was no sign of Mark, but she heard him talking to Vicki and then Peter.

During the night a noise woke Judy. She heard someone moving around in the kitchen. Quickly putting on her brunch coat and slippers, she hurried out in case Nan had taken a bad turn.

"Oh, it's you, Mark. I thought Nan might not be feeling well."

"Judy, I'm sorry, I was just making some coffee. Did I wake you up?"

"What on earth is the time?" asked Judy, rubbing her eyes.

"About one o'clock. I was busy doing my paper work. I've just finished. Seeing I've woken you up, would you like a cup of coffee?"

Judy walked over and stirred the fire. "By the look of the table you've had quite a bit to do."

Mark collected his papers and tidied them up. He poured Judy a cup of coffee and brought it over to her, then sat down opposite her.

"You understate the case. I've had a monumental task. I hate doing my bills. They always tell such a disastrous story. I keep putting if off. I usually pick a wet day, you know: dismal day—dismal task; but I didn't feel like bed tonight, so I thought I'd do a bit on the budget.''

"Well, did you balance it?"

"You have to be joking!" Mark laughed without mirth. "However, I have a few more months left. To be exact, four, November, December, January and February. Not long considering the state of my books at the moment. But believe me, Judy, I'm going to have this farm. I've sweated my guts out here for five years, I'm not going to lose it.''

Judy sipped her coffee. There didn't really seem anything to say. She knew so little of the situation. Mark lit a cigarette and stretched his long legs out in front of the fire. "The set-up here is a bit difficult. My uncle had a peculiar sense of humor. He left me the farm provided I could double the production in five years. Then he added quite a few strings. He socked me with a high rent, stipulated of course that I was not to borrow, and then threw in a delightful saver. I'm not boring you?"

"Not at all. What was the saver?"

"Oh, really very cute. His old friend Duke Morrison has a lovely daughter Zelda, and Uncle Jack thought he would play Cupid. If I marry Zelda before first of March I'll get 10,000 dollars. This, I may add, I am allowed to use to balance the budget, and so gain the farm. The old reprobate!''

Judy's eyes were enormous. "That was an awful thing to do.''

"Oh, I don't know." Mark's expression was enigmatic. "He never married and was always on at me not to leave it until too late. He thought Paul was fortunate marrying young and having a family. This was his way of making his point.''

"What is Zelda like? Do you love her?"

"She's a very nice girl. When she's at home we go around a lot together. I've known her for years."

"Does she know about the will?"

"Of course not. Only the lawyer, Nan, and myself and Paul know the contents of the will. Oh, I forgot to mention the twins."

"Would she marry you?"

"I think she might."

"But what would she think if she found out that you'd only married her to get the farm?" Judy was horrified.

"I didn't say that was the only reason I would have for marrying her. Anyway, she's a very sensible girl. I'm sure she would think it a good idea."

"Sensible? I think it's shocking! However, it's none of my affair." Judy stood up and put her cup on the table. "It beats me why you bother working so hard, or trying to balance your budget when you have the problem already solved."

"Why are you so angry, Judy? —not that it doesn't suit you to look angry. I think I've mentioned it before."

"I'm not angry, just disgusted. I didn't think you were like that."

"Like what?" He was laughing at her.

"Miserable, calculating, someone who would marry for money. I hope you have all the happiness you deserve, but I'm sorry for the girl. Goodnight!"

"Judy, you're always jumping to conclusions. I never said I was going to marry her. I was just telling you the terms of the will."

"I'm not interested." Judy would have liked to slam the door, but was scared of waking the whole household.

Judy was so angry she thumped the pillow with rage and then burst into tears. After a while she stopped and tried to work out why she was so angry. It wasn't because Mark was going to marry Zelda. If he had said he was in love with Zelda she would have accepted that, but he had implied that it would be a sort of arranged marriage.

He was just despicable. How could she have been so mistaken in his character? She had admired him so much. He was so good with Vicki and Peter. He and his mother shared a wonderful relationship. He worked so hard and was so cheerful—so kind. She had liked him, more than liked him—not loved, that would have been stupid.

I hate him, she told herself firmly. He's just not worth thinking about. I can't leave here because I've found out what he really is. I love Nan and the children. It wouldn't be fair to leave them in the lurch. I will wait until after Christmas. They should have some definite word about the twins' parents by then. And she had to admit it—she wanted to see Zelda. What could she be like? Sensible! Ugh!

Judy fell into an uneasy sleep just before dawn. She didn't wake at the usual time and Nan was surprised to see her come into the kitchen.

"Oh, I thought you were over at the shed, Judy. Didn't you sleep well?" Nan's voice was sympathetic.

"Not very," admitted Judy. "I don't think I'll go to the shed this morning. I'll do the lunches, and then start the washing. Do you think it will keep fine? It looks a bit cloudy."

"The weather report is for rain. We might be lucky. We can always finish the clothes off in the drier if it does rain."

When Mark and the children came in laughing together, Judy decided grimly that Mark wouldn't get around her as easily as he did the twins.

"Why weren't you at the shed, Judy?' Vicki demanded. 'Were you sick?''

"No, darling, I wasn't sick. Now eat your breakfast, or you'll be late for the bus.''

"Oh, I think your prize Judy is just a oncer, kids. You won't see her back in the shed.''

Both twins defended Judy loyally. Peter wasn't having his star pupil maligned or criticized. "You will come over tonight, won't you, Judy?''

"Of course. Really, you must hurry. Get your books.'' She refused to look at Mark. Drat the man! She had intended keeping as far away from him as possible. Now to pacify the twins she would have to spend a couple of hours a day in his company. After the twins left Judy cleaned the table and stacked the dishes.

"Will you come and give me a hand to move the sheep, Judy?''

"No, I'll be busy in the house today,'' she replied brusquely.

"Oh, don't tell me you're still mad at me.'' Mark put a friendly hand on her arm.

"Don't touch me!'' Judy flared, shrugging away.

"Temper, temper!''

"What's the matter with you two?'' asked Mrs. Palmer. "Have you been teasing her, Mark?''

"No, Nan my pet, I haven't been teasing her. She's disillusioned. She has discovered that I have feet of clay and is very angry with me.''

"You do flatter yourself, my son. Only finding that their idols have feet of clay upsets people. I'm sure Judy is much too intelligent to have ever thought you perfect.''

"But you think I'm perfect, don't you, Nan?'' queried Mark in a plaintive tone.

"I do not,'' replied Nan severely. "I think you can be

most aggravating sometimes. Now get off to work and leave Judy and me in peace."

"Right, I'm off. Who would want to stay in a house with two bad-tempered women? 'Bye!'"

Judy worked furiously. She hung out the washing, then scrubbed the kitchen, wash-house and veranda. Then she polished the kitchen floor. She tidied and vacuumed the bedrooms, cleaned the bath and basin, moving like a whirlwind.

Nan called, "Judy, stop work this minute! Come and have a cup of tea. It's poured out. Come on, now, the house is as clean as a new pin."

Judy came through to the kitchen reluctantly. She took her cup of tea, but did not drink it. She was ashamed of her bad temper. She knew that she was being unreasonable. Mark meant nothing to her. The very fact that she was being illogical made her even more angry.

Nan's quiet voice interrupted her thoughts. "What's worrying you, Judy? Can I help? Have you and Mark really quarreled? Are you angry at him for upsetting the twins last night? Is that it?"

"No, of course not. It's nothing to do with Peter and Vicki. Really, it's nothing at all. I'm just being silly," Judy said unhappily.

"We're all silly sometimes." Nan's voice was sympathetic. "Tell me what it is. I'm fond of you, Judy. I don't like to see you upset."

"Mark told me about his uncle's will last night, and that to make sure of getting the farm he'll have to marry a girl named Zelda. I thought Mark was such a wonderful person, and now I think he's despicable. To marry a girl for money . . . !" Judy pushed her cup away and walked over to the window, fiercely fighting back the threatening tears. What was the matter with her? She rarely cried, but now she was becoming a real crybaby.

She stared out of the window until she had control of herself, then realized that Mrs. Palmer had not answered her. She turned. "Don't you think that's terrible, Nan? To marry a girl to get money. Not because he loves her, but because it would be a satisfactory arrangement."

"Did he tell you that he didn't love her?" questioned Nan.

"No. I asked him if he did, but he didn't say yes or no."

"Did he definitely say he was going to marry her?" Nan persisted.

"Well, not a definite statement," Judy spoke as if the words hurt her, "but his intentions are quite obvious. First he said he couldn't balance his budget, then he said he wasn't going to lose the farm, then he said if he married Zelda Morrison before the first of March everything would be all right."

Mrs. Palmer sighed. "Well, Mark and Zelda have been friends for years. It's quite on the cards that they will marry. But I can tell you one thing for certain, he won't marry her unless he loves her. Mark talks a lot of nonsense at times, but he has often said to me that unless he's as lucky as Paul in finding a real mate he would never marry. So you can be assured that if they do marry it won't be just for the sake of the farm. Does that make you feel any better?"

"Yes, yes, it does. If it's true," said Judy doubtfully. "It was the thought of him being so calculating, so cold-blooded, that upset me. It didn't seem in character. It shocked me. Why do you think he misled me like that?"

"Perhaps to get your reaction?"

"Oh, he had that all right," said Judy and laughed.

"That's better, you're smiling again. He was probably only teasing you—or maybe he had some other reason."

"Nan," Judy hesitated for a moment, then continued, "I want to ask you something. How do you know for sure when you are in love? Is there any test? Let me tell you about Bruce. I would like to ask your advice."

Mrs. Palmer listened carefully. Judy told her the whole story from the time she had met Bruce in England until she had given him back his ring.

"Honestly, Nan, he was a completely different person in his own home. In England he was wonderful, light-hearted, and full of fun, but once he was with his mother. . . . " Judy shrugged her shoulders hopelessly.

"Thank you for telling me, Judy. Mark did tell me, when you first came, that you were only here until you sorted out a personal problem. Have you come to any decision yet?"

"No. That's what's so awful. I've been here nearly two months, and I'm still undecided. Bruce is becoming impatient, and I can't blame him really. I've been wanting to talk it over with you. I want to ask you what I should do. Should I marry Bruce?"

Nan looked into Judy's trusting eyes. "My dear, I wouldn't dream of telling you what you should do. It must be your own decision. It is your life. But I will say this, if you have any doubts, any doubts at all, don't marry him. You must be absolutely sure that he's the right man before you commit yourself."

"But how can I be sure?" Judy cried. "How did you know that Mark's father was the right man for you? Were you really sure before you married him?"

Nan's smile was sweet. "Quite, quite sure. When he told me he loved me I felt I was walking on air. When he held my hand I felt safe. His presence gave me comfort, courage, and a sense of belonging. When he kissed me I knew I could never love anyone else. Whether he made me happy or miserable didn't seem important, just so long as I could be with him. Perhaps I was one of the lucky ones, because I knew from the day I met him that he was the only man in the world for me."

"I don't feel like that about Bruce," Judy said sadly. "Yet I like him very much. It seems so unfair to keep him waiting."

"It would be much more unfair to marry him before you were sure. Take your time, perhaps something will happen to point the way for you."

It started to rain later in the afternoon, and Judy had to race out to the line to rescue the washing.

"Wasn't I lucky? They're all beautifully dry," she said as she placed the basket on the table.

It rained steadily all the night and the next morning it became heavier. While they were milking, the noise of the rain pelting on the shed roof drowned out the sound of the radio and milking machines. Thunder rolled ominously in the distance. As they finished, the storm moved closer. The sky lit up with vivid flashes of lightning. As the thunder crashed overhead the ground actually trembled. Judy was soaked to the skin by the time she reached the house and was glad to change into dry clothes.

"I've never seen anything like it, Nan. It scares me, yet it's exciting," remarked Judy as she sat down to breakfast. "Does it always rain like this? Look at the windows. The water is just bucketing down."

"I wish we didn't have to go to school," moaned Peter. "We'll miss all the flood. The kids on the other bus are lucky. They usually get sent home early when it floods."

"Do you like floods?" asked Judy, turning to help Vicki button her coat.

"Yes," said Vicki, her eyes sparkling. "Last time we had a raft out on the lawn. It was great fun. Oh, I do hope it comes up properly."

"You little horrors! What about all the sheep and cattle?" Judy scolded, but the twins did not stop to answer as they ran for the bus.

"Where's Mark, Nan? Isn't he having any breakfast? Whoo! that was close," Judy cried as the lightning flashed, making the telephone ring.

"He went down to check on the river. I don't think it will be up yet, but it won't be long if this deluge keeps up."

"How long does it have to rain before it floods?"

"It depends on how heavy the rain is. Rain like this will bring a flood in about five hours. Sometimes it can rain for weeks without flooding."

"I think that's Mark on the porch now," said Judy, getting up to put the kettle on. She put his bacon and eggs in the pan and made some toast.

As Mark sat down to the table he looked worried. "It's going to be a real, old man flood. The paddocks are covered with surface water now. I reckon we've had nearly an inch of rain this morning. I'll start moving the stock as soon as I've had this."

"Can I help?" offered Judy hesitantly.

Mark grinned, "Decided to forgive me, love?"

"There's nothing to forgive," Judy replied stiffly.

"Let's say you don't think I'm such a bad guy after all?" His eyes were amused.

"I'll reserve judgment," answered Judy.

"You're a hard woman," Mark laughed. "I don't think you'd better come with me. It's raining cats and dogs out there. I can manage. There's no need for you to get wet."

"But I would like to help." Judy persisted. "It's not cold rain. I've been wet before. I won't melt."

"Please yourself, but don't say I didn't warn you."

Just then the phone rang. Mark answered it and came back. "Well, if I had any doubts, they're gone. That was Jim—he says it's been raining in the back country all night and the river there has burst its banks. We have about two hours at the outside."

All morning Judy helped him bring the sheep, the cattle and the calves up onto the road. The stock were stubborn and hard to move. Judy was appalled at the sight of the Grey River in full flood. It was terrifying to see the ugly, brown water surging and boiling past. It was two miles wide from bank to bank, and Judy saw huge trees being washed down, some of them being hurled end over end in the raging torrent. She saw some cattle being swept down, far out from the bank. It made her sick to watch their feeble efforts against the tremendous current.

"Some of them will manage to get ashore farther down where the river takes a big swing just before the gorge," Mark told her. "I've heard that the police stand on the Grey River bridge at Greymouth and put a bullet into the ones that get that far. At least it puts them out of their misery before they get swept over the bar and out to sea. I don't know if it's true or not. I've always been too busy saving my own stock to worry much about anyone else when the flood is on."

As they mustered the last lot of stray sheep and drove them over to the road, they found that the water had risen alarmingly. It covered the bridge and about a chain each side. The sheep would not face it.

Mark and Judy pushed, shoved, and yelled. The dogs barked, but still the sheep would not move.

"We haven't much time. In five minutes it'll be too late.

Push your way through to the front, Judy!'' Mark yelled. "Then lead them in. I'll stay here with the dogs and keep them bunched.''

Judy struggled through the flock of wet, bewildered sheep, and waded into the water. It was well over her boots, but by now she was so wet it didn't bother her. Miraculously the sheep followed her and were soon safe on high ground.

"That's great,'' said Mark as he splashed through the water. "To think I was going to leave you at home! I would have lost that bunch if you hadn't been here. Well, I think we have the lot. Let's go home and get something to eat. That was close, you know. The river is coming up much more quickly than I expected. I wouldn't have managed without your help. You're a great girl.'' He put his arm around her and gave her a hug. "You poor little thing! You look like a drowned rat.''

"I've had more attractive compliments in my time.'' But she smiled as she said it.

To Judy's amazement, Koromiko Creek, the little creek by the house, was a raging river. It had overflowed its banks. The water was flowing all over the lawns, the paths and the gardens.

"Oh, poor Mac! Look at his garden. What a shame! Will it come into the house, Mark?'' she asked apprehensively as she rescued some of the twins' toys that were bobbing about in the water.

"No, it's never been through the house to my knowledge. It pours through the washhouse, but stops an inch short of the top step. Whoever built this place put it on high piles, I wouldn't mind if they had put it up another foot. An inch to spare doesn't give a real feeling of security, does it?''

Nan was delighted to see them home and learn that all

the stock was safe. She bustled about putting a hot meal on the table while they changed into dry clothes.

"Won't the dairy cows be in danger, Mark?" asked Judy as she drank her second cup of tea.

"They should be safe for a while. I'll milk early this afternoon in case the power goes off. Then I'll bring them out in the road for the night. There's no use upsetting them too early, and they are pretty safe in that paddock."

"It wasn't safe enough once," Nan reminded him.

"Oh, that was years ago." He explained to Judy, "The chap who owned the farm then left the cows in that paddock while he came home for a cup of tea. Poor devil! A wall of water came down on the valley and picked up the cows and left them stuck in those big old black pine trees in the bottom paddock. Those trees are about 100 feet high and half a mile from here, so you can imagine the force of the water. They say the county trucks were carting them out of here for days."

"How terrible," cried Judy. "How can you sit here calmly drinking your tea when the same thing may happen to your herd?"

"Don't worry. I wouldn't be here if I thought there was any risk. That time the embankment about six miles above us gave way. It won't happen again."

It rained incessantly all afternoon. Mark was out all the time, but he would not let Judy go with him. Judy, heard the milking machine start about half past three, and she waded across to the shed. At one part she had to climb along the calf yard rails, because the water between the house and the shed was three or four feet deep with a strong current.

Mark looked up when she came in. "Why didn't you stay at home? There's no need for you to be out in this mess."

"I'll stay and help. I'm wet through now, there's no point in going home again."

As they finished the twins came splashing in. "Isn't it fun, Judy?" cried Vicky joyfully.

"I'm not sure if you'd call it fun," smiled Judy.

They all helped to drive the cows through the flood to a special yard behind the house. The rain stopped suddenly. Within half an hour the sky was blue, and the sun shining. The twins played happily on the lawn until dark.

"Well, it's all over now," Judy remarked as they sat by the fire after dinner.

"Not quite," Mark told her. "The water is still rising, at least it was the last time I was down the road."

About ten o'clock when Mark went for a last look at the stock Judy went with him. He had a series of gates dividing off each lot of animals. Judy found the sight of the flood eerie. The still, black water covered the whole farm. Here and there a patch of bush or the top of a fence showed, but the most uncanny part was the light. It was as bright as day. The huge moon reflected on the flood waters, and the stars were out in all their glory.

"It's dropping," Mark said with satisfaction. "By morning there won't be a sign of water. But there will be a sign left by the flood, most of my fences will be flattened. Home to bed, Judy, we'll worry about that in the morning. The main thing is that I didn't lose any stock."

CHAPTER SIX

On Monday Judy received a letter from Bruce. He had arranged his transfer from Wellington and was leaving Christchurch in three weeks. He wanted to come and see her. In his letter he poured out his love for her. As Judy read it she felt guilty that it did not awake any response in her own heart. She felt detached, as if she was reading a letter meant for someone else.

Perhaps when she saw him it would be different. Bruce had suggested that he come next Sunday if it suited Judy. He would arrive about ten o'clock. She asked Nan if it would be all right for her to take the day off.

"Of course, Judy. Pack a picnic lunch and get Bruce to take you out to Lake Moana for the day. It's not far and is a really lovely spot. You're quite welcome to have Bruce here to lunch, of course, but I'm sure you would rather be on your own."

"Oh, that's a lovely idea," replied Judy gratefully.

All the week she was irritable, absentminded, and unsettled. She was disgusted with herself because the thought of his visit did not thrill her. She only felt the pleasure she would feel at seeing any acquaintance. She tried to recall him to mind, but he seemed a nebulous figure, indistinct and vague. She gazed at his photograph, but it did not help to bring him to life. She could not marry him feeling the way she did, but the thought of hurting him made her so very unhappy. He loved her so much, and once she had loved him. It seemed so cruel to dash his hopes for the second time.

For hours she brooded, worried, and came no nearer to finding the answer. She liked him, better than any man she had ever met. Mark? Angrily she tried to erase that thought from her mind. Mark was going to marry Zelda. She must come to a decision. The uncertainty was wearing her down.

On Saturday morning Peter rushed into the kitchen. "Judy, Uncle Mark is going to the islands to get a load of sand. Will you come with us?"

"No, but thanks for asking me."

Mark and Vicki came in as she refused Peter. Vicki, always direct and to the point, cried angrily, "You've been crabby all week. You won't go anywhere with us. We wanted you to help us birdnesting last night, and you wouldn't. It's frightfully important to Peter. You just don't care. Don't you like living here any more?"

Judy saw their angry, disappointed faces and was instantly repentant. "Of course I do, Vicki. I'm sorry I've been crabby."

"Then you'll come?" urged Peter. "It's a great place. We have to go across the creek, and up through the bush. Then we cross a few streams of the river onto the island. It's the only place Uncle Mark can get good cementing sand. I have to get some birds eggs for my project. We'll find a lot there."

"Do come," said Vicki, sensing that Judy was weakening. "I want to find some stones. Teacher said if we bring him some pretty ones he'll put them in his tumbler and polish them for us. You can make them into lovely brooches or pendants. I want to get a special one for Mommy for Christmas."

"Leave Judy alone, you brats. She has a lot on her

mind. She doesn't want to be bothered by your chatter today. If you're coming with me you'd better look slippy," said Mark as he walked out.

The twins stood silently pleading. Suddenly Judy made up her mind. "I'll go. Run out and tell Mark to wait a minute."

Mrs. Palmer encouraged Judy, "Good girl! You'll enjoy yourself. The fresh air will do you good. You've been looking quite pale this week."

"But the work? I'm going to be away. . . . "

"Bother the work," replied Nan. "You've hung the washing out and done the rooms. I'll be glad to have the house to myself; old ladies need peace and quiet."

"Old ladies, poof! You know you're not much older than Vicki at heart," laughed Judy. "In fact compared to you, I sometimes feel positively ancient. However, thanks for your blessing. I'd better hurry, or Mark will drive off and leave me."

Judy scrambled onto the trailer with the twins. She was going to forget her problems today and have fun. The ground was rough, and they were bounced around on the trailer. The twins growled about Mark's driving and giggled happily. It was a beautiful day, warm and sunny. They drove down the farm lane that was lined with hawthorn trees, in full bloom. They reminded Judy of home in England, but as soon as she lifted her gaze and saw the majestic Southern Alps her memories fled. How grand they were, providing a permanent backdrop of beauty to every view.

Mark drove past the old orchard and crossed the Koromiko Creek, then across some open country to stop by a lagoon bordered by huge kowhai trees and willows. Flax bushes edged the lake, and a flock of wild ducks took wing as Mark stopped the tractor. Judy was spellbound when she heard the clear, liquid notes of the mocking bird. Two pigeons flew to another tree with a soft whirr of wings.

"See, Judy, up there, that's a tui—see his white throat. He's sometimes called a parson bird," Peter pointed out. Suddenly a tiny fantail flew inquisitively nearer. Judy was fascinated.

"Oh, isn't he beautiful? So tame." She stretched out her hand to touch it, but it flitted a little farther away and continued its erratic dance. Mark started the tractor and drove on.

They traveled through some bush, then out onto a green river bank, forded several small streams, and stopped by a huge sandbank.

"Well, off you go while I load up," said Mark.

The twins needed no second bidding. Judy followed as they ran off. Vicki searched diligently for unusual colored stones, exclaiming in delight whenever she made a find. Peter hunted for nests, but had no luck as they had been swept away in the recent flood. They found a small, clear pool with cock-a-bullies in it and spent a happy time trying to catch them, but the tiny darting fish were too clever at camouflaging themselves.

They heard Mark returning for his second load and hurried back to him. They put their treasures carefully in the tool box. Judy stood admiring the effortless ease with which Mark shoveled the sand. He was stripped to the waist and deeply tanned. His muscles rippled as he dug, then threw the sand onto the trailer. How fit and active he was!

"Come on, Judy," called Peter. "We'll go over to the big trees on the river bank. We're sure to find some nests there. Can we, Uncle Mark?"

"Sure, go ahead, but don't go too far away from the

track. I'll be leaving in about 20 minutes, and I'm in a hurry.''

Judy and the twins were quickly on the river bank searching for birds' nests in the high trees.

"There's one!" shouted Vicki excitedly, pointing upwards.. "No, not there, farther out, just above that dead branch."

"Good. Help me up to the first branch, Judy," demanded Peter. He climbed fearlessly higher and higher.

"Be careful, Peter, do be careful," called Judy anxiously. "That branch doesn't look very safe."

"I can't reach it, Judy. Do you think you could come up here? You're a lot taller than me. I'm sure you could get it. Oh, do have a go." He peered down at her.

"You come down first. I don't think I could even get to the first branch," Judy answered reluctantly.

Peter was down in a flash and examined the situation. Then he marshaled his forces like a general in the field. "It's only the first branch that's difficult, after that it's easy. Now, Vicki and I will kneel down and you stand on our backs. That ought to give you a start."

"Oh, I couldn't! I might hurt you," Judy protested.

"You're only skinny, you wouldn't be as heavy as me. You're not scared, are you?" There was a world of scorn in his voice.

"Of course not," replied Judy hastily and stepped gingerly onto their backs, then reached up and grasped the branch.

The twins stood up as soon as they felt her weight off them. "That's it, Judy," encouraged Peter. "Swing your leg over. Yes, like that. Now pull yourself up. Hurry, we haven't much time. I can hear the tractor."

Judy panted and heaved and searched desperately for safe holds as she climbed higher. If she hadn't been so short of breath she would have told Peter a thing or two. Skinny indeed! Little horror!

Now she was opposite the nest and began inching her way out along the dead branch.

"A little bit farther, Judy. Just a little bit farther. You can do it," Peter called helpfully.

As she took the nest, she heard the branch crack frighteningly, and she began to fall. Twice she nearly saved herself, but each time the branches tore from her hands.

Her head was throbbing violently. Slowly she opened her eyes. Someone was bathing her face with a wet cloth. "What happened?"

"Oh, Uncle, she's not dead." Peter's voice was shaky.

"No thanks to you. You limb of Satan, sending her up that tree. . . . I'll tan the hide off you when I get home!"

"Judy, we're sorry. Truly!"

That sounded like Vicki. She must sit up.

"Take it easy, Judy. Just rest for a bit. You've had a nasty fall. What in the world possessed you to climb up there?"

"A bird's nest. I wanted to get Peter a bird's nest," Judy answered, still feeling slightly muzzy.

"My God, you frightened me to death. The twins came screaming out onto the track, yelling that they'd killed you. When I found you, I thought they might be right." He wiped her face again.

"I'll be fine. I'm sorry to hold you up."

"Don't be so silly. I'm thankful you didn't break your neck. I don't think you've broken any bones. Next time you go climbing, take a parachute."

"Help me up, Mark." He lifted her carefully to her feet, and she leaned against him for support. "I think I have twisted my ankle." She grimaced with pain. "I can't put my weight on it."

"You twins shoot off and make a comfortable place ready on the trailer for Judy. I'll carry her along in a few minutes when she's feeling better."

He helped her to a fallen log and lifted her up, then took off her sandal. "Yes, you've broken or sprained your ankle. Is your head better now? I'd like to get you to a doctor as soon as possible."

"Yes, I'm feeling much better. I was really lucky, having all those fallen leaves to land on. The branches broke my fall. I'm ready when you are." She eased herself down off the log. "If you give me an arm I could hop along to the trailer."

"Just one arm? Oh, I think two would be much better." He put his arms around her and held her close, "What am I to do with you, Judy' There's your intended coming tomorrow to claim you, and you'll be hobbling around on crutches. You'll have bits of bandages here and there, and if I'm not mistaken, a lovely shiny, black eye."

She looked up at him, intending to make some light remark, but the look in his eyes silenced her. She felt breathless—shaky—it must be the effects of the fall.

Mark said, "I know it's mean to take advantage of an injured person, but do realize that tomorrow you may well be engaged to be married and quite out of my reach. You'll just have to forgive me, the temptation is just too strong to resist."

Slowly his arms tightened, and his lips came down on hers. As she surrendered to the sweetness of his kiss, she knew with blinding certainty that she could never marry Bruce. So this was love!

As he drew away she looked into his face. How long had she loved him and not known it? How stupid she had been! Wonderingly she put her hand up to touch his cheek.

"I'm sorry Judy. I shouldn't have kissed you. Even if you're free, I'm not. I was crazy, a thoughtless fool." His face was pale under his tan. "Judy, you're crying! Oh, my dear, forgive me."

He swung her into his arms and carried her along the track to where the children were waiting.

"Good kids. You sit this side, Peter," he said as he lowered Judy onto the trailer. "That's right, Vicki, you sit here. Don't talk to Judy, let her rest, and I'll drive as carefully as I can."

As soon as they arrived home Mrs. Palmer took charge calmly and efficiently. She soon had Judy in a warm bath and gently washed the bruises and cuts. "You were very fortunate, Judy, to get off so lightly. Oh, I know you're stiff, sore, and scratched, but you could have so easily been seriously injured. Those wretched grandchildren of mine . . . !"

"You won't let Mark punish them, will you Nan?" Judy interrupted. "It wasn't their fault."

"Of course not. He knows how upset they are because you're hurt." Nan helped her dress, and after lunch Mark drove her into town to the doctor.

Doctor Jones gave her a thorough examination and pronounced her quite sound except for her ankle. "I'm sending you to hospital for an X-ray. If they find a break they'll put you in plaster. If it's a sprain, they'll strap it up for you. Keep off that foot for the first three days and then use crutches. They'll give you a pair at the hospital."

He went to the door and called Mark in. "Right, you can take her away. Bring her back in a week. You, young lady, leave climbing trees to those more suited to it, and then you won't interrupt my weekend again." But he smiled to take the sting out of his words.

Judy was exhausted by the time they left the hospital.

Her foot was neatly strapped and felt more comfortable. They had had a long wait, and she felt so tired. They drove home in silence.

At the gate Mark helped her with her crutches. Judy said, "I'm sorry you've had to waste all afternoon with me. You won't get any cementing done now."

"Damn the cementing!" He saw her safely inside and then left abruptly.

Judy sat on the sofa, while the twins took turns trying out her crutches. When Mark called them at milking time Judy asked Mrs. Palmer to put a call in to Bruce's number in Christchurch.

Mrs. Palmer came back from the telephone. "There's a 20 minute delay, Judy. I wish you'd go to bed and have a rest."

"I want to speak to Bruce first. I'm going to ask him not to come over tomorrow. It's no use, I can't marry him."

Mrs. Palmer looked at Judy anxiously. "Are you sure, Judy?"

"Quite sure, Nan," Judy replied, wishing that the phone would ring. Now she had made up her mind she wanted to get the ordeal over. "Something happened today to show me that I can't marry him." She lay back on the sofa and closed her eyes. Mrs. Palmer wisely left her in peace.

When the phone shrilled, she felt quite sick as she gathered her crutches and hopped through behind Mrs. Palmer.

"It's Bruce, Judy," said Mrs. Palmer, handing her the receiver; she walked out, shutting the door behind her.

Judy explained to Bruce that she had had a fall and was unable to go out with him on Sunday.

"I don't mind, Judy. I want to see you. Surely I can come to the house and visit you?"

So she steeled herself and told him she could not marry him. It was not easy; she hated to hurt him.

"Don't upset yourself, Judy," Bruce said quietly. "I was half expecting this. I could tell from your letters that there wasn't much hope for me. I love you, Judy. I think I always will. You're not a girl anyone could forget easily. I realize that I lost you through my own stupidity. There doesn't seem much more to say, except that I hope some day we may meet again as friends. If you ever need me, you have my address. Goodbye, Judy, my darling."

She heard him hang up and walked through to her room feeling mentally and physically exhausted. Oh, why was life so difficult? Who said that being in love was a wonderful experience—it wasn't, it was painful, it tore you to shreds, it hurt. She crawled into bed, and her pillow was wet with tears before she slept.

She woke up to find Vicki by her bed. "What's the time, Vicki? Have you finished milking?"

"It's late, we've had dinner ages ago. Nan sent me in to see if you were awake and would like something to eat. You're not to get up. You scared us when you fell out of that tree." Vicki looked at her reproachfully.

Judy laughed, "It scared me too, Vicki. What happened to the nest?"

"You squashed it. All the eggs were broken."

"Oh well, that's life, Vicki," Judy smiled. "Tell Nan I would love a cup of tea if it's not too much trouble."

A few minutes later Nan came in followed by Mark carrying a tray. He put the tray down. "I'll be back to collect this later."

"Oh Nan, I feel terrible giving you this extra work. I'm supposed to be here looking after you, and here I am lying in bed, with you doing all the work. I'm feeling fine now."

"That's good. Now I'll leave you to have your dinner. I told Mark you'd called Bruce. You don't mind?"

"No, not at all. I would rather he knew. It's all over now. It wouldn't have worked out. Thanks for letting me talk to you, Nan. You helped me more than you'll ever know."

"I'm glad," answered Nan. She patted Judy's shoulder and went out.

When Judy had eaten the delicious meal she put the tray away, lay back, and closed her eyes. This was the first chance she had had to examine the exciting discovery she had made this morning. She loved Mark. Even thinking of him gave her a feeling of excitement. No wonder she had been unable to think seriously about marrying Bruce—she had been unconsciously comparing him with Mark, always to his detriment. She must be careful. Mark must not suspect that his kiss had been the reason for her breaking off with Bruce. It would only embarrass him. He was going to marry Zelda. He had only been flirting with her to pass the time, she knew that. He had been honest with her. Even this morning he had told her he wasn't free.

"You asleep?" It was Mark taking her tray.

Judy opened her eyes. "No, just thinking."

"I'd like to talk to you if you're not too tired."

"Go ahead, I've had a good sleep. You're not going to start growling at me again for climbing trees?"

"No," Mark replied as he sat down on the end of the bed, taking care not to disturb her foot. "Nan tells me you're not going to marry Bruce."

Judy watched him carefully. She wished she knew what he was thinking and blushed. It was lucky he didn't know what she was thinking. She looked down and started pleating the sheet between her finger, nervously. "No. I've thought it over carefully, and I don't think we would have been happy together."

"I'm glad. He wasn't the man for you, too wishy-washy."

Judy smoothed the sheet out and started pleating it again as if it was her only interest in life. "What sort of a man do you think I need?"

"Someone to boss you. Bruce would have let you have your own way all the time—very bad for your character. Are you very unhappy?"

"No, just relieved."

"Good. Now that's settled, let's talk business. You came here to have a place where you could think until you could come to a decision. Now that a decision has been made, what are your plans? Will you stay on here a few more months? At least until we get some definite news from abroad. What do you say?"

Judy had been trying to concentrate on his words, but her thoughts were chaotic. "Oh, Mark, Mark," cried her heart, "I'd stay forever if you'd ask me." Had he no idea what effect he was having on her? He was so close she could put her hand out and touch him. He was waiting patiently for her answer.

"I haven't made any plans yet. I want to get back to nursing eventually, but there's no rush. I love Nan and the children. I know it sounds funny, but I feel closer to Nan than I do to my own mother. I would like to be here when the news comes, just in case it isn't good. They'll need me then." She looked directly at him.

This time it was Mark who turned away. "I'm very grateful, Judy. I don't know how to thank you. Will you stay until March? Would you be prepared to stay that long?"

Judy's heart sank. He would not need her after that date

because Zelda would be here to take care of Nan and the twins. "Yes, I'll stay."

"Will you promise me that no matter what happens you'll stay until the beginning of March? I would like something definite so that I can plan my work."

"Yes, I give you my word," Judy answered quietly. How funny listening to him begging her to stay, when that was the only thing in the world she wanted to do. Just to be near him was heaven, but he couldn't know that. How dear he was to her! How could she leave without seeing Zelda? She wouldn't have been human if she did not hope for a miracle. That something might happen.

Three months was quite a long time. Who knows?

CHAPTER SEVEN

Judy enjoyed her three days of enforced rest. She felt relaxed and happy as she sat on the sofa, doing small jobs that normally she had little time for. She sewed buttons on, darned sweaters, and caught up on her correspondence. She had received letters from her mother and father the previous week. As she answered them, she felt a greater affection for her parents than she had felt for years. Who was she to judge them? She had nearly made the same mistake as they had. Her mother had been just 18, and her father a year older when they had married. As the years passed they had drawn further and further away from each other. They had quarreled incessantly, and while her mother had loved company, loved parties and outings, her father had been a quiet, bookish person. They had rubbed each other raw. Perhaps they had been wise to part. In fact they were now better friends than they had been when they were married to each other. She realized now that they did love her, that they had always tried to minimize the effect of their divorce on her. It had been she herself who had held aloof, blaming them for her unhappy childhood. With this new understanding, she felt all the bitterness drain away.

At the end of the week the doctor checked her ankle. He advised her to keep off it as much as possible for the next two weeks, otherwise she would have a permanently weak ankle. Mark put a comfortable chair out in the garden, where Judy spent much of her time watching Mac at his work. She had become quite good friends with Mr. McTaggart over the past two months. She had come to respect and admire the old man for his wisdom and honest, upright standards. He did not talk a lot. Judy had to work hard to extract any information she wanted. She knew that he had been a miner most of his life, and since he retired he had a gold claim that he worked in his spare time. He had promised to take Judy up to see his claim.

Judy hopped out on her crutches to her chair and sat enjoying the warm sunlight and listening to the birds singing. She noted the meticulous care with which Mac transplanted the tiny lettuce plants. She was beginning to feel restless, tied to her chair. The first week she had been as happy as a lark. Her love for Mark had been so new, so precious, she had hoarded it like a hidden treasure, content that she loved him, not worried whether he loved her in return. She loved him, she could see him every day, that was all she asked for then. As the days passed she began to long for some sign that he found her attractive, that he liked her more than as a friend. But there was nothing. He was friendly, teasing, cheerful, and that was all. Since the day she had fallen from the tree, and he had kissed her, he had erected an invisible barrier between them.

"Well, lassie, you're improving on those contraptions," Mac's voice interrupted her thoughts.

"Yes, I am. By the end of this week I should be able to return them to the hospital."

Mac had finished the transplanting and sat down on the wheelbarrow, beside her. He lit his pipe and puffed away contentedly.

"Were you ever married, Mac?" she asked.

"I was."

Judy waited patiently. There was no use trying to

prompt him, that much she had learned. If he had something to say he would tell her in his own good time.

"Ah, she was a bonnie lassie. Her hair was the same color as your own, like fire in the sun. My bonnie Jean, wilful, wayward, loving, and kind. She had plenty of spirit, and a heart as big as the whole world. You make me think of her, only her eyes were blue."

"How long have you been on your own, Mac?" Judy's voice was soft.

"A long time," he sighed. "Thirty years, yet sometimes it feels like only yesterday she was by me. She drowned saving a young boy. Two children were swept out to sea in a rip tide. She managed to save one, but perished with the other. She should not have gone back in after the other boy, but it was like her not to count the cost. When they came to tell me, I couldn't believe it at first, that anyone as full of life as she. . . . " He drew on his pipe. "Time is a marvelous friend, Judy. Time heals all wounds."

They sat in silence for a long time, then Judy asked, "You never thought of marrying again? You must have been a young man when she died."

"No, never. Who could take my Jeannie's place?"

"Do you believe there's someone special for each person?" Judy persisted.

"Yes, and I found mine," Mac smiled at Judy, "and I think you've found yours."

Judy blushed. "How do you know?"

"I may not say much, but I see a lot. Mark is a fine man. You have a good chap."

Judy burst out, "That's just the trouble, Mac, I don't have him. He doesn't love me. He's going to marry Zelda Morrison."

"Rubbish!"

"It isn't rubbish, he told me so himself—or as good as,"
Judy said miserably. "In three months' time."

"Is she wearing his ring?"

"No."

"No, and she never will, if you have any gumption. Go
in and fight for him if you think he's worth it. You have
everything on your side; you live in his house, you work
with him. In three months, my Jeannie could have moved
mountains, and so can you. Think on, what does he want
most in the world?"

"To get this farm," replied Judy.

"Well, help him win it. By the time he has achieved his
ambition, it will be you he turns to, mark my words."

"I wish I had money," said Judy desolately.

"Don't be so foolish, woman. What can money buy?
Can it buy happiness? Can it buy health, or love? Do you
think if you had money Mark would take it or marry you
for it? You don't know your man. He wouldn't want to be
beholden to any woman, least of all his wife. Mark wants
the satisfaction of beating this on his own. What would he
have gained to have it handed to him on a plate?"

"A farm," said Judy bitterly.

Mac stood up and knocked his pipe out. "I must get
back to work, instead of blathering here all day. When
you marry Mark, I will have your wedding ring made
from gold I've won from my claim. Now put on that loving smile of yours and remember that no one ever won
anything worthwhile without a bit of a struggle."

Perhaps Mac had something there, Judy thought. It
would do no harm to try. She loved Mark enough to want
to see him get the farm, whether he married her or not. If
she helped him, maybe he would be able to finance it
himself. He would not then need extra money. He would
not need to marry Zelda—but what if he loved Zelda?

November passed and then December. Day by day Judy worked beside Mark, always cheerful and willing to help. He gratefully accepted her offer to milk each night, with the twins to assist her. It gave him another two hours to work. And how hard he worked! During the day he ploughed, worked, and sowed the paddocks. At night he sheared the sheep. Each afternoon Judy would bring in about 50 sheep, and after dinner Mark would shear them. So, slowly, the flock was shorn and the bales filled and railed away. Nan worried and scolded him for working too hard, but it made not one iota of difference; he drove himself to the utmost.

Christmas passed with scarcely a ripple. Mrs. Palmer was very worried that the twins would miss their parents badly at Christmas; however, the parcels that their parents had left ready in case they were not back by Christmas seemed to satisfy them. As they opened them and read the cards they were reassured of their parents' love and talked eagerly of their return.

It was school holidays now, and they were enjoying themselves immensely, helping with the haymaking, going swimming, and in general keeping everyone on their toes waiting for the next disaster.

Early in January Mark had another letter from the leader of the expedition. He wrote saying there was a rumor that two white people were known to be living with a tribe far in the hinterland. He begged them not to be too hopeful, as it could be two missionaries, or some government officials. However, he felt that he could not leave with a clear conscience unless he checked the rumors out on the off chance that it could be Paul and Betsy. He warned them that the chance was slight and that he would visit them on his return to New Zealand in February.

Mrs. Palmer was confident that it would prove to be her

son and his wife. Nothing could shake her. "Oh, I'm glad we have kept all this worry from the twins!"

Mark was not so sure and tried to caution her against a further disappointment. They all watched anxiously for the mail each day.

Judy often went down to the Stillwater tennis club after dinner. She enjoyed a game of tennis and played well. Mark had taken her down and introduced her. She knew Claire and Steve quite well now. They had been friends since the first night that Claire had played chaperon, and of course Steve was quoted daily by the twins as "teacher says." They were enthusiastic members of the club, so Judy saw quite a lot of them.

Mark had told her, "I won't be able to take you very often, but you can take the car whenever you wish."

Judy often went home with Claire for coffee after a game. One evening after she had helped Claire put the children to bed and Steve had gone back to school to work, they sat chatting.

"What is Zelda Morrison like, Claire? I often hear her name mentioned at the club, and I gather she's Mark's girlfriend. Where is she, anyhow?" Judy sounded deliberately casual.

"Oh, Zelda? She's a nice kid—sort of small, blonde, and sweet. You'll like her, everyone does. Yes, she and Mark have always been close. Her father was a domineering, old pig, and I think she used to head for Mark whenever the going got rough. He would set her on her feet and give her the necessary courage to stand up to her old man. I don't know if they're any more than good friends, but you never can tell.

"No, you can't," answered Judy lightly.

"Where is she now?"

"In Australia. She's very artistic and won some sort of

designing competition. Look, I'm not really sure of my facts, but one thing I do know, she's coming home at the beginning of February. I heard her cousin say so the other day."

Mark sold his wool in the January wool sale. The price of wool had slumped badly at the Wellington and Auckland sales, and dropped again disastrously at Christchurch. Mark's wool check was 600 dollars less than he had allowed for in his budget. His face was set and stubborn after he had spent a night working on his accounts. The next morning he said, "Right, Nan, there's no other way out, I'll have to make up the deficiency by cutting flax. Provided I really go at it, I can make 600 dollars by March. I get nine dollars a ton here at the gate—say 60 tons, I can do it."

"I hate you starting that, Mark. It's such heavy work— not so much the cutting but the carrying out. I'm always scared you'll cut yourself, or tip the tractor up. The ground is so rough up there. Isn't there any other way?"

"Cattle prices are good at the moment, but they could drop. I can't afford to count on them to adjust the balance. I have to keep the stock numbers up anyhow." He turned to Judy. "Do you mind keeping on with the evening milking? If it's too much for you tell me. I don't want to kill you with work."

Judy noted the new lines of strain around Mark's eyes and answered unhesitantly, "It's no trouble Mark. I love the work, and the twins are a great help."

So each morning after milking, wet or fine, Mark set off with his lunch to cut flax. He sometimes took a morning off for stock work, but never any time for relaxation or pleasure.

Judy went up with him occasionally, and sat and watched as he swung the sharp sickle-shaped knife in a steady, rhythmical movement, slicing through the flax just above the roots. He tied each bundle of flax with a special knot at each end—24 bundles to the ton. Working steadily all day with only a short break for lunch, Mark could cut three tons a day. He then had to carry them over rough country to the trailer and bring them home. The flax-mill lorry picked it up at the gate.

Judy marveled at the terrific pace he worked, never stopping, never flagging. One day she stayed to share his lunch.

"Why are you killing yourself like this, Mark? Surely there's no need to work so hard. You said you're going to marry Zelda, and then you'll get the farm. What's the point of this effort?"

Mark grinned his old, wicked, teasing grin, that she saw so rarely these days. "You would rather I didn't work? You think I should sit back and wait for Zelda to come home?"

"No," Judy stammered.

"Wouldn't it be a shocker if she turned me down? I just have to cover all bets."

"But you are going to marry her?" Judy persisted. In spite of the ache in her heart, she had to know.

"I want to make this on my own, Judy, it's something I have to do. When or if I'm successful, I'll marry the girl I love."

"So you think love is important?"

"Perhaps. Now off you go home. I'm not wasting my time talking when I could be working. Go away, you're distracting me."

"I wish I could distract you," she muttered under her breath as she walked away.

She had followed Mac's advice to the letter, and where had it got her? Nowhere. Mark was friendly and deeply grateful for her help. He teased her, growled at her, laughed at her, but really he treated her no differently from the way he treated Vicki. Well, Judy decided, she was no child. She would show him. She was sick of playing little-goody-two-shoes; not that she minded helping him, but romance-wise it was not getting her anywhere. Zelda would be home soon, and her chance would be gone. What he needed was a good shock, someone else on the scene, perhaps? Come to think of it, the last time he had kissed her was when Bruce was due for the day. Since that day he had kept his distance, behaved so very, very brotherly. Well, bother it, she did not need a brother!

When she came to Koromiko Creek, she sat down on the bank to think out some plan. Competition, that was the answer—but who? Her eyes gleamed as she cast her mind over the available material. There were not many eligible men about. Most of the male visitors to the farm were married. The young student teacher who boarded with Claire and Steve? No, he was too young. One by one she discarded the prospective males from her list. The vet?—now he was really something, quite a dish. Unfortunately he had recently become engaged. She had no intention of hurting anyone by her schemes, yet it had to be a man who would make Mark sit up and take notice. She had to find out if he had any feeling for her at all. If he ignored the fact that she was going out with someone else, then she would know that he didn't care. She had to find out.

Suddenly she laughed out loud. Right under her nose all the time, and she had missed him! The herd-tester, who was due any day now. He usually arrived about two in the afternoon, took samples at the evening milking, stayed the night and left after lunch the following day. Lucky Costelle was a strange man. Mark seemed to get on with him quite well, but Judy noticed none of the other farmers had a good word to say for him. He had apparently built up a fairly shocking reputation as far as women were concerned. When she asked Mark if the stories were true he had laughed and said "Oh, I don't think he's as bad as they make out. He told me once that he considered himself as God's gift to the farmers' wives. He brightened the lives of the lonely ones. He said the farmers were always much nicer to their wives when he was around—just in case. You keep out of the shed when he's here. After all, there's no smoke without fire."

She had been looking forward to meeting him, expecting to see someone looking as handsome as a Greek god, but Lucky wasn't handsome. In fact his thin, angular face had just missed being ugly. It was his eyes that fascinated Judy—deep brown, almost black—and hard, as if they had looked on this world and found nothing good. He was over 30, and moved with the grace of a panther. He made Judy feel rather uneasy at first. He was cynical and sarcastic. Yet there was something appealing about him, a little-boy-lost look. She thought that must be what attracted the women to him.

He treated Mrs. Palmer with graciousness and charm, and he was always extremely polite to Judy, but he adored the twins. They thought he was utterly wonderful and hardly left his side from the time he arrived until he left. Judy thought of the way Claire had described him, "a lean and hungry man, with magnetism you could almost touch, a danger to any female between eight and eighty." Hmm—well, Judy did not intend to become one of his conquests, but if she went out with him she was sure Mark would have something to say. After all that was the object of the exercise.

Judy stood up and waded through the creek, breaking

off a sprig of koromiko tree. She admired the small clusters of pale-lilac-to-white flowers and carried it home with her. Mrs. Palmer was talking to Mac in the garden, when Judy joned them.

"You're up to something wicked, lassie. Come on, out with it!" Mac demanded.

"How can you tell?" Judy wanted to know.

"My Jeannie used to get the very same look in her eye when she was bent on mischief. Are you going to let us into the secret?"

"No, I'm not. It wouldn't be a secret any more then, but I'll make you both a cup of tea," and she ran gaily inside. Nan liked Lucky, so he couldn't be that bad, although Mark always said Nan would make excuses for the Devil himself. Nan had told Judy that Lucky was either separated from his wife or divorced. She was not sure, but she knew there were children involved.

Shortly after Lucky arrived on the following Saturday, it seemed as if Fate were playing into Judy's hands. The telephone rang while they were having afternoon tea, and it was for Lucky. As he left the room Judy thought again how gracefully he moved, like a cat stalking its prey. Maybe she was mad to think of trying to use him.

As he returned to the table he said, "Well, I've suffered a grievous disappointement. The lady who was to accompany me to the cabaret tonight has been forced to forgo the pleasure of my company. Her husband has returned home—so disobliging of him, don't you think? It does seem a shame to waste these tickets. Perhaps you could use them, Mark? Give Judy a night out?"

Judy held her breath. Silently she begged him to take them.

"No, thanks all the same, Lucky. I think I'll have an

early night. I'm sure you won't have any difficulty getting another partner."

Judy was sick with disappointment. Serve him right if he did get upset when she went out with Lucky she thought viciously! Well, that was provided Lucky would take her. She had to wait until she could get Lucky on his own. When Mark sent the twins for the cows and went himself to set up the shed, Judy followed Lucky out to the front gate where he had parked his van.

As he was about to get in Judy called, "Wait a minute, Lucky, I want to talk to you, please."

He stopped and leaned back against the van. His stillness frightened Judy. Her courage nearly failed. He made her feel so young and immature. He was waiting; she could not back out now. "If you haven't anyone to take to the cabaret, would you take me?"

He raised his eyebrows, and Judy felt a crimson tide of color sweep her face. "Why?" His voice was soft as velvet.

"I never go out anywhere. I thought I'd like a night out."

"Not true. Tell me your real reason."

Judy turned away for a moment. She would have to tell him the truth, or he would not take her. She took a deep breath. "Because I want to make Mark jealous."

Lucky half closed his eyes and smiled. "Your Mark is a formidable rival. What happens to me if you're successful?"

Judy gave him a steady look. "You're not scared of any man."

"True, but also I'm not a fool. You're in love with Mark?"

"Yes."

"And he's not—how shall I put it delicately—not coming up to scratch?"

"No, he's not," admitted Judy. "He says he's going to marry another girl."

"You don't easily accept defeat. I like that; we shall get on well together. You have unsuspected depths, my dear. Fancy me writing you off as a sweet young thing. Perhaps you have possibilities? What's in this for me?"

"Nothing," Judy answered flatly.

"You know my reputation?"

"Yes," Judy answered without faltering.

"You have courage, but no intelligence. Mark is a man who will brook no competition. He won't share you, I warn you."

"He's not being asked to share me. I'm his if he wants me. At the moment I can't find out if he cares for me or not. If he blows a fuse because I go out with you, then I'll know that there's some hope."

"My motto, young Judy, is I shall do nothing for nothing. You may not get out of this as lightly as you imagine," Lucky smiled cynically.

"I'm not scared of you." Which is a whopping lie, thought Judy, crossing her fingers.

"You think I go around like Cupid patching up unhappy romances? You insult me."

"I think I'll be quite safe with you," Judy replied quietly.

"That's an even bigger insult. I'll take you to the cabaret, if that's what you want. You'll enjoy yourself. If Mark hangs one on me we'll then know we've been successful, huh?" His smile had genuine humor in it this time. "Be ready at seven. We'll have dinner in town. This van is my only means of transport. You don't think it too humble a conveyance to take a lady on such a dangerous mission?"

Judy laughed, "I'll be honored to ride in your van."

As Lucky slipped into the vehicle and slammed the door, she stepped forward. "Thank you very much for being so nice."

Lucky growled, "If this gets out it'll ruin my reputation. We shall have to select some very public spot, and you can slap my face so that people will know I'm not losing my touch!" He waved and drove off.

Judy felt her spirits lift. Lucky was nice, it was going to be fun. She danced along the path and into the kitchen. She smiled to herself as she helped Nan prepare the dinner.

"You're looking very pleased with yourself, Judy," said Nan with an inquiring glance.

"Oh, I am, Nan. Lucky is taking me to the cabaret. We're having dinner in town."

"Splendid. I hope you have a lovely evening," Nan smiled.

"You do like Lucky, don't you, Nan?"

"Yes, I do. He's so gentle and kind with the children. They bring out the best in him. He has been very badly hurt at one time. It's very easy to preach when you've never met real trouble. He's very bitter, but life hasn't been kind to him."

"You don't think I'm stupid to go out with him?" Judy asked anxiously.

"Not at all. I think an evening out with Lucky would be a very exciting and memorable experience. Now run along, dear, and make yourself pretty, while I do the dinner."

Judy bathed luxuriously, after adding her most wickedly expensive bath salts with a generous hand. It was fortunate that she had washed her hair that morning. She brushed it until it shone and was glad that she had decided to grow it long. Usually she wore it loose, or in a ponytail to keep it tidy, but tonight she swept it high on her head giving her an elegant, sophisticated look. She did her nails with care, and spent a considerable time on her make-up.

Tonight Mark was going to see a very different Judy. Gone were her shirts and jeans, gone were her fresh little cotton dresses. In their place she chose from her wardrobe her most glamorous full-length evening gown. As it fell in soft folds to her feet, she smoothed it gently into place. When she had been nursing in England she had been chosen with six other nurses to model clothes at a charity fashion show. The object of the show had been to raise funds for special equipment for the hospital. A famous dress designer had provided model dresses. Her father had attended, and when he had seen her in this one he had bought it for her, for a present. It was a creation of green and gold, cut and swathed with the utmost cunning, and showed Judy's perfect figure off to great advantage.

Judy put on her matching green pendant and earrings, a present from her mother, and stood back to get the full effect. She smiled, well pleased with her efforts; the Grecian style of the dress that left one arm and shoulder bare looked even more attractive now that she had acquired a light tan. Also her face was thinner than the last time she had worn the dress.

Mrs. Palmer knocked on the door and came in. "Oh, Judy, my dear, you look beautiful! What a dream of a dress. The children will be thrilled to see you."

"Does Mark know I'm going out with Lucky?"

"No, I'm sure he doesn't. Lucky is ready whenever you are. He has an evening suit on and looks most dashing and distinguished. You look simply wonderful, I hope you have a very happy evening." She kissed Judy lightly and walked to the door, then turned and looked at Judy again as she said, "Mark is a stubborn fool, but I can't interfere." She went out and closed the door.

Now the time had come to face Mark, Judy felt scared. Perhaps Lucky was right, perhaps she was a fool to go out with him. It was a ridiculous idea. She must have been crazy to think of it—still, she would have to go through with it now. She dabbed a little perfume on, then picked up her matching stole and went slowly along the passage to the kitchen. As she opened the door she heard Mark speaking.

"Well, apparently you've found yourself a partner for tonight, Lucky."

Judy slipped into the room, "Yes, Mark, he found me." She looked at Mark, her eyes bright and challenging, her chin high. Mark just stared at her, while Lucky was on his feet in an instant. "Exquisite, my dear, exquisite. That dress suits you to perfection."

The twins hung back for a moment, then Vicki clapped her hands, "Oh, isn't she gorgeous, Uncle Mark? Look, she's almost as pretty as Mommy."

Mark spoke at last. "Yes, Vicki, Judy is beautiful. I've told her so before. Do you remember, Judy?"

Judy remembered very well the night they had walked home from the orchard and how he had looked at her that night. She felt the lump in her throat would choke her.

Mark continued as if her answer did not matter, "Lucky, you can't take that vision out in your old van. Borrow my car for the night. It's at the front gate. The keys are in it."

"Come with me, Judy," Lucky said, offering his arm. "We'll travel in style tonight. Thanks for the car, Mark. I really appreciate your offer. I'll take good care of it."

"It's more important that you take good care of Judy," Mark replied.

Judy's eyes were bright with unshed tears, as she walked down the path. The dress meant nothing at all. Mark did not care who she went out with. Lucky closed the door, then went around to the driver's seat. He started the car and moved off smoothly. "Beautiful car, it was decent of Mark to lend it to us," he commented.

"He didn't care, Lucky. I shouldn't have bothered you to take me out."

"You think he didn't care? You're very much mistaken, my chicken. He was boiling mad at me. Now cheer up, you're going to enjoy yourself tonight, make no mistake about that. No girl goes out with me and sits weeping over another man; I wouldn't allow it."

They had an excellent dinner at a hotel, then went to the cabaret. Perhaps it was because Judy had not been out since she arrived on the Coast; perhaps it was because she had Lucky for a partner, but whatever the reason the evening began to swing. It was one of those evenings when everything goes well; a night to remember for years. Judy loved dancing, and Lucky was a superb partner. The music was wonderful. In between dances they talked and laughed, or were entertained by interesting and exciting floor shows.

The party they were with were all older than Judy, and they made much of her. The women were frankly envious of her dress, and the men showered her with compliments. The drinks were cold, the music intoxicating, and the conversation at the table was witty and sophisticated. Judy loved the laughter, the excitement and the gaiety. Her eyes sparkled with fun.

Some time after supper Lucky asked her if she was tired, and if she wanted to go home.

"No, not yet, I'm having a wonderful time. But of course, if you have had enough I don't mind leaving."

"No, I don't want to go," replied Lucky. "I can't remember when I've enjoyed myself more. You certainly have a way of spreading joy around the place, but you make me realize my age. I think dancing around and around this room is harder than going up on the tops."

"On the tops of what?" asked Judy.

"Up in the mountains, on top of the hills," explained Lucky. "Each month I get three or four days off because I work straight through Saturdays and Sundays, you see. Well, if the weather is good I get away up the bush and do a bit of shooting. I'll take you with me next time I go. It's a great feeling to get away up there, away from everyone. You come back refreshed and ready to take your place in this dingy, old world with more tranquility. How about it?"

"No, thanks, although I would love to go. I think I'd better stay on the flat and admire them from a distance."

At last the band played "Auld Lang Syne," the party broke up, and the couples left the hall.

Lucky asked as they drove away, 'Have you any idea what time it is?"

Judy giggled happily. "Haven't a clue. Does it matter?"

"Four-thirty. We're going to get home with the milk."

"Oh, milking! I forgot you'll have to get up for milking. You'll only get half an hour in bed."

"It causes you some amusement? You think it funny?" Lucky growled.

"Hilariously funny," laughed Judy, knowing she could go to bed and sleep as late as she wished.

As they walked through the gate and stopped by the back door the sky was turning pearly pink with the dawn. "Thank you, Lucky, for the most wonderful evening. I loved every minute of it."

"Did you think of Mark?"

"Not once."

"Liar! I saw you looking dreamy-eyed during some of those oh-so-sad love songs—however, I'll forgive you. You don't think I'll let you off with a pretty thank-you, do you?"

Judy leaned up and gave him a kiss on the cheek, as light as a butterfly.

Lucky laughed, "Go on, get to bed. I must be getting soft!"

It was after ten when Judy awoke. The children were at Sunday school, so she had tea and toast with Mrs. Palmer and told her all the highlights of the evening.

"I'm glad you went out and had such a good time," smiled Nan. "Listening to you tell about the entertainment is nearly as good as being there to see it for myself."

Judy wandered over to the shed to see Lucky. As she walked under the louver windows, she heard her name mentioned so she stopped.

"You leave Judy alone, Lucky. She's not your type of girl."

"Do tell?" Lucky's soft voice made Judy giggle, but she clapped her hand over her mouth quickly. She knew she shouldn't listen, but she could not resist.

"Yes, you keep away from her. I'm warning you, if she gets hurt through you I'll break every bone in your body. She's had a pretty rough time since she came to New Zealand. I don't want to see her get mixed up with you and your crowd. I don't see why you invited her out in the first place."

"You'd be surprised if I told you why." Judy held her breath. He wasn't going to tell!

There was a silence for a minute or two, then she heard Lucky again. "What's it to you anyhow? You're a proper dog in the manger, Palmer—you don't want her yourself, and you don't want to have anyone else take her out and give her a good time. I think she's an attractive young lady, and I'll ask her out if I want to, so belt up.''

"You'll bring her nothing but trouble, Lucky. You're a married man, so leave her alone. I have nothing against you personally except that your reputation with women stinks. Judy is a nice girl.''

"Have you never heard of divorce? What say do you have anyhow? She's not your girl. I tried to give you the tickets yesterday.''

"She's living in my house and under my protection. Understand?''

"Protection?'' Lucky roared with laughing. "That girl needs protection like I need a hole in the head! She's quite capable of looking after herself, believe me.''

Judy decided it was time she moved unless she wanted to be caught. She returned to the house with a happy smile on her face and a lilt in her walk. She knew she should be ashamed of herself, but all's fair in love and war, and she did love Mark. She loved him with her whole heart. Lucky? Judy gave a little pirouette. Lucky was a darling. She had been right to trust him.

After lunch, when Lucky was leaving, he asked Judy to walk out to his van with him. "So, my young Judy, I think you may consider your campaign a success, because Mark had a go at me this morning. I'll give you a call occasionally during the month to keep the kettle on the boil, so to speak. When I come back next month we'll have another night out.''

Judy put an impulsive hand on his arm. "I can't thank you enough, but I don't want to become a nuisance to you.''

"You're not a nuisance, chicken. I find I'm enjoying myself in a very novel way. Don't look now, but Mark is watching. Would you like me to seize you in a passionate embrace and give him a display of my magnificent technique?''

Judy laughed delightedly. "No, thanks, you've done more than enough already.''

"Whew! I was scared you would say yes, and the way your Mark is scowling at me I think I would have been lucky to leave here alive!''

Judy waved goodbye and then sauntered by Mark on her way inside. As she passed he caught her wrist. "Do you like playing with fire?''

Judy smiled sweetly, "If you mean do I like Lucky, the answer is yes!''

At that moment the twins arrived home from Sunday school and further conversation was impossible.

Vicki ran up. "You stayed in bed awfully late this morning, Judy. I wanted to hear all about the dance. Mommy used to tell me what people wore, and what she had to eat. Will you tell me now? Nan wouldn't let me wake you up this morning.''

"Yes, I'll tell you everything. Come on in, so I can talk while I put lunch on.''

The next day Mark went up to the flax and forgot to take his lunch, so Judy carried it up to where he was working beside the deep black lagoon. As she stood watching him work, she had a feeling he had left his lunch behind on purpose so that he would be able to talk to her without interruption. He had been very quiet and stiff since lunch time yesterday. As he tied off a bundle of flax with unnecessary force, he threw it aside and turned to Judy. "Thank you for bringing my lunch. Put it down there. I want to talk to you.''

Judy put down the lunch carefully, surprised to find her hands were shaking. Perhaps this was going to be the moment she had waited for, perhaps Mark was going to tell her he loved her. As she turned toward him she realized that there was no love in his eyes, only anger. Immediately her fighting spirit was aroused.

"Are you going out with Lucky again?" His voice was hard.

"I might," replied Judy casually.

"You're not very particular, are you?" Mark glared at her.

"Oh, I wouldn't say that, but he did take me out, which is more than I can say for you. A girl likes to be told she's pretty and fun to be with. Makes her feel good." Judy was being deliberately provocative.

"I suppose he kissed you last night."

"Well, not last night, actually, it was this morning," she said blandly.

"And you enjoyed that too?" demanded Mark savagely.

"Since you ask, yes, I did rather."

"You don't care who you go out with—any man will do? You don't care who kisses you—any man will do, is that what you mean?"

"You're catching on fast." Judy moved farther along the lagoon edge, "Enjoy your lunch, Mark. I'm going home."

In two strides he caught her, and holding her in an inflexible grip he kissed her three or four times—ruthless, insulting kisses with no love or affection in them.

"If that's all you want, why didn't you say? I don't mind obliging you."

Judy's face was white. "You beast, I hate you!" Her green eyes were flashing fire. She rushed at him, catching him off balance, and pushed him backward, into the lagoon. Then she turned and ran for her life. She headed away from home and down toward the river.

Her tears blinded her, and she did not see Mac on the river bank until he touched her arm. "What's the matter, lassie? Has someone been hurt?"

"No—yes, I have. I hate Mark, I hate him, I hate him!" And she threw herself down on the grass and cried as if her heart would break.

Mac sat beside her and gently stroked her hair until she lay quiet. "Poor wee lassie, tell me about your trouble."

Judy sat up wiping her eyes. "Mark kissed me," she sniffed.

"Did he now?" asked Mac without a glimmer of a smile. "But I thought you wanted him to kiss you?"

"No, not like that! Oh, Mac, he kissed me as if he hated me!"

"Now why would he do a thing like that?" Mac pretended to be puzzled.

"Because I went out with Lucky on Saturday night," Judy explained.

"Oh, ho, ho, ho, ho, fancy that? You went out with Lucky, and Mark is angry with you? That's very good, and I'm sure it was what you had in mind. You scheming little minx!"

"Ye-e-s," Judy answered hesitantly.

"Well, what are you complaining about?"

Judy brightened up and gave a small giggle. "I pushed Mark into the lagoon, and I'm scared to go home. He looked so mad I think he'll kill me."

"He will no kill you," Mac hastened to assure her, "but he may beat you, which would be no more than you deserve. Come on home with me, now. There's no use me staying here any longer. You've scared away all the fish."

"I can't go home, Mac. I can't face Mark," said Judy,

getting to her feet. "I'll have to leave. I can't stay here now."

"I didn't think you were a coward, lassie. I'm disappointed in you."

"It's all right for you to talk, you're not living in his house. He thinks I'm cheap. I'm going to pack my case."

"You will do no such thing. You will say you are sorry to Mark for trying to drown him, and you will stay here until March. You told me you'd given your word to do that."

"I won't say I'm sorry!" cried Judy passionately. "Why should I? He deserved to be pushed in."

"Now, now, lassie, you must apologize. It's always easier for a woman to say she's sorry than for a man. You don't want to leave in anger and not see Mark again, do you?" He strode along briskly, letting Judy trail behind while she tried to decide what to do.

When they came across the small bridge over Koromiko Creek, Mark was unloading the flax. As he was in dry clothes Judy presumed he had been inside to change. He still seemed to be very angry. Mac waited for Judy to catch up. "Don't let your pride get in the way, Judy," he said softly, then as they came closer to Mark he pushed her forward. "Judy has something to say to you Mark. I'll be on my way," and Mac walked off.

Judy stood irresolute. If she walked away now there would be no returning. What was stopping her? Pride? She was to blame for the situation; she faced that honestly. She had meant to upset Mark, and he couldn't be expected to react just as she wanted him to. Suddenly she wanted to see him smile more than anything in the world. A wave of love for him swept over her, leaving her weak and shaken. What was pride compared to being friends with him again?

She put out her hand in a pleading gesture. "I'm sorry Mark; please forgive me. I can't bear it if you're angry with me." She looked at the ground, fighting the tears. "I didn't mean what I said up at the lagoon. You know I'm not like that. I was only trying to hurt you."

The silence was unbearable. Wasn't he ever going to speak? She felt his hands gently on her shoulders and then she was drawn into the wonderful comfort of his arms. She knew what Nan had meant when she said that love was comfort, courage, and a sense of belonging.

Mark whispered against her hair, "Judy love, you make me feel even more of a heel than I was feeling already. If I forgive you will you forgive me? Oh God, Judy, don't cry. I can't stand it. We're friends again now. Stop crying. First you push me in the water, and now you're soaking my shirt. Do you want to give me pneumonia?"

Judy buried her head in his shoulder. Just a few minutes more in his arms, and then she would go. She had her answer; if he loved her he would have said so. All he could offer was friendship. She would always treasure even that much of him.

"Please, Mark," her voice was muffled. "I want you to release me from my promise to stay here till March. I want to go away. Zelda will be home next week, your mother told me. She can come and stay and look after your mother and the twins. Will you let me go?"

"No, you promised to stay no matter what happened, remember?"

Judy pushed herself away from him. "Why wait until March to marry her? You could get married straight away, and then I could leave. Please, Mark," Judy pleaded. "I must go."

"Yes, I'd look fine asking any girl to marry me now, wouldn't I, Judy? What would I say? Darling, would you marry me? I can't offer you much except love. I have a farm that I may lose before the end of the month. I have a mother to support. If Paul and Betsy don't turn up I'll have a set of twins to bring up as well. If I lose the farm and go back to my job you'll get damn all to live on. Do you think any girl in her right mind would say yes to a proposal like that one, Judy?"

"If she loved you she would jump at the chance." Judy's voice was low.

"Well, she isn't getting the chance." Mark's voice was strained. "I may be an optimistic fool to think I can swing this farm, but I'd be crazy to contemplate marriage with all the rest hanging over my head. Now go and make me a cup of tea. If you ever shove me in the lagoon again I'll put you over my knee and paddle your bottom. Now get going!"

CHAPTER EIGHT

The next week was one of the happiest Judy had ever spent. She went fishing with Mac and Peter and earned their praise by catching a three-pound trout.

Peter was so proud of her, his very own pupil. He was not a bit deterred when Mac warned him that he would end up in jail with Judy for encouraging her to fish without a license.

"If the ranger came along, I'd take back the rod," he explained happily. "Course, Judy is so pretty she would only have to smile at him and he'd let her go."

On Sunday Mark took them all out to a speedboat regatta at Lake Moana. Friends there gave Judy the thrill of her life by letting her try water-skiing. She spent more time in the water than on it, but it did not weaken her enthusiasm for the sport.

On the following Wednesday afternoon she came home to find Nan entertaining a visitor. Judy knew before Nan introduced them that this was Zelda. Judy had been prepared to hate her on sight, but before she had been in her company very long she knew she could not hate her. Zelda was small and slender, a quiet, shy girl with a very sweet smile. No wonder Mark felt protective toward her; any man would. Zelda spent a lot of time at the farm. She followed Mark around, and Judy saw them having long, earnest conversations.

Judy was jealous, horribly jealous. She could not bear the bitter heartache that came when she saw Mark put a carelessly casual arm around Zelda, or took her hand walking down the path. Judy despised herself for being resentful. She liked Zelda; she loved Mark; if she was a decent person she should have been pleased to see them so happy.

One night as she leaned out of her window gazing at the stars she saw them walk out to Zelda's car. Zelda's voice carried clearly to her. "Oh, Mark, you are a silly fool! Money is nothing. You have your values mixed. It's love that makes the world go around."

Judy did not hear Mark's reply, but she did see him put his hands on Zelda's slight shoulders, just as he had done to her only a week ago. Judy turned away from the window. It was no use tormenting herself. Mark was her friend, but he loved Zelda. Three weeks more, and she would be able to leave. Tomorrow she would go into town and buy her ticket. That would help her to accept the reality of her eventual, but definite, departure. She lay in bed, but did not sleep, nor did she cry. The pain she felt was too deep for tears; it was a tearing, aching loneliness for Mark's arms to be around her, for his lips to be on hers.

As she drove from Greymouth the next day she could see the huge mountain range, the Southern Alps, stretched out before her, in the distance. Strange how they had fascinated her from the day she had come to the farm. Suddenly she decided that before she left New Zealand, she was going to take a trip to the mountains.

She remembered Lucky offering to take her that night at the cabaret. Of course she knew that he had been joking. She had laughed at his offer, but she wasn't laughing now. Her determination strengthened as she drew nearer the farm. She would go. Mark did not care where she went, or who she went with now; he had Zelda home.

The next time Lucky called her she asked him when he was going on the tops again.

"It all depends on the weather, Judy. I have three days off next week, starting Wednesday. Why do you ask?"

"You offered to take me with you once. Well, now I want to go."

"You have to be joking!"

"No, I'm quite serious," Judy assured him. "I'm leaving for England on the first of March. It's something I want to do before I leave. Will you take me, Lucky?"

"Like that, is it, chicken? Well, you can't win them all. I'm sorry."

"Will you take me?" Judy pleaded.

"Sure, I'll take you. Let me think a minute. I know just the place for you. It's a stiffish climb, but you should manage it okay. Are you sure you want to go? Mark may not let you."

"Mark won't be worried. He's otherwise occupied at the moment. What do I have to wear?"

"A comfortable pair of boots or shoes for a start, shorts and shirt if you want to, but bring a pair of slacks and a warm sweater in case it turns cold. We can go up and back in the one day, if we get an early start."

"What's the name of the mountain I'm going to climb?"

"Round Hill."

"I don't want a hill, I want to climb a mountain," Judy argued.

"It's quite a hill. You'll do very well if you get to the top of it. It's about 4000 feet or a bit over. Do you want me to pick out a bigger one?" laughed Lucky.

"No, Round Hill will do nicely, thanks." Then she had second thoughts. "I've never done any climbing, Lucky. I don't know anything about ropes and all those fancy things you have to do on rocks. Perhaps I might cause you too much trouble.''

"Oh, there's no need for roping, you'll do fine. It will be tough going for you, though. But let me warn you that once you start I won't let you turn back if I have to drag you to the top by your hair. Still game to give it a go?''

"Yes."

"Right, I'll give you a call Tuesday night, just in case you change your mind. We'll have to start from here at four-thirty in the morning. See you!'' and he hung up.

Judy listened anxiously to the weather report and was reassured to hear "fine weather" predicted. On Tuesday night after Lucky called, Judy returned to the dinner table.

"May I have the day off tomorrow, please, Mark?''

Mark looked surprised. "Why, sure. Going somewhere?''

"I'm going away for the whole day. I'll be leaving at four-thirty a.m. and won't be back until quite late. You don't mind, do you, Nan?''

"Not at all, dear. Don't worry about me, I'm disgustingly healthy these days.''

Judy knew this was far from the truth, because as day followed day, and no news came from South America, Nan seemed to grow more frail. Judy worried about her, but there was nothing she could do except insist on her resting each afternoon.

"Where are you going, Judy?'' asked Vicki.

"I bet I know,'' Peter said. "Someone is taking you to Christchurch and back. Am I right?''

"No, guess again.''

"I know, I know!'' shouted Vicki. "You're going to the glaciers?''

"Wrong again," teased Judy. "You'd never guess in a 100 years."

"The Pancake Rocks?—no, you wouldn't have to start that early," Peter guessed again.

"The glow-worm caves and the greenstone factory at Hokitika?" When Judy shook her head Vicki urged, "Tell us, Judy, where are you going?"

"I'm going to climb a mountain."

Peter questioned, "Which one? How high is it? Who's taking you?"

Judy smiled, "Well, it's not really a mountain. The name is Round Hill, and it's over 4000 feet high. I'm going right to the very top."

"Have you had any climbing experience, Judy?" Mark's tone was cautious.

"None at all, but I'll have an expert guide," Judy answered pleasantly.

"Lucky?" Mark spat the name out.

"Yes, Lucky." Judy's own temper started to rise. He was not going to stop her.

"You're very foolish. I warned you not to go out with him. I thought you had more sense."

"Don't you think Lucky is a competent guide?" Judy asked innocently.

"Oh, he's good all right, one of the best—half mountain goat, but that isn't what I meant, as you very well know."

"Oh, you're still carrying on about his reputation. I've booked my ticket on the plane, and I'm leaving in ten days' time. I want to go up to the mountains before I leave. In fact, I want to enjoy as many new experiences as I can before I go." Her green eyes challenged him.

"I forbid you to go!" Mark shouted.

Judy pushed her chair away from the table. "You can't stop me. You have no right to try. You look after Zelda.

I'll look after myself." She turned and ran from the room, out of the gate and up onto the bridge. Leaning on the rail, she looked down into the swift-moving water. Why did she have to lose her temper and make a mess of everything? She had intended to be calm and collected even if Mark tried to stop her, but she had shouted back at him, like a virago. She was bitterly ashamed of herself. Only a few weeks ago she had been so happy and content to be his friend, but that had been before Zelda had returned. Since then she had tried to control her feelings. Tonight, in one flash of temper she had spoiled her hopes of being able to leave here pretending she did not care. Mark, oh, Mark! She loved him so much she would have died for him. But she wouldn't die, she thought drearily. She would go on living. Back in England the days would pass, and the pain would gradually grow less. Some day she would be able to look back on her visit to New Zealand as a wonderful memory. Nursing would fill her life. She would make it do so. She returned to the house in a more reasonable frame of mind.

Nan had started the dinner dishes, so Judy picked up a tea towel. "I'm so sorry, Nan. I hope I didn't upset you, but Mark had no business trying to stop me from going with Lucky."

"I'm not upset, Judy dear. You have a perfect right to go where you like, but do be careful."

"Be careful of Lucky, or of the mountain, Nan?"

"Both," answered Nan with a wicked smile. "He's a most attractive man."

"I'm in no danger from Lucky's charms. He doesn't interest me, except as a friend, but as I'm leaving, I would like to do this trip. The mountains have fascinated me ever since I came here. I have a feeling that when I get to the top of my mountain, my troubles will look very small and insignificant."

"I understand, Judy." Nan's voice was kind.

They finished the dishes in silence, both busy with their own thoughts. As Judy hung up the tea towel she asked, "Where are the twins? Have they gone to bed?"

"No, they went to see Mac. Oh, Judy, I am upset over you leaving. I never interfere with my children's lives, but this time I've been sorely tempted. I had hoped that you and Mark. . . . " She sighed deeply.

"Don't, Nan!" Judy's voice was sharp. Then she took a deep breath. "I love Mark. I suppose you've guessed that, but he loves Zelda, so I must leave. I thought I'd like to tell you. It's nice to know that you would have welcomed me, but don't let us talk about it any more, please."

"The twins were worried about your leaving. That's why they went over to see Mac; they head for him when they feel Mark and I are not coping with their problems in a satisfactory manner. They're going to miss you terribly, and so am I. You must write to me when you leave here. I'll remember your kindness always; you've become like one of the family, and I hate to see you go."

Judy's eyes were bright with tears. "I've loved it here . . . " her voice shook. "I must be tired. If you don't mind I'll go to bed. I have to get up so early in the morning." She kissed Mrs. Palmer and went through to her room. Only ten more days to go. Could she stand ten more days of this stupid, self-inflicted torture? Of hoping for the impossible? Hoping that perhaps at the last minute Mark might find out that he loved her and not Zelda? It was a good thing that she would be away tomorrow. Even one day in the mountains might give her the tranquillity that Lucky spoke of. She certainly needed something to carry her through these next few days.

Judy set the alarm for four o'clock. That would give her time to have something to eat before Lucky came.

When the alarm shrilled she quickly switched it off, jumped out of bed and washed and dressed. She wore her slacks over her shorts because it was still fairly cold. She could take them off later if she felt too hot. A feeling of exhilaration took hold of her. Today she was going to climb her mountain. She picked up her thick sweater and hurried out to the kitchen, then stopped dead at the sight of Mark by the stove.

"Come on, sit down—one breakfast coming up." He spoke quite cheerfully. "It's a long drive out to the Kopara. You'll travel all the better for eating a good meal before you start."

Judy felt rather bewildered. "Why, thanks, Mark. You shouldn't have bothered. I could have made something myself. You're not trying to stop me, then?"

The smile he gave her was warm and friendly. "No, I was stupid, not you. I'm very glad you're having this trip. Lucky is a good chap in the hills, but you must be careful. Take it easy for a start and take a rest when you need it. Don't let Lucky hurry you too much. I've done that climb many times. If I had known that you wanted to go I would have taken you myself."

Judy felt a pang of regret. I would have been marvelous to go there with Mark. Then she remembered how he could not take a day off work for any relaxation. "Yes, it would have been nice to go with you, Mark, but you're always so busy. You couldn't spare the time. You have to use every minute trying to save your farm."

Mark had a peculiar expression on his face. "It isn't the farm that has come between us, Judy. I would chuck the farm tomorrow—" He stopped suddenly. "Forget it, nothing has changed. Drink up your tea. I can hear Lucky's van coming down the hill.''

Just as they were going out the door, the phone shrilled. Mark said, "Damn, I'll have to answer it, or it will wake the whole household. Have a good day.''

Judy walked slowly out to the truck. For a moment back there in the kitchen, for one whole heart-stopping, breathless moment, she had thought her dreams were coming true. Of course that was impossible. She had too much imagination, that was the trouble. She kept trying to read hidden meanings into Mark's words and glances, and there was nothing there at all. Snap out of it, Judy, she told herself. This is your day to climb to the sky, to pack up your troubles and throw them to the winds. She greeted Lucky with a gay smile. "Hello, I'm ready. Let's get going.''

"Good girl! You know, I could get attached to you. You never keep me waiting," remarked Lucky as they drove off. "It will take us about an hour to the old Mill, and then you're for it. It takes me about an hour and a half by myself to climb to the top. Dragging you with me, we should take an hour longer, maybe more. I'd like to get a shot if I can, might get some good velvet.''

"What do you mean, velvet?" queried Judy.

"Each year the stags shed their antlers and grow new ones. While they're soft and new they feel like velvet to touch. The stags are said to be in the velvet. Later the antlers harden in time for the mating season. That's when the stags roar for their mates. They need their antlers nice and sharp to fight their rivals off.''

"But what do you want the velvet for?"

"Money. They pay big money for a good set of velvet. It's exported to China. I believe they grind it up and use it for medicinal purposes, but I don't much care. Just as long as they keep paying out fantastic prices for it."

"Why don't you settle down, Lucky? Don't you get sick of being in a different house every night?"

"Now, Judy, we'll remain friends on one condition, and that is you must not try and reform me. How did we get onto this subject, anyhow? My mother is always telling me a rolling stone gathers no moss, and who wants to gather moss? Not me, I can assure you."

"I was wondering, that's all. However, if it worries you, I can promise you I won't try to reform you. For one thing, I have only nine days left. I'm sure reforming you would take me much longer."

"True," answered Lucky with a grin. After they had driven about 20 miles, he said, "In a few minutes I'm going to show you something special."

"What is it?"

"Wait and see." They were driving along a narrow, gravel road, that spiraled down a steep hill. The bush was so close on either side that the tall trees sometimes met overhead, making an archway of green. Lucky stopped the van. "Well, what do you think of that view?"

Judy looked out at a beautiful lake, which was as smooth and still as a mirror, reflecting the snow-capped mountains in all their glory.

"Oh, what a wonderful sight!"

"Not too bad," replied Lucky as they drove on. "Won't be long now. In about ten minutes I'll be able to show you Round Hill. We'll stop on the Bluff, and you can see it clearly. Then I'll take you up for a closer inspection."

When he stopped, he pointed. "See, over there—no, not the high craggy one with the snow on, the one to the left, that's Round Hill. The big one is Mount Elizabeth. You would need a bit of training before you could tackle that one." He let the clutch out gently, and the car moved on down the hill. They drove about three miles up a farm road and stopped by an old abandoned sawmill.

"From here on it's Shanks' Pony," said Lucky. "The old van wouldn't make it far in the bush."

Judy noticed how much more natural and relaxed Lucky had become as they came nearer to the bush. He had lost that bored, cynical expression he usually wore.

They set out, Lucky leading and carrying the pack, Judy behind with the rifle. The first quarter of an hour was easy: a gradual climb along an overgrown, disused road. Although little more than two ruts up the ridge, it at least gave good footing and free passage for their taut, straining bodies. The second growth and rushes underfoot were still wet with the heavy overnight dew. The road petered out into a creek bed, wide at this point and scoured with past flooding. It was caused by the torrential rains that fell frequently and without warning in these mountains, Lucky explained to her.

They followed up the creek, gaining altitude until the gully began to close in, and there was only just room for Lucky to squeeze through with the encumbrance of his pack. When a narrow, side stream came tumbling in on his left Lucky turned toward the opposite face and started to climb.

"Give me the rifle, Judy, and take a breather."

Judy's legs were trembling, and her mouth was parched and dry. She was only too pleased to hand over the rifle that had seemed so light when they started and now weighed a ton, by the feel of it.

She climbed after Lucky, following in his footsteps, grasping the trees he grasped, and being determined not to be left behind. After 15 minutes of almost vertical climb they came out onto a ridge, and the going became easier.

Below them she could still hear the creek bubbling and gurgling its way down to the river, although the sight of it was denied her by the steepness of the face they had just climbed. On either side, the ridge fell away steeply to disappear into an impenetrable wall of green forest.

Above them a brief glimpse of the sunlight could be seen through a gap in the green canopy caused by the falling of a huge rimu tree. Lucky told Judy that these trees lived to be over 100 years old. She wondered what sort of life people lived in New Zealand when it had been a seedling the size of the one beside her. It was at least 50 feet tall, reaching for the sunlight, dead straight and no thicker than her wrist. Then she chided herself, there were probably no people living here then—after all, New Zealand was only discovered by Abel Tasman in 1642, and the Maoris had migrated here about A.D. 1350. At least she had learned that much by helping the twins with their homework.

"We mustn't stop for more than a couple of minutes," said Lucky, "or your muscles will stiffen up on you. Have to keep a sweat up. Come on!"

"Ladies don't sweat, they perspire," argued Judy as she scrambled to her feet.

"Same difference," remarked Lucky. "And you don't fool me. You're just trying to start an argument so that you can get a longer spell."

Ahead of them the ridge rose steadily, and the footing was much better. They were walking on a carpet of leaves and moss; there was silence except for the harshness of their breathing. Twenty minutes after their brief rest by the creek bed, Lucky pointed out to Judy that they were leaving the rimu trees behind. The birch trees were becoming smaller, and their branches nearer the ground.

When she asked about a big tree beside the track Lucky

answered, "That's a rata. You can pick them out easily from the flat when they're in flower. They have a brilliant, scarlet flower. Ten years ago this hill used to be a mass of scarlet blooms in January, but a blight attacked the trees, and now only the odd one flowers. Some people say that the opossums killed the trees, but it's not so. Most of the opossums hang around the edges of the bush and eat the farmers' turnips and grass."

An hour and a half away from the van, after taking a two-minute rest every 20 minutes, Judy thought she must be going delirious with fatigue. She suddenly smelt her favorite fruit—bananas.

She stopped, wiped the perspiration out of her eyes and looked around. She noticed that they had left all the big trees behind. The ridge had broadened out, and she could see for several hundred yards. Beside her grew a tree about 20 feet high from which came the delicious banana smell.

"Banana tree," replied Lucky in answer to her query. "Don't get excited, though, they don't have any fruit on them. They look like the real thing with their broad leaves, don't they? The smell comes from the bark that they shed every year. It's saved plenty of blokes who've been bushed overnight, because the bark and limbs will burn easily even when they're wet. We're getting well up the mountain now, because they only grow around the 3000- to 3500-foot mark."

Judy found everything Lucky had to say of absorbing interest. He was a wonderful guide, but she did not see how he had the breath to talk, when she needed every ounce of strength just to keep walking.

"Same as this stuff," continued Lucky, pointing to a scrub about a foot high. "Monkey scrub. It's a fair cow if you get off the track. This stuff grows very thick around

3500 feet up. The snow gets on it, and crushes it down. It doesn't die; just spreads out and grows up again all around. It's sometimes so thick and matted that you have to go over the top of it like a monkey would. Hurry up. We'll be out in the open in about 20 minutes."

Gradually the scrub became more sparse, and the mountain top came into view. The track was not so steep now and almost disappeared among the flax bushes that were no more than three feet high. Then they came to a small waterhole set in a tiny flat at the foot of a ridge: the junction of two gullies. The flax here was taller, and the banana trees and monkey scrub afforded them some protection from the keen early morning breeze, still chilled by the light dew.

"Let's have a tea," Lucky said. "There's still a lot of mist on the tops, and we'll have to wait for it to lift if we want to get a good shot."

Judy sagged to the ground and was content to watch Lucky busy himself preparing a fire and filling a billy. "How far to the top?" she asked.

"It will take us about half an hour or a bit more, but there's quite a good view from here. Have a look when you've recovered."

Immediately below them they could see the lake still covered here and there with wisps of early morning mist. From the lake shore the bush ran away into ridges and gullies rounded off and softened by the trees' leafy camouflage. Green gave way to white as the snow caps of the main divide followed through to Mount Cook, the monarch of them all, looming high even at 100 miles away.

Lucky showed her on the right where the green gave way to blue: the deep blue of midnight, the turbulent Tasman Sea. Through the hills he plotted the course of the Grey River wandering on its way to the Tasman. Pockets of mist clung here and there in the valleys. Where the Grey River finished, its joining at Greymouth could be pinpointed by the tinge of red from the red-painted roofs.

"It's about 30 miles to Greymouth, as the crow flies," remarked Lucky. "Come on, finish your tea, and we'll get on to the top."

"That was a great cup of tea, Lucky. It's given me enough strength to make it to the top, I hope. Nice to find a waterhole handy, just when I was about to die of exhaustion!"

"Tarn, Judy, not waterhole." He pulled her to her feet. "Walk, or I'll drag you, caveman style!"

Judy forced her aching limbs to carry her up the last ridge. Finally she made the summit. What a grand sense of achievement she felt!

"Well now, I'm going to cross over to the second peak. Do you want to come with me, or do you want to stay here? There's nothing on these hills to hurt you. It's ten o'clock; it will take me a couple of hours to go over and back."

"I'll stay here," said Judy. "This is the nearest I've ever been to heaven. I could sit and look at this view for hours. Why didn't you tell me to bring a camera?"

Lucky raised an eyebrow. "Do you think you could have made it carrying a camera?" he laughed. "You did jolly well. I shouldn't tease you. You were much better than I thought possible. Well, I'm off. You're as safe as a church here provided you don't wander off. Move down by that tarn if you feel cold. We'll have venison for lunch." He moved off with the easy, tireless tread of an experienced mountaineer.

Judy lay back in the tussocks and gazed at the blue sky with the little white clouds scuttling across it. This was her mountain. With Lucky gone she had it all to herself. She was completely alone and filled with a strange sense of peace; and something more, a touch of excitement and expectancy. This was her mountain. Somehow, some time before she went down it was going to give her the courage she needed to smile when Mark and Zelda announced their plans. Something would be given to her to help her hold her head high for the next nine days. She wasn't in a hurry. She just relaxed and waited. Slowly her eyes closed, and she fell asleep.

When she awoke the sun was high over head. Lucky would be back soon. She went down to the tarn and washed her face and hands in the cool, clear water. She watched the water settle and become smooth, then looked at her reflection in the water. She stiffened and stared. The water reflected the figure of a man standing behind her, and it wasn't Lucky. Nervously she turned.

"Mark!" she said incredulously. She could hardly believe her eyes. She put her hand out and touched him, just in case she was dreaming.

"Oh, I'm real enough," Mark said, smiling that wicked teasing smile that she loved so much.

"What are you doing here?" Judy could not accept the fact that he was on the mountainside with her.

"I came up here to ask you to marry me."

Judy shut her eyes. It must be a mirage. She had never heard of people seeing a mirage in the mountains, but this sudden vision of Mark could not be real.

She felt his arms enfold her and draw her close. "Will you marry me, Judy, love? I love you so much. I can't let you go. I won't ever let you go. Say yes, my darling."

For an answer she opened her eyes and put her arms around his neck, drawing his lips down to hers.

A long time later he asked, "Where's Lucky?"

"He went across to the second peak shooting. He should be back soon."

Mark held her tight, "Oh, Judy, how I've longed to take you in my arms and call you my own. You have no idea the control I've had to keep on myself to stop me from doing so, and damning the consequences."

"But why, Mark, why didn't you tell me?"

"When you left this morning as the phone was ringing, I was feeling quite desperate. I thought I'd lost you forever. I cursed the phone. But when I answered it, it was the exchange to say that there was a call coming through from South America and to wait around for it. I had to wait for over an hour before the call came through. It was Paul, to say that he and Betsy were safe and returning to New Zealand by plane next week."

"How wonderful!" Judy's eyes shone. "Oh, dear Nan will be so relieved. At last her faith has been rewarded."

"Yes, it's great news, in more ways than one. It meant that I could ask you to marry me. I nearly started off after you there and then, but first I had to wake Nan and tell her. She was rather overcome, so I made her stay in bed. When I told the twins their mother and father would be home next week they went completely crazy, like a pair of lunatics. It took me ages to get their lunches ready and feed them breakfast. I thought they were better at school. It would help them to settle down. By the time I put them on the bus I was hours late with the milking. The more I hurried to get to you the more things went wrong." He pulled her close and kissed her.

As Judy drew away she asked, "But why did you have to wait to hear from Paul before you could ask me to marry you? You would have saved us both so much pain and heartache. You knew I loved the twins. Had their parents not returned, I would have loved to help you with them. Didn't you trust me that far?" Her voice was sad.

"Of course I trusted you, darling, and loved you. I loved you from the moment I found you, oh, so beautiful, and oh, so angry, in my car. But how could I ask you to marry me? There was not only the twins, but also Nan only has her pension. She was also my responsibility and would have had to live with us."

"As if that would have worried me!" Judy interrupted indignantly.

"I know, I know, but there was always the chance I would lose the farm. If I could have counted on swinging the farm I would have risked it, but it's always been so close to the margin I couldn't be sure. If I lost that and had to take another farm advisory appointment, my salary wouldn't have stretched to you, as well as Nan and the twins."

"And now it can." Judy nestled closer to him.

"Yes, now Paul and Betsy will come home and take their horrible little brats away. Nan will live with them as she has always done. You and I will be together, perhaps not on the farm, but I don't care, just as long as we're together."

A thought struck Judy. "What about Zelda? Is she going to be terribly hurt?"

"She is not, you silly goose. Zelda has been a good friend to me, and always will be, but nothing more. She's keen on a chap she met in Aussie. She's been giving me the works because I wasn't honest with you. I felt it was better, if you had to go, not to complicate matters further by telling you I loved you, but had no hope of being able to marry you."

"Okay, okay, break it up!" Lucky was back.

"You'd think when a chap brings a girl 4000 feet up a

mountain that he could at least be sure of being safe leaving her alone for a couple of hours. I came back an hour ago, but saw you were busy, so I roamed around being tactful, but enough is enough. I'm starving. We're having venison for lunch—that is, if food isn't too mundane a subject to mention.

Mark built the fire while Lucky prepared the venison. Judy thought the meal was delicious; she was really hungry after the climb, and even being in love had not affected her appetite.

As they tidied up Lucky remarked, "I suppose congratulations are in order. You want to watch her, Mark, she's too fond of getting her own way. Don't ever let her get the upper hand, or you're done for!"

"I'll keep your advice in mind, Lucky," Mark replied with a grin.

"Well, seeing you're here, you can have the responsibility of taking her home. I'll stay up here the night and have another go tomorrow, if that's okay by you."

"Thank you for bringing me, Lucky. It has been a marvelous trip," said Judy as she watched Lucky pack his gear into the pack.

"Right, that's settled," Lucky said as he straightened up and looked at Mark. "As I won't be at your wedding, do you mind if I kiss the bride now? I've danced miles around the ballroom with her, dragged her miles up this damned hill without getting a kiss, and I reckon I deserve one. So with your permission . . . ?"

To Judy's surprise, Mark nodded. Lucky took her in his arms and kissed her with practised skill. "If he doesn't treat you right, chicken, you just let me know." He picked up his pack and gave them a mock salute. "So long, guys, see you around."

Judy watched him striding away and thought what a

good friend he had been to her. Just now his words and action had been to clear any small doubts that Mark might have been harboring in his mind concerning their friendship. Lucky reached the ridge, turned, waved, and disappeared from view.

Judy and Mark did not hurry home. Their love was so precious, so new. They wished to keep their wonderful experience to themselves, if only for a few hours.

The wedding was over, and Judy sat by Mark as he drove the car through the traffic. On her finger was a square-cut emerald ring and a wide band of bright gold, her wedding ring. Mac had provided the gold for her ring and offered it with his customary dignity, wishing them lifelong happiness. A tender smile touched Judy's lips as she thought of Nan's loving kindness and Vicki's wild excitement when she and Mark had returned from the hill. Peter had been quite smug, pointing out that he had suggested Mark should marry Judy ages ago. Paul and Betsy had arrived home, and then the wedding had been arranged. Zelda had been delighted when Judy had asked her to be bridesmaid. Vicki had been a beautiful flower-girl. Judy turned to smile at Mark, her husband; all the love in her heart shining in her eyes.

Mark pulled over onto a quiet part of the road. "Don't you dare look at me like that when I'm driving, my lovely, lovely wife, or you may have us off the road!" He took her in his arms and kissed her.

Later he said, "You know, I'm a remarkably lucky fellow. Today I have myself a wife. She may not be much to look at, but she can cook, and a man can't have everything. Now, now control that nasty temper!" He kissed her again, then continued. "I haven't had time to tell you, but I also own a farm. Yes, old James, the lawyer, gave me the title deeds at the wedding—a present from Uncle Jack, the old rascal. He apparently wanted me to have the farm all the time, but he also wanted to make me sweat a bit first. The clause about me marrying Zelda was only to make sure I *didn't* marry her. He told old James that she wasn't the girl for me. He knew me well enough to know that if he put that clause in the will, Zelda would be the last girl I would marry. Cunning old devil! I wish he could have seen the beauty I picked for myself."

"Oh Mark," whispered Judy as he drew her close, "I love you so much . . . " and that was all she had time to say.

THE UNKNOWN MR. BROWN

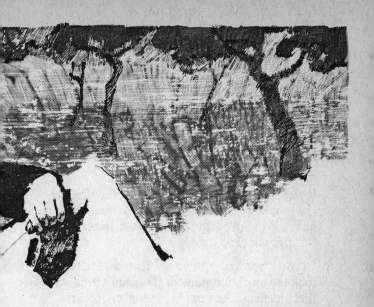

The Unknown
Mr. Brown

Sara Seale

From the age of 14 Victoria was in the care of a benefactor she was never able to meet, the unknown "Mr. Brown."

It was no wonder then that, starved for affection, she should weave romantic dreams about him and be ready to fall for the first man who took a flattering interest in her.

"I was green and gullible," Victoria admitted. "I took too much for granted. If it hadn't been for that practical joke I might have taken Robert seriously, so perhaps it's all worked out for the best."

But she knew now with depressing certainty that, whatever the future held for her, she would go on loving Robert.

CHAPTER ONE

The impatient schoolgirl had waited in the outer office of Messrs. Chapple, Chapple & Ponsonby's city premises on the occasion of that first extraordinary interview. It had seemed a long time before the elderly clerk ushered her into the presence of the senior partner.

"I'm Victoria Mary Hayes," she had announced confidingly almost before the door had closed hehind her. "Are *you* Mr. Brown?"

The benevolent-looking old gentleman who was rising to greet her paused halfway and sat down again. His deceptive air of bonhomie momentarily vanished behind an expression of prim disapproval.

"Certainly not," he replied, sounding faintly shocked. "And I might remind you, young lady, that the identity of your—er—benefactor is no concern of yours. You are very unlikely to meet."

"Oh!" She sounded both disappointed and justly reproved, but the next minute had returned to the attack with, he thought, a most improper want of respect. "But it sounds so unlikely. Complete strangers don't adopt you out of the blue. If they did they would surely want to have a look at you first—not buying a pig in a poke, if you see what I mean."

"Mr. Brown has not adopted you, as we've been at some pains to point out in our correspondence," the lawyer retorted a little sharply. "As to having a look at you, as you rather baldly put it, I have already explained that he saw you in court and for reasons best known to himself decided on this rather unusual course of action. Since he has followed the case he is quite aware of your history. Whether he is—er—buying a pig in a poke will be up to you," he added with a somewhat wintry smile. "It would seem that, unlike counsel for the prosecution, he was—er—not unmoved by your evidence."

"Counsel for the prosecution was too busy having a ball at my expense to worry about my feelings. He got a kick out of every minute of it," she retorted with some venom, and he frowned.

"My dear child! Robert Farmer is too able and too experienced in cross-examination to—er—get a kick out of making mincemeat of a schoolgirl," he said with some sharpness. "In my opinion, you should never have been called in the first place. Had Farmer been defending he would not have made that mistake. Your evidence did your father no good."

"No," she answered quietly, sounding suddenly grave and older than her 14 years, "they told me afterward I had let him down. You see, Mr. Chapple, I hadn't understood that I must give prearranged answers even if they weren't strictly true."

"Yes, well . . . your evidence was clearly ill-prepared, but it's all over now. At least you will not have to suffer for your father's mistakes," the lawyer said rather testily, but he observed her uneasily across the imposing width of his desk. She sat there staring beyond him at the impressive rows of deedboxes, looking as she had looked that day in the witness-box, withdrawn to the point of stupidity, with those wide, blue eyes staring blankly over Counsel's shoulder. She was too thin and her face was all angles with ears that were not only a peculiar shape but seemed to be much too large. He wondered what young Farmer, who was said to have an eye for the ladies, had made of her when he rose to cross-examine. He had dealt with her gently enough to begin with, mindful of Mr. Justice Seldon's well-known prejudices in the matter of children giving evidence, but she had proved a stubborn and argumentative witness. Farmer could hardly be blamed for a little rough handling toward the end.

It had been an unsavory case altogether, uncovering shady financial transactions that had put several small firms out of business, Mr. Chapple reflected distastefully. Grahame Hayes had been a dupe rather than a principal and might have got off lightly. But the defense had been mishandled, and he made a bad impression in the box. The court had adjourned, leaving the judge's summing up for the next day. Bail having been granted upon a large security, Hayes had returned to his home. Unable to face a prison sentence, he had taken an overdose that, if unsatisfactory from the point of view of justice, at least saved the country expense, thought Mr. Chapple with his usual cynicism.

It had been tough on the girl of course. The mother had been dead for some years, and there were no relatives to offer a home or financial security. The expensive education her father had planned for her would certainly have come to nothing but for the whim of an eccentric client with more money than sense and a taste for playing providence, thought Mr. Chapple.

"Well now," he said briskly, "returning to Mr. Brown . . . have you quite understood this situation?"

"Understood what?" she asked vaguely.

"The arrangements that have been made for your future," the lawyer replied impatiently. Really! The child could look almost half-witted at times. That wide, unblinking stare, and the mousy hair dragged back from those prominent ears gave her a skinned appearance.

"Oh yes," she answered with disconcerting composure. "A Trust has been formed that operates until I'm 21. I'm to finish my education along the lines my father had laid down, spend the holidays at places appointed by Mr. Brown, apply to this office for money when necessary, send periodical reports of progress to Mr. Brown and be responsible to Mr. Brown for good behavior. I suppose," she added with a sudden grin, "there really *is* a Mr. Brown?"

"Oh yes, my client exists and will expect a reckoning," he assured her with a heavy attempt at roguishness, "so don't run away with the idea that you can play ducks and drakes with his money, young lady."

She gave him a long, considering look as she stood up slowly, smoothing down her skirt with unchildlike carefulness. Then she bestowed upon him that unexpected slow, beguiling smile that, he remembered, had momentarily halted Counsel in the early stages of his cross-examination.

"I think I've learned my lesson regarding other people's money, Mr. Chapple," she said in a cool little voice and, for almost the first time in his professional career, he found himself put out of sorts. He did not like the girl, he decided uncomfortably, and understood very well what had prompted Robert Farmer's subsequent harshness.

"My dear child, I had no intention—I was merely using a colloquialism—the sort of—er—avuncular jest not intended to be taken seriously," he said, red in the face, heaving his corpulent figure out of his chair with some effort.

"That's quite all right, Mr. Chapple. No hard feelings," she told him kindly, then suddenly reverted to her proper age. "Mr. Brown must be stinking rich—stinking rich and slightly mad, wouldn't you say?" she observed. "That isn't his real name, of course, is it?"

"It's the name my client chooses to be known by. As to your other assumption, had I observed any sign of—er—derangement, I would scarcely have been a party to such an undertaking," he replied rather pompously.

"No I suppose not. Still, you must admit it all sounds a bit cock-eyed—unless, of course, he had something to do with my father's trouble and is salving his conscience. Is he—salving his conscience, I mean?"

Mr. Chapple's countenance assumed a purple tinge.

"That is a most improper suggestion," he snapped severely.

"Improper? I don't understand. I wasn't suggesting that the old gentleman was indecent, or anything."

He shot her a suspicious glance, resolving firmly to delegate future interviews to one of his partners, but she was gazing at him with what appeared to be honest perplexity. He cleared his throat gustily.

"Merely a legal use of the term and not intended to imply—er—indecency. However, you will be well advised to check your quite natural curiosity," he told her, his hand already on the bell that would summon his clerk. "Your—er—benefactor has particularly stressed that he wishes to remain anonymous, neither does he desire any personal contact with you. Just think of him as someone in the background holding a watching brief for you that, if I may say so without offense, is more than you could rightly expect in the—er—circumstances."

"Oh, I entirely agree with you," she said obligingly, edging toward the door. "If it wasn't for this mysterious Mr. Brown I would be begging my bread in the streets like the unfortunate heroines in our cook's favorite romances." She paused at the door as a fresh thought struck her. "Perhaps I remind him of someone he has lost, that of course would explain things—a much loved only daughter?"

"As far as I am aware, Mr. Brown is unmarried," he replied somewhat stiffly, then aware that even this much information was a breach of professional etiquette, he pressed his bell with determined finality.

She looked surprised, but made no comment, then apologizing politely for taking up so much of his valuable time, she departed abruptly without waiting for the clerk to show her out.

Now, four years later, Victoria found herself traveling to the same destination on the top of a city-bound bus, summoned at last to a meeting with Mr. Brown. He had assumed so many different disguises through the imaginative years of her schooldays that she told herself the reality was sure to be a let-down. Whether he was a crusty recluse who had been crossed in love, or a reformed criminal expiating his past through charity, or just a rich eccentric with a taste for power, she owed him the security that her father had planned for her. She hoped he would not regret his munificence when they met.

She had been accustomed for so long to her situation that she had ceased to regard it as strange. She had, as required, written regularly to Mr. Brown; stiff, impersonal little letters, dutifully reporting progress in her studies and receiving in due course brief acknowledgements from Chapple, Chapple & Ponsonby. She wished that Mr. Brown would sometimes reply in person, but he never did. Neither, despite vague promises, had he ever attended prize-givings or end-of-term theatricals, occasions when the presence of parents and guardians afforded much consequence to the participants.

The London house had been sold to meet the demands of creditors, but the weekend bungalow in the country had been retained for the period of her schooling. Here the holidays had been spent with Dora Scott, her father's onetime secretary who had dealt with his private affairs and run his house ever since he had become a widower.

Upon leaving school Victoria had been against the doubtful advantages of being finished abroad.

"It's silly these days when most girls are finding jobs and saving their parents unnecessary expense," she had told Scottie, "and specially so in my case. When the Trust is finally wound up, I'll presumably have to earn a living, so why waste time and Mr. Brown's money playing at being a future deb? It's time I met this Mr. Brown and put him wise. Who do you think he is, Scottie? One of Father's less respectable cronies doing penance?"

"I've no idea. Your father had many contacts in all walks of life. Any one of them might conceivably be repaying a favor and, whoever he may be, it doesn't do to look a gift horse in the mouth. As least he's giving you the start in life your father had planned for you."

"Well, things have changed since then, and I am done with school now. Far better to send me to some training college where I can learn something useful instead of wasting time being groomed for social occasions that I'm never likely to grace."

"Well, why don't you write and suggest it?" Scottie had said to end the argument, and Victoria had. She not only firmly stated her views, but intimated that it was time she was summoned to a personal interview with Mr. Brown. And summoned she had been to attend the offices of Messrs. Chapple, Chapple & Ponsonby at eleven-thirty on the following Friday when her remarks would be given attention. So here she was, riding on the top of a bus, her anticipation mounting with every mile, determined to like and even to love Mr. Brown in whatever guise he should present himself.

The bus halted to set down passengers outside the Law Courts, and she watched the gowned and bewigged figures hurrying to and fro amongst the loitering sightseers, sharply reminded of her own unhappy experience. She could look back now on that brief interruption in the ordered pattern of her schooldays with discomfort rather than sorrow. But as she gazed down upon those forbidding halls of justice, certain faces rose clearly in her mind as if she had seen them yesterday. Her father, pale and uneasy, sporting the inevitable carnation in his buttonhole and refusing to catch her eye; the judge heavily aloof on his bench, looking like a sad, elderly bloodhound whose drooping ears had turned gray, and the thin-lipped, ironic face of the prosecuting counsel as he stripped her of dignity and assurance. She had little recollection of Counsel for the Defense who had taken her so gently through the preliminaries. But Robert Farmer's face with its fastidious, chiseled look; cold and colorless as the dusty gray of his wig, she would remember always with that same hurt resentment she had felt as a child. Until the advent of Mr. Brown had directed her fancies into other channels it had afforded her pleasure to invent crushing defeats for Mr. Farmer, even bodily harm. She had been delighted to learn from the gossip columns in the Sunday press that his engagement to some well-known socialite had been broken off on the very eve of marriage. It had been distinctly soothing to the spirit to picture Mr. Farmer suffering the pangs of unrequited love, and although by now he had probably married someone else, Victoria still liked to imagine that things had turned out badly for him.

The bus dropped her within minutes of her destination, and as she mounted the dark staircase to the first floor, the same musty smell of ancient archives greeted her. In the outer office the elderly clerk regarded her over his spectacles with the same air of faint disapproval.

"I don't suppose you remember me?" she said gaily, hoping to astonish him with her newly acquired emancipation, but he replied with a discouraging lack of surprise as he rose from his desk.

"Certainly I remember you, Miss Hayes. Please be seated. Mr. Ponsonby will see you in a few minutes."

She had not met Mr. Ponsonby and for a moment forgot that he was a partner in the firm.

"Is that his real name?" she asked eagerly and felt reproved once more by the chilly glance the old man bestowed on her.

"It is not the custom of this firm to shelter behind false identities when receiving clients," he replied coldly, and she gave a small, nervous giggle.

"I thought you meant Mr. Brown," she said, feeling both foolish and disappointed.

"Indeed?" he countered with raised eyebrows, then a buzzer sounded with peremptory impatience, and he rose to his feet.

"Mr. Ponsonby will see you now, miss," he murmured and ushered her over to one of the closed doors that separated the office from the partners' private rooms.

True to his previous resolution, Mr. Chapple had delegated this interview to his junior partner, and Mr. Ponsonby rose to receive his client with only a faint flicker of curiosity in the gaze that he allowed to dwell on her with momentary appraisal.

"Well now, Miss Hayes, come, sit down and let's hear your objections to our arrangements for you," he said, indicating a chair by the desk. "An opportunity to round off your education abroad isn't given to many these hard times, I may say."

"For that very reason—" she began, then her eyes came to rest on a door at the far end of the room. "Is he in there?" she asked.

"Mr. Chapple is in occupation, naturally, but he is busy with a client. Did you wish to see him particularly?" Mr. Ponsonby replied.

"Not Mr. Chapple. Mr. Brown," said Victoria impatiently, and the little lawyer's rather sparse eyebrows climbed up his forehead.

"Mr.—er—Brown is not on the premises as far as I am aware," he said with some surprise. "Had you expected to see him?"

"Yes—yes, I had. He was obviously the person to discuss my future with and—from the way your letter was worded, I thought—"

"In that case, there must have been some slight error in the drafting," Mr. Ponsonby interrupted with a thin smile. "Mr. Brown had no appointment with us and merely gave instructions to deal with any queries as we saw fit. Now—" he glanced at his watch yet again "—if you would state your reasons for requesting this interview we can clear up any little misunderstanding and set your mind at rest."

"You can set my mind at rest best by letting me talk to Mr. Brown," she answered stubbornly. "Why do I never meet him?"

"Mr. Brown is a very busy person. He has many commitments."

"Such as?"

"Oh, this and that. His interests cover a wide field."

"Who is he, Mr. Ponsonby? Surely you can tell me that much?"

"I am not in a position to say," the lawyer replied stiffly and, as it happened, with perfect truth.

Victoria sighed, feeling not only disappointed, but cheated into the bargain. She had been so sure that this summons to the lawyers' office was in the nature of a rendezvous, but it looked very much as if the elusive Mr. Brown was determined to remain a myth.

On being pressed again to state her objections to their arrangements, she did so. Her old assurance had deserted her, knowing the battle to be lost already. Mr. Ponsonby swept aside her ill-expressed opinions with tolerant amusement, read her a short homily on the need to accept good fortune with grace, and pointed out somewhat acidly that most young women in her position would jump at the chance for betterment and not confuse the issue with foolish fancies.

"In other words, don't look a gift horse in the mouth," said Victoria, remembering Scottie's crisp retort to her protests.

"Exactly," Mr. Ponsonby observed with satisfaction, and rose hastily after another and more pointed look at his watch. "Now, everything is quite clear in your mind, I trust. Arrangements have already been made with the Paris end, and the excellent Miss Scott has her instructions regarding travel and any personal requiremnts, so you have nothing to worry about. One day, my dear young lady, you will be grateful for these advantages."

"Perhaps," she agreed politely, but without conviction. "I can only hope that if I ever do get around to meeting Mr. Brown, he will feel he's had his money's worth," she concluded.

So Victoria had completed the educational program laid down for her. The faceless image of Mr. Brown receded once more into the background. She dutifully resumed the obligatory correspondence, reporting progress, and trying to convey her impressions of this new life in more colorful terms than the stilted accounts of her schooldays in England. It was difficult to maintain contact with a person one had never met and who never replied. Her letters became briefer and duller as time went on.

And so the year had slipped away with so much to offer that was new and delightful that the days seemed scarcely long enough. Victoria made few intimate friends among her fellow pupils. They seemed to be always newly arrived, or finished and leaving, transformed at great expense into polished young ladies ready to reward their parents' efforts by attracting suitable husbands. Sometimes she wondered whether the unknown Mr. Brown was conducting some cranky experiment and had some such plans for her. It seemed unlikely unless he was proposing to take her into his home and launch her upon society, which was more unlikely still.

All too soon the time had approached when she, like the other girls, would be packing up to go home. Her thoughts turned once more to the question of earning a living. She could not feel that the social accomplishments insisted upon by Madame would stand her in much stead with prospective employers when set against a lack of more rudimentary abilities. Deportment and a sense of chic were all very well for those destined to grace society, but for her, a course at a training college might have been more useful. Still, she was emancipated enough now to be grateful for that year of leisurely transition from child to adult. Her French was very passable, she could discuss the Arts intelligently, and she had learned discrimination in the choice of food and wine. If she did not rate herself very highly in the matter of chic, having only a passing interest in fashion, she had learned to make the best of her appearance.

Altogether, thought Victoria, having completed an assessment of her possible assets with modest satisfaction, she had not done too badly by Mr. Brown. It seemed a pity, though, to have acquired the superficial trappings of a finished young lady when there seemed little chance of profiting by them.

She would, she supposed, be returning to the bungalow and Scottie's chaperonage until such time when Mr. Brown should consider her competent to earn a living. But it was Scottie herself who determined the immediate future. She was, she wrote, shortly to go into hospital for an operation, and since convalescence was likely to be lengthy, and it was not considered suitable for Victoria to live alone, the bungalow was to be rented furnished temporarily. The lawyers were making arrangements with a small hostel in the Swiss Alps that took in a few advanced students for a limited period during the winter sports season. Victoria must consider herself fortunate that such an opportunity should come her way.

The first weeks in that small, unfashionable winter resort high up in the Alps were a revelation, for after the discreet supervision of Madame's select establishment, the freedom provided by the little hostel was both unexpected and stimulating. Victoria proved herself an apt pupil in the arts of skiing and skating. Although, as in Paris, she made few intimate friends of her own age, she became pleasurably acquainted with a young widow who was stopping at the nearby hotel with her small, rather delicate son in hopes that he would benefit by the invigorating mountain air.

The boy, who was slightly lame, had taken an immediate fancy to Victoria whom he seemed to regard as not very much older than his own five years. An attachment sprang up among all three.

"You should be flattered. Timmy isn't given to crushes," Kate Allen had said at one of their early meetings. She did not add that she herself had felt drawn to this solitary girl with the inquiring eyes and delicately angled face, looking so impossibly slender in her tight, black ski suit.

Victoria had been not only flattered, but ready to return the compliment in full measure. Timmy, flaxen-haired and smoothly pink, had engaging ways. She thought his mother fussed a little unduly, but upon learning later something of Kate's history she supposed it was only natural. Jim Allen had been tragically killed in a car accident before his son was born. Kate who had been with him blamed herself bitterly, not only for insisting on accompanying him against his better judgment, but for the child's slight infirmity that she believed to be a direct result. Kate, who had taken to inviting the girl over to the hotel for tea or aperitifs, was never very forthcoming about her own affairs. Victoria understood that Kate had been left badly off and now lived in an old Sussex farmhouse, writing children's books to augment her income. It seemed a little sad to Victoria that Kate with her gift for homemaking and regrets for the denial of other children should resign herself to widowhood at the early age of 30. Although she was too sensitive to another's reserve to elicit confidences that were not freely offered, she hoped very much there was some man in Kate's life who was waiting to fill the gap.

Kate, on the other hand, soon knew all about her Mr. Brown, and his strange beneficence. She remembered the

Hayes scandal, but the case had made little impression on her at the time, coinciding as it had with her own personal tragedy. It had only been brought to mind by a casual reference before she left England, suggesting that she might get acquainted should she happen to run across the girl.

Christmas had come and gone and with it many of the tourists. Soon Victoria realized with a pang, the Allens would be leaving, too. The boy had certainly benefited from the mountain air but, said Kate a shade wryly, it was time she settled down to work again and replenished her dwindling coffers.

They were sitting on the terrace of the small hotel watching the beginners on the nursery slopes staggering about and falling down, Victoria with amused recollection of her own first efforts. She had progressed quickly to better things, being light and supple with an excellent sense of balance, thanks no doubt, to Madame's tedious insistence on deportment. For her, too, the interlude was coming to an end and only that morning she had received disturbing news from Scottie. Although the operation had been over and done with months ago, convalescence had been retarded with several small setbacks. Now Scottie wrote from the nursing home that she had once more returned to, explaining with her usual calm acceptance that as it was considered likely that she would remain a semi-invalid for the rest of her life, it would seem wise in the circumstances to accept her sister's offer of a permanent home in Wales. She had already informed the lawyers who would be making fresh arrangements for Victoria. Although she much regretted being unable to complete her undertaking with Mr. Brown, doubtless it was all for the best.

"Well," said Kate when she had digested the news, "so

your Mr. Brown will have to think again, won't he? Perhaps at long last, he will decide to reap the benefits of his unsolicited philanthropy and invite you to share his hearth and home and be a comfort to his old age.''

"Oh, do you really think so? It would, of course, be the natural way to repay himself for all his expense and trouble.''

"No, I don't,'' Kate answered rather sharply. "If his thoughts were running in those channels he would have made his intentions clear long ago. You should have grown out of romantic fantasies of father-figures and star-crossed lovers awaiting rewards. For all you know, your Mr. Brown may be no one person, but a hard-headed syndicate of old cronies of your father's with a debt to pay. Have you thought of that?''

"Often. It's the most likely explanation, isn't it? Still, when one is growing up, it's important to have something, or someone to fix one's sights on. It was much more satisfying to invent images for Mr. Brown than to think of him just as a Trust,'' Victoria answered, and there was a touch of apology in Kate's smile.

"Yes, it must have been. Well, what are your own ideas in view of this latest development?''

"To find a job, obviously, and since poor Scottie's no longer available to make a home for me, Mr. Brown may have to revise his antediluvian ideas.''

"Antediluvian?''

"Well, stuffy, anyway, considering the times and my situation. So far, any suggestions to become self-supporting haven't met with much success.''

"And what would you like to do?''

Victoria twined one long, black-clad leg around the other and gazed out across the snowy slopes with that inquiring consideration that always intrigued Kate.

"Oh, impossible things, of course. Becoming a great ballerina, discovering a lost land, riding the winner of the National to victory—fantasies with the ignoble end in view of thumbing my nose at Mr. Brown," she answered.

"In point of fact, I suppose my qualifications can't have a very high rating commercially, but there must be someone somewhere willing to employ me after such an expensive education."

Kate smiled without making any immediate comment, and sat turning over a half-formed project in her mind, then she said casually, "Would you care to give the Allens a trial if it could be arranged?"

The girl's thin face became instantly so alive with naïve delight that for a moment Kate regretted having made an offer that might well be vetoed in other quarters.

"Work for you, Mrs. Allen?" Victoria exclaimed ecstatically. "But that would be pure heaven! What would I do? When could I start?"

"Gently, child, it's only a tentative suggestion to fill in time while you were looking around for something more suitable. You mightn't find life at Farthings such heaven after the advantages of being finished abroad. We live very quietly and don't entertain."

Victoria regarded her with grave, suddenly unchildlike eyes, the vivacity dying out of her face, leaving it blank and a little pinched.

"But don't you understand?" she said like an anxious child. "I'm grateful, of course, for what has been done for me, but I've never had any feeling of permanence. You treat me as a person, you see, and Farthings sounds like a real home."

"Yes," Kate answered with gentleness, "I think it has that quality. I only rent it, you know, but it's mine for as long as I need it."

"Need it? But won't you always need a home for Timmy?"

"Yes, of course, but one day he'll grow up and I won't want to be tied to one place forever. In the meantime Farthings serves us very well, but there are domestic problems. Timmy needs companionship while I'm working. My old Elspeth who's been with us since he was born has enough to do with cooking and running the house without being at the beck and call of a child. He doesn't need a nursemaid now, but someone young enough to play with him as well as teach him his alphabet. You and he seemed to click at once. Do you think you could be happy being a general dogsbody for a time?"

"I don't need to think. I can imagine nothing more—more rewarding than to share in your family life at Farthings for a little while. Oh damn, there's Mr. Brown!"

For a moment Kate looked up, startled, half expecting to see an elderly stranger bearing down upon them, then she laughed.

"Don't cross your bridges. Just write to the lawyers and state your wishes. After all, you're nearly 20 and entitled to order your own life within reason," she said.

"Yes, I am. But they don't treat me as an adult. They won't consider my wishes if they have other plans."

"Well, you can write and find out. I'm quite willing to present myself and my credentials for their inspection if necessary."

"Do you know any influential people—the sort, I mean, to impress lawyers?" Victoria asked hopefully, and Kate laughed.

"One or two, I expect," she said. "The cousin from whom I rent my house would doubtless put in a word if asked, but you must put your own case first. After all, it's possible that your Mr. Brown is faced with a problem owing to this fresh development. You can hardly stay on here indefinitely now that your education is finished.''

"Mr. Brown is never faced with problems, and if he was Mr. Chapple or Mr. Ponsonby would devise means to iron them out with prompt dispatch. It's being borne in on me of late that they must have made a very good thing out of Mr. Brown's little ploy all these years,'' said Victoria astutely, and Kate's eyebrows went up.

"Very likely, but one must assume that rich eccentrics expect to pay for their whims, so run along and get that letter off before it's too late to alter plans.''

CHAPTER TWO

But as the days went by with no reply to her letter, Victoria's spirits sank. At first she had consoled herself with the thought that negotiations would have to be effected with Mr. Brown who might well be at the other ends of the earth engaged on one of those nameless projects that Mr. Ponsonby had said covered such a wide field. But when, still without news, the day came for the Allens to leave for England, their departure seemed to put an end to her hopes.

"After all, it was only a dream," she said as she bade them goodby, and Kate gave her a quick kiss.

"Cheer up! One's never sure what's around the corner, and for all you know, your Mr. Brown may be laid up with some dire complaint and unable to conduct any business," she said lightly and was amused to see Victoria's face undergo one of its lightning transitions.

"I never thought of that!" she exclaimed. "Oh, poor Mr. Brown! And all this time I've been thinking unworthy things about him. I must write at once and tell the lawyers not to worry him."

"I wouldn't bother," Kate retorted somewhat dryly. "I doubt if they would be impressed by a belated concern for their client. You have, I fancy, a secret fondness for this unknown patron, Victoria, or is it just wishful thinking?"

Victoria stood considering with that grave deliberation that she employed at times before answering the question.

"Perhaps," she said then. "Perhaps everyone needs a

figurehead—a kind of touchstone against adversity. I hardly knew my father, you see, for I so seldom saw him. I admired him tremendously from a distance, but he wasn't much more real than Mr. Brown, so if ever I do meet Mr. Brown, I shall find something to like in him—even to love, if necessary.''

"In that case content yourself with your own creations, the reality may turn out to be a big letdown,'' Kate retorted with some crispness. As the sound of approaching sleighbells announced that the hour of departure was upon them, Victoria turned to her with a forlorn attempt to smile.

"Oh, I shall miss you—and Timmy, and all the fun we've had. Perhaps it was a pity we met, after all.''

"Nonsense, child! Even if you aren't allowed to accept employment with me we shall meet when you're back in England. You can at least come on a visit to Farthings and we'll pick up the threads again.''

"That will be nice,'' Victoria replied politely, but without conviction. Then Timmy created a timely diversion by clutching Victoria tightly around the legs and bursting into anguished wails.

"Don't want to go home . . . don't want to leave T—Toria . . . I won't, I won't, I *won't*!'' he shouted, scarlet in the face. By the time his mother and Victoria had soothed him into a hiccoughing state of compliance, there was no margin left for prolonged farewells.

Victoria picked up the bundle of English periodicals that Kate had left behind for her and sat down to idle away the time, reluctant to return to the hostel. Most of the magazines were filled with seasonable snapshots of notable winter sports enthusiasts holidaying at the more fashionable resorts. Under one of them a familiar name caught her eye, and she read the caption: *Mr. Robert*

Farmer, who has recently added fresh laurels to his legal reputation, relaxing in the sun. Mr. Robert Farmer was certainly relaxing with a glamorous blonde alongside, but since an enormous straw sombrero was tipped well over his face, he could have been anyone. Victoria, upon picking up *Country Life*, was irritated to find that he figured here too. *Our candid camera catches Mr. Robert Farmer in holiday mood on the slopes at St. Moritz,* she was informed cosily. *A little bird whispers that this brilliant young junior Counsel might be thinking of settling down, so we may expect to hear an important announcement soon.* So he hadn't married after all, thought Victoria, hoping the little bird might still be a forerunner of disaster, at the same time examining the photograph for remembered characteristics. Here, too, Mr. Farmer was effectively disguised by a large pair of dark glasses. It was odd how the mention of him could still rankle, she reflected as she made her way back to the hostel, and was thankful that this modest little holiday resort was not smart enough to attract a more publicized clientele.

There was a postcard from Kate at the end of the week announcing their safe arrival, but nothing from Chapple, Chapple & Ponsonby. Victoria sat down to pen a tactful reminder that she was still awaiting instructions, and were they aware that the hostel would shortly be closing down for its spring respite before the start of the climbing season?

When at last the reply came, she opened it with no anticipation of agreement, but whether her arguments had at last found favor, or whether Kate's efforts had proved more persuasive and her credentials suitably impressive, permission was granted for a trial run agreed upon with Mrs. Allen on certain terms. There followed precise instructions as to dates of departure and modes of travel and concluded wih prim good wishes for the future.

From then on the days seemed to fly past. All too soon she was making her farewells and discovering with some surprise that she would be missed. For a moment as her plane took off from the airport, she experienced regret for those carefree months that would never come again and could be grateful now for that meticulous attention to her father's wishes that at the time had seemed so pointless. Later as the plane passed over the English coast and touched down on English soil, such philosophic musings vanished on a wave of eager anticipation. She was a child again, returning for the holidays, but this time it was a real homecoming. There was Kate waiting at the barrier and signaling frantically. All around her was the almost forgotten buzz of English voices, and the inevitable patter and hissing of English rain.

"Oh, *Kate*! If it wasn't so wet and dirty, I'd fall on my knees and kiss the ground like what's-his-name," she cried as she was clasped in a warm embrace, then grew pink with embarrassment. "Oh, how awful! I've never called you that before, and now you're my employer! It was just that I was so pleased to see you that I didn't think."

"Well, please go on forgetting," Kate replied, her brown eyes twinkling. "I hope we're going to be friends rather than mistress and mother's help for which neither of us are very well fitted. Come along now—we have a fair drive ahead of us and it's a stinking day."

It was, indeed, a most unpleasant day, but to Victoria, repeatedly rubbing a clear spot in the condensation on the passenger window and peering out at familiar surroundings, it seemed only right that the weather should be traditional on her return to her native land.

"How did you work it? Did you blackmail old Mr. Chapple? Did you even, perhaps, get into the Presence and do a spot of persuasion on Mr. Brown?" she asked among other less relevant questions. Kate laughed.

"No, I did *not* get into the Presence—it didn't occur to me to try," she replied. "As it happens, Chapple, Chapple & Ponsonby handled my affairs when my husband died, so I wasn't unknown to them."

Kate turned her attention again to the countryside. New estates and factory sites seemed to have encroached still farther on green fields and commons, but gradually these were left behind. The car took a sudden plunge down a steep, winding hill into the narrow lanes and wooded pockets of the Sussex Weald. Every so often a gap in the trees would reveal an unbroken vista of rolling country, but the line of downs lying beyond was hidden in a misty curtain of rain. Another hill was climbed, twisting sharply through the trees. At the top Kate turned the car into a rough, puddle-pitted lane that ended at a pair of white gates standing open to the long, mellow walls of an old farmhouse.

Even in the rainy bleakness of a March afternoon, Farthings offered a welcome and a sense of homecoming. Victoria fell in love with it on sight. Kate gave her no time to stand and stare, however, but hustled her in out of the wet. There was Timmy clutching her around the legs with the remembered tenacity, though this time his fervor found expression in piercing squeals of delight.

"You've come for always, haven't you, Toria? Elspeth *said* it was just to visit, but it *isn't*, is it?" he said as she hugged him in return.

"Now, young man, don't plague the young leddy as soon as she's set foot through the door," said a big, capable-looking woman hurrying to relieve them of their luggage. "Losh me, Mrs. Allen, don't you go out in the wet again. Sam will fetch in the rest of your traps and put the car away, too."

"Very well," Kate smiled. "Victoria, this is my dear Elspeth of whom you've often heard me speak. She manages the house and us with equal impartiality. I expect she'll manage you, too, if you don't make a stand from the start. Elspeth, this is Miss Hayes who is going to take Timmy off your hands for a bit and think up fresh uses for magic for me when I run out of plots."

"How do you do?" Victoria said, disentangling herself from Timmy and holding out a hand.

Elspeth took it after an instant's deliberation and Victoria, watching the woman's shrewd gray eyes traveling over her face, knew that she was being silently appraised.

"We're pleased to welcome you here to Farthings, miss," she said politely, but there was reserve behind the pleasant burr of her native Scotland. Victoria knew that Elspeth would accept her only when she had formed her own assessment.

"Well," said Kate, hoping that her old servant would not extend her past distrust of the au pair girls to Victoria, "I expect you'd like to see your room and freshen up generally. After that we'll have our well-earned tea. I know Elspeth was making a batch of her special griddle scones in your honor, so come along and I'll show you the lie of the land."

Very soon it seemed to Victoria that she had known Farthings all her life, or perhaps, as Kate pointed out, it was simply her first real experience of home.

Mr. Brown was forgotten for days on end in the pleasure of fresh discoveries. She loved the old, rambling house with its many passages, hidden stairways, and rooms opening invitingly one upon another. Elspeth grumbled at the inconvenience when it came to carrying coals and trays, but she kept the place spotless with only the help of a daily girl from the village and a youth who periodically dug the garden and cleaned the car. She would allow no one but herself to wax and polish the fine period pieces that graced many of the rooms. It was a long time before Victoria realized that the contents of the house that seemed so much to reflect Kate's tastes belonged to her no more than the house itself.

"Took the whole lot furnished at a nominal rent for these times, and no strings attached," Elspeth told her. "It was a merciful dispensation at the time of her trouble, for poor Mr. Allen left very little money and the bairn needed special care and quiet, born as he was. Aye, there's some good folks in this world yet."

Victoria remembered that Kate had said she leased Farthings from a cousin for as long as she might need it. She must be a very nice and devoted cousin, Victoria thought, to offer her home for an indefinite period, unless for some reason she had never cared for it herself.

"Yes," she said, "that was generous of the cousin, but perhaps she's old, or maybe lives abroad?"

Elspeth paused in her attentions to a piecrust table long enough to favor Victoria with a look of amused surprise, then fell to again with renewed vigor.

"Neither old nor female, and as far as I know has no thoughts of settling abroad," she retorted.

"Oh, I see. I suppose I took the sex for granted because this house has a sort of family feeling, if you know what I mean."

"Aye, I ken what you mean, but the leddy didn't share your views, it seems."

"What lady?" Elspeth so often had the trick of presupposing you could follow her line of thought.

"The leddy who should have come here as a bride, of course. The poor gentleman couldna be expected to fancy the place on his own, so Mrs. Allen keeps it warm for him. Now will you leave me to get on with my redding, Miss Toria? The bairn won't hurt in the woods this fine morn, but mind that weak leg of his on rough ground."

Victoria could hear Kate tapping away on her typewriter as she passed the study on her way to the nursery and wondered vaguely what sort of person the male cousin might be; elderly, one might suppose, and contemplating a second marriage, since Farthings and its contents had all the familiar hallmarks of a previous home. The nameless lady of his choice must have been hard to please if she could resist the charms of such a place, Victoria reflected, then felt a guilty sense of thankfulness for the timely misfortune of another.

March had slipped into April. The banks were starred with primroses, and the woods with the first leafy freshness of spring. In the little orchard the tight pink buds on the apple trees were ready to burst into blossom.

One morning when Victoria was helping Elspeth in the kitchen, they heard a car stop at the gates, followed by Timmy's delighted squeals of recognition.

"Now, who would that be just when lunch is ready to go on the table?" Elspeth exclaimed with annoyance. "If it's a body dropping in expecting a meal there'll no be enough to go around. The butcher brought three chops the morn instead of the wee roast I ordered."

"It's probably Dr. Squires fitting us in between calls," Victoria said. Kate had few visitors, but the doctor frequently dropped in to keep a professional eye on Timmy, although Victoria suspected that he had more than a passing regard for Kate.

"Aye, very likely. Well, he'll be no trouble. Bread and

cheese and a dram is all he'll have time for, no doubt. Run and tell Mrs. Allen. She'll not be taking any heed if she's stuck in the middle of a chapter."

But Kate was already hurrying across the hall, holding out welcoming hands with much less restraint than she accorded the doctor. The tall man who stepped over the threshold with Timmy tugging violently at his leg took her hands in his and kissed her affectionately.

"*Rob!*" she cried with surprised delight as he released her. "Why on earth didn't you let me know? It's been such an age that I thought you must have forgotten us."

"That's blatant fishing, as well you know," he replied. "I've been snowed under lately, or I'd have cadged a weekend before now. Can you do with me at such short notice? I hadn't time to do more than fling a few things together and hop into the car."

"Of course we can do with you. Your old room's always ready and we only have to make up the bed. Timmy, for goodness' sake stop tugging at Uncle Rob's pants—there won't be any crease left!" Kate laughed, then became aware of Victoria waiting a little uncertainly to be introduced. "Oh, I'm forgetting my manners in the unexpectedness of the moment. This is Timmy's Toria who has nearly cut you out, so you'll have to be very tactful if you want to share his affections."

Victoria came forward to shake hands. There had been something vaguely familiar about the stranger's voice, but the light had been behind him, so that his features were indistinct. When he turned to acknowledge the introduction however, she encountered a pair of cool, appraising eyes under hair that was dark when it should have been gray and experienced an unwelcome shock of recognition. When she had last seen him he had been gray; the gray of a wig pushed carelessly back from his forehead matching the gray of his cold, fastidious regard. The memories of that bewildering day in court had faded like the recollections of a nightmare, but Mr. Robert Farmer had never been forgotten. For a moment, old impressions renewed themselves so vividly that she found herself stammering when she responded with conventional greetings and knew the color had risen in her cheeks.

He shook hands, making some mock-rueful reference to Timmy's vacillating affections, but there was no recognition in his eyes. After a moment of incurious attention he turned back to Kate with whom he was clearly on excellent terms.

"Darling, run and tell Elspeth that my cousin is here, will you?" Kate said to Victoria. "She'll be very angry with you, Robert, for not giving her a chance to provide your favorite lunch, but I expect you'll get around her as you always do. Now come along into the parlor for a glass of sherry and tell me all you've been doing since last we met."

Victoria thought it tactful to leave them to themselves until luncheon was ready and stayed in the kitchen admiring the resource with which Elspeth contrived to make a substantial meal from the meager rations of the butcher's chops. All the time she chattered reminiscently about Mr. Rab, who was plainly a favorite. Victoria learned with growing surprise that he was the self-same cousin from whom Kate rented the house.

"Then it was Mr. Farmer's bride who wouldn't live here, was it?" she asked.

"Aye. A fasionable besom with a taste for parties and fine clothes, so I'm told. She ran off with one of those rock singers and divorced him within the year, it's said."

"Oh!" said Victoria, wondering how much the jilted

Mr. Farmer had minded. "Has he married someone else?"

"If he had, Mrs. Allen would hardly be living here, would she?" Elspeth retorted with a certain asperity. "I'd like to think—still, it's no, my business, nor yet yours, so I'll be obliged if you'll carry in the vegetables for me, Miss Toria, and then tell them lunch is ready."

By the time she sat down with them at table, Victoria had recovered her self-possession, enjoying the knowledge that she had the advantage of Mr. Robert Farmer in the matter of acquaintance. It was hardly surprising, of course, that he had failed to recognize an unremarkable schoolgirl. Save for provoking him to a fine display of fireworks, she could have made little impression as an individual out of the scores of witnesses that must be his daily lot. She had to admit that off duty he possessed a degree of easy charm that found a ready response in Kate and, remembering Elspeth's unfinished remark in the kitchen, wondered if there might be more to a benevolent concession in the matter of his house than cousinly kindness.

"You've been exceptionally silent, darling." Kate observed as they left the dining room, "still, I'm afraid we've been holding the floor. You and Robert must get acquainted, for you'll be seeing plenty of each other if we can persuade him to come down more often. You can't think, Rob, how nice it is to have a man about the house again."

"Has the good doctor given up calling, then?" he asked with a faint twinkle, and she made a face at him.

"Certainly not. He's most attentive to Timmy's needs," she replied primly. "But poor Victoria has little chance to show off the finished results of her expensive education. There aren't many eligible young men in these parts, and if there were her rather stuffy guardians would probably disapprove."

"Guardians?"

"One, to be precise, and he isn't really a guardian at all. Victoria, take Robert around the garden and tell him about your mysterious Mr. Brown while I finish correcting those proofs. I really must try to get them off by the afternoon mail."

Victoria, not relishing the prospect of a *tête-à-tête* with the stranger until she had decided on her line of conduct, made hurried excuses, but Kate said nonsense to all of them and went away to her study. Victoria, catching Mr. Robert Farmer's eye resting upon her with somewhat sardonic amusement, knew that he was fully aware of her reluctance and enjoying himself.

"Are you shy, Timmy's Toria?" he inquired a little mockingly, and now that they were alone together, her old antagonism revived.

"Certainly not," she replied, endeavoring to sound cool and assured. "At my Paris establishment we were taught that it was impolite to appear gauche whatever our provocation."

"Very proper, but weren't you taught that it was also impolite to leave a guest to his own devices?"

"Of course, but you're Kate's guest, not mine. Since you're related and this house is yours, I didn't suppose that you needed entertaining."

"*Touché.* Still, if I were to ask you very politely if you would be so kind as to take me around the garden perhaps you would stifle your disinclination and oblige?"

"Certainly, Mr. Farmer, if that's what you want," she said at once. "We'll find Timmy and take him with us."

"I've always understood that Timmy rested at this hour, but perhaps you've instituted a new regime," he said, and Victoria could have kicked herself. She had quite genuinely forgotten that Timmy would not be available for another hour, but in saying the first thing that came into her head, she could only have confirmed whatever he was probably thinking.

"Of course, I'd forgotten. We have so few visitors here, you see, that your sudden arrival has thrown out our routine." It was a feeble enough explanation and had a distinctly governessy flavor, she thought crossly; then saw him grin with a most unexpected touch of mischief and found herself grinning back.

"That's better," he said, taking her by the arm and piloting her out into the garden. "You shouldn't try conclusions with me on such short acquaintance, you know. I have quite a reputation for dealing firmly with evasive witnesses."

"So I believe," she replied rather tartly. "It must be very uplifting to the ego to browbeat witnesses who can't answer back."

"Oh, but some of them do, and I only browbeat the stubborn ones. Tell me about your mysterious Mr. Brown. Is he an admirer?"

Victoria was not given to inventing fantasies to boost her own consequence, but Robert Farmer seemed to have the knack of making her feel a child again. It would do him no harm to keep him guessing.

"Mr. Brown . . ." she repeated musingly. "Now, there's a man who thoroughly understands the romantic approach."

"By being mysterious?"

"That and other things."

"What other things?"

"You're very inquisitive, aren't you, Mr. Farmer, considering we've only just met."

They were strolling through the little orchard that bounded the neat approach to Farthings. Here nature had been left to run wild, and the grass was already ankle deep. The fruit trees were long past bearing, but they still put forth blossom. Victoria paused now to reach up to a low-hanging branch and shake the last of the petals about her. Robert stood and watched her with obliging attention, thinking that she was probably quite aware of the charming picture she presented. Then she laughed as a shower of dew fell on her upturned face and opened her mouth like a child to catch the drops.

"Very pretty," he observed with a certain dryness. "No doubt the romantic Mr. Brown would immediately respond in the appropriate manner were he here to observe."

She looked at him with a moment's surprised inquiry as if she had temporarily forgotten him. Then she let the branch spring back with a final shower of dew and blossom and stood trying to shake the petals out of her long hair.

"Allow me," Robert said and neatly removed those that clung more tenaciously.

"I never said he was romantic," she protested while she stood passively under his ministrations.

"No? Well, I certainly thought that was implied. A man who thoroughly understands the romantic approach should have all the right answers. Is he romantic-looking too, this paragon?"

"I don't know."

"You don't *know*?"

"I've never seen him," Victoria snapped, wishing that she had not embarked on such an unrewarding line of evasion.

"Dear me! Does he appear masked?" Robert absently

tucked a piece of hair behind her ear as he spoke, and she shook her head impatiently to free it.

"Of course he doesn't. Don't do that, please. I like to keep my ears covered."

"Why? Do you suffer from earache?"

"You are the most aggravating person I've ever met and ask far too many questions," she replied, exasperated both with him and with herself. "No, I do *not* suffer from earache, but my ears are my worst feature, if you must know. I've been taught to hide them."

"*Are* they? Let me look again." He restrained her with a gentle hand before she could break away from him and swept her hair to one side to inspect her ears with earnest attention.

"H'm . . . a trifle large, possibly, by fashionable standards, but they are most engagingly pointed, like a faun's. Perhaps you're a changeling."

She ducked under his arm and backed away from him, her eyes bright with anger.

"Well, now that you've had your fun at my expense, Mr. Farmer, perhaps you'll consider yourself sufficiently entertained for one afternoon and allow me to get on with the chores for which I'm paid," she said.

"Now that," he retorted with infuriating good humor, "is a splendid exit line. Puts me in my place and reminds me of yours with admirable restraint. Still, you will admit that you've had your bit of fun, too."

"What do you mean? I was only following Kate's instructions and trying to amuse the guest."

"With some success, though possibly not as you intended. I have a longer memory than you give me credit for."

"What do you mean?" she said again, but with less assurance. "I'm a stranger to you."

"No, no, Miss Victoria Mary Hayes, I recognized you at once. I hasten to add that the transformation since last we met is quite charming, but I couldn't be mistaken in those ears," said Robert Farmer and, turning on his heel, strolled back to the house.

CHAPTER THREE

"You might have warned me," Victoria said to Kate after Robert had returned to London.

"Warned you of what?"

"That the cousin who owns this house was Mr. Farmer."

"I'm afraid it never occurred to me that you would be interested."

"But you must have known he was involved in my father's case."

Kate's eyes rested on her thoughtfully for a moment, and her eyebrows rose a fraction.

"Yes, of course I knew, but you were a child at the time. I didn't suppose you'd even remember him."

"Not remember! It's true I was too young to understand the rights and wrongs of the affair, but Mr. Robert Farmer I've not forgotten. He made a nonsense of my evidence and enjoyed every minute of it."

"Dear me!" said Kate midly. "I'd no idea you still cherished a grievance. I can understand that the experience must have been bewildering and alarming, but you must surely realize now that there was nothing personal in Robert's methods of cross-examination. The only enjoyment he would derive would be the satisfaction in establishing and winning his case. You've never mentioned him before, Victoria, and I didn't suppose you'd even remember his name."

"I used, when I was younger," said Victoria reminiscently, "to make up splendid stories of dire retribution overtaking Mr. Farmer. Like Mr. Brown, he stuck in my mind, but for different reasons." She spoke with an effort to minimize any suggestion that Kate had been remiss, by admitting to childish fantasies as if they were well behind her. For once Kate did not respond with her usual amused tolerance.

"It's to be hoped then that you're adult enough by now to have grown out of such pastimes," she said a little sharply. "Mr. Brown, I suppose, is fair game since he chooses to pander to your fancies by remaining invisible. Robert is a different kettle of fish, and I'm very fond of him. I'm sorry that you evidently can't bring yourself to think more kindly of him, since he will be coming down here quite often, I hope; but you can always keep out of his way."

"I'm sorry," Victoria apologized. "I didn't mean to be personal in any way. It was so unexpected meeting him again and finding you were both related that it threw me a little, I hope I wasn't rude."

"Oh no, just a little prickly and on your dignity. It's a sure way to bring out the worst in Robert, let me warn you, so if you don't want him to tease, stop trailing your coat."

"Do I do that?"

"Well, perhaps not consciously. Robert's a bad person to tangle with when it comes to disagreement, as you must have discovered years ago, so be careful." Kate spoke with a return of her old affectionate lightness, and Victoria wondered if she had imagined that touch of resentment earlier. She remembered Kate's pleasure in the weekend, and Elspeth's unspoken approval and thought more humbly of her own objections. Since she was fond of Kate and knew something of her earlier tragedy she could

not feel that a man as cold and sharp-tongued as Robert
Farmer was right for her, but if Kate's inclinations lay in
that direction, then the least she could do was to accept his
occasional presence at Farthings with good grace.

It was not so easy, however, to remain impartially in the
background. Robert, whose last-minute descents upon
them became more frequent as summer approached,
showed a perverse liking for her company when Kate was
not available. Although she did not flatter herself that his
casual attentions were inspired by anything other than a
desire to provoke her into argument for the pleasure of
proving her wrong, she found herself having unexpected
moments of doubt when he chose, instead, to charm her.

"Why are you so quick to take my harmless pleasantries amiss?" he asked her once and was intrigued as Kate
so often was by her grave deliberation before replying.

"Possibly because I'm never sure that your pleasantries
are harmless, Mr. Farmer," she said then, and his eyebrows lifted.

"Dear me! I don't seem to be making much headway,
do I? And can't you bring yourself to address me less
formally?" he said. She twisted around on the bench to
regard him with more indifference than she felt.

"I will call you Robert if you prefer it," she answered
with rather prim composure, "but I hardly think that you
would concern yourself over making headway or not."

"Wouldn't you? But then you don't know me very well,
do you?"

"Well enough. You forget I've already had a taste of
your humors in court."

They had been sunning themselves on the sheltered
patio behind the house waiting for Kate to summon them
in for tea. Without any warning his fingers closed on her
shoulder in a none too gentle grip.

"The taste you had then, my child, was mild compared to what you would get now," he retorted, and the lazy banter had gone from his voice. "I would advise you to think twice before trying to get your own back with childish attempts to sting me. My sting can be a great deal more deadly than yours, so don't tempt fate."

"Do you keep your sting in your tail, like the scorpion, Mr. Farmer?" she said, unable to resist retaliating even while she knew she was no match for him.

"That you will doubtless find out in due course, Miss Hayes," he replied mocking her but with an underlying note of warning. Victoria was relieved when Kate appeared to announce that tea was ready.

As always when Kate was present, the tempo changed to a pleasant impression of family unity. Victoria could forget her easily aroused hostility listening to their warm exchanges and watching Robert's ease and patience with the little boy. Timmy plainly adored him, and sometimes she would catch Kate looking at her son and her cousin with a rueful expression as if she were regretting some unexplained decision in the past.

"Robert's very fond of Timmy, isn't he?" she said to Kate when they were alone again.

"Well, he's Timmy's godfather, so I suppose there's a special bond," Kate answered tranquilly. "Timmy, of course, is too young to miss a father he never knew. Robert makes a very good stand-in."

"Would you marry again, Kate?" Victoria asked, remembering Elspeth's hints. Kate, if she was aware of the obvious train of thought, avoided any direct admission.

"I don't know," she answered placidly. "Timmy will need a father when he's grown beyond my capabilities, but marriage embraces more than that."

Victoria's eyes were at once apologetic. "Yes, of course.

And when one has loved very much once, it wouldn't, I imagine, be easy to put up with second best.''

Kate glanced at her with amusement. "Easier than you think, my dear. Compromise isn't such a bad thing if you look it squarely in the face. Jim—my husband—and I were very happy during the short time we had together, but I was in love with someone else when I married him. Don't look so shocked, Victoria, the world isn't really well lost for love, you know. It's silly to go crying for the moon when a lesser light will suit very well.''

Victoria said nothing while she tried to readjust her ideas. She had taken for granted that Kate's marriage had been a love-match, and she was still young enough to feel cheated out of a romantic ending.

"This other man—why didn't you marry him?" she asked. "Had he a wife already?''

"No, but he was engaged to somebody else. I've never believed much happiness would come from breaking up a love affair.''

"So you married your Jim to make things final. No going back.''

"There's never any going back whatever you may decide.''

"Isn't there? No second chances? No opportunities to begin again?''

"Well that might depend on circumstances, I suppose. I doubt, in my own case, whether my decision made much difference except to me, as the other engagement came to nothing.''

"What a waste of noble intentions! If only you'd waited, Kate!" Victoria sounded so outraged that Kate had to laugh.

"Nothing of the kind," she retorted with some brisk-ness. "I was never very good at waiting, and Jim made me an excellent husband. I've never had regrets, so don't go investing me with a tragic past to lend color to those imageries of yours. Stick to your creations for Mr. Brown which will never give you cause for disillusionment, since it seems unlikely that you will meet him in the flesh."

"But I will one day," Victoria said softly, diverted as Kate had intended back to her own affairs. "In 15 months the Trust will be wound up, and I'll be responsible to no one for my bed and board. He can hardly refuse a meeting then to round things off—besides, however old or busy he may be, he must surely have some spark of natural curiosity as to how his human experiment has turned out."

"Well, time will show," said Kate, refusing as usual to commit herself, "but don't build too much on conventional happy endings. I fancy your Mr. Brown is not overmuch concerned with the human angle, or he would have made himself known before now."

"Yes, I suppose you're right, but I shall track him down somehow. Apart from anything else, I couldn't bear to spend the rest of my life with my own curiosity unsatisfied," Victoria said, and although she would have liked to return to the more present subject of Kate's affairs, she had too much sensibility to probe.

They did not see much of Robert for some time, for the courts kept him busy. An ever-growing practice made demands that Kate said put an unnecessary strain on a man who could well afford to turn down cases.

"Well, I suppose he needs the money. It must take quite a packet to pay for all those expensive aids to gracious living," Victoria said, and Kate gave her a sidelong look.

"You sound censorious," she said mildly. "There's nothing pretentious about Robert's mode of living. He just has a taste for quality, and since he can afford the best he naturally sees that he gets it."

Victoria glanced across at her in surprise, imagining a touch of resentment in her reply.

"I didn't mean to be. I was only countering your suggestion that he could afford to turn down cases," she said.

"Well, so he can. He inherited quite a sizable fortune from his father who made money in oil and could pick and choose without running himself ragged."

Victoria's eyes widened. It was true that such indications of Robert's well-lined pockets were sober and unobtrusive, but she had rubbed shoulders too long with Madame's richer pupils not to appreciate the cost of such niceties.

"Perhaps he can't resist living up to his reputation and keeping in the public eye," she suggested without any intention of sounding critical, but Kate frowned.

"I wish you liked Robert better," she said. "His manner can be misleading, but he's a tender-hearted creature at bottom. He's been a very good friend to Timmy and me."

"Yes, I know."

"He should have married, of course, but he took that business of Irene pretty hard. Apart from throwing his affections back in his face, she made a laughing stock of him running off with that frightful rock heart-throb. Robert's a proud man. It's partly the reason he works so unneccessarily hard, I often think. Stops you from brooding at first and then becomes a habit."

"Kate—have you ever thought—" Victoria began impulsively, but checked herself as she caught Kate's cool glance. Friendship had ripened pleasantly between them during the past weeks, but Kate was rarely addicted to confidences.

"I've thought a lot of things too trivial to be of value," she said, neatly evading a direct answer, "but one thing I *can* tell you without betraying any promises, that might make you feel more kindly toward Robert. You primarily have him to thank for being here."

"What on earth can you mean, Kate? We met by chance in Gruse, and it was chance again that Robert turned out to be a connecting link."

"Not entirely. He knew I might run across you in such a small place and suggested you might be suitable for Timmy. I was to form my own judgment and act accordingly."

"But how on earth could he know I was there?"

"He presumably made inquiries. Chapple & Ponsonby have put work in his way from time to time. He's on good terms with the old gentleman. Don't you remember I told you at the time I had a cousin who might put in a good word should your Mr. Brown prove difficult?"

"Yes, I do, but I never dreamed—and I thought the cousin was a woman, anyway. How very odd that he should have remembered all this time."

"Not really. I told you Robert has an unsuspected soft center. He was upset by the case at the time. No one could foresee that your father would take the way out that he did, but it left a nasty taste, all mixed up with the mess of Robert's own affairs."

Victoria was silent. It was surprising to learn Robert must have kept track of her from time to time. For the first time, she began to think of him as a human being who could be subject to hurt like any other.

"Well," said Kate who had been watching her swift changes of expression with interest, "have I succeeded in getting you to have second thoughts?"

"Second thoughts?"

"More adult ones, shall we say, than those you've cherished since the age of 14."

"Yes, it *was* childish. I suppose, comforting myself with imaginary scenes of dire retribution was as silly as inventing impossible images for Mr. Brown," Victoria said, trying to laugh at her fancies, and Kate smiled.

"Mr. Brown was a natural in view of the circumstances, but I wonder why Robert stuck in your mind with equal vividness," she observed a little dryly. Victoria frowned.

"I suppose because he made a deep impression on me at a time when everything familiar seemed suddenly to be swept away," she said slowly. "There has to be a villain in all self-respecting fairy tales, as you should know. Mr. Robert Farmer filled the part to a T."

"While Mr. Fairy-godfather Brown reigned smug and aloof on his pedestal."

"Yes, perhaps he is a bit smug," agreed Victoria seriously, "but I expect you get that way if you dwell upon Olympus."

"Very likely. Well, at least you can absolve Robert of that. He may be provocative and often infuriating, but he's never smug," Kate said.

Victoria asked a little tentatively, "Why are you trying so hard to convince me, Kate? It can't really matter to Robert whether I like him or not."

"I daresay it doesn't, but it matters to me. I like harmony in the home and since Farthings belongs to Robert he's entitled to treat it as such."

"Yes, of course, I keep forgetting. Farthings doesn't seem at all the sort of place an oil magnate would have chosen to settle down in."

"Neither did he. Old man Farmer had a taste for roving, I understand, and seldom saw his son. Farthings belonged to an aunt of Robert's who used to have him for the school holidays. She was a maiden lady with no family ties and left it to him when she died, together with all the treasures she had collected over the years."

"And he's never lived here?"

"Only as a boy for holidays. Of course he intended settling here when he married and using the town apartment as a convenience for work, but Irene had other ideas. She insisted on a house in London, and wanted Robert to sell Farthings and buy a place in some fashionable resort where she could entertain her weekend guests with a nice display of chic. Such a silly thing to quarrel about."

"And Robert wouldn't?"

"No. He didn't insist that they live here if Irene didn't care for it, but he wouldn't agree to selling. There was no reason why Irene should have made an issue of it except that she was vain, spoiled and had always had her own way. But she did, and when threats and recriminations failed to move him she up and ran off with this frightful young man and lived to regret it, I'm glad to say."

"So you ill-wished her," Victoria said, and Kate looked quite startled.

"Yes, perhaps I did," she admitted ruefully. "Does that exonerate your own revengeful thoughts?"

"No, but it makes me feel less foolish for having had them. She can't have cared for him very much, can she, to demand her pound of flesh just to gratify a whim?"

"I don't think Irene would ever care for anyone as much as herself. She was quite proud of having hooked Robert who was much sought after and never doubted she could twist him around her little finger."

"But the perspicacious Mr. Farmer so adept at putting his finger on any flaw in evidence—shouldn't he have seen through her?"

"Still not allowing poor Robert any human weaknesses? When a man as heartwhole as Robert becomes emotionally involved for the first time he's no wiser or less vulnerable than the rest of us, and Irene was very lovely."

"So he let you have Farthings instead," Victoria said, her first suspicions returning. "Perhaps it's the case of an ill wind."

"Perhaps it is, but that's another story," Kate replied rather sharply and stood to lean out of a window to call to her son playing with his blocks on the lawn. It was a definite intimation that confidences were at an end. Victoria was too wise to persist, but she wondered again if Kate, so calm and well adjusted, was biding her time until Robert should come to share her view that compromise was no bad substitute for the unattainable. But what of Robert, so deeply in love once, it seemed, that he could scarcely have been aware of another woman's feelings for him? Could he ever recapture what he had felt for Irene, or would he just be content with second-best and a wife who would not expect too much of him?

When Robert next came down he was tired and over-worked following a gruelling session in the courts. He spent most of his time stretched out on one of Kate's sun-cots in a sunny corner of the patio. Perhaps, Victoria thought, she was looking at him with new eyes as a result of Kate's disclosures. She found herself experiencing a most unfamiliar desire to afford him small attentions, even to dispersing the headache, that she was sure caused that little frown of discomfort, by smoothing it away as she did for Timmy after a bout of crying. She restrained herself, however, from such an uncharacteristic offer that would surely be received with derisive comment, but Kate watched her with amusement, gratified to note that the silly child had evidently profited by her casual hints. She hoped Robert would not nip a better relationship in the bud by administering one of his put-downs, but although he caught her eye with a quizzical glance from time to time, he forbore to tease.

When she left them, however, to plan the evening meal with Elspeth, he opened his eyes and inquired lazily, "What's come over you, Victoria Mary Hayes? Do I imagine a brief cessation of hostilities, or have you just run out of ammunition?"

"You won't provoke me, Robert, not today when the sun shines, and you're enjoying a hard-earned rest," she countered, smiling at him while she mentally decided that she liked his cold, clever features in repose.

"Won't I? How disappointing. You rise so beautifully when you think I'm laughing at you."

"But half the time you are, aren't you."

"Only with amused affection."

"Affection?"

"Don't sound so incredulous—I'm not entirely devoid of the more tender emotions. He spoke with a tinge of the old mockery, but she did not counter with her usual scorn.

"Perhaps I haven't had a chance to know you as you really are. It's awfully easy to take people at face value, isn't it?" she said with an unfamiliar touch of shyness and his face immediately resumed its mask of hardness.

"Am I to gather Kate has been talking?" he asked with a touch of distaste.

"Well, I think she thought I had the wrong idea of you. She only told me very briefly about that old affair—just to prove how wrong one's judgment could be. Kate's very fond of you, you know."

"Yes, Miss Prim, I do know and don't let undigested notions run away with you. You're a little young to be

sitting in judgment on your elders and betters, anyway,"
he retorted with a decided bite to his voice, but although
she colored a little, she smiled back at him with a serene
refusal to be snubbed.

"I won't be put in my place by that old cliché. Perhaps
you haven't realized I'll be 20 next week. In another year
even Mr. Brown will have to acknowledge my adult
status," she said and he smiled back at her a shade wryly.

"*Touché*," he murmured, raising a hand to sketch a
vague salute. "What a pity we invariably have to come
back to the egregious Mr. Brown as arbiter."

"Well, he is for the time being, but why should you
care?"

"I can't say I do very much, but I find his recurrence as
a theme somewhat tedious."

"Well, he's a theme I've grown so accustomed to that I
shall quite miss him when he disappears from the background," Victoria said, sounding both regretful and a
little surprised. Robert gave her a sharp glance.

"I believe you will. Well, I suppose there's something to
be said for a nameless deity who supplies one with security without any obligations," he observed with some dryness, and she looked slightly shocked.

"Oh, but I have obligations and, even if I didn't get a
sharp reminder when I'm remiss in reporting progress, I
would feel a personal responsiblity toward him," she said
quickly. "I hope, when the time comes, he'll come out of
hiding and let me thank him properly."

"Aha!" he exclaimed triumphantly. "I believe, despite
the lack of evidence, that you've been fostering romantic
dreams all along. Mr. Brown is the Frog Prince, or Beauty's Beast who will claim his reward in the usual way and
suffer disenchantment for his pains."

"What *are* you talking about? I'll admit at first I had

rosy hopes of getting adopted and becoming an old man's darling, but I never went further than that!''

"Didn't you, now? Well, there's yet time for a reshuffle. Since, as you have pointed out, you've already reached the years of discretion, adoption must have gone by the board, but there's still the other alternative. What would you say if you found that marriage had been the end product in mind all along?''

"It would depend entirely on whether I found him acceptable or not,'' Victoria answered with engaging primness, and he laughed.

"But you might consider it—as a token repayment of benefits received, shall we say?''

"Oh, you're being absurd! Whoever he may be, he'd scarcely cherish dreams of marrying a complete stranger seen only once as an unprepossessing schoolgirl.''

"Well, by the laws of average you will marry some worthy young man and solve both your own and your unknown benefactor's problems,'' Robert said, raising his long body from its recumbent position with an impatient jerk and getting to his feet.

"How cross you sound, suddenly,'' she said, her eyes on his elongated shadow stretching across the paving stones as he stood looking down at her. "You don't know me at all well, really, do you? No better than Mr. Brown does.''

"Be damned to Mr. Brown! Can't we have any discussion without coming back to him?'' Robert snapped, and reaching down a hand, pulled her smartly to her feet. It was the first time he had ever touched her and perhaps because their recent exchanges had been devoid of that more usual undercurrent of hostility, she became aware of him in an entirely different dimension.

"No, you don't,'' Robert said, anticipating flight, and his fingers tightened on her shoulders. But she had made no attempt to break away and stood there passively with her face uplifted. "After all, you're full of surprises, as befits a true daughter of Eve," he murmured with unexpected tenderness and bent his dark head to kiss her with gentle insistence.

The sun was already gone from the patio leaving behind a sudden coolness to remind them that summer had not yet come. Kate's voice from the doorway had a matching crispness.

"You'd better come in now, both of you, it's getting chilly," she said, and Victoria slipped a little awkwardly from Robert's grasp and began picking up the scattered cushions.

"Dear Kate, do I detect a note of disapproval in your untimely summons?" Robert asked on a teasing note that held no embarrassment.

"Not at all. Perhaps I should have coughed discreetly in the best tradition," she replied lightly, but she did not smile. Victoria, standing irresolutely with the pile of gaily colored cushions clasped to her chest, remembered too late her own suspicions regarding Kate's feelings.

"Can I do anything to help Elspeth?" she asked hurriedly.

"No. She won't thank you for getting under her feet when she's preparing a meal, but you might go up to Timmy and treat him to an extra bedtime story. He's been feeling a bit neglected," Kate said. "Robert, you're looking very tired. Come in and have a whisky and soda to warm you up before supper. I've lighted a fire in the parlor."

Victoria went upstairs. Robert followed his cousin into the small, charming paneled room that was used by Kate when she was alone in preference to the larger drawing room. It still retained the old-fashioned name it had been known by in Miss Eva Farmer's day. He poured himself a drink while Kate, her back turned to him, busied herself unnecessarily with the fire.

"Was that quite fair?" she asked suddenly.

"Kissing your paid employee, you mean?" he said, employing a cool inflection that she knew only too well.

"Don't be deliberately obtuse," she answered impatiently. "I wasn't suggesting that you were amusing yourself with the housemaid, but I'm responsible for Victoria, and she's not been around much."

"You're not, you know. Mr. Brown is responsible for her," Robert retorted provocatively.

"Oh, Mr. Brown! And how do you suppose he will react if he suspects my notable cousin has been making idle passes under my own roof?"

"Your notable cousin doesn't make idle passes, my love, so stop being angry and doing your best to wreck that nicely burning fire," he said. She put down the poker at once and rose from her knees looking a little sheepish.

"Sorry, Rob," she said, moving over to the tray of drinks to pour herself a sherry, "I've no business to take you to task in what is virtually your own house, I suppose; but that little episode looked suspiciously like a pass to me, idle or otherwise."

He sipped his drink in silence for a moment regarding her affectionately across the width of the hearth. Then he said with a complete change of tone, "Dear Kate, your concern for your ewe-lamb is very right and proper, but you should know me better after all this time than to suppose I would take unfair advantage. Today I progressed a little way because the sun was shining, and your delightful young *protégée* forgot to keep stoking the ancient fires. By tomorrow she'll have had time to reach your own conclusions, and hostility will take over. By the way, did you know your young *protégée* will be 20 next week?"

"Yes, of course I knew. Could you get down for the night, Rob? I've asked John Squires for dinner to try to make the occasion a little festive, but it won't be very exciting for Victoria."

"Sorry, it's impossible mid-week. I'll send her a birth-day card instead."

"That won't exactly send her into transport. You might at least manage a handsome floral tribute. Do you know that child's never had so much as a bunch of violets as a gesture from Mr. Brown? A check comes from the lawyer on the appropiate occasions, but never anything personal. You might trot around to your pet florist who kept Irene so well supplied and give them a nice expensive order."

"Really, Kate! You do want the best of both worlds, don't you?" Robert laughed. "If I followed up today's little pleasantry by sending flowers, it could put all sorts of ideas into her foolish head, as you should be the first to point out."

"I don't see why—" Kate began stubbornly, then caught his eye and joined reluctantly in his laughter. "Yes, I see what you mean," she said. "Oh, well, perhaps when you next come down we'll have a second party and crack a bottle of champagne. Only—"

"Only what?"

"Nothing that you mightn't consider an impertinence. Do you ever see Irene now that she's back in circulation again?"

"That was a very transparent line of thought. Yes, we meet occasionally at parties when I can get to them; yes, she is as lovely and sought after as ever; finally and in the hope of convincing you of complete recovery, I have no regrets except for the wasted years. Does that answer you?''

"Yes, dear Robert, and I won't worry again. I, too, have regretted the wasted years and grieved for you,'' she said just as Victoria ran down the little winding stairs in a corner of the room to tell them that supper was ready. Kate saw her hesitate on the bottom step before she spoke and mistook the quick glance she gave them both for one of belated embarrassment.

"Come and have a quick sherry before we go in,'' she said, holding out a welcoming hand. "Robert and I have been reminiscing shamelessly—a sure sign of encroaching age, so one's told. Robert, fill a glass for the girl and help yourself at the same time. Since it's Sunday supper and traditionally cold, we won't incur Elspeth's wrath by keeping it waiting. Come to the fire and warm up, Victoria—these late spring evenings can catch one out once the sun is down.''

CHAPTER FOUR

Victoria had ample time in the watches of the night to review not only her own disturbed emotions but Kate's too. As Robert had predicted, by the morning hostility had returned. He was stopping over Monday as a brief concession to overstrain, and her elaborate maneuvers to keep out of his way apparently passed unnoticed. He made no attempt to seek her out.

John Squires looked in on them before lunch to run a professional eye over Timmy, evidently surprised and not too pleased to find the weekend guest was still with them. Victoria liked the quiet, uncommunicative doctor who was a widower with a growing practice in the district. Listening to the two men's casual exchanges over their beer, she realized that neither much cared for the other. She had long suspected that John Squires had more than a friendly interest in Kate and no doubt resented Robert's easy claim to her hospitality. Familiar now with the betraying nuance that could creep into a desultory remark almost unnoticed, she thought that Robert, too, was not immune from the natural antagonism of the possessive male.

"Still waiting and hoping, seeking no reward but the comfort of your smile and, presumably, the periodical settling of his bill?" Robert said when the doctor had driven away.

"Don't be so absurd, Rob. John takes a great interest in Timmy and has always thought that something could be done about that leg when he's older," Kate said a little brusquely. She flushed very slightly and Victoria, because she considered that if he was aware of Kate's feelings for himself, Robert had no right to make fun of her in this fashion, remarked with some tartness,

"It's easy to jeer at qualities one doesn't possess oneself."

She should have kept her mouth shut, of course, for Robert turned around to look at her absently as if he had forgotten her presence and observed with amusement, "Dear me! Is it possible that you, too, have fallen a victim to the good doctor's hidden virtues? Kate, you must look to your laurels in the face of unexpected competition."

"Be quiet, Robert! Your humor is ill-placed since it's obvious neither of us has anything but honest liking for a very good friend. I don't know what's come over you since yesterday," Kate said with most unusual asperity.

"I must have got out on the wrong side of my bed, as they say in the nursery," he replied meekly. "And here's another who made the same error, didn't you, Victoria Mary?"

"I'll go and get Timmy cleaned up for lunch, Kate," Victoria said, pointedly ignoring him, and went out of the room.

"You see!" Kate said as the door closed with the faint suggestion of a slam.

"What am I supposed to see? A little girl who takes teasing as a personal affront when she should know better?"

"I'm not at all sure that wasn't your intention. You may be regretting your lapse of yesterday, Robert, but you don't need to rub it in by being deliberately hurtful. Victoria may be inexperienced, but she has enough *savoir faire* to take such things at their proper value."

"What things?"

"Oh, don't be so tiresome. I was only trying to say that she's unlikely to have taken your advances seriously."

"Advances—what a delightfully old-fashioned expression. But only yesterday, sweet Kate, you were trying to convince me of the opposite. Putting ideas into her head, you said."

"On the contrary, it was you who said that when I suggested you might send her some flowers for her birthday."

"So I did. Anyway, don't you think we're making too much of a very commonplace incident?"

"Not so commonplace in Victoria's reckoning, I don't mind betting. Now, will you do some chores in the village for me after lunch? Timmy is dying for a drive in your new and opulent car. You can take Victoria, too, and establish a truce."

But the outing was not a success. Before starting off Victoria, who had not wanted to go, viewed the Bentley's elegant lines without enthusiasm. When asked by Robert for her opinion, she observed rashly, "Sleek and superior—like you," that she had to admit later was not a promising overture to friendly relations. Robert insisted on Victoria taking the wheel, thinking, no doubt, she would enjoy handling a quality car after Kate's ancient and sober, old Morris. She had passed her test some time ago and was quite confident when driving the familiar Morris. Robert's Bentley was a different matter altogether and he made her nervous.

"For goodness' sake, don't stamp on the accelerator like that! This car's a high-powered, lethal weapon and will rocket us straight into kingdom come if you don't watch out," he exclaimed on one occasion.

"You do it on purpose for the fun of it—just the same

way you enjoyed tearing strips off me that day in court,"
she said, and he was surprised to see tears in her eyes.

"Oh, come now! I don't enjoy the mishandling of a fine
piece of machinery. It sets my teeth on edge," he protested, ignoring her accusation.

"Then why insist that I drive the beastly thing when
you know very well I'm inexperienced?"

"I merely thought it would give you pleasure. Tell me,
Victoria, is all the sudden antagonism a result of yesterday's charming little interlude?"

She sat very still beside him, blinking back the tears
that already shamed her. She wanted to dismiss that episode as casually as he seemed to regard it and hurt him if
she could for supposing that it might have meant anything more to her. He unexpectedly cupped her averted
chin in gentle fingers, turning her around to face him, and
she remembered only the pleasure of his touch and Kate's
overheard words as she came down the stairs.

"Dear Victoria Mary, don't turn me into an ogre just to
satisfy your belief that there must be a villain in every self-
respecting fairy story," he said softly, and she smiled a
little tremulously.

"I suppose Kate told you that."

"Oh yes, among other things. I suppose I should feel
flattered that I unknowingly shared the honors with Mr.
Brown in your flights of fancy, even if I *was* cast for the
part of the Demon King."

He was smiling at her with that cajoling tenderness that
only yesterday had surprised her into compliance. She
experienced a brief return of that curious desire to forget
her preconceived notions and simply please him. She
made a small gesture of hesitancy toward him, but they
had both forgotten Timmy.

"Why've you stopped? What you want to quarrel for?

Where's the Demon King? Want to *see* him!" he wailed. When Victoria, remorseful at her own neglect, reached back to draw him to her, he struck at her outstretched hands, called her a rude name and started to bawl.

"That's enough, young man," Robert said, his laughter gone and lifted the child over the back of the seat and deposited him in the road with one quick movement. "Now, Timmy—little boys who behave badly aren't wanted on car drives. Are you going to say sorry to Toria for hitting her, or do we leave you behind in the road?"

The boy stood, scarlet and hiccoughing on the grass staring up at his godfather, dimly aware that something besides his own behavior had sparked off this unfamiliar anger, but unwilling to admit defeat.

"You—you wouldn't *really* l-leave me here, Uncle Rob," he spluttered, torn between doubt and defiance.

"Oh yes, I would. It's time you learned that boys don't hit girls, whatever the provocation."

"Toria wouldn't let you—besides, I'm lame. Lame boys have special attention."

"Toria will do as I tell her if she knows what's good for her, and you're no more entitled to special attention than other children. You were born lame, so you've known nothing different."

There was silence, punctuated only by Timmy's hiccoughing sobs and the cackling of hens from a nearby farmyard. Victoria, who had slid over into the passenger seat, made no further move to intervene, but watched the small contest of wills with interest. It was rare in her experience for Robert to use his authority with Kate's son, but it was evidently not the first time.

The little comedy by the roadside came to an abrupt end when Robert reached out a hand to the dashboard and switched on the ignition. To Timmy, the sound of the gently idling engine was the final proof that desertion was imminent, and without more ado he flung himself upon Victoria in a fierce abandonment of remorse.

"Good!" said Robert cheerfully, taking his seat behind the wheel. "Now that we're all friends again you shall sit between us in the front, Timmy, and if you're very quiet and good I'll let you steer between my hands."

Timmy, thus reinstated to a position of importance, held their attention all the way home, but once there he did not take kindly to being banished to the kitchen to take tea with Elspeth. Kate, obliged to deal both with tears and Elspeth's ruffled feelings, was in no mood to bear tolerantly with her cousin's amused explanation of the original cause of the trouble.

"Yes, that's all very well," she said, for once finding no favor with Robert's handling of her son, "but Timmy isn't as strong as other children, and when he gets overexcited, trouble can start. You at least should know that by now, Victoria—or were you too much engrossed with your own affairs to give a thought to your charge?"

The sudden attack was so uncharacteristic that Victoria was too taken aback to make any coherent reply, and it was Robert who answered for her.

"Your young employee had been suffering discomfort on her own account and might therefore be excused," he said on a faint note of irony. Kate looked up quickly.

"And what might that mean?" she asked sharply, but he gave her one of his slow, tantalizing grins.

"Not what you're obviously thinking, careful Kate. I had mistakenly urged the poor girl to try the Bentley thinking only to give pleasure, and she didn't take kindly to my comments on her driving."

There was a moment of flat silence during which Victoria could find no gratitude for Robert's intervention. Kate then gave a small apologetic laugh and hastily pressed fresh cups of tea upon them.

"I'm sorry, Victoria, I've been making mountains out of molehills, I'm afraid. Forgive me and have some more cake."

"Yes, you have, haven't you?" Robert said before Victoria could reply. "I wonder what can have provoked such an unusual display of feminine pique."

But Victoria had a strong suspicion, and since she judged by Robert's false air of innocence that he was equally aware of the answer, hostility rose in her again.

"Since you're a man you'd only recognize one reason for feminine pique, whatever that may mean. Women, let me tell you, allow small trivialities to upset a mood that have nothing whatever to do with the sexes," she said, putting down her empty cup and getting to her feet. "If you'll excuse me, Kate, I'll go up and read to Timmy until it's time to put him to bed."

"Well, there's gratitude for you!" Robert exclaimed as the door closed behind her. "I strive to excuse your employee's imagined shortcomings by stating the facts and get put in my place for my pains."

"Serves you right, too! You know very well, Rob, that your intentions were anything but altruistic. You wanted to embarrass the child, didn't you?" Kate replied, and somewhat absently poured herself a third cup of tea.

"It's not easy to embarrass Miss Victoria Mary Hayes when her hackles are up, but I confess I find her unpredictable reactions endearing," he said and received a straight old-fashioned look from his cousin.

"If I didn't know you better I'd have serious misgivings on the wisdom of encouraging these odd weekends," she said bluntly. "It would be a pity if you succeeded in turning the girl's head just because you find her unpredictable reactions endearing.''

"Would you say there was any chance of her head being turned when the remembered image of the first Mr. Robert Farmer is forever looking over my shoulder?'' he asked her with mock despair, and she shook her head at him.

"Don't play games just for masculine satisfaction in breaking down resistance. It wouldn't be fair,'' she answered soberly. The humor went from his face leaving it grave and suddenly tired.

"No, it wouldn't be fair,'' he said gently. "Don't anticipate contingencies that may never arise, sweet Kate; just remember that I'm grateful for the past years; your unfailing support and hospitality and wouldn't willingly give you cause for concern, imagined or otherwise.''

"Dear Rob . . . '' she said with a little smile of acceptance, "has the thaw set in at last?''

"The thaw?''

"That protective wall of ice you fashioned for yourself to shut Irene out. It's been so long.''

"Yes, I suppose it has. Well, don't be too hasty with your metaphors, my dear. If ice melts too quickly it leaves nothing behind but a puddle of dirty water—no solid foundation on which to build again—so leave me a few stubborn icicles to bolster up my morale,'' he said with a return to his old manner. She knew that the moment for confidences had passed.

"Well,'' she said, "I'd better go up to the nursery and do my share of story-telling. Will you come up later to say good night? Timmy's very jealous of his Uncle Rob's attentions.''

"Yes, I'll be up. I don't think you'll find my halo's

slipped, you know. Timmy was quite aware that he was being not only rude but wrong in hitting out at Victoria."

"Yes, and of course you were quite right to check him. I don't know why I made such a thing of it."

"Don't you? Well, never mind. It's been quite an unsettling weekend altogether, so perhaps we've all been acting a little out of character."

But although with Robert's departure the next morning the household appeared to settle back into its normal, quiet routine, Victoria was conscious of change. Perhaps she imagined a slight withdrawal in Kate and only fancied a certain coolness in Elspeth. She found herself hoping that pressure of work would keep Robert away from Farthings for a time. Not the least of her doubts was the curious effect on her own emotions. She did not flatter herself that his behavior on Sunday afternoon meant any more than an impulse of the moment born of idleness and a masculine desire to experiment, but she wished now that she had slapped his face in the traditional manner instead of responding with such undisguised pleasure.

With the dawn of her birthday, however, such fancies were dispelled by the goodwill and small attentions surrounding her. Kate, very conscious that their quiet country life offered little in the way of excitement to a young and attractive girl, had tried to make the day a festive one with small surprises and presents hidden in unlikely places, just as she planned for Timmy on like occasions. Elspeth contributed with a splendid cake ablaze with 20 candles.

The morning's mail had brought the usual small check from the lawyers, together with the customary handkerchiefs from Scottie and Robert's promised birthday card. Kate privately thought Robert might have found time to choose a personal gift, knowing that Victoria had no relations to remember her. But if Victoria was disappointed there had been no time to dwell on it, for all her pleasure had culminated in the biggest surprise of the morning. Five dozen red roses had arrived by special delivery packed with all the extravagant trimmings of ribbons and bows and a card attached by a silver cord which read simply: *With the compliments of Mr. Brown.*

Amazement turning to pure bliss had illuminated the girl's thin face with such startling happiness that Kate had known a prick of irritation. It was absurd in this day and age that flowers from a perfect stranger should evoke such astonished delight.

"Well, it's a handsome gesture, even though some might call five dozen of the best a trifle excessive," she had said with some dryness. Victoria had only smiled and alternately stroked a petal and the plain white card with equal tenderness.

"It wouldn't have hurt him to add a message—many happy returns or even just best wishes," Kate went on, wondering why she should feel so put out. Victoria smiled again, the affectionate smile an adult might bestow on a complaining child.

"He never adds anything but his name," she said serenely, "I suppose the lawyers see to it for him, but he's never sent me flowers before, so perhaps, this time, he chose them himself."

"Hardly, when it's simply a matter of picking up the telephone, stating your requirements and leaving the rest to the florist. Is it his writing on the card?"

"I don't know. He never writes letters. The only other time he sent me a present Mr. Chapple or Mr. Ponsonby signed the card."

"Then the florist's assistant probably did the same. It's

not a particularly distinctive hand. Never mind," she added hastily with a belated resolution not to spoil the day, "nothing can take away the compliment of five dozen, expensive, hothouse, red roses to grace our rooms, so I, too, must be grateful to your Mr. Brown."

But she need not have troubled herself with regrets for her lack of enthusiasm. Victoria, her pleasure in the day enriched by such an unexpected tribute to her consequence, shared none of Kate's misgivings. The occasion was made perfect by the lavish abundance that greeted her eyes in every room, coloring her thoughts and filling the day with promise. Even Timmy, inevitably playing up at bedtime from overexcitement, failed to spoil the evening for her. She was glad, though, for Kate's sake when John Squires, arriving with a large box of chocolates to mark the occasion, went up to the nursery and restored peace with little apparent effort.

"You have as much influence over him as Robert," Kate told him with some surprise when later they were drinking their sherry while awaiting Elspeth's summons to dinner. He gave her a rather curious look.

"Well, of course your cousin has the advantage of occupying a pedestal, but even a dull country doctor can cultivate a way with children," he replied with a twinkle, and Kate smiled demurely.

"You shouldn't begrudge Robert his place in the sun—he's known Timmy ever since he was born," she said.

"Consequently the natural father-substitute in your eyes?"

"Not necessarily, but it's become rather a habit to depend on Rob. He's been a good friend to us both, as I think you know, and helped me through a bad time after the accident. I wasn't very good company then."

"Very likely, but you had no reason to blame yourself for the boy's infirmity."

"If I hadn't insisted on going in the car with Jim that day, Timmy wouldn't have been born as he was."

"That's only surmise. Shock can certainly cause damage to the unborn child, but no doctor would care to commit himself on the evidence in your case, so bury that bogey where it belongs, in the unalterable past."

Victoria had moved away, feeling she was eavesdropping as the conversation became unexpectedly personal. She stood now in the shadows at the far end of the room, rearranging one of the many bowls of roses.

If the doctor had momentarily forgotten Victoria's presence, Kate had been perfectly aware of her tactful withdrawal and the mischief was back in her voice as she said, "You're quite oblivious of your social obligations when you get on your hobby horse, John. Here's our birthday girl politely trying to efface herself when you should be paying her compliments instead of forgetting it's her party."

"Victoria is much too sensible to take offense, since I'm neither particularly young nor one of her attendant swains," he answered, quite unabashed. "But evidently somebody is sufficiently *épris* to spend a small fortune on flowers. I've never seen such an extravagant display of horticulture in all my life. Who is he, Victoria?"

"Only Mr. Brown, but as he's never done such a thing before, it's rather special," Victoria replied, returning to join them again.

"What! The eccentric old gentleman who pays the bills but remains unseen? How very disappointing."

"Oh no," Victoria said, her eyes bright with her inward thoughts, "it's crowned the whole day. Nothing that Mr.

Brown has ever done for me has given me quite the same pleasure."

Kate said rather quickly, "I'm afraid Victoria, for all the advantages of being finished abroad, still tends to cling to her schoolgirl daydreams."

"There's nothing wrong with a bit of daydreaming—we all indulge at times—and even to my untutored eye, being finished abroad has paid off handsomely. It's a pity there's only myself here to appreciate the results," John replied with quiet sincerity. Indeed, he thought she looked charming and refreshingly free of the modern tendency to picturesque squalor: sitting there in her white, full-skirted dress, the soft hair with its demure center parting falling in a shining curve about her neck and shoulders. She was the sort of daughter he would have liked himself, had he not been fated to be childless. He found himself wondering what sort of a chap this unknown benefactor might be to content himself with periodic reports of progress and nothing more. By the same token his thoughts wandered to the possible effect a young and unspoiled girl might have on a man of Robert Farmer's caliber. He was aware that Kate's too well-endowed cousin was not without interest in her *protégée*. He wondered, with mixed feelings, how long it would be before Kate herself became conscious that she might have dallied too long in making up her mind.

It was a relief to Victoria that Elspeth chose that moment to announce that dinner was ready, but her pleasure in Kate's well-intentioned plans to mark the day as something special was beginning to dwindle. It had been a mistake, she thought, to invite the doctor as the sole guest to lend the occasion a party air. She would have been better pleased to sit down with Kate as usual than make up an ill-assorted trio. Although John, doubtless aware that he had started the evening off on the wrong foot, made gallant efforts to amend his shortcomings, she was faintly embarrassed by his avuncular attempts at chivalry. They drank champagne with forced gaiety, and only Elspeth, summoned to join in a toast to Victoria, treated the occasion as a ceremony. But Elspeth, having excelled herself in the matter of choice dishes, was entitled to insist on ceremony despite the absence of guests. Victoria knew it would be useless to excuse herself tonight with offers of help with the washing up.

After dinner they watched television, that last standby for filling an empty evening. John did not stay late, saying he had a call to make on the way home, and Kate made no effort to dissuade him.

"I'm afraid it's all been a flop," she said to Victoria as she emptied ashtrays and collected glasses after he had gone.

"Oh no, Kate!" Victoria protested, distressed beyond measure that such good intentions should only bring disappointment. "It's been a lovely day, and you thought up so many nice surprises."

"Rather as if you were Timmy's age and expected juvenile treats," Kate said, and there was a tinge of bitterness in her voice. "But your reactions were irreproachable, Victoria. Never for a moment did you let me feel I was treating you to nursery entertainments."

Victoria stooped to pick up a cushion and restore it unhurriedly to its proper place, then she said deliberately,

"What's the matter, Kate? It's not like you to have doubts without foundation. Is it John?"

"That was my worst mistake. I should have known better than to ask him because I felt you should have a party.

It made a dull evening for you, and a not very profitable one for him."

"It wasn't dull, just a little out of my element. I think John's in love with you."

"I know. He's a dear; good and dependable, and I owe him so much for his care of Timmy, but sometimes—"

"Sometimes those very virtues work against him."

"Yes, they do, but how can you know?"

"I don't really, but I can imagine. Scottie was like that, you know, and Father never really appreciated her. I like your John. I don't find him dull."

"Neither do I, oddly enough. I'm past the age of demanding pretty speeches and scintillating wit in an admirer, and John would make an excellent husband. His own marriage was a failure, so he wouldn't expect too much."

Victoria considered this aspect carefully before answering. She could not altogether feel that not to expect too much was a virtue. On the other hand, her own upbringing had taught her the virtue of security and having someone in the background to depend upon, even though it was only the intangible presence of Mr. Brown.

"Well," she said then, "I wouldn't know about marriage, of course, but I would think there would be something more than just mutual tolerance."

"Mutual tolerance is very important, let me tell you, but then you're young, and romantic fervor would naturally come first. Don't look as though I'd insulted you, darling—it's only right at your age to think no further than falling in love and living happily ever after."

"I don't think I do—think much about falling in love, I mean. If I marry I would certainly hope to feel more than mutual tolerance for my husband, but I've already learned that other people seldom have the same needs as oneself."

"Well, don't go ascribing false needs to the self-sufficient Mr. Brown on account of one uncharacteristic gesture. I doubt if the flowers mean any more than a belated act of conventional politeness," Kate said, speaking more brusquely than she meant because Victoria's uncertain future had begun to trouble her.

"Of course not. All the same—" The telephone rang, cutting short Victoria's response. Kate went to answer it, relieved that these slightly disturbing exchanges should be broken, but impatient with John Squires, whose voice she expected to hear, for thinking it necessary to apologize for the party's failure. But it was not John, and she handed the receiver over to Victoria, saying a little irritably,

"It's Robert for you. A little late with his birthday greetings, but at least he remembered to send a card." She did not leave the room, but resumed the small chores she had started at the beginning of their conversation. If she listened for any betraying nuances in Victoria's replies, it was quite unconscious. Victoria, remembering the look on Kate's face that Sunday afternoon, felt awkward as she answered Robert's frivolous inquiries as to how the party had gone.

"It was a pity you couldn't be here," she said a little coolly. "It would have been so much nicer for Kate to have even numbers."

"Do I gather that the worthy doctor paid all the attention to you and none to poor Kate?"

"Certainly not. In point of fact—"

"In point of fact, it's you and not Kate who would have benefited by my presence for the feast. Did you play gooseberry?"

"Really, Robert! You have a very good opinion of yourself. As to your last remark, I had no chance to do anything else since it was my party."

"Kate's listening, is she? Well, what shall I say to provoke further tantalizing observations from your end? Didn't the conscientious Squires rise to compliments, or avail himself of any chaste avuncular salute?"

"No, he did not. Why are you being so nosy, not to say infuriating?" Kate gave a faint, unmatronly giggle, and Victoria made a face at her.

"Naturally I'm nosy about what goes on in my absence. I have prior claim in the matter of chaste salutes. Are you being unfaithful to me?"

"Have you been drinking?" she snapped back so sharply that Kate looked around in surprise.

"No, no, I'm most regrettably sober, not having had your excuse for champagne," he answered. "I was only trying to imagine the festive scene. If there was no excitement beyond Elspeth's doubtless lordly offerings, what did you do with the rest of the evening?"

"We watched television," said Victoria primly and felt herself coloring at his burst of ribald laughter.

"Well, well . . . I should certainly have been with you to put a stopper on that. And did you have some nice presents?"

"Very nice, and thank you for your card. Did you choose it yourself?"

"Certainly. I thought hearts and flowers very appropriate."

"Did you? I can't think why." But the mention of flowers distracted Victoria from thinking up retorts to put him in his place, and she added in quite a different tone of voice, "And what do you think, Robert? I had five dozen gorgeous red roses from Mr. Brown by special delivery."

"Did you indeed? So the Sphinx has spoken at last, has he? And that, of course, made your day, and probably encouraged unlikely fancies," he answered. The mockery in his voice came to her very clearly over the line.

"It made my day, certainly, but I'm a little old now to cherish unlikely fancies," she said, and Kate, with a quick glance at her face, at last left the room.

"Of course you are—and done with the foolish pretenses of childhood, but no doubt you have changed them for other and more romantic expectations suitable to your new estate."

"You," she shouted down the telephone trying to disguise a sudden desire to cry, "are as unfeeling and—and beastly as you were that day in court, mocking and—and brow-beating just for kicks. Why don't you pick on someone your own size?"

"Has Kate gone?" he asked with seeming irrelevance. "Yes? I thought she must have, or you wouldn't have dared to talk to me like that." But he must have heard the tremor in her voice, for his own suddenly lost its provocative raillery and became gentle. "Don't think badly of me, dear Victoria Mary. The habit of levity grows upon one as a necessary defense. I have no wish ever to hurt you by banter, so bear with me kindly if you will."

His capitulation was so unexpected, and the warmth in his voice so beguiling that her tears waited no longer.

"Are you crying?" Robert asked after a long silence, and when she answered "No" in a suspiciously shaky voice, he swore softly at the other end of the line.

"Now I've spoiled the day for you. Go on hating me if it eases you, my child. One day I'll hope to show you a different Robert Farmer. Till then, dream your dreams and fight your dragons to your heart's content. Good night, now, and a belated but very sincere many happy returns."

He had hung up before she had time to thank him, or

adjust her mood to his. As she turned to replace the receiver she saw Kate standing in the doorway watching her.

"Well, have you made your peace?" she asked, but her voice held none of its usual indulgence, and Victoria was again reminded that where Robert was concerned Kate had very definite reservations.

"I suppose I should know him better by now than to take his teasing seriously," she answered evasively.

"Yes, you should. And that could apply to other things, too. It would be a pity if you allowed your head to be turned for want of a little worldly experience."

Victoria stared at her, the tears still bright on her lashes, and felt the color begin to creep up under her skin.

"Kate," she said gravely, "I'm not so inexperienced that I'm likely to read more into a casual incident than was intended."

For a moment Kate looked embarrassed as if she had not expected to be met with such a direct response. Then she rubbed her eyelids as though they ached and sat down on the arm of a chair.

"I'm sorry, Victoria, I shouldn't have said that," she replied, sounding suddenly tired. "I'm very fond of Robert, you see. I wouldn't like him to be hurt all over again."

All at once Victoria lost her temper.

"Why can't you come straight out with it and tell me not to trespass?" she demanded. "If it gives you any comfort, Robert is the last man who would turn my head, so don't let a casual kiss disturb any personal claims. If he flatters himself he's made an easy conquest, then you can disabuse him in no uncertain terms. I'm sorry you happened to witness that incident, but don't lose any sleep on his account or mine."

"Oh dear! I have made a mess of things!" Kate said,

looking defeated and surprised. "I'm afraid you've completely misunderstood my well-intentioned efforts, but, like everything else today, I seem to have made errors of judgment."

She sounded so tired and unsure of herself that Victoria immediately felt ashamed of her outburst.

"I'm sorry," she said, "I shouldn't have spoken to you like that, Kate. You've made me feel so much one of the family that it's difficult sometimes to remember my place."

That made Kate laugh, and she stretched out a conciliatory hand.

"What an idea! Your place is here at Farthings and has nothing to do with employment. And if you can bring yourself to accept Robert along with Timmy and me, I for one will be grateful to you." It was graciously spoken, Victoria thought, considering the probable state of Kate's affections. She would have liked to assure her that far from leading Robert Farmer up the garden path, she had every intention of discouraging further opportunities when next he came to Farthings. But too much had already been made of a situation that should never have arisen, and she could only smile apologetically and take herself off to bed.

CHAPTER FIVE

It was June before Robert paid them another visit. Despite her hope on the last occasion that pressure of work would keep him away, Victoria found that she had missed him. Kate's circle of acquaintances was small and consisted largely of young marrieds with growing families that kept them too busy for cultivating more than a casual neighborliness. Sometimes Kate would look at Victoria a little ruefully and apologize for the dullness of country life.

"I've let myself drift since Jim died, I suppose," she said on one occasion. "Timmy occupied so much of my time when he was a baby that it was easy to drop out. Now I'm just selfishly content with my own company, and the peace and pleasant monotony of Farthings. But you should be having fun, admirers like other girls, and justifying the expense of that finishing abroad."

"You needn't feel anxious on my account. It's still a novelty to have anchorage after years of being pushed from one select establishment to another and very restful," Victoria replied, sounding old-fashioned and a little pedantic. Kate frowned.

"Well, I suppose that's natural considering the unusual circumstances, but I can't feel the aim of all this careful preparation was to bury you in the country where chances to benefit by it are few," she said, and Victoria laughed.

"Well, I wasn't being prepared for a London season and the chance of an eligible husband, if that's what

422

you're thinking was the aim—unless of course it was Mr. Brown's original intention, and the idea just died on him."

"That's possible, I suppose, and rich cranks who indulge in the whims of the moment are notoriously unreliable."

"Do you think Robert knows who he is?"

"Rob? I shouldn't think so for a minute. He'd know better than to abuse professional etiquette by pumping old Chapple to satisfy your curiosity."

"Yes, of course. Only sometimes he's so ribald about poor Mr. Brown that I've wondered if he thinks he doesn't exist."

"Well, whatever he may think, five dozen roses would seem to settle that doubt. Have you had any reply to your letter of thanks?"

"Only from the lawyers, but they never do more than acknowledge mine. I had thought that as this was something more personal they might have mentioned it, but I expect the roses, like the checks were just so much routine to them. When is Robert coming down again?"

She asked the question casually enough, but Kate glanced down at her curiously. She was lying on her back in the long grass by Kate's deck chair thoughtfully chewing a piece of clover. There was a withdrawn look about her as if she was indulging in one of her private fantasies.

"I don't know," Kate said, careful to sound equally casual. "Why? Have you missed him?"

"I suppose I have—like the way one misses a tooth when it stops aching."

"Well! Robert *would* be flattered," Kate exclaimed, not knowing whether to be relieved, or mildly indignant. "I must certainly remember to pass that compliment on."

Victoria giggled, unabashed, and rolled over on her stomach.

"Well, you know what I mean. An irritant keeps you on your toes even while you wish it would stop. I have the same effect on Robert, judging by his behavior, so I'm sure he'd understand."

It was not the sort of remark to give Kate any real clue as to the measure of Victoria's feelings, but she had to admit to a superficial element of truth. It was, she thought, unfortunate that owing to Mr. Brown's liking for wrapping his *protégée* in cotton wool, the only man she was likely to get to know well would be her own cousin.

"Oh well," she said a little helplessly, "if you feel Robert is neglecting us, you'd better write and suggest a visit. I had a notion that his reasons for staying away were not entirely unconnected with yourself."

"I could hardly do that since it's your house, and he's your guest," Victoria answered with a polite air of rebuke and impatiently tucked her hair behind her ears to stop it from tickling her.

Kate observed those faun-like features with interest, remembering Robert's teasing, and said lightly, "A guest in his own house, not mine," and Victoria gave her a quick inquiring look.

"Well, it's yours for the present, since you pay rent," she replied and would have liked to follow up the statement with queries about the future of Farthings when Kate's lease was up. It might be premature to press for an answer, neither did she particularly relish a too definite reply.

"Yes, of course. Still there's always been an understanding that he should treat the place as his home, so he'll come without being asked when the mood takes him," Kate said with an air of closing the subject. Victoria thought she sounded a little short.

During the week, however, it was easier to avoid the unwelcome thoughts that these chance remarks could cause to flourish unsatisfied. Kate, on the final chapter of her latest book, was closeted with her typewriter for long hours. Victoria, in sole charge of Timmy, delighted in sharing in his games and inventing fresh amusements of her own.

John Squires, who privately considered Kate's concern for her son excessive, if understandable, approved the ease and youthful casualness with which Victoria handled the boy.

"You'll make a charming mother when your time comes," he told her once when he had met them in the village and paused for a chat. "You'll not grow old in heart like so many women. Do you want children of your own?"

"Oh yes, but first I have to find a husband," Victoria replied demurely, but her eyes were dancing. She had always found it very easy to get along with the doctor when she had him to herself.

"Well, that shouldn't present any difficulty. If I was a younger man—" he said, shamelessly dismissing Kate's image in an effort at gallantry that Victoria found touching.

"You say the nicest things, John, but I know where your true heart lies," she said affectionately.

"Do you indeed? Well, it's your prospects we're discussing, not mine, and I have to admit there's not much choice to be had in these parts. How long will you be staying with Kate?"

As long as she'll keep me—that is, if the lawyers allow it. It's supposed to be a trial run, you know."

"Ah, yes. The omniscient Mr. Brown who pays the piper and calls the tune."

She looked at him, and her eyes were startled.

"Yes, I suppose that's the whole answer," she said, sounding surprised. "Well, in less than a year the piper will have been paid off, and that will leave *me* to call the tune."

"So . . . and what are your plans?"

"I haven't any. It wasn't any use making plans for earning a living. My suggestions were either stamped on, or there was a last-minute postponement. It was really a most unexpected concession to be sent here, but I suppose Kate's credentials were so exemplary that no objections could be raised."

"Or your Mr. Brown is shrewder than you think. Not much chance of unwelcome competition in a village as remote as this."

"Competition? But there's nothing personal in the arrangement. I've never even met him."

"For all that, I understand a pretty observant eye has been kept on your activities. If admirers are to be discouraged, Farthings is a pretty safe place for a young girl's first job."

"Yes, I suppose it is. Only there doesn't seem much point, does there, if, when the Trust is wound up, I'm free to do what I like?"

"No, it doesn't sound very logical, but who's to know what twists and quirks govern the actions of rich eccentrics with a taste for power?"

Victoria giggled, "You make him sound sinister—a kind of Svengali chuckling in the wings and casting spells."

"Farmer hasn't been down for some time. When is he next expected?" John observed casually.

"I don't know. I believe the courts are very busy for this term," Victoria said, and he glanced at her speculatively.

"H'mmm. . . . Kate seemed to have an idea—still, she could well be wrong."

"Kate, like anyone else, can jump to wrong conclusions," Victoria said, choosing her words carefully. "She's been working long hours lately, finishing the latest children's epic. Imagination can carry over into real life without much distinction."

"You're a wise child, aren't you, Victoria? I wonder how you came by your perceptions so young," he said, looking down at her with a measure of wryness.

"Well, when one's self-appointed mentor is never there to give counsel, I suppose one learns to seek it in oneself. Poor Mr. Brown! What a lot he's missed by sitting on a horse so high that they're both lost in the clouds," she said, deliberately making light of the matter. He smiled, his blue, observant eyes momentarily losing their thoughtful gravity.

"Yes, poor Mr. Brown!" he echoed with his mock solicitude. "What a strange, unloved individual he must be, if, that is, he exists at all, outside that fertile imagination of yours."

"Well, *someone* exists. I haven't imagined the monthly checks and the other evidences of a directing power," Victoia retorted. As if she had invoked some mysterious agency to give credence to her statement, a second delivery of roses arrived the very next day with an identitical card attached.

This time the roses were pink, but their number no less extravagant. Kate, observing the girl's heightened color and the tenderness with which she arranged her flowers, felt a shade uneasy. It was not fair of Mr. Brown, whoever he might be, to start playing games of this kind, she thought; and wondered for an unreasoning instant if the thing could be some kind of crazy hoax on the part of staid old Mr. Chapple.

"Well," she said trying to sound flippant, "if this sort of thing goes on, you'll be raising false hopes again of a happy-ever-after ending,"

But Victoria smiled at her with that secret air of withdrawal and replied gently, "Oh no, Kate, I don't live in a fairy tale any longer. You'll have to admit that, however disinterested this sort of gesture may be, it at least has the virtue of adding to one's stature."

"What a queer mixture you are," Kate said, reassured but not wholly satisfied. "Sometimes you talk like a woman twice your age, but I get your point regarding the tonic action of floral tributes, whoever they may come from. You're growing up, darling."

"Oh no, I grew up a long time ago, I think," Victoria said reflectively, and Kate sighed, aware that there might be a rather sad truth in this observation.

"Yes, perhaps you did," she agreed, remembering her own childhood secure in the ties of a family united in love and wellbeing. There had not been the money to afford her the educational advantages bestowed upon Victoria, but neither had she been obliged to create images for herself in return for the chilly dispensations of an unknown benefactor.

Kate was to spend the following weekend in London which made quite a break in the household's routine. Her book was finished, her publishers anxious to discuss a fresh contract, and John Squires had been urging a short change of scene for some time. There was no reason to worry about Timmy with Victoria in charge, and himself within easy call, he had said.

Victoria drove Kate to the station, attending gravely to the last-minute instructions of an anxious mother, solemnly offering assurances in the matter of her own competence until they both began to giggle.

"I'm not naturally a fusspot," Kate excused herself a trifle sheepishly, "but it's such an event for me to leave Timmy just to go on the razzle that I suppose I'm reverting to type. Are you sure you won't be lonely, Victoria? I wish there were a few nice young people you could ask over to Farthings to keep you company."

"For heaven's sake stop feeling guilty because you're treating yourself to a holiday!" Victoria told her. "If you want to know the truth, I'm looking forward to playing mistress of the house in your absence and pretending Farthings belongs to me. I would be most intolerant of nice, young people distracting me from my simple pleasures, so you can be thankful we don't know any."

So Kate went away satisfied and refrained from a warning not to build dreams around Farthings, a much more tangible fantasy than Mr. Brown. Victoria drove home with a mounting sense of delight in the novel experience of being answerable to no one but herself for the next two days.

Elspeth had set out a cold lunch for them in the shade of the patio. Afterward, with Timmy settled on a suncot for his rest instead of being sent upstairs, Victoria wandered through the rooms of the house, enjoying her game of pretense. Here in the drawing room filled with the elegant cabinets of china and bibelots treasured by that unknown maiden lady she would entertain friends after dinner; here in the cool, flagged hall, masculine belongings would clutter up the brassbound chest, together with the discarded toys of children. Here in the white-paneled parlor she would sit and dream when she grew old and remember the follies of her youth with gentle amusement. . . .

"There's no call to run your finger along the mantelshelf for dust, for it was done the morn," Elspeth's voice observed disapprovingly behind her, and she jumped.

"I wasn't thinking of dust," she said, her mind still focussed on that other world. "I like to touch things for remembrance."

"Are you thinking of leaving us, then? That'll no be good news for Mrs. Allen to come back to. I'd thought you were different to those foreign hussies who'd up and go as soon as they'd unpacked their trays for want of a gay time." Elspeth spoke in the uncompromising tones that Victoria first remembered and she said quickly:

"Oh *no*! I was—was only storing up memories for much later on. Sometimes, you see, I pretend to myself just to make things seem real—like inventing personalities for Mr. Brown."

Elspeth gave her a curious look, and her eyes narrowed in dry comprehension.

"Making believe you're mistress here and planning your alterations, I suppose," she said, dismissing Mr. Brown whose existence she privately doubted. Victoria, if a little astonished at being so promptly understood, hastened to disabuse her.

"If that were true and just a game, I wouldn't alter one single thing. My plans were just make-believe too—imaginary domestic pictures, like children's toys scattered about, and pipes and old coats belonging to the master of the house."

"And who, pray, might he be, or hadn't you got so far as that?"

"Of course I hadn't. Only Farthings was real—the rest were ghosts—even me."

"You're forgetting mebbe that the place already has a master. There may come a time when Mr. Rab makes up his mind to settle here."

"With a wife?"

"Aye, with a wife, if it's not already too late for courting." Elspeth, having delivered her ambiguous parting shot, left the room before she could be questioned further. Victoria stood, her fingers still absently caressing the smooth, weathered surface of the mantelshelf, wondering if it had been intended as a warning.

The day was too fine, however, to waste time indoors indulging in unrewarding fancies. The rest of the afternoon passed pleasantly enough. Timmy was on his best behavior, joining happily in whatever game Victoria thought up to amuse him, and was clearly enjoying the novelty of being left in her care while his mother was away.

John Squires looked in for a few moments before dinner to inquire whether Victoria was lonely, and Kate rang up from London to satisfy herself that all was well at home. She had spent more than she should on clothes and had been squeezed into the latest triumph in expensive foundations that, though certainly doing something for one's bulges, would be too agonizing to wear to justify the expense, she said. She sounded young and excited, was just off to the theater following a chance meeting with a man she hadn't seen for years. She hoped Victoria wasn't finding her solitary state too dull. She hung up without prolonging the conversation, and Victoria put down the receiver feeling staid and elderly.

"You'll have your turn when the right man comes along," Elspeth said as she brought in the supper, evidently mistaking Victoria's absent manner of imparting this information for disappointment. "Is it Mr. Rab who's taking her to the play?"

"I don't think so. She spoke of someone she hadn't seen for years."

"Then let's hope it's no' that other one turning up like a bad penny," Elspeth sniffed and went away before curiosity could be satisfied.

Victoria did full justice to the meal, musing happily on the events of Kate's day. She was pleased that Kate was not enjoying herself alone, but secretly glad that Robert was not her escort.

When the supper things had been cleared she watched television for a while. The program did not accord with the peace and quiet of the summer night so she switched it off, together with the lamp, and curled up in a chair to float on a gentle tide of contentment and dreams that mingled so pleasurably with the scents and sounds drifting in from the garden.

She must have slept, for she had no conscious knowledge of hearing any sounds of a late arrival. When she opened her eyes moonlight was flooding across her face through the uncurtained window, and the tall figure of a man stood looking down at her.

"Well," said Robert Farmer softly, "the Sleeping Princess in the flesh, and floodlit, too. I was, alas, a little tardy with the traditional awakening, but I can soon remedy that."

He bent over her, his face etched in unfamiliar lines as the moonlight caught it. She was too bemused to do more than give him that slow, uncertain smile that sometimes seemed an echo of her secret dreams, and he kissed her very gently on the mouth.

"Well . . . " he said as he straightened his long back,
" . . . that was a distinct improvement on your usual welcome. Perhaps I was wise to stay away."

She struggled into a more upright position, uncurling
her long legs from under her to allow her feet a more
decorous place on the floor, and stretched out a hand to
switch on the lamp beside her.

"Why didn't you let us know?" she asked, blinking
sleepily in the light.

"Because, as usual, I didn't know myself until the last
minute. Has Kate gone to bed already?"

She stared up at him, suddenly aware of the awkward
timing of his visit. Kate was so seldom away from home
that it would not have occurred to him to make sure
beforehand.

"She's not here. She's gone to London for the weekend
and won't be back till Sunday evening," she said, adding
with genuine regret for a wasted journey, "Oh, Robert, I
am sorry!"

He ran a hand absently over his chin as if he suspected
he needed a shave, but looked amused rather than
disappointed.

"Well, that may be unexpected, but no setback to my
plans. I'll go and find Elspeth," he said, and left the room
to return very shortly with an Elspeth already divested of
overall and shoes, evidently preparing for bed.

"What's got into you, Mr. Rab?" she was saying a trifle
crossly. "You've been later than this and not disturbed
the household. You know very well your room's always
ready, and there's no need to announce your presence till
the morn."

"Well, since Mrs. Allen is away, I thought I'd better
have your approval. The local hostelry would hardly take
me in at this hour, and I don't fancy a long drive back to

London." Robert spoke with an air of humoring possible opposition, but Elspeth merely looked surprised.

"And what has Mrs. Allen's absence to do with that? You've no' considered the proprieties when she lived alone, and I'm still here to make your visiting respectable," she retorted. "If it's Miss Toria having doubts, she can make her mind easy. We're both of us paid employees here and not concerned with the habits of guests. I was just coming down to lock up, but perhaps you'll do it as usual before going up." She bade them both good night in matter-of-fact tones and retired upstairs once more. Robert glanced quizzically at Victoria and asked with faint mockery, "*Were* you having doubts, Miss Toria?"

Victoria, who had harbored no such thoughts, being largely concerned with his disappointment at finding his hostess absent, replied with a certain asperity, "Why should I? Kate will be sorry she missed you as you haven't been down for some time, but if you don't mind putting up with your own company, it's no skin off my nose. As Elspeth pointed out just now, I'm a paid employee and am not concerned with the habits of guests."

"How prim you sound, suddenly. Did Elspeth's pointed reminder sting?" he asked teasingly and caught a glimpse of that inviting smile that she hurriedly tried to suppress.

"Of course not," she answered with amused indulgence. "She evidently thought I was having maidenly scruples and was putting me in my place. Would you like a nightcap, Robert, before you go up? You know where Kate keeps the whisky, so just help yourself."

"You know," he said, availing himself unhurriedly of the offer, "you've changed for the better since last we met. I was right when I said I was wise to stay away."

"I hardly imagine you were influenced by anything other than pressure of work," she replied, watching him run appreciative fingers over the delicately cut pattern of his Waterford tumbler and thinking what well-shaped hands he had.

"Don't you? But then you've never credited me with much sensibility. Have you missed me?"

She thought of her remark to Kate that had met with such amusement and smiled reminiscently.

"Oh yes," she said. "You keep my wits up to scratch if nothing else. Kate is too calm and too kind to argue with to score a point, and Timmy too young. You, on the other hand, are fair game since brow-beating witnesses is your stock in trade, and there's no need to consider your feelings."

He looked at her thoughtfully for a moment or two before replying, then he said quite gently, "Haven't you lost that penchant for creating false images yet? A brow-beating counsel may have his feelings, even if it does serve as an excuse for working off old scores; but there comes a time when the game resolves into a one-sided contest. You are too intelligent, my dear, to cling so obstinately to old misconceptions."

She was aware not only of a disconcerting change in his attitude, but one of unexpected compliance in herself. From the moment she had awakened in the moonlight to find him bending over her, the old hostility had slipped away. She knew that although she might try to revive it by whipping up imagined grudges, the desire to sting him into retaliation would never be quite the same again.

"You sound," she said at last, "as if you minded what I might think of you."

"Certainly I mind. Verbal friction can be amusing and often stimulating, but I wouldn't be human if I desired nothing more than that."

"And do you?"

"Oh yes. I have, perhaps, a greater understanding of the real Victoria than you suppose. And, without wishing to sound complacent, you aren't, I think, as indifferent to me as you would like to believe."

"I've never been that," she said quickly, uncomfortably conscious of his attraction. "You're hardly indifferent to a person you perpetually wrangle with."

"True, but has it never struck you that that in itself should be a warning? There's a very thin dividing line between hate and love, so we're told."

She met his quizzical gaze with a composure she was far from feeling. She was not so untutored as to confuse his meaning, but neither did she jump to romantic conclusions. She remembered Kate saying: *Robert is fastidious, and you are very much to his taste, I should say. . . .* This was seemingly not so unlikely as might have been supposed, but Victoria was no longer ruled by the fanciful flights of her adolescence. Robert was probably no different from any other man in the matter of casual affairs.

"No, it's not what you're thinking," he said suddenly, and there was a decided twinkle in his eye as he observed her betraying color. "All the same I *have* a proposition to make. Shall we, just for this one weekend, forget our differences and try getting to know one another instead? It's unlikely such a suitable opportunity for better acquaintance will occur again."

He put his half-finished drink on the mantelshelf and held out both hands to her. She unhesitatingly gave him hers. His eyes were still quizzical, but not cold at all as they searched her face. She found herself wondering why she had once built up such an unflattering image of a stranger she was unlikely to meet again.

"Am I to take it you're in agreement?" he asked, watching her changing expressions and trying to guess at her thoughts. "I'd like the chance to show you a different Robert Farmer from the one you've created for yourself."

"You said that when you called the night of my birthday," she said. "Till then, 'dream your dreams and fight your dragons,' you said. What did you mean?"

"Just that the time wasn't ripe for the dragon's transformation. Like all the sorely tried victims of spells in the best fairy tales, I was still condemned to enchantment."

"It sounds very odd for you to be talking like this—very odd and quite out of character," she said frowning.

"That, young woman, you have no right to judge until you know me better. Even brow-beating attorneys have their moments of fantasy," he retorted and, releasing her hands rather abruptly, turned to pick up his glass again.

"What shall we do tomorrow?" he asked conversationally, firmly dismissing any further flights of fancy. At the same time he observed the lavish arrangements of roses that so far had escaped his notice and whistled softly.

"Oho! More floral tributes! Has Mr. Brown been at it again?"

"Yes, he has," Victoria answered a little shortly, wishing for the first time that she could have presented Robert with the existence of a genuine suitor.

"Dear me, how remarkable! Are you celebrating another birthday?"

"Of course not. The lawyers probably slipped up and forgot they'd been ordered the first time."

"Very likely. Still, they've come at an opportune moment, for I, too, had notions of a belated celebration but no time, alas, to say it with flowers."

"Say what with flowers?"

"Happy birthday, of course. Kate suggested that when I next came down we'd have a second party and crack a bottle of bubbly. Well, I've brought the bubbly and a few *recherché* trifles, so we'll have to celebrate without her."

"Oh, Robert! That *was* nice of you," she said, flushing with pleasure like a child. "I will admit to you that everything fell flat that night. Poor John did his best, but he would much rather have had Kate to himself. Kate was terribly conscious that it had been a mistake to whip up a spurious gaiety."

"Spurious gaiety . . . what a dismal picture that conjures up," he said with a wry grimace. "Well, I'll promise you this, Victoria Mary, there'll be nothing spurious about our gaiety, unless, of course, you've quarreled with me by then."

"I don't think I shall quarrel with you, Robert," she said, rewarding his efforts with that sudden endearing smile and added curiously, "Why do you so often address me by both my names?"

"Because their prim respectability amuses me. Victoria Mary has a delightfully Edwardian flavor, and you with your demure center parting and little nipped-in waist can look misleadingly decorous at times. No doubt I must thank your Mr. Brown for succeeding in shielding you from the pitfalls of this permissive age."

"Well, if I'm a milk-and-water miss you sound positively Victorian!" she exclaimed a shade indignantly. "Are you really old-fashioned, Robert, or do you just like to tease?"

"A little of both, perhaps, and I certainly wouldn't liken you to a milk-and-water miss. No well-brought-up young lady of earlier days would dream of being so free with her tongue and opinions," he retorted. She giggled with what he told her reprovingly was an unbecoming lack of respect for his superior judgment and approaching gray hairs.

"Your judgment may be superior, my learned friend, but you're not old enough yet to demand respect as your right," she retorted, enjoying the small exchange with none of the old resentment, and suddenly liking him very much.

"Well, that at least should encourage my self-esteem. When one is over 30 one tends to get written off by young things in their teens," he said, and her eyes became thoughtful.

"But I'm not in my teens," she reminded him gravely, I'm 20 and quite adult."

For a moment his eyes rested on her with an answering thoughtfulness, and the lines in his clever face seemed to deepen and sharpen.

"So you are," he said then, "and in less than a year Mr. Brown's jurisdiction will be at an end. Are you going to miss this unseen influence that has colored so much of your life?"

He had turned away from the light to rest his arm on the mantelshelf, so that his face was now in shadow. She could no longer read his expression, but she thought there was a touch of irony in his voice.

"Yes, I suppose I will," she answered slowly, aware of a curious blankness lying ahead, but not knowing how desolate she sounded until he moved impatiently and inquired whether she was still banking on that improbable happy ending.

"Not in the way I used to when I was young," she answered carefully, "but I see no reason why we shouldn't become friends, once we've met."

"And suppose you don't meet? Your Mr. Brown, judging by past eccentricities, is perfectly capable of vanishing into thin air if it suits him," Robert said, unkindly refusing to pander to hope.

"Then," she replied with fresh determination, "I shall set about finding him myself, if only to say thank you and satisfy my curiosity."

"And how would you do that?" he asked with some amusement. 'The lawyers won't betray a client, you know, however charmingly you may try to wheedle."

"I wouldn't waste time trying to wheedle Mr. Chapple, stuffy old bore," she replied with her nose in the air. "There are better ways of finding out—private eyes for one. It can't be so difficult to trace a person of Mr. Brown's peculiar habits, for he's sure to have other benevolent schemes on hand. Also, there's bound to be someone willing to give him away for a small consideration."

Robert burst out laughing.

"Well, for pity's sake! Private eyes and mercenary inducements! And how do you suppose such methods would endear you to your erstwhile patron?"

"Yes, that's a point," she admitted, looking crestfallen, but she rallied at once as her eyes came to rest on the roses' mute assurance of an awakening interest.

"You won't blight my expectations with legal objections, Robert," she told him cheerfully. "Those flowers and the others are my guarantee of good faith. There was no need, after all, to depart from the custom of years unless something more personal was intended, was there?"

He moved his hand with a quick, irritable gesture, knocking a china figurine onto the hearth where it smashed with a melancholy sound of finality. Victoria went on her knees to pick up the pieces.

"Oh dear, Kate *will* be upset!" she exclaimed, forgetting both Robert and Mr. Brown in this unfortunate mishap. "It was one of a pair she particularly liked."

"Nothing of the sort, she thought them hideous," he countered rather crossly, "but they belonged to my Aunt

Eva and came with the house, so Kate tactfully left them where they were.''

"Oh, what a good thing," Victoria said with relief, getting up and disposing of the remains in the wastepaper basket. "I keep forgetting your aunt left everything to you. Nobody can complain if you break your own ornaments, can they? But returning to Mr. Brown—''

"I have no wish to return to Mr. Brown," Robert interrupted with unusual sharpness. "I'm heartily sick of Mr. Brown, and I must beg you to keep him out of the conversation for the rest of the weekend, unless you want to try my patience too highly."

"*Well!*" said Victoria, her eyes growing wider and wider until her face seemed all angles and hollows, "Of *all* things! If I didn't know you better, Robert, I'd think you were jealous of poor Mr. Brown."

"You don't know me at all as yet, so don't make rash pronouncements," he retorted, but the irritability had gone from his voice. "I think, however, we'll postpone our further acquaintance till tomorrow as it's getting late. Go to bed, Victoria Mary, and may your dreams bring sense, if not satisfaction. Good night."

CHAPTER SIX

If she dreamed at all, Victoria remembered nothing upon awakening. Last night's promise of felicity remained with her, stirring a sense of expectancy for which she could not altogether account. The morning fulfilled the pledge of the day before with a heat haze already shimmering over the still countryside, and she resolved that nothing should spoil the day through retaliation on her part should Robert choose to provoke her.

There was no need, however, to guard her tongue. His teasing had lost its sting or, perhaps, she understood him better. He very skilfully set about the business of proving her first conceptions wrong.

"You know, Robert," she told him as they lay soaking up the sun in the orchard after lunch, "I wouldn't have believed a month ago that I could feel so completely at home with you."

"A month ago you were intent on fighting dragons. I don't doubt the urge will arise again once the novelty of peaceful companionship has worn off," he retorted with his more customary dryness, but she only laughed.

"It isn't likely that companionship with you would remain peaceful indefinitely. You're too used to slapping people down in court to give in meekly," she said, and he reached out a hand to administer a more literal slap on one bare leg.

"And you, young woman, are too fond of trailing your coat to encourage meekness."

"Only with you. I'm really very accommodating in regard to most people. Ask Kate."

"Really? Accommodating is hardly a description that would appeal to Mr. Brown, I fancy."

"I thought his name wasn't to be mentioned over the weekend," she murmured demurely, and he raised himself on one elbow to look down at her stretched out beside him. Her eyes were closed against the sunlight that, filtering through the branches of an apple tree, cast provocative shadows across her throat and breast, and the slender thigh exposed by the drawn-up hem of her cotton dress.

"Your innocent air of abandonment is curiously inviting—but perhaps you knew," he said softly, and her eyes flew open. She sat up abruptly, pulling her dress over her knees. Grace was suddenly lost in awkwardness.

"Ah, now you've spoiled it," he said regretfully, lying back again with his hands behind his head, aware at once that he had been premature.

"No, it's you who've spoiled it," she replied, remembering Kate's well-meaning hints. "I'm not accommodating in that sense of the word, I can assure you."

"Hush, child, don't pick a quarrel with me on that score," he said with lazy good-humor. "I spoke without consideration, for which I'm sorry, but you can set your mind at rest as to any dubious intentions. They're strictly honorable."

She caught the note of gentle mockery in his voice that he intended she should and immediately felt gauche and immature.

"I beg your pardon," she said with prim politeness. "I'm not at all used to remarks of that kind, you see Mr. Brown has never encouraged followers."

He, in his turn, caught the veiled provocation in her last statement and propped himself once more on his elbow.

"Is that a direct invitation to quarrel? I thought we were agreed that mention of that gentleman might lead to trouble."

"Well, you mentioned him first," Victoria retorted, her resilience restored. "I was only trying to excuse a lack of *savoir faire* in myself."

"Were you, now? Well, despite the alleged scarcity of followers, you've no need to trouble yourself on that score, my dear. I suspect you'll have no difficulty in dealing with suitors when they start lining up."

"Suitors? Where?"

"Wherever you may happen to be after your next birth-day—unless, of course, the unlikely occurs, and you finish up as a substitute daughter after all—in that case," Robert concluded on a distinctly dry note, "your chances of selecting the man of your choice would seem to be remote, if past history is anything to go by."

She hugged her knees and giggled appreciatively, no longer ruffled by his tendency to poke fun at Mr. Brown.

"Well, since that contingency is equally remote, I won't need to please anyone but myself when and if the time arises," she said.

"*If?* Do you have doubts, Victoria Mary? I thought all attractive girls took a future husband for granted," he said lightly and watched the untroubled look in her eyes change to one of grave consideration.

"I haven't really thought that far," she said, after some deliberation. "Time for me has been here and now, with everything arranged for me, and my opinions not asked for. I suppose I've been too occupied in guessing at Mr. Brown's intentions to look ahead to any future without him."

"The gentleman is still an obsession, I see, despite this assurance that you've grown out of your infantile fancies," he observed none too sympathetically, and she smiled.

"Not an obsession, only a background and natural spur to curiosity," she replied. "However short of reality my infantile fancies may have been, he can't be dismissed as a figment of the imagination."

"You would be bitterly disappointed if he turned out to be no more than the collective contributors to a trust, wouldn't you? he asked more gently.

She looked at him gravely as if she suspected him of possessing knowledge that she did not share, then smiled at him again rather abstractedly and replied, "Yes, I would because it's comforted me to think there was someone who cared, even in an impersonal sort of way, what became of me. Even if your guess is right, you won't convince me those roses were thought up by a board of directors—or even a computer!"

"A computer . . . now that's a thought," he said appreciatively. "How would you feel if your elusive Mr. Brown turned out to be nothing more rewarding than an efficient machine?"

"You don't really think, do you—" she began, looking suddenly stricken, and he moved a little impatiently.

"Of course not, but I *do* think we've had enough for one day of that gentleman's tiresome intrusion into our affairs, to say nothing of the fact that, like all women, you aren't sticking to your bargain," he retorted.

"But we haven't quarreled and I hope your patience hasn't been tried too highly," she countered demurely, adding as she saw him smile, "You really shouldn't generalize like that, you know, Robert. Women don't follow the same pattern just because they're female. You might find yourself in a lot of trouble one of these days by overlooking that fact."

"Might I, indeed?" he said with some asperity, reaching out a hand as if he meant to administer another salutary slap. She twisted away from him, springing to her feet in one lithe movement of returning grace and stood leaning against the trunk of the apple tree laughing down at him.

He was reminded vividly of the occasion of their first meeting at Farthings when Kate had told her to take him around the garden. She had stood in the orchard shaking blossoms onto her head with charming inconsequence while she spun him ridiculous yarns about Mr. Brown, imagining he did not remember her. He had, perhaps, been a little unkind in keeping up the fiction until he was ready to prick her innocent bubble of pretense. He had been both surprised and piqued by the hostility she did not try to disguise, forgetting that youthful impressions went deep and tended to magnify with the years.

As if she, too, remembered and was deliberately recreating the scene, she stretched up a hand and picked off an overhanging apple. A leaf or two settled on her hair.

"Not quite so effective as a shower of blossoms, but nicely staged all the same," he observed, wondering if she knew how instinctively she had responded to his tentative overtures and whether she realized she was nearly ready to accept a new relationship. She merely looked puzzled by his comment and bit into the apple with no sign of connecting the two occasions.

"Blossoms?" she murmured vaguely and had clearly not been listening. "Shall I pick one for you? They're not very ripe, but quite nice."

"No, thanks. Eve tried that one, too, but I prefer to do my own picking," he retorted. For a moment she looked inquiring, then she laughed, tossing the half-eaten apple into the long grass and reached up for another.

"Oh, that old gag," she said. "I wouldn't be surprised if it wasn't Adam who did the picking, then blamed the whole thing on Eve."

"The woman tempted me . . . an unfair apportioning of the blame, you think?"

"Well, don't you? They say it takes two to make a quarrel, so I expect it takes two to share the blame. Anyway, it was really all the Serpent's fault, and he got off without a scratch, which all goes to show."

"You talk a lot of charming nonsense, don't you? No, don't start on another. It would be a pity if our little celebration tonight had to be postponed because you had a pain in your stomach," he said, getting to his feet and confiscating the fruit already half-way to her mouth. He picked a leaf out of her hair just as on the other occasion he had disentangled petals. This time she did not try to free herself, but stood looking inquiringly up at him. He smiled and dropped a light kiss on the top of her head.

"We mustn't prolong this delightful idyll at my godson's expense, or he'll feel neglected," he said. "Go and get him up from his rest, and we'll play a game with him until teatime.

Victoria hurried into the house, guiltily aware that with Robert's unexpected advent it had been all too easy to forget her responsibilities. She had devoted the morning to the boy while Robert drove to the village for extra stores to oblige Elspeth. She informed him with slight asperity, she had been counting on a quiet weekend with Mrs. Allen away, and only Miss Toria and the bairn to cater for. She had looked with faint disfavor at the ready-prepared delicacies he had brought with him to augment their board and expressed the opinion that Mrs. Allen was more likely to appreciate out-of-season luxuries than a young girl with little or no palate as yet,

"You forget the advantages of being finished abroad," he had reminded her with a grin. "If nothing else, young ladies about to take their places in society are taught discrimination in the matters of food and style."

"And what good will that do this poor lass with never a chance to show off her tricks at balls and parties and suchlike?" Elspeth had demanded indignantly. "The daft old gentleman would have done better to have the girl trained for a sensible career than pay for fancy trimmings abroad to please himself."

"Perhaps he had reasons that will come to light in due course," Robert had answered, cocking a cynical eyebrow at her. She gave an unmistakable snort, then smiled reluctantly.

"As to that I ha'e ma doots," she retorted, her accent broadening uncompromisingly as it did in moments of disagreement. "Still, you'll do no harm with your wee celebration if you mind your tongue and your teasing ways. It was no' a very gay birthday dinner with no man of her own to admire her looks and the doctor doing his best, poor man, to hide the fact that he wanted Mrs. Allen to himself."

"Would you say my cousin was—interested in that quarter at all?" Robert asked with deliberate casualness, and Elspeth gave him a distinctly old-fashioned look.

"That wouldn't be for me to remark on," she replied repressively. "I had my own ideas once, but mebbe I was wrong. Mrs. Allen's no' the sort to wear her heart on her sleeve. Now don't waste my time any longer, blethering, Mr. Rab, when I've the lunch to re-plan to allow for one extra."

Timmy, with a child's sharp perceptions, had, when they all three met for lunch, sensed a difference in his two favorite grown-ups despite their joint efforts to amuse him. Now when Victoria came to waken him from his afternoon nap, he was ready to assert his rights by being contrary. His favorite games were no longer to his liking, neither it seemed was his Uncle Rab, making jokes he did not understand and taking too much of Victoria's attention.

Both Robert and Victoria did their best to keep him amused and ward off the probability of a scene at bedtime. Elspeth's preparations in the kitchen together with Victoria's efforts to get him settled for the night in good time betokened something special in the way of a party from which he was to be excluded, and he took refuge in the only form of protest he understood.

Neither Victoria's blandishments nor his godfather's offer of a piggyback up the stairs could persuade him into compliance, for both of them were now out of favor. He was making such a noise that none of them heard a car pull up outside, or were aware of John Squires following his usual practice of entering the house unannounced until he spoke from the doorway.

At the time Victoria could only regard his intervention as mercifully opportune. Timmy's tears stopped instantly and, with very little persuasion he allowed himself to be hoisted triumphantly onto the doctor's broad shoulders and carried hiccoughing up to bed. But when he came down again to announce a little brusquely that the boy was quiet and ready to be tucked up for the night, she was not so sure.

"I used to flatter myself that I could always coax Timmy back to reason, but I seem to have lost my touch," Robert said, smiling a little wryly at the doctor, but John did not smile in return.

"Children are extraordinarily sensitive to atmosphere. The boy probably sensed he wasn't wanted," he said quite shortly. Robert raised a quizzical eyebrow, but made no comment.

Victoria protested indignantly, "We've both been leaning over backward to keep him amused, but he got wind of the party and that finished it."

"What party?"

"Oh, not a real one—at least in a way it is. Robert had the idea of giving me a second party because he couldn't get down on my birthday."

"I see. A private celebration to make up for the awkwardness of the first. Well, I looked in for a while in case you should be lonely, but I can see I needn't have been anxious."

She could not understand why he should sound so stuffy, but it seemed clear that he had evidently been aware that Kate's party had been a mistake. She did not want him to feel hurt.

"It was a lovely party and not awkward at all. It was only Kate who minded because she didn't know any young men to make up the numbers," she told him anxiously and was at last rewarded with an unwilling smile.

"That's nice of you, my dear—all the same it's time you met young people of your own age and weren't obliged to fall back on Kate's old cronies for your entertainment."

Robert was busy mixing drinks and had his back to them, but he said over his shoulder, "If that was a crack at me I take exception to being dubbed an old crony." He turned as he finished speaking, holding out a glass of sherry to the doctor, a faintly malicious twinkle in his eye. "You won't, I trust, be too disapproving to accept my wine and drink Victoria's health."

"Oh dear. . . . " Victoria thought unhappily. "Robert's in one of his infuriating moods. . . . " That the two men were incompatible she had put down to their conflicting interests in Kate. Although John Squires's sentiments could well be guessed at, Robert's were less easily divined.

"Well, now, since my cousin isn't here to set the conversational ball rolling, what shall we all talk about?" Robert asked, imitating the bright, encouraging accents of the professional hostess. "Victoria, you aren't drinking."

"I'll have mine later," she said rather hurriedly. "I must go up and settle Timmy, then it will be time to change my dress."

She thought Robert gave her a sardonic look as she turned toward the corner staircase in the parlor that was a short cut to the bedrooms and heard him say, just as she reached the top, "You really shouldn't try to cramp my style by bracketing me with your own age group, my dear chap. I'm no beardless youth, I'll admit, but optimistic mammas still regard me as an eligible *parti*."

Really, she thought, suppressing an unseemly giggle, Robert could be quite impossible when he set out to provoke.

To her relief, she found Timmy sleepy and obligingly ready to forget his grievances. With an extra cuddle and the promise of something saved from the party to provide a treat for the next day, he was content to let Victoria go without demur. She wondered how the two men were faring over their drinks. She did not go down again. Very soon she heard John's car start up. Later, the sounds of water running into the bath accompanied by the familiar explosions emitted from the ancient boiler, and Robert shouting down to Elspeth for fresh towels. He banged companionably on her door on the way back to his room to let her know the bathroom was free, and she went to perform her own ablutions, unconsciously renewing yesterday's game of pretense. With just such trivial domestic intimacies she would feel cherished were she mistress of Farthings; part and parcel of the masculine belongings and children's toys that she had mentally scattered about her make-believe home. It did not seem strange that Robert should now be playing an unrehearsed part in the fantasy, for although her imagined master of the house had been no more than a faceless figment in her mind's eye, Robert was not only very real but would one day claim the place as his own.

When she was dressed she stood in front of the long mirror as she had on the night of her birthday and surveyed herself critically. She wore the same white dress, remembering how she had wished he could have seen her in it and tried to view herself through his eyes. Would he find her pleasing, she wondered with recollections of his reputed fastidiousness, or was he too familiar with the image she had chosen to present to him to look upon her as a woman? It was, she supposed, unreasonable to desire his approval when she had shown so often that she was indifferent to it, but today had not been like any of the others.

The evening was all she could have wished it to be. Robert, who had put on a dinner jacket to grace the occasion, made every effort to charm her. He succeeded so well that she found herself wondering why she had ever thought him cold and bitter-tongued.

"You were very rude to poor John who had only looked in out of the kindness of his heart, thinking I was alone," she admonished him as they went to dinner.

"Poor John was, I fancy, harboring unworthy suspicions and deserved all he got," he retorted unrepentantly, and she giggled.

"Don't flatter yourself," she said. "He's only concerned with Kate's good opinion, not yours."

"Exactly. Now stop taking me to task. It's not becoming in you when I'm only trying to please," he said with mock severity and seated her at the table with ceremonious courtesy.

He must have inspired Elspeth with a sense of occasion, Victoria reflected, for not only did she serve them an excellent meal, but had set out the best china and glass. She placed an old many-branched candelabrum in the center of the table to add the elegance of candlelight to their feasting.

"What a shame Kate's missing all this," Victoria said, much impressed by all the festive touches, and Robert raised a sceptical eyebrow.

"Do you think so? Be honest, Victoria Mary, and admit that a small celebration *à deux* is infinitely more pleasing to you."

"How conceited you are!" she countered, but her smile held shy agreement, and her eyes were bright with anticipation.

"But of course," he retorted, his keen regard capturing each changing expression and getting much enjoyment from her naïve responses. "Conceit is an essential part of one's armor if one wants to survive the rat-race—or if it comes to that, convince others of one's worth."

"I wouldn't have thought you cared enough to bother," she said, busily intent on extracting the very last morsel from her lobster thermidor.

"Ah, but then you're not acquainted yet with my secret aims and desires and the need to establish a footing—you really can't dig any more out of that empty shell, my dear child—didn't they teach you to restrain your unladylike greed in that Paris establishment?"

"Yes, they did, but I don't count you as polite society, so you must bear with my manners for just this once. Who do you want to establish a footing with? I would have thought you were well able to call the tune."

"Would you, indeed? And I'm not sure that I take it as a compliment to be excluded from polite society."

"Then you should, Robert. It only means that I'm at last feeling at home with you, and—and isn't that furthering this better acquaintance you've talked so much about?"

"In that case, I'm both touched and honored," he replied gravely, "so don't take it amiss any more if I tease. Your first dislike for me was natural enough in the circumstances, but you're too old to carry a childish grudge into adult life you know."

"Yes, I suppose I am, but it isn't easy to shed first impressions. Mr. Brown has dominated so much of my life in a remote kind of fashion, and you were all mixed up with the start of it."

"So you turned Mr. Brown into the traditional Fairy Godfather, and I was naturally cast for the Demon King. I should, I suppose be flattered at having made an impression at all, though it was hardly the equivalent of a school-girl crush—or was it?"

He added the last provocative query so softly that she was taken off guard. She did not, however, immediately retaliate with outraged denials, but sat staring absently beyond him while she deliberated with that thoughtful gravity that so often took him by surprise.

"I wonder if it could have been—in a topsy-turvy kind of fashion," she said then, slowly.

"Well, Victoria Mary, you never cease to astonish me!" he said, sounding for once a little at a loss. "I would never have expected you to appreciate the psychology of that, much less admit it."

"Wouldn't you? That side of my education wasn't neglected, you know. The French take a deep interest in what makes them tick, and we had to read up the accepted works in order to be able to converse intelligently at imaginary select dinner parties," she retorted, helping herself lavishly from a dish of salted almonds. His smile, if appreciative, was a trifle wry.

"Dear me! How alarming that sounds! And what else were you required to store away for the edification of imaginary guests?"

"Oh, the usual things—current affairs, the arts, of course, and the latest play or book. We were expected to be reasonably well informed on any topic of social interest, but never to air our views to the discomfort of the gentlemen."

Robert burst out laughing.

"Well, that should rule you out of court!" he said. "I've noticed precious little consideration for the gentlemen when you've had views to air."

For a moment she looked startled, then she sighed.

"You're quite right, of course, Robert," she said, reaching absently for another almond. "I suppose I never thought of you in that category."

"I see. You're informing me now that I'm no gentleman."

"Of course not! I meant the sort of young gentleman Madame imagined would be taking me out to dinner."

"Well, I'm taking you out to dinner now even though we're having it here at Farthings. Next time I'll arange something smarter and more conventional so you'd better get in shape for a proper display of all these social graces."

"Next time?"

"Certainly. This is just the curtain-raiser. On the next occasion you'll get the full treatment—the latest in fashionable restaurants, attentive waiters, and a still more attentive host."

"But—" she began, her eyes growing bigger and bigger. He reached for the bottle in its basket of ice to top up her champagne and said firmly,

"Now don't come out with the old statement that Mr. Brown doesn't encourage followers. It's time that gentleman ceased to be a convenient excuse, unless, of course, you have personal objections that you're too polite to state."

"Oh no," she said very seriously, watching the bubbles dancing merrily to the surface as he filled her glass, "I would find it most exciting to be entertained by you, Robert. I'm sure you're very expert at the job once you've made up your mind the end in view is worth your while."

"Well, I'm not altogether certain that was intended to be complimentary, but let's drink to our better acquaintance just the same," he said with a wry little smile. Then he raised his glass to her and, for a moment, his eyes were grave and inquiring, belying the lightness of his words. She lifted her own glass in silent reply to his toast, and her eyes held a shy promise of acceptance of which she was quite unaware.

Afterward she could not remember very clearly how they had passed the rest of the evening, only that there had been sweetness between them, and a growing sense of communion.

They talked, covering a multitude of subjects; sometimes they just sat in companionable silence; once he stretched out a hand to tuck a strand of hair behind her ear, saying he found its faun-like resemblance vastly intriguing. His fingers lingered, tracing the lines of her neck and bare shoulder with a delicate touch. The old house settled about them with its familiar nocturnal creaks and whispers as the first pale shaft of moonlight crept slowly across the floor. Elspeth could be heard moving from kitchen to dining room laying the breakfast things for the morning, but she did not disturb them, and presently they heard her go upstairs to bed.

"And we, I suppose, should do likewise," Robert said, getting lazily to his feet. He stood looking down at Victoria curled up in the big chair, clearly reluctant to move, and held out both hands to her.

"Come along, my child. This is only a beginning, and tomorrow is another day," he said and pulled her up into his arms.

She stood expectantly between his hands, blinking up at him, her eyes already clouded with sleep, and reached up a hand to explore the sharply chiselled outlines of his prominent bones.

"I've often wanted to do that," she said.

"Have you, indeed? And why, might I ask, since you apparently found me so objectionable?"

"Only to make sure I wouldn't cut myself if I did," she retorted with a sleepy smile, and he caught her straying fingers, imprisoning them firmly against his chest.

"What impudence! For that you should be made to pay forfeit," he exclaimed, but when she obligingly offered him her lips, his mood changed. He cupped her upturned face gently between his hands and said softly, "Have you understood, I wonder, that I've been making tentative love to you all evening?"

"Oh yes," she answered serenely, "and most of the afternoon, too, I think."

"Oh you do, do you? And have I made any progress?"

But her new-found consequence was weakening. Tonight she had been delicately courted with the sophisticated accompaniments of food, wine and the attentions of a man probably well used to easy conquests when he troubled to exert his charm. She had no measure by which to gauge the depth of his intentions. He had teased her and kissed her, but made no demands on her charity other than that repeated desire for a better acquaintance. She became painfully aware that the answer to his question must betray more than she was prepared to acknowledge, even to herself.

"Dear Robert . . . if by making progress you mean am I suitably impressed by your well-planned celebration, then you've certainly earned full marks," she said, but refused to meet his eyes. His smile held a trace of appreciative irony.

"Very nicely evaded, Miss Hayes, and I'm encouraged by such early signs of maturity. It's possible, though, that you have mistaken my intentions," he said and was amused by the confused uncertainty with which she tried to withdraw from him. "Now, don't jump to extremes. As I told you this afternoon, my intentions are strictly above board, so there's no need for maidenly scruples."

"I'm not given to *them*!" she replied with scorn.

"You relieve me mightily. In that case, you'll doubtless take any future slip on my part in the spirit in which it is meant."

"What sort of slip?" The conversation was becoming confusing, or she was too sleepy and too content in her new-found felicity to follow him.

"Oh, just the occasional lapse into unrestraint that can overtake the impatient lover." He spoke lightly enough, but she was suddenly wide awake. Surely even Robert wouldn't carry his mockery to these lengths.

"Are you joking?" she asked, and the quizzical amusement immediately died out of his face.

"No, my bewildered sleepyhead, I'm not joking—just feeling my way. Do you find it so difficult to visualize me in the light of a lover?" he said, and the tenderness that she found so difficult to resist was back again in his voice.

"No—oh, no," she replied; then, because her conscience would continue to prick until she could silence those early unconfirmed suspicions, she added with naïve abruptness, "But what of Kate?"

"Kate?" He sounded faintly surprised, then one eyebrow rose a shade cynically. "Well, I wouldn't advise a spate of girlish confidences at this early stage. Kate takes her responsibilities seriously and tends to be over-anxious."

"That isn't what I meant."

"No? Well, whatever you meant, you can safely leave Kate to draw her own conclusions."

It was not, Victoria thought, a very enlightening reply, but short of asking him point blank if Kate had once been in love with him there was nothing more she could say to clarify the situation. She stood there a little hesitantly while he closed the window and switched off the lights, and wished she had not rubbed off some of the evening's magic by mentioning Kate. Perhaps Robert, too, was aware that something had been spoiled, for he opened the long window into the garden again and said, "Come out for a few minutes before I lock up. It's a perfect night for making promises under the stars."

She went with him willingly, grateful for that touch of fantasy that seemed to bring him closer. In the moonlit garden with shadows etched sharply across the dewy lawn, and the warm air sweet with night-scented stock and new-mown grass, the magic returned.

They lingered for a while in silence, listening to the owls calling from the woods below, and the myriad small night sounds that stirred in the leaves and grass about them. He made no move to take advantage of the romantic setting, and suddenly a brilliant point of light detached itself from the glistening galaxy above them and swept down to earth to be forever lost.

"Oh, look—a shooting star!" Victoria cried in delight. "You must wish, Robert. You must always wish on a shooting star, and this is the first I've ever seen."

"Then let's hope it's a good omen," he said observing with tender amusement the way she instantly closed her eyes and moved her lips as if in unconscious prayer.

"Did you wish?" she asked anxiously, opening her eyes again, but he gave her no reply, only stooped to kiss her good night so lightly that she was scarcely aware of his lips touching hers.

"Bed," he said, brushing off a white moth that had settled on her hair, as long ago he had brushed away the white petals of apple blossom, then turned her gently back toward the house.

CHAPTER SEVEN

Sunday proved a sad disappointment after such seemingly settled weather, for rain had come with the dawn. The leaden sky gave no promise of lifting.

"You'd never believe things could change so quickly after the heat of yesterday, would you?" Victoria said to Robert when they met for breakfast. "Everything seemed set for a lovely weekend."

"That just goes to show that you can't trust nature any more than your own feelings," he replied with that discouraging promptitude, and she eyed him uncertainly.

"What, exactly, do you mean by that?" she asked, wondering if he already regretted his mood of yesterday.

"Nothing very profound, merely a passing comment on life's depressing uncertainties," he answered, extracting a wasp from the jar of marmalade and squashing it irritably on his plate.

"*Are* you depressed, Robert? The weather certainly isn't helping, I'll admit, but we can find plenty to do indoors. Timmy will welcome an excuse for his uncle Rob's undivided attention," she said, not realizing how wifely she sounded until he cocked a sardonic eyebrow at her across the table, observing acidly:

"Trying your make-believe out on me?"

"Not consciously," she replied, making an effort to laugh at her own absurdities. "I suppose Kate being away gives me a false feeling of being mistress of the house, but it's only pretense."

"And what part am I playing in this pretense of yours?" he asked in the suave, misleading tones he had employed for his cross-examination.

She was not going to be trapped into incoherent admissions or denials as she had been then, and replied coolly, "I haven't got as far as casting you, yet. My imaginary master of the house is a very intangible character—just a dim figure in the background."

"Like Mr. Brown?"

"Not at all like Mr. Brown. I picture *him* living in some remote mansion in chilly isolation except for minions he pays so well that they never give him notice. I don't think he'd suit Farthings at all."

He laughed then and seemed to shed some of his early morning irritability.

"Poor Mr. Brown! I fear that his star is at last on the wane for want of a more substantial identity, and a good thing, too," he said, sounding pleased with himself. She remembered the roses, undeniable evidence of an interest not wholly dutiful, even, perhaps, of a change of heart, and felt she had been unduly flippant.

"Oh no," she said softly, "it wouldn't be a good thing at all. Even if we never met I would still feel bound to him in a queer sort of way."

The look Robert gave her was neither conciliatory nor particularly sympathetic, but he spoke quite gently, "In that case you seem likely to be caught in your dream world for the rest of your days. I wonder if you could meet this ubiquitous ghost would the spell be broken."

"What spell?"

"A spell you have made for yourself, I fancy, but no less potent for that. I'm not at all sure it isn't you who are awaiting the traditional disenchantment and not me."

Despite the prosaicness of the breakfast hour and the

discouraging sound of rain beating on the windows, something of last night's magic returned with his words.

"I'm glad you haven't forgotten all those things you said to me, even if you didn't mean them," she told him. That unconscious smile began to turn up the corners of her mouth and then stopped abruptly as if uncertain of a welcome.

"I meant them, but possibly you misinterpreted my reasons," he said, but she answered quickly, instinctively avoiding a reply that could pin him down to more concrete explanations.

"There dosen't have to be a reason in make-believe—that's the beauty of it."

For a moment it seemed as though he would have liked to dispute the point, but he evidently had second thoughts. He only shook his head at her and rose from the breakfast table to stand staring out of the window at the rain-soaked garden.

"Well, what shall we do with ourselves this uninviting morning? Shall we take advantage of the contrary weather and go to church?" he asked.

"I would like to," she said, "but I don't think I ought to leave Timmy to his own devices. Elspeth will be busy with the Sunday dinner and won't want him under her feet. Why don't you go?"

"I think perhaps I will," he replied. "You didn't expect that, did you?"

"Well, you've never bothered much when you've been down before."

"To everything there is a season and a time for every purpose under heaven—or didn't your expensive education include a bowing acquaintance with the Bible?"

"Oh yes, that was one of my favorites. A time to be born and a time to die . . . a time to weep and a time to laugh, a time to mourn and a time to dance . . . a time to love and a time to hate . . . practically everything's catered for, isn't it?'' she said, delighted, if surprised by this fresh twist in his personality.

Although his eyes softened as they momentarily dwelt on her eager face, his voice held a hint of asperity when he countered swiftly, ''A time to keep silence, and a time to speak . . . you've forgotten that one, possibly the wisest of them all. Well now, it's certainly time for me to get cracking if I don't want to be late for church, so I'll leave you to your nursery duties.''

Up in the nursery, Timmy was contrary and inclined to be fretful, alternating between affectionate demonstrations that became a trifle exhausting and sudden withdrawals into silence that were equally difficult to treat with patience. Nothing she suggested for his amusement seemed to please him. Robert, returning from church with an hour before lunch to devote to his godson, fared no better. In the end his patience gave out.

''Very well,'' he said firmly but kindly, ''since you prefer being rude and naughty to behaving nicely, you can have your lunch up here, instead of with us. Elspeth will bring up a tray.''

''But it's *Sunday*!'' Timmy protested, too astonished to resort to more usual methods for the moment.

''I know it's Sunday, but you should have thought of that before, shouldn't you? Come along, Victoria, we'll leave this naughty, little boy to his own company. Perhaps we'll find him in a better mood after lunch,'' Robert said, extending a helping hand to Victoria, who was on her knees picking up tiddlywink counters from the floor where they had been thrown in a temper.

''Well, perhaps if he says he's sorry, we'll let him come down after all,'' she said, aware that the boy, jealous and provoked, was quite quick enough to imagine he wasn't wanted.

"Certainly, if he's really sorry. Are you, Timmy?" Robert asked pleasantly. "Your mother won't be pleased, you know, if I have to tell her you've behaved badly while she's away."

Timmy, it was plain, had been wavering, but the mention of his mother brought his grievances to a head. He shouted. "*No!* I hate you! I want my mommy!" stamping his feet and bursting into angry tears.

"Oh dear!" Victoria exclaimed, wondering how best to quell the noise and offer comfort at the same time. Robert said, "Leave him," in no uncertain tones and taking her by the shoulders pushed her firmly out of the room.

Down in the parlor Robert poured out drinks and Victoria, accepting hers with the comment that she had earned it, relaxed in a big armchair feeling tired and discouraged.

"Have I slipped up somewhere, do you suppose?" she asked him a little anxiously. "I've never known Timmy to be so unreasonable before. I generally manage him so easily."

"Don't upset youself. The boy's merely suffering from his first introduction to the green-eyed monster. It's time he learned he's not the only pebble on the beach, anyway," Robert said. "Kate, with the best of intentions, keeps him too much apart from other children. You and she teach him his letters, I know, but there's no earthly reason why he shouldn't be attending some kindergarten school like others of his age."

"I understood John was against it. Kate sets great store by his judgment."

"The gallant doctor obliged with the desired medical opinion to establish his own standing, but he won't subscribe to sentiment much longer, from what I gather. Though we've little enough in common I have a great respect for Squires's professional integrity.''

"Well, that's something of an admission,'' she retorted, eyeing him with faint disfavor. "Why, in that case, do you go out of your way to bait him?''

"For the same reason, probably, that you go out of your way to be upsides with me,'' he replied promptly. "Something in the worthy doctor brings out the worst in me.''

She was silent, digesting the implication, then she said, sounding a little surprised, "But I don't any longer, or haven't you noticed?''

"Oh yes, I've noticed, my naïve little charmer, but then I've been exerting myself in no mean measure to that end, or hadn't *you* noticed?''

"That's a silly question, considering you must know the answer, but Robert—'' she stopped, leaving the sentence unfinished with an unspoken question in the way she pronounced his name. His eyebrows lifted quizzically.

"But Robert what?'' he asked, mocking her gently, and she looked away.

"Nothing, only—I wouldn't care to be just an experiment to bolster up your masculine ego,'' she said, and quite suddenly he became angry.

"How dare you credit me with such shallow motives out of your prejudice and colossal ignorance!'' he exclaimed in his courtroom accents. "Do you imagine I'd waste my time trying to make a conquest of one stubborn little girl when there are those less averse to being charmed?''

She was a little shaken by such an unexpected reaction, but not prepared to capitulate without a struggle.

"I may have been prejudiced, but I'm not so ignorant as to be unacquainted with the rules of human behavior,'' she told him calmly. "I can imagine that if conquests, as you call them, have come easily, the one stubborn exception could present a challenge."

For a moment he looked as if he would like to shake her, then the hard lines about his mouth slackened, and he laughed.

"Well, I'll give you this, Victoria Mary," he said, "for all your uncomplimentary opinions of my methods in court you need never number yourself among the browbeaten witnesses! I'd back you to stand up to the toughest cross-examination."

"But I didn't, did I?" she said, forgetting the present in being reminded of the ignominious past. "They told me afterward my evidence had lost the case."

"Who told you?"

"I forget. My father's lawyer, probably."

"Then forget that too. The case was lost before you ever went into the box, and your evidence, even had you been better briefed, could have made no difference. It was just a last throw for leniency on the part of the defense, gambling on old Seldon's distaste for children being forced to give evidence, and it didn't come off. Had I been able to see you afterward I could at least have relieved your mind on that score."

"I wish you had. I wish I'd known that you tried."

"Would it have made any difference to those uncharitable thoughts you've harbored ever since?"

"Yes, I think it would. There was nobody, you see, who seemed to care until Mr. Brown stepped in. Even he wasn't much use as a comfort, as I never met him."

"Yes, well . . . possibly he was afraid of involving you in some emotional entanglement out of a sense of obligation that you might later regret," Robert said absently, and she looked at him in surprise.

"Do you know, Robert, that's the first time I've ever

heard you refer to Mr. Brown as if he was human with possible problems of his own," she said. He sent her a quick, wary look as though she had caught him out in an unintentional slip.

"Well, if one accepts the fact that your patron is unlikely to be the equivalent of a computer, one must, I suppose, allow him a modicum of natural feelings—but enough of Mr. Brown. Having exchanged a few home truths on the matter of my dubious attentions I insist upon spending the rest of the day in amicable harmony and the hope of furthering my private aims, despite your doubts," he said. He reverted firmly to his more usual manner and held out a hand for her empty glass.

She thought it wiser not to pursue the ambiguous subject of his private aims by asking awkward questions, but she hoped very much for a return of yesterday's felicity and knew in her heart that she no longer had any wish to withstand his persuasions.

There were few opportunities, however, for recapturing the mood of yesterday. Rain persisted steadily through the afternoon, putting paid to Robert's original plan for a trip to the coast and a swim.

Robert had lit a small fire in the parlor to offset the gloom of the afternoon, although it was warm enough. Victoria was grateful for the cosiness and an illusion of continued intimacy, but she could not quite recapture the magic of yesterday that had ended so fittingly with moonlight and the miracle of a shooting star. Robert, too, seemed in no hurry to renew his attentions or, perhaps, he was too wise to try to recall a mood that was already in the past. Although he still contrived to coax responses from her with a skill she was as yet too inexperienced to appreciate, he made no move to kiss her, or even to touch her.

Kate, expected back that evening, had been vague about

her train and said she would take a taxi up from the station. Victoria, as time went on, found she had an ear alert for the sounds of arrival distracting her attention from Robert. When Elspeth brought in the tea, delivering Timmy at the same time, she was grateful for the chance to revert to her more customary place in the household before Kate returned.

Robert watched her with amusement, admiring the determination with which she sought to ignore the subtle implications of the past two days; knowing with increasing tenderness that however in the future she might regret her weakness in accepting his overtures, she would never again be able to whip up that old animosity with quite such uncaring ease.

When tea was finished he obligingly joined in the games Victoria devised for Timmy, sitting on the floor and devoting his attention entirely to his godson. Although the boy received his efforts with satisfaction, his response was a little wary. To him the weekend had not only been a bitter disappointment, but filled with uneasy doubts. The godfather so long admired and taken for granted had in his mother's absence seemed different and like a stranger in a grown-up sort of way. Even his dear Toria had become grown-up too and had secrets with his Uncle Rab and not with him. He wished that Uncle John was his godfather, for, though not so entertaining as Uncle Rab, he never laughed at you or made funny jokes you couldn't understand. He was always exactly the same. He was thinking all these things as they played Snakes and Ladders, a game he had been newly introduced to and hadn't quite got the hang of. Robert chose that moment to point out that he had cheated.

"What's cheated?" he demanded, sounding immediately truculent, for he knew very well it was something bad, even if he didn't grasp the implication. Robert explained patiently, giving demonstrations with the counters, making a joke about the snakes that you must always come down because they were slippery, so that it was cheating to try to go up them.

Timmy listened unsmilingly, then firmly announced that if he wanted to go up a snake he would, so there!

"In that case nobody would play with you, so you'd have to play by yourself," his godfather retorted good-naturedly, and the boy's face began to grow scarlet. Victoria, knowing the signs tried hastily to find excuses for him, but she was too late.

"Don't care, don't care! Who wants to play with silly old snakes, anyway? *You're* a snake, Uncle Rab—a big, ugly, slippery snake, and I hate you!" he shouted, snatching up the board with its remaining counters and hurling them at Robert.

"Now this is where you learn your lesson, young man," Robert exclaimed, getting to his feet and picking up the child in one swift movement. He sat down in the nearest chair with the boy across his knee. Timmy let out such a roar that Victoria clapped her hands to her ears. He was making so much noise that none of them heard a car draw up outside. His screams must have sounded alarming to Kate, for she did not wait to pay off the taxi but ran into the house and flung open the door of the parlor just as Robert brought his hand down on the child's wriggling bottom.

"For heaven's sake! What's going on?" she demanded breathlessly. At the sound of her voice, Timmy twisted out of his godfather's grasp and flung himself upon her, his bellows changing to gulping sobs.

"Oh dear, oh dear! What a moment to pick for a welcomed return to the bosom of your family," Robert observed, getting to his feet. "I'm afraid you've caught me in the act of administering a long-delayed spanking to your son and heir."

If Kate heard him she was too concerned with soothing her child to pay very much heed. She was on her knees, with her arms tight around him, trying to elucidate the flood of grievances that poured from him. Her eyes, meeting Victoria's, were reproachful.

"What have you been doing to him?" she demanded. "He's feverish and probably has a chill."

"The feverish appearance is due to temper, not a chill, dear Kate," Robert interposed, with that suggestion of amused tolerance for human unreason that he could assume so devastatingly at times. Kate looked at him angrily.

"Then you've probably upset him. If I'd known you were thinking of coming down for the day I'd have come back in the morning, and none of this would have happened," she replied with a sweeping disregard for cause and effect. Robert grinned.

"Well, I suppose it's possible you might have averted trouble, but it would have been a shame to cut your holiday short before you'd even got started. I came down on Friday," he said quite gently. She disengaged Timmy's clinging hands and rose slowly to her feet.

"You mean you've spent the weekend here?" she said, her voice sounding tight and unfamiliar.

"Yes, do you mind? I wasn't to know, of course, that you wouldn't be here, but Victoria kindly made me welcome."

"I'm sure she did. It's even possible she made the suggestion herself. She's been concerned at your absence for some little time," Kate snapped.

"Has she indeed?" said Robert with interest, but made

no attempt to corroborate or otherwise. Victoria, convinced now that Kate's feelings for her cousin went only too plainly deeper than friendship, experienced an unreasoning sense of guilt as if she had, indeed, been responsible for engineering the visit. This was no time, however, for denials, with Robert standing there, quite undisturbed, and clearly enjoying the situation.

"I'm sorry you should think that, Kate," she said in a cool little voice. "I had no more idea than you of Robert's intentions, but since he looks on this as his home and seldom does give notice of his arrival, it never occurred to me to refuse him a bed."

She was aware that Robert's eyes were resting on his cousin with an enigmatical expression. Kate colored faintly as if conscious that in the heat of the moment brought about by matronly concern she had spoken without her usual logical calm. She smiled a little ruefully at Victoria.

"Of course it didn't," she said. "I'm afraid I spoke without thinking. All the same, Robert should have known better."

"What! Waken up the inn at that hour of night to take me in in case the neighbors talked?" Robert exclaimed. Victoria felt greatly relieved when Elspeth, appearing in the doorway to welcome Kate back, arrived im time to catch his remark and said in her nursery voice, and with a significant broadening of accent, "You'll surely no' be fashin' yoursel' with gossiping tongues after all this time, Mrs. Allen. There's many a weekend Mr. Rab visited here, with only mysel' to presairve the proprieties. No talk ever came out of that, to my sairtain knowledge."

"That was different. I'm a widow with a child and old enough to ignore the conventions," Kate replied, but she sounded as if she knew it to be a weak defense. Elspeth sniffed.

"Widows are no less immune from gossip as far as I know, and you're no' so old that a man wouldna look at you twice," she retorted tartly, "but let me take this laddie off to his bed now he's stopped his bawling. You sit down and rest yourself until he's ready to be tucked up. Run along, Timmy, your mammy's back safe and sound and she'll be up in a wee while to read you a story."

Robert, taking the hint, was already filling glasses for the evening aperitif, and Timmy allowed himself to be led away without protest. Victoria, anxious not only to fulfil her duties, but to leave the two cousins to settle their differences without being hampered by her presence, ran up the little corner staircase as a short cut to the nursery. She hoped that Kate's homecoming hadn't been spoiled by such an explosive reception.

"That's better," Robert said as Kate took off her hat, tossing it carelessly onto the floor, and relaxed in a deep chair with her drink. "I can appreciate that arriving at such an unpropitious moment you were naturally thrown off balance, but you were acting a little out of character, don't you think?"

"No, I don't. I'll admit that in the heat of the moment I probably said more than was wise, but I'm concerned for that child's reputation so long as I'm responsible for her. You should have had more sense than to invite trouble with the authorities."

"What authorities? I'm not aware that one requires a license for weekend visiting."

"Oh, don't be so deliberately aggravating! You know very well I was alluding to the lawyers and their charges upon my responsibility. What do you suppose their reaction will be when news of this innocent weekend reaches them?"

"Not so obvious as yours, one must hope. In any case there's no reason to suppose your absence from home would be unduly noticed."

"I daresay not, since the girl isn't without tact and a sense of discretion—still, I can hardly tell her not to mention it when she writes without giving her ideas she's better without."

"Then you will have to keep your fingers crossed and rely on that sense of discretion, won't you?" he replied, sounding, she thought, reprehensibly unconcerned.

"You don't seem to realize how tricky this situation could be," she said sharply. "It's not a question of morality, or even of outdated conventions, but the peculiar conditions laid down by Mr. Brown. Any minute Victoria could be removed from my care with no reasons given. Old Mr. Chapple made it very plain at the time that a concession had been made in the matter of temporary employment only so long as I complied with certain provisos. It puts me in a very awkward position."

"Not so awkward as that of poor Victoria Mary should your forebodings come to pass," he retorted with unseemly levity, and she glanced up at him, frowning.

"Oh, you're in one of your tiresome moods!" she exclaimed crossly. "I've no doubt the whole thing strikes you as a trivial storm in a teacup, which it well may be. At least you might consider Victoria's point of view. She's happy here with a pleasant illusion of home and wouldn't take at all kindly to being uprooted again for lack of a little forethought."

"All of which is unlikely to occur for such far-fetched reasons, but even if it did—" he said, and stopped.

"Yes? Even if it did?"

"It would scarcely be the end of the road for Victoria, only for Mr. Brown," he concluded softly, and she glanced at him suspiciously.

"What do you mean by that ambiguous remark?" she asked and went on without waiting for an answer, "Incidentally, I've a bone to pick with you—quite a large bone in view of this surprise visit."

"What have I done now to flaunt the conventions, or is it merely a matter of personal annoyance?"

"Nothing personal as far as I'm concerned, but I happened to run into Irene in London, looking very glamorous and expensive, bursting with well-bred curiosity about your latest conquest."

"What on earth are you talking about?"

"Only that she apparently happened to meet you one day coming out of Flora's where you used to spend such a fortune on flowers for her and had the inquisitiveness to go inside and make inquiries. They were most discreet, of course, and mentioned no names, but the address you had written out was still lying on the counter. Since it was only too familiar to Irene, it set her thinking."

"And her thoughts presumably fixed on you."

"Oh no. Irene may have been piqued by our long friendship, but she never considered me worth a jealous pang—besides, the name of the mysterious recipient of five dozen highly priced roses was plainly written above the address and, being a new one to Irene, set her agog with speculation."

"Very likely, since women are never content to relinquish old claims, but it's scarcely a matter of much moment, is it?"

"Perhaps you've forgotten," Kate said deliberately after a glance at his face, "that Victoria received five dozen roses from Mr. Brown on her birthday, but only a card from you.''

"Well, what of it?" Robert retorted and turned to replenish his glass, so that she had no means of reading anything from his expression.

"What of it? Well, surely there must be an explanation, unless you were just amusing yourself at her expense, which wouldn't have been very nice. What *are* you up to, Rob? Flowers purporting to come from a stranger you've always ridiculed, and now picking the one weekend to appear yourself, when I'm conveniently out of the way.''

"That was just the luck of the draw—I'd really no idea you were in London," he answered casually. "As for the flowers, it seemed a pity not to give Mr. Brown's image a boost by crediting him with something warmer than the dictates of cold charity.''

All at once Kate was angry. She knew from past experience that she would learn nothing from Robert by calling him to account, but she had a sudden clear picture of the soft radiance lighting up Victoria's face as she looked down at the roses in her arms and said wonderingly, "They've crowned my whole day . . . '' and suddenly itched to pick a quarrel with him. "Cold charity is at least more honest than an attempt to bamboozle an unsuspecting innocent for one's private amusement," she snapped at him. "You must have a peculiar sense of humor, Robert, if playing tricks of this sort affords you entertainment.''

"I think," he replied with the sudden, icy politeness of a stranger, "we won't pursue this subject any further. I have nothing to say that would satisfy you at this juncture, neither am I prepared to justify my actions. However, I would strongly advise you to keep your knowledge to yourself unless you're out to make trouble.''

"I wouldn't dream of reducing that bright bubble of happiness to the ugly reality of an ill-timed jest for my own satisfaction, but watch your step, my dear. It isn't wise to tread on dreams lightly, and the young have a right to theirs however foolish they may seem to others," Kate said, and jumped, spilling her drink on her smart, new suit as Victoria's voice said from the bottom of the staircase:

"Thank you, Kate, but I'd rather know. It's much more humiliating to be bolstered up with fairy tales to save one's pride than to face the fact that one has been made a fool of."

There was an instant of shocked silence. Kate dabbed ineffectually at the stain on her skirt while she sought vainly for the right words: Robert, standing by the fireplace, put his half-empty glass down on the mantelshelf, creating a staccato sharpness of sound, but otherwise did not move. Victoria remained where she was at the foot of the stairs. Her face was white; its planes and angles sharply accentuated giving her a curiously fragile look, but she held herself very erect with an odd kind of stillness that was strangely moving.

"How much have you heard?" Kate asked at last realizing the futility of trying to cover up with soothing improvisations.

"Oh, everything, I think," Victoria answered still in those cool, unhurried tones. "I listened, you know. I listened quite deliberately. I was coming down to tell you Timmy was ready to be tucked in, and I heard you reproving Robert for coming down this weekend. I thought he might say something that would give me a clue to—to certain things I wanted to know. Then you sidetracked him with your discovery about the roses, so I just sat at the top of the stairs till you had both finished. As you said yourself, Kate, it wasn't a very nice trick to play, knowing how much I've always hoped for some sign of interest from Mr. Brown, but I suppose I was fair game. Robert, I realize now, is fond of playing tricks to pass the time, but I won't be had again. Will you go up to Timmy? He's looking forward to his bedtime story."

Robert still said nothing, and Kate rose slowly to her feet, uncertain whether it was best to leave them alone, or try to minimize the consequences of a crisis she had unwittingly brought about.

"Victoria . . . " she began hesitantly as she crossed the room " . . . it's no use saying I'm sorry you overheard our conversation, but you mustn't think you were being made a fool of. I'm sure there's a perfectly good explanation for Robert's odd behavior, so don't. . . . " She trailed off rather lamely, and Victoria prompted politely, "Don't what?"

"Nothing. There's nothing I can possibly advise in the circumstances. I'll be in the nursery if you want me, but I won't come down till I'm called," Kate replied, adding over her shoulder as she passed Victoria at the foot of the stairs, "And you'd better make your excuses good, Robert, if you want to keep your newly won advantage."

Robert stooped with leisurely deliberation to throw another log on the fire.

"Well . . . " he said at last as Victoria did not move, " . . . hadn't you better come and sit down? There's no point in us shouting abuse at one another across the width of the room."

"I haven't been shouting, and I see no reason why you should need the support of abuse," she replied with that strange, unnatural composure. He frowned, impatient of his careless phrasing.

"Quite right. I was presuming, I'm afraid, on experience of other occasions when sparring matches between us took on a flavor of high school retaliation," he said. He deliberately used the teasing intonation that used to rile her in the past, hoping to goad her into an outburst that would relieve her feelings.

"Yes, well . . . " she said a little absently as if the past no longer greatly mattered, "I daresay I was easy prey, not being at all experienced in the art of repartee, but you hadn't much in the way of opposition to sharpen your wits on, had you?"

"You think not? Well, Victoria Mary, it may please you to know that I found your repartee exhilarating and by no means adolescent, if that's what you were implying," he answered, still with that light raillery. She looked at him with grave consideration, then said bleakly:

"It doesn't please me at all. It only points out an obvious truth that I was a convenient butt to provide entertainment for your idle moments."

His manner underwent a subtle change, and when next he spoke it was with the measured coolness he employed in court. His face became the cold, clever mask she had first known and disliked.

"If that's what you think you can hardly absolve yourself entirely," he retorted. "You would have been willing enough, I fancy, to come to terms with me had I pressed my advantage this weekend, despite these unflattering opinions. On second thought, perhaps I was too forbearing and merely disappointed you."

He regretted his words as soon as he saw the color flooding her cheeks. Her slender body seemed to shrink from an unexpected blow, but at least, he reflected wryly, he had succeeded in breaking through that alarming composure.

"That of course is what I should have expected from

you," she countered swiftly, and there was already a hint of tears in her voice. "All right, then! I'm too honest, or too silly to deny that I was willing to be made love to because I thought. . . . Well, it doesn't matter now what I thought, but you at least might have had the decency to leave me my illusions . . . to pretend, even though it was only make-believe, that you had found me p-pleasing."

She was crying now, quite unaware of it. He gave a sharp exclamation and crossed the room in two strides to take her by the shoulders.

"You foolish, pig-headed little idiot! What do you suppose I was doing if I didn't find you pleasing?" he exclaimed, shaking her quite hard. "I may have made a mess of the whole damned business, but I wasn't scheming to seduce you, whatever you may think now."

"I don't know what to think," she said on a note of distraction and stood very still, weeping on his shoulder for a snatched moment of comfort, then tried to pull away from him.

"No, you don't," he said, tightening his grip. "Not until we get this nonsense sorted out. Will you listen, now, while I plead my case?"

She nodded.

"You'll remember we talked of a time that would be ripe for disenchantment," he began, leading her to the fire and putting her gently into a chair. "I don't think that time is quite yet, but I'll have to take a chance on being premature and crave your indulgence."

She had stopped crying and was listening to him politely, but without much comprehension. He realized he had made an error in trying to pave the way by wrapping his intentions in a semblance of make-believe when she said in a tired voice, "You don't have to go on pandering to my adolescent dream-world. I'm quite capable of distinguishing between fantasy and reality, even though I still sometimes like to make images.''

"I'm sure you are. Very well, I won't waste time any longer trying for the delicate approach. Will you marry me, Victoria Mary Hayes, and try to overcome that aversion for browbeating lawyers?''

He had in sheer self-defense dropped back into flippancy to cloak a proposal that might come as something of a shock. He was unprepared for the naked pain that suddenly darkened her eyes, or the swift dismay with which she sprang to her feet.

"That was quite unnecessary, Robert,'' she said, and her voice was now completely steady and devoid of tears. "Whatever the unlucky results of this weekend, there's no occasion to make things worse with gentlemanly offers of rectitude.''

"Good God!'' he exclaimed, uncertain at that moment whether to laugh or be angry. "Where on earth do you get such phrases from? I can assure you that gentlemanly offers of rectitude wouldn't in my opinion be any sort of foundation for a successful marriage, or even as the price of seduction. Don't go weaving more fantasies to confuse the issue.''

"I'm sorry you should think so poorly of my efforts to be practical. I was merely trying to relieve you of a misplaced sense of duty, and there's nothing particularly fanciful in that,'' she said. He regarded her in thoughtful silence for a moment, cursing the impulse that had led him to speak against his better judgment, and wondering how best to deal with an intelligence temporarily closed to reason.

"You have a most curious trick of relapsing into slightly pompous pedantry on certain occasions,'' he observed, hoping to give her time to readjust her ideas. She looked at him as if he had been guilty of some trivial irrelevance and replied without humor:

"Then I must have caught the trick from you. After all, I haven't had much chance since coming to Farthings of associating with men of my own age and habits of speech, have I?"

"All right, you've made your point," Robert said, and the bite was back in his voice. "I realize that it could be said that I've taken advantage of your unique situation, but there's no need to throw it in my face. It seems I've misjudged both the moment and your own misleading behavior, so we'll shelve your answer until a more propitious time."

"My answer?"

"Perhaps you've already forgotten that little item, or wasn't it important? Never mind, the time wasn't ripe, so we'll let that pass, but there's one thing I *would* like to know. Was I only deceiving myself by imagining a change of heart in you?" His voice softened as he asked the question; the ghost of that tender smile touching his lips. For a moment Victoria wavered. It would be so easy to abandon resistance, shut one's eyes both to disillusioning reality and to the pricklings of conscience. Because her conscience had never been entirely easy in regard to Kate, she could only answer him indirectly by blurting out as she had once before, "And what of Kate?"

"Kate?" He frowned impatiently. "Oh yes, Kate. . . . It was a pity you had to find out about those roses. If you hadn't succumbed to temptation and eavesdropped on our conversation, you'd have been none the wiser, so don't blame poor Kate for giving the show away."

She, in turn, supposed him to have purposely side-tracked her, but the casual mention of that most bitter hurt to her pride successfully silenced any qualms of conscience in regard to Kate.

"Why?" she asked. "Why did you have to play such a pointless, practical joke on me? To make fun of me by letting me believe in something that wasn't true was not only stupid but heartless."

"Stupid, possibly, but not intentionally heartless," he replied, but there was little of warmth in his voice now; only a cool note of tolerance as if he was humoring an unreasonable child. Like a child, she stamped her foot at him.

"That's no excuse and no answer either," she flashed out. "If I could understand what prompted you—but I can't."

"Can't you? Well no, how could you? Let's say, then, that it seemed a pity not to endow unimaginative Mr. Brown with a little fictional awareness of his more tender obligations in view of past omissions. You must admit, Victoria Mary, that true or false, the result was fully justified."

"Don't go on addressing me in that silly manner as if my names as well as my greenness amused you," she snapped back, sounding, at last, more like her usual self. "Nothing's justified as it's turned out, unless you count your success in making a fool of me. For that I can't forgive you."

"No, I suppose not," he said, sounding suddenly tired and not very interested. "Well, I'll just have to make the best of it, won't I?"

"Is that all you care?" she asked, but if he caught the tentative plea for assurance in her voice he ignored it.

"You're not, I fancy, in the right mood to assess degrees of emotion, so the answer had better be yes. I care to the extent of not wishing to hurt you unnecessarily, but I'm too old and seasoned not to have learned acceptance. You might with good effect apply a little of the same philosophy to your own situation when you've recovered from your disappointment regarding Mr. Brown. There are worse things in life than the loss of one's youthful illusions."

"None of which explains anything," she protested, striving to capture a shred of dignity. "It's very easy to wrap things up in a lot of high-sounding nonsense that doesn't mean a thing, but you owe me more than that, Robert. So far, you've offered me nothing definite to come to terms with."

"I've offered you marriage, but perhaps you don't consider that definite enough," he replied quite gently.

"But that," she countered quickly before her resistance could be further weakened, "was probably a hoax. It was all a hoax, wasn't it? The roses, the surprise weekend, even the moonlight and the shooting star—everything laid on to lend enchantment where none existed."

He made a small involuntary movement toward her, then thrust his hands in his pants pockets and leaned back against the mantelshelf.

"You must, of course, draw your own conclusions about that," he said with cool deliberation. "I'm not prepared to make palatable concessions as a sop to hurt feelings. You must take me as you find me, my dear, or not at all."

"Then," she replied with a studied politeness that she hoped would match his own coolness, "it will have to be not at all, if you really need an answer. I must apologize, Robert, for being so dumb that I mistook fantasy for fact, but it won't occur again. I'll go up and tell Kate she can come down now. It must be nearly supper time."

She turned as she finished speaking and crossed the

room to escape up the staircase that had provided such disastrous facilities for eavesdropping. Robert watched her go, but made no attempt to call her back. When, a few minutes later, Kate came down, he was already collecting his personal possessions that lay scattered about the room and paused only to say, 'I'll pour you a drink in a moment, Kate, then I'll go upstairs and pack.''

"But you don't need to do that yet," she said, switching on lights and drawing curtains to shut out the depressing view of the lingering daylight. "You never do leave till late on Sundays."

"There are Sundays and Sundays, and I won't stay for your cold collation if you don't mind," he replied. She glanced quickly at his face, then as quickly away.

"Oh dear! Didn't you straighten things out?" she said and sounded faintly exasperated. She had not expected to return to her home to find complications leading to strained relationships and no one very interested in how she herself had spent the weekend.

"Quite the opposite. Confusion was only piled upon confusion," he replied, pouring her a drink. His voice held such a touch of bitterness that her eyes became thoughtful.

"Well," she said, "leaving aside the question of whether or not your visit was wise, I'll confess I find your prank with the roses a little hard to take. How did you explain that away to Victoria?"

"I didn't, neither am I going to explain it to you. You will just have to write it off as an eccentricity and blame that peculiar sense of humor that you accused me of earlier."

"And is that all the satisfaction you afforded Victoria? I wonder she didn't up and dot you one!"

He smiled then, but his eyes were a little sad as he handed her the drink he had poured for her.

"It would possibly have saved a lot of heartaches if she had," he replied, "but Miss Victoria Mary Hayes showed a remarkable restraint for the most part. I—well, I probably took up the wrong attitude and discovered it too late to start afresh."

"Are you serious, Rob?" she asked him curiously, not very sure what answer she wanted him to make. He raised one eyebrow with that trick he had when he chose to be uncommunicative.

"I'm perfectly serious in regretting my own shortcomings," he replied, "and will you now, please, revert to your usual tactful self and forbear to plague me with awkward questions?"

"No, I will not," she retorted with spirit. "I'm very fond of you, Rob, and grateful for all that you do to make life pleasant for Timmy and me. I have a responsibility to the girls I employ, and Victoria in particular with all those tiresome provisos I've had to comply with. She's not, thank heavens, a silly young miss with her head full of romantic nonsense, but she's had little chance to be courted and admired in the usual way. You, after all, are a very attractive man when you set out to charm. I wouldn't like to think you've embarked on making a conquest just for the sake of amusement. There! Tell me to mind my own business if you like, but don't be surprised if I claim the rights of an old friend, to say nothing of a relation."

"A very distant one—just sufficiently connected to make our association respectable," he said with a grin. "Are you by any chance asking my intentions, sweet Kate?"

"Yes, I think I am. I think I hope that you are serious, for it's high time you settled down with someone who could make you happy. You've waited too long as a result of overdone caution. Irene was simply typical of her own set and upbringing, and the only mistake you made was in thinking you could change her. But you're older now, and possibly not so exacting in your demands for perfection. Whether Victoria is old enough or experienced enough to satisfy you, I wouldn't know. The pernickety Mr. Brown has certainly seen to it that there's been small chance of her developing a taste for riotous living, so at least you'd be spared a repetition of the Irene fiasco. There—I've said my piece, and if you don't like it you'll just have to lump it!''

"Well, that was quite a speech, Cousin Kate," he said, sounding amused and slightly surprised. "I must say I admire the temerity with which you stick to your guns, and I'll reward it this much to relieve your doubts. I asked Victoria to marry me just now, so you can put your mind at rest concerning my intentions. Unfortunately she didn't take the same view, dismissing my proposal either as a gentlemanly offer to offset gossip, or a hoax on the same lines as that unfortunate affair of the roses.''

"So she turned you down. Well, I can't say I'm surprised, all things considered. Why on earth, if you were building up to a romantic scene, didn't you send your wretched floral offering from yourself instead of foisting it onto Mr. Brown, who for all we know, is still trying to work out how the mistake occurred?"

"Now that, as they say, is another story, and not one that I'm prepared to embark upon. You will, I hope, Kate, be discreet if Victoria sees fit to confide in you—no well-intentioned persuasions on my behalf, please. This is something she will have to work out for herself. Now, I really must get my things together and be off before the poor child appears for supper; bracing herself to sit through an embarrassing meal as if nothing had happened.''

"Rob . . . " Kate said, catching at his sleeve when he kissed her quickly in passing, " . . . won't you-
. . . wouldn't you like to . . . ? I can tell Elspeth to put supper back and retire upstairs to my room.''

"No, I wouldn't like, dear Kate. The moment isn't propitious for the recapturing of magic. Poor Victoria's dream world has taken a hard knock. I won't come down here again unless you send for me, so I'll say goodby now and slip away when the coast is clear,'' he said and left her, instinctively avoiding the habitual short cut to the bedrooms provided by the corner staircase.

CHAPTER EIGHT

But Victoria did no confiding. Kate, remembering that disconcerting trick of cool withdrawal, if disappointed, was unsurprised. Robert, she thought had not allowed for a maturity of mind that the years of enforced dependence had fostered early.

When they met at supper that Sunday evening, it had been Kate who appeared awkward and at a loss for conversation. Victoria might had wept in the privacy of her room, but she was composed enough at the supper table. If she ate little, she gave no other sign of being distressed, relieved no doubt by Robert's decision to absent himself. Kate found herself answering polite questions and giving dutiful accounts of her doings in London as if it were she who were required to be set at ease. Although she tried once or twice to provide an opening for reciprocal confidences, she was neatly sidetracked. No mention was made of Robert's sudden departure, or the extraordinary trick he had seen fit to play; but the next morning, Kate found the roses had been replaced with hastily picked oddments from the garden.

"What have done with them?" she asked casually, wondering whether Victoria had, on a sentimental impulse, removed them all to her own room to brood over them in solitude, but felt snubbed when she was answered equally casually:

"I threw them away. They were beginning to drop."

"Oh, what a pity!" was all Kate could find to say.

"They may have been dropping, but they weren't nearly dead."

"They were to me. I find I don't care for roses as much as I once did—they're an overrated luxury if you don't grow them yourself," Victoria said and began to talk brightly of something else.

As the days went on, a sense of unease troubled them both. It seemed to Kate that that unfortunate weekend had sparked off something that affected the whole household.

"I wish I'd never gone away that weekend. Nothing's been quite the same since," Kate confided in John Squires on one of her customary stops for a glass of sherry on her way home from the village.

"In what way?" he inquired cautiously. He had never alluded to Robert's visit during her absence. Quite apart from the fact that, like himself, she probably thought it unwise, he imagined she could well have been hurt by this show of interest in a younger woman.

"Oh, I don't know. Perhaps leaving home unsettled me. I'm not really cut out for the gay life, and I bought a lot of new clothes I could quite well do without."

"Haven't they been properly appreciated?"

"Oh yes, Victoria is most approving, and even Elspeth pays me a grudging compliment or two. It was she, as a matter of fact, who persuaded me into extravagance in the first place. Lately she's been a bit crotchety, as though she regretted departing from her native caution."

"And the attentive cousin—wasn't he impressed?"

"Robert? Well, there was scarcely time for him to notice new clothes. He went back before supper. There—well-,there had been a little disagreement with Victoria over something, and he thought it better not to stay late."

"I see. It might have been wiser if he hadn't stayed at all in the circumstances. Did you mind, Kate?"

"Not really," she answered evasively. "I did think at the time it might have caused awkwardness if it traveled to the ears of that tiresome Mr. Brown, but it was probably only due to a slight sense of guilt."

"Why on earth should you blame yourself?" he exclaimed angrily. "Farmer should have known better than to upset you with thoughtless behavior."

"Oh, I don't really—only to the extent of having Victoria removed from my employment as a result of any carelessness on my part. You've no idea how fussy those pompous lawyers are, but Robert didn't upset me for that reason."

"Oh, I see." He did not inquire for the true reason, having no wish for his suspicions to be confirmed. Kate, mistaking his reticence for censure of Robert, found herself on dangerous ground. He had not sworn her to secrecy in the matter of his rejected proposal, but she felt it was premature to discuss his prospects when so much lay unresolved.

"I don't think you do, John dear, but it wouldn't be fair to Robert to discuss his affairs at this juncture, so just forget my little burst of discontent," she said, and wished as she saw the familiar expression of patient resignation in his steady blue eyes that she could have sought his counsel and understanding for the doubts that still troubled her.

"This weather's enough to breed discontent in the hardiest of us," he replied, taking his cue and thankful for the never-failing excuse of the weather's vagaries. She smiled at him gratefully.

"Yes, it is, isn't it?" she agreed, getting up reluctantly to go. "The weekend I was in London was so hot that I thought nostalgically of the country, and now this! Timmy, incidentally, hasn't been himself lately. I think he has a bit of a chill and hasn't shaken it off. I was sure he was running a fever then, though Robert said it was only spleen."

"And Farmer was probably right," John said briskly. "We don't see eye to eye on many matters, but we do share the opinion that you fuss too much about the boy."

She was used to his plain speaking and respected his medical skill, but he had never before accused her quite so openly of maternal foolishness.

"But, John, he's all I have! I can't help being overanxious at times," she said and stood looking at him a little helplessly with hurt, brown eyes. He became suddenly too impatient of the strictures that clouded his own situation to offer the usual soothing assurances.

"It's no fault of the child's that he's all you have," he retorted bluntly. "Being a born mother, you're simply suffering from frustration. You should marry again and have other children to keep you busy and happy in the way you were meant for."

"*Well!*" she said a little blankly, and found to her surprise that she was blushing. "If anyone but you had said that to me, John, I'd—"

"You'd what?"

"I've really no idea! I think I'd better return home before you offer me any more surprising advice."

"I could offer advice that might surprise but probably wouldn't please you," he said soberly, "so I won't risk our valuable friendship by being too outspoken. Do you want me to come up and run the thermometer over Timmy to prove your anxieties groundless?"

"Yes, if you would. I'm not really so anxious as all that, but it makes a nice excuse for your company. Besides, Victoria and I need cheering up," she said. She returned to Farthings feeling suddenly gay and indifferent to the weather and pleased that she had spent more than she should on some becoming new clothes.

But if Kate contrived to ignore the discomforts of the rest of that chilly June, Victoria found the gray skies and perpetual drizzle a discouraging if fit complement to her own disturbance of mind. She became morbidly conscious of a sense of guilt. However trivial Robert's attentions had turned out to be, the fact remained that she had been ready and willing to receive them because for her he had ceased to be the enemy of old. She did not blame him now for having misled her, or for that ridiculous proposal that she supposed was his way of offering amends, but taken all together with that pointless practical joke involving Mr. Brown, the whole sorry affair was reduced to bitterness.

"The courts will be rising soon," Kate said to her one day with apparent irrelevance, adding when Victoria looked politely inquiring, but made no rejoinder, "Robert was going to spend part of the Long Vacation here, you know."

"Was he?"

"Yes, he was. He usually has until this year."

"Well, I suppose he's changed his plans. People do," Victoria replied, trying to sound rational and disinterested. To Kate's over-sensitive ears she appeared to be offering a polite snub.

"Well, you needn't be so smug about it," Kate retorted sharply. "I've no doubt a change of plans suits you, but this is Robert's home when all's said and done. It's a little hard that he should feel obliged to stay away in order not to upset a young girl I happen to employ."

"That," Victoria replied, sounding strained but still infuriatingly polite, "is surely an exaggeration. Robert, I imagine, would hardly consider the feelings of an employee if it interfered with his own convenience. Aren't you making too much out of that unlucky weekend?''

"No," said Kate, seizing her opportunity when at last it was offered with an uncharacteristic abandonment of reserve. "It's you who, I suspect, has magnified things out of all proportion. I can respect your effort to cover up hurt feelings with a show of indifference, but not this refusal to come to terms with yourself."

"Oh, I've done that," Victoria said quietly, her eyes grave and curiously wordly-wise. Kate blurted out before she could stop herself:

"Are you in love with him, Victoria?"

"I don't think you should ask me that, Kate. I may have been silly and extremely green, but my feelings are my own business and quite unimportant."

Resentment began to stir in Kate. Although she could, in her rational moments, allow that everyone was entitled to privacy, it was humiliating to be put in one's place by a chit of a girl who, unintentionally or not, was causing so much trouble.

"Very well," she said, controlling an impulse to quarrel vulgarly by taking refuge instead in the authority of an employer, "you are, of course, entitled to keep your own counsel; but if, as you state, your feelings are unimportant, I would be glad if you didn't let them interfere with your obligations here at Farthings. Elspeth tells me you spend too much time in the kitchen asking vague questions about the past that she's in no position to answer. You seem to have temporarily lost your touch with Timmy. Children's attachments can, I know, be fickle and subject to change, but it would be a pity if he turned against his godfather for want of a little tact on your part."

Victoria had listened without interruption or protest, but her face had grown whiter and more sharply angled.

She looked as she had that evening standing at the foot of the stairs saying so quietly that it was more humiliating to be bolstered up with fairy tales than to face the fact that one had been made a fool of. For a moment Kate felt ashamed of resorting to cheap criticism to relieve her feeling. Before she could add a word of retraction, Victoria said in a voice that had lost its cool confidence and sounded bewildered and very young:

"Then it would be better if I went away. I—I'm sorry Kate, if I've been the cause of—of any trouble, but Timmy will soon forget his resentment of Robert once I've gone. He was only jealous. I shall miss you, Kate, but it will be better this way."

Kate watched her with troubled eyes. She wanted to take the girl in her arms, to tell her the whole thing was a storm in a teacup and was best forgotten by both of them. Yes there was too much truth in Victoria's sad conclusions and, for her own sake, it might be wiser to make a break while there was still time to forget.

"Yes, perhaps it would," she said with a regretful sigh. "Not because I was finding fault, perhaps unfairly, but because I think it might be best for you. I shall miss you, too, very much, but it needn't be the end of friendship. You'll come back here one day for a visit."

"You said that in Switzerland when I thought Mr. Brown wouldn't agree—do you remember? Even if he won't, you said, you can at least come on a visit, and we'll pick up the threads. How long ago it all seems," Victoria said and thought as she had then that those sort of promises were usually doomed to be unfulfilled, but Kate frowned.

"Yes, I'd forgotten Mr. Brown. I'd better write and make tactful explanations; perhaps suggest some alternative plan to see you through the next few months."

"No, I'll write. A course at some commercial college would fill in the time nicely before the Trust is wound up. The lawyers, at least, would see the sense in that and point out to Mr. Brown that I could hardly be expected to earn a respectable living without some sort of training. He should, of course, have thought of that long ago."

Victoria, having delivered her little speech with matter-of-fact finality, was gone before Kate could form any suitable reply. She sat down limply in the nearest easy chair, feeling despondent and somehow at fault. She considered calling up Robert to ask advice, but she knew him too well to expect interference in a situation that involved himself. He would find his own way of resolving his difficulties when and if the time came. Whether or not Victoria had been near to loving him before being shocked into apathy by that pointless deception, it would be better to allow her time to readjust in some other environment than stay on at Farthings with perpetual reminders of a spoiled dream.

She remembered now that it had been Robert who had casually acquainted her with the girl's whereabouts and suggested the possibility of arriving at some mutual agreement. He must, she supposed with slight surprise, have kept track of the child's progress through the years, owing to his irrational sense of responsibility at the outcome of the trial.

Had Robert been merely curious to see how she had turned out, thanks to a benefactor who must have shared something of his own disquiet, or had he more definite plans that he hoped would mature given the appropriate environment and careful handling? And why, thought Kate with a fresh renewal of exasperated curiosity, when he was so nearly within reach of his goal, had he chosen to play a trick that, if discovered, could only result in wreckage? As it was, she had no doubts that the watchful Mr.

Brown would be prompt in removing his *protégée* to more suitable quarters. Since it was only too likely that Robert's name had appeared with increasing regularity in Victoria's duty letters, it would not be difficult to arrive at a reason for her sudden request to leave. Robert was too well known in legal circles to escape censure should her letters have been indiscreet, and one thing could lead to another. . . .

The lawyers' reply to the letter Victoria had written about her plans was unexpected and far from helpful. Mr. Brown, they informed Victoria, was entirely satisfied with the present arrangement and saw no reason to make any changes, providing that Mrs. Allen was still willing to offer employment. They trusted that Miss Hayes was not being so inconsiderate at this late date as to indulge in girlish fancies and remained hers faithfully.

"Girlish fancies indeed!" she exclaimed indignantly, shaking back her hair like a startled pony. Kate had been watching her across the breakfast table as she read the brief communication and gave a sympathetic smile.

"Yes, I've heard too," she said, meeting Victoria's outraged gaze with some wryness. "It looks as though we'll have to make the best of it, doesn't it?"

"You could always write and say you've fired me. Even Mr. Brown could hardly insist on my remaining here in that case," Victoria replied, and Kate sighed.

"Probably not, but since the decision was yours and not mine, the question of firing doesn't arise," she said briefly.

"But you agreed. You thought it was best in the circumstances. You could say with perfect truth that you found me unsatisfactory."

"I could, but I haven't. I thought it best only for your

own sake. As you evidently didn't see fit to explain your reasons for wanting to leave, you can't blame your Mr. Brown for not taking you seriously."

"It should have been sufficient that the arrangement didn't suit me. I'm not a child any longer to be dismissed as inconsequent and tiresome. Surely they must realize that I've rights that weren't in existence when the Trust was drawn up. If you can marry at 18 without the consent of parents, and vote and be allowed to buy on credit, there's no power that can stop you ordering your own life at 20."

"No, there isn't," Kate admitted. "Still, I suppose one can't entirely rule out one's obligations. Your Mr. Brown may be a crank and a bit of a despot, but he's entitled to expect some return for his generosity. Well, it looks as if you'll have to submit with a good grace to remaining here for a time. I can't in all honesty fire you to force a different decision. I don't suppose Mr. Brown or the lawyers would know what on earth to do with you if I did."

"No, I suppose they wouldn't. Oh well, I'm sorry if you're stuck with me after all. Perhaps I should have made my reasons plainer," Victoria said, sounding flippant, but looking as if she wanted to cry. Kate's eyes grew soft. So the child hadn't played her strongest card and alleged unwelcome masculine attentions.

"Perhaps you should—" she said gently, "—if, that is, you think you were being taken advantage of."

Victoria lowered her lashes, but did not quite succeed in hiding the brightness of tears.

"I try not to think at all," she replied, keeping her voice quite steady. "I was green, gullible, and took too much for granted, I expect. If it hadn't been for that practical joke I might even have taken Robert seriously, so perhaps it's all worked out for the best."

"But, Victoria—"

"Don't try to explain things away with feeble excuses out of loyalty, Kate. I can guess that your own feelings were no less sore than mine, but I'm out of your way now—if I ever was in it."

"What on earth are you talking about? Is it possible that—"

"Can I speak to you a moment, Mrs. Allen?" said Elspeth's voice from the doorway. "If Miss Toria is leaving us shortly, you'd do well to be thinking of a replacement. I'm no' so young that I can take over Timmy for more than a wee while, so you'd best get out an advertisement for the local paper. A daily girl might suit us better than someone living in." She spoke as if Victoria were not present, and Kate frowned. The implied rebuke was no less annoying than the untimely interruption.

"Miss Toria isn't leaving us, after all, so there's no need for you to fuss," she said a little shortly. "You should know, in any case, that I'd not expect you to add Timmy to your other commitments."

"Verra guid," said Elspeth primly, pulling down the corners of her mouth and registering her displeasure by reverting to the well-trained servant whose opinions were neither asked for nor heeded. As she turned to leave the room, however, she added with the habit of long privilege, "You'll no' throw dust in my eyes, missus, by reminding me of my poseetion. There's a deal of nonsense goes on in this hoose that a mite of common sense would clear up without setting us all at odds."

"Oh dear!" said Kate as the door closed behind her. "Now I've offended her. What were we saying, Victoria? I've an idea we were interrupted at a crucial moment."

"Nothing of any importance," Victoria answered. "I'd become tangled up with a lot of foolish thoughts as a result of Mr. Brown's refusal to play ball. If you really want me to stay, Kate, that's all that matters. Let's forget the whole thing."

"Very well," Kate replied a shade stiffly, conscious of being gently put in her place. She did not find as the days went on that it was easy to dismiss the matter so lightly. She was troubled not only by the girl's air of withdrawal, but the slight sense of strain that seemed to have crept into their pleasant relationship.

"It's a ridiculous situation," she complained to John Squires on one of his hurried visits. "I've no desire to get rid of Victoria, but I think she's beginning to feel she's here on sufferance thanks to the uncooperativeness of this tiresome Mr. Brown. Timmy seems to have forgotten his temporary resentment. That is something to be thankful for, I suppose, but Elspeth's particularly crotchety these days, and Robert keeps away."

"And that, of course, is the reason for your disquiet, my dear," John said with some dryness. She looked at him in surprise.

"Are you implying that I'm jealous?"

"Well, aren't you? I have no means of knowing what, if any, understanding lies between you and Farmer, but you've regarded him as your special property for so long that it's only natural to be a little piqued."

"You have no earthly right to take me to task—to suggest motives that you can't possibly be sure of. You'll be accusing me next of being Robert's mistress and resenting the attractions of a young woman!" Kate cried, but he had smothered his own feeling for too long to choose his next words with care.

"If that should, by any chance, be true, I would be the last to blame you," he said, refusing to raise his voice to match hers. "You are a young woman still, with healthy desires and appetites that should not be denied. You'll need more than that to satisfy you later on. You'll need marriage, children, and the security of a legitimized union as you grow older. It's time we, both of us, took stock."

Kate stared at him speechless for a moment while she sought vainly for the remnants of her old composure.

"Your tolerance is as insulting as your well-worn advice," she flung back at him then. "I suppose you'd be complacent enough to offer to supply all these things and kindly overlook any little lapse on my part."

"Hush, my poor, angry dear, don't throw my ill-expressed intentions back in my face. Whatever you may or may not have been to Robert Farmer has no bearing on my own feelings. I would have you, Kate, on any terms if I thought I could make you happy," he said, his blue eyes suddenly a little shy. She burst into tears.

"Oh, go away . . . go away!" she wept, touched and exasperated at the same time. Because it had been too long since he had learned to deal persuasively with a weeping woman, he got up at once and took his leave of her. He had scarcely reached his car, however, when he was confronted by Victoria, who demanded indignantly to know what was the matter with him.

"Nothing that concerns you," he replied with unusual asperity, but she refused to be snubbed.

"Then you shouldn't quarrel with all the windows wide open," she retorted. "Why couldn't you take poor Kate in your arms and knock some sense into her instead of slinking off as if you'd put both feet in it?"

"I may very well have put both feet in it, but I wasn't aware of slinking off," he replied with the ghost of a smile. "Were you listening under the window, young woman?"

"Of course not, but I couldn't help hearing when Kate

started to shout. Why do you let yourself be used just as a safety valve?"

"It's not a bad thing to one's credit if it eases the mind. It's scarcely becoming in you to take me to task in the circumstances. Whatever Farmer's intentions may have been, Kate was happy enough in their association until you came."

She stared up at him, her eyes suddenly clouded with the old doubts. When she spoke her voice had lost its assurance.

"Do you think she's in love with him, John?" she asked, and he gave a little shrug.

"I don't know. It's always possible that the situation suited them both so long as there was no need to make decisions, but women can be possessive, even if they're not in love. It can't have been very pleasant for Kate to have to acknowledge a shifting interest under her very nose. You should think of your own part in the affair, Victoria, before you accuse me of being chicken-hearted."

She went a little white, but her eyes were steady.

"Yes, I suppose I deserved that, but you don't know the ins and outs of that business," she replied. "I should have kept my head and written off the fruits of that weekend for what they were, instead of—"

"Instead of what, my child?"

"Oh, not what you were thinking. I didn't jump into bed with Robert, neither, to be honest, did he ask me to."

"It wasn't what I was thinking at all. You were going to say, I fancy, instead of falling in love with him," John replied gently. Her eyes filled with sudden tears.

"All right, and if I did?" she answered swiftly. "At least I've never admitted as much to Kate. She may suspect a mild affair and have the normal feminine reaction, but she has no reason to suppose I would take Robert from her—just the opposite. Kate is quite safe from losing Robert if she wants him.''

He observed her thoughtfully, but with a more professional eye, noting that her face was a little thinner and she was making an effort to control her voice.

"You should get away," he said. "Find another job until you're your own mistress and can please yourself."

"How can I? Mr. Brown won't hear of a change. It's no good running away. The allowance has always been paid to whoever was in charge of me, and now it comes through Kate. I could hardly expect to find a job that would keep and house me as I am trained for nothing that's marketable."

"Yes, I see. A strange man, your benefactor—possibly a mild pathological case, if one but knew. What reason did you give for wishing to leave?"

"Oh, just that the place didn't suit me. Kate wouldn't fire me, so I had to be a bit vague."

"It didn't occur to you to give the real reason?"

"The real reason?"

"Emotional disturbance—even, being the object of unwelcome attentions. I would have thought in the light of this gentleman's apparent views on unsuitable admirers, it would have been your strongest card." There was a definite twinkle in his eye as he spoke, and she gave him that slow, engaging smile.

"Yes, it would, wouldn't it?" she said. "And I could come clean with impunity as Mr. Brown is a stranger and doesn't know any of us. I could confess without naming any names that I'd had the misfortune to fall for a man whose intentions were none too clear and would he please see fit to remove me from temptation."

"Very masterly! I can see your imagination will never

let you down in a crisis," he said with some dryness. Her eyes immediately became grave.

"It isn't all imagination," she told him frankly. "I have a horrible feeling that if the weekend hadn't ended as it did, I might have been persuaded to whatever course Robert had in mind for the future. Now you know what I wouldn't confess to another living soul, John. Doctors are safe, though, like priests and lawyers, aren't they?"

"Yes, my dear, and I'm honored by your confidence," he said a shade formally and wondered for the first time if he had misjudged Robert Farmer. For all his dislike, he did not think he was the type of man who would seduce a young girl in his cousin's employ. It was more likely that he realized the child was becoming fonder of him than he wished, and for that very reason was keeping away.

"Thank you," she said and reached up a hand to him. "Dear John . . . I do hope things turn out well for you. Even if Kate is still fond of Robert in that way, she's very practical when it comes to deciding what's best for Timmy. A doctor would be far more satisfactory as a father than an up-and-coming attorney with his nose forever stuck in his work from morning to night."

At this he burst out laughing and got into his car.

"Well, I don't know that that's a very encouraging comparison, but I'll take it in the spirit in which it was meant. Look after yourself, Victoria, and remember the world is seldom well lost for love," he said, turning on the ignition.

"Kate said the same thing to me once, so you must think alike on certain matters, mustn't you?" she replied, sounding suddenly quite gay. He made a wry face out of the window and drove away without comment.

July brought a return of more settled weather. Victoria, when Timmy did not need her, found compensation for the rejection of her plans by working in the garden, weeding and trying to catch up on the vigorous signs of Sam's neglect. But if the warm summer days restored her to an acceptance of her situation, they did little to soothe Elspeth's temper. She remarked rather acidly after some trivial domestic argument one morning that it was high time Mr. Rab paid them a visit and put an end to moods and contrariness. It was plain as the nose on your face, said she, that the house hadn't been the same since he was last down, and if Mrs. Allen was too stiff-necked to invite him then Victoria should do it instead.

"Oh no, it's not my place," Victoria answered primly, but received a withering look in exchange.

"Hoots! Do you think I don't ken what goes on in this house, under my verra nose?" she retorted, her native burr becoming very apparent. "Since you saw fit to quarrel with the gentleman and send him from the house without his supper it's for you to swallow your pride and call him back. You can tell Mr. Rab that Mrs. Allen is missing him, and it's time Timmy had that present he was promised a long time since."

Victoria obediently wrote to Robert, adopting Elspeth's suggestions and rather overdoing Kate's need of his company. She also wrote to Mr. Brown reiterating her desire to leave Farthings. Remembering the doctor's advice, she set down a candid analysis of the regrettable state of her heart. It was not, she thought upon re-reading this effusion, a very lucid explanation of the situation, since Robert must necessarily remain anonymous. It was difficult to bare one's soul to a perfect stranger who, for all she knew might not even trouble to read the letter.

It was Kate who heard first, and as she passed the letter to Victoria across the breakfast table it seemed plain from her expression that she was both hurt and displeased.

"I thought we had agreed to forget this business and carry on as before," she said. "Why have you stirred up fresh trouble?"

Victoria made no reply until she had digested the ambiguous contents of Mr. Chapple's careful communication, then she said quietly, "I suppose they wanted to be sure I wasn't just romancing. There's no suggestion of blame where you're concerned, Kate. They only want assurance that you consider the situation warrants the inconvenience of making other arrangements."

"And were you romancing? Since, with typical legal caution, they are careful to avoid direct accusations, it's not very clear what the situation amounts to. Had you implied that you were being subjected to unwelcome attentions?"

"No—no, of course not! I—I simply tried to explain my real reasons for wanting to leave without involving anyone."

"Which are?"

"But you know, Kate. It clearly cut no ice to say the place didn't suit me, so I thought I'd better come clean."

"And lay the blame at Robert's door, I suppose, by way of clinching the matter. Why in that case, have you written asking him to come down?"

"Have you heard from Robert, then?" Victoria asked.

"He called up last night about another matter and mentioned it in passing."

"Oh!"

"Your invitation hardly accords very well with the tale you seem to have spun for Mr. Brown's benefit, does it?"

"Oh, Kate, can't you see?" Victoria exclaimed, wishing she had never paid attention to either John Squires's or Elspeth's counsel. "I only tried to convince him that I'd involved myself in an emotional tangle. I wrote to Robert because I thought he might be staying away on account of that, and it wasn't fair to you."

"Somewhat muddled reasoning, but I suppose I must accept it. Are you sure you're not trying to deceive yourself because you're still smarting from that unfortunate affair of the roses?"

"Perhaps it wasn't so unfortunate as it appeared at the time. Unkind practical jokes have a very salutary effect on emotional misconceptions," Victoria replied with gentle evasion, and Kate sighed.

"Yes," she said, "I can understand that. Still, you've had time to reconsider. Though I hold no brief for silly pranks there must have been some good reason to trigger off that one."

"Such as?"

Kate hesitated.

"Well," she replied a little lamely, "he probably thought roses from Mr. Brown would crown the birthday for you, as indeed it did. If I hadn't unwittingly caught him out and you hadn't eavesdropped, you would have gone on living quite happily in your fool's paradise, wouldn't you?"

"Yes, and that should answer you, Kate. No one but a complete moron is satisfied to go about in blinkers," Victoria retorted. Kate, regretting too late her choice of words, folded the lawyer's letter back into its meticulous creases and sat tapping it irritably against her thumbnail.

"Yes, of course. Well, what do you want me to answer to this?" she said, and her voice was cool and brisk again.

"You could say," Victoria suggested gravely, "that young girls are sometimes apt to mistake idle attentions for something deeper and you think, in the circumstances, a change would be advisable."

"And did you?"

"If I did it's all in the past, but it's a good enough reason for the lawyers. They can hardly refuse to regard the matter seriously if you back me up."

"Very well. I wish, though, you could bring yourself to confide in me. Robert has a right to know where he slipped up, quite apart from those wretched roses."

"If he slipped up at all it was in thinking a proposal of marriage would cancel out other bad jokes," Victoria answered. Kate smiled, her resentment ebbing a little.

"Poor Victoria," she said softly, "I suspect that you care more than you'll admit."

"I don't care at all, and if I did I'm not so far gone that I couldn't get over it."

"In that case you'll have no objection if Robert comes down again soon?"

"Of course not. Would I have written to suggest it if I did?"

"I don't know. I gather you took great pains to put the onus on me."

"Well, you've missed him, haven't you? He may or may not have stayed away on my account. As Elspeth pointed out, it's not right that the mistress of the house should be deprived of visitors to suit the whims of a paid employee."

"Dear me!" said Kate quite mildly. "You do seem to have got yourself in a tangle! Who else has been proffering well-meaning advice?"

"Only people who have your well-being at heart."

"I suppose you mean John. And what was his reason for wanting to get you out of the house? Has he, by any chance, fallen a victim to more youthful charms and distrusts Robert's evil influence?" Kate spoke with such sudden bitterness that for a moment Victoria could only sit and blink at her.

"Kate!" she exclaimed then, her own anger flaring up, "you know very well John only has eyes for you. He's the sort of quixotic fool who'd hand you over to someone else without a struggle if he thought it would make you happier. He probably only wants me out of the way to ease the situation for you."

"I'm sorry, I shouldn't have said that," Kate said a little stiffly. "All the same, I think you've probably been more honest with John than you have with me."

"And that was possible because he's only concerned indirectly with my affairs. You should know better than to be jealous on that score. If you want the truth, I think you treat him abominably! You use him so long as it suits you and trade on his dog-like devotion."

"Victoria—be careful!" warned Kate, going a little white. "I've allowed you the freedom of a friend and an equal since you've been here, but I won't put up with impertinence. I'll go and reply to that letter now. You can mail it when it's ready. I shall have no difficulty this time in persuading the lawyers that a change is not only advisable but necessary—both from your employer's point of view and your own. If they are still unwilling to make other arrangements for the little time that's left, then I must demand an audience with the reluctant Mr. Brown in person: a demand you could well have insisted on yourself in the circumstances had you not been more content to dwell in your cloud-cuckoo-land." She stood up abruptly as she finished speaking, the letter in her hand, and left the room, closing the door behind her with a sharp click of finality.

A gust of wind caught the curtains at the open casement windows and sent them spiralling out into the room. In the distance the first faint growl of thunder echoed over the downs. Victoria, still sitting stiffly in her place at the breakfast table, suddenly bowed her face in her hands. She wept not only for the unthinking dissolution of a friendship, but for the lost felicity of her foolish dreams.

CHAPTER NINE

It was to be a week of thundery weather with storms that threatened but never came to much, leaving the atmosphere sticky and oppressive. The heavy showers that punctuated the sultry closeness pressing down on the countryside were never long enough to relieve the thirsty earth. They only beat down the tall flowers in Kate's herbaceous border that Victoria had tied up and staked with such care only a week ago.

"I wish," she observed after days of exhausting heat, "we could have one good, cracking storm and have done with it."

"That, perhaps, is being held in reserve," Kate answered ambiguously, using the polite, measured tones she had employed since their disastrous altercation. Victoria's enquiring glance held a modicum of wariness.

"Was that a metaphorical observation?" she asked, trying to match Kate's casual coolness.

"You can take it how you like," Kate replied, raising her eyebrows. "Perhaps I was simply anticipating a final clearing of the air."

Victoria, taking the remark literally, asked quickly, "Have you heard from the lawyers, then?"

"Not yet, but I've heard from Robert. He'll be down this weekend."

"Oh!"

"Perhaps," observed Kate, catching a suggestion of dismay in the exclamation, "you've had time to regret your hasty intervention on my behalf. It's a pity your excellent Miss Scott lives so far away in Wales, or you might have begged a bed for the weekend.''

"I'm not,'' replied Victoria, stung to retaliation, "in the least anxious to avoid a meeting with Robert, but if I'm going to be in the way I can quite well make myself scarce.''

"What nonsense! If you're going to be tiresomely tactful without any encouragement, you'll simply embarrass us both. Now, run along and get Timmy up from his rest. After tea we'll play Happy Families and allow him to cheat a little because he's being extra good.''

As the week drew to a close, Victoria found herself looking forward to Robert's visit with a mixture of anticipation and dread. Whatever his intentions might once have been he was, she knew, much too experienced and worldly-wise to allow awkwardness to spoil his weekend. Neither was he likely to commit the folly of arriving with floral tributes as a peace-offering. She wondered whether he would allude at all to his last visit, or whether absence and time for more reflection had turned his thoughts back to Kate. It was, she realized with a sudden sharp awareness, very likely the last time she would see him, for soon Mr. Brown must make his intentions known. When next he came she would be gone, and life at Farthings would go on without her. For one panic-stricken moment she wished with all her heart that she could have been gone before the ordeal of another meeting. By constantly reminding herself how successfully he had made a fool of her, she was able to whip up a comforting illusion of indifference.

Robert was expected in time for dinner on Friday. All day the house had exuded an air of occasion. Elspeth, miraculously restored to good humor, was clearly determined to show her approval by excelling herself in culinary skill and set Victoria to work washing the best china and polishing silver between numerous errands to the village for forgotten delicacies. Timmy, neglected in consequence, caused a minor panic by taking himself off unaccompanied down the hill, to be brought back by John Squires, who had chanced to spot him making a determined assault on a neighbor's strawberry beds. The doctor was not unwilling, Victoria thought, to find a legitimate excuse for calling after his last unhappy visit. Kate could do no less than offer him a glass of sherry together with demure surprise at his absence. She seemed a little piqued when he observed that Victoria was looking washed out. She airily blamed the weather, adding innocently that Elspeth was killing the fatted calf in honor of Robert's arrival, and poor Victoria was being run off her feet with last-minute preparations.

"Oh, I see. And is it an occasion of any special significance? I thought, since he's practically part of the family, he's used to just taking pot luck," John said casually. His eyes still rested thoughtfully on Victoria's averted face, and Kate gave a small, indecisive shrug.

"Yes, well . . . he hasn't been down for some time, and you know what Elspeth is. Nothing's too good for Mr. Rab. We're all of us a bit in need of cheering up," she replied, and his eyebrows lifted.

"Really? This young woman looks more in need of a tonic than a gay weekend. Come to my office next time you're in the village, Victoria, and I'll give you a prescription," he said.

"I've no doubt she'll pick up once she's away from here," Kate observed before Victoria could reply. He smiled, but his eyes were a little rueful as he said to Victoria:

"So you took my advice, and it's done the trick?"

"I don't know. We're still waiting to hear," Victoria replied, not caring very much for the trend the conversation was taking. Kate said as she observed the doctor's quick frown:

"Don't you think you were rather rash to meddle, John? Whatever Victoria may have told you, she was settled enough here until her head was turned by a couple of well-intentioned admirers." She spoke quite pleasantly, even with a touch of amused indulgence. Victoria sprang to her feet, the color standing out sharply on her cheekbones.

"If you'll excuse me, Kate, I'll go and get Timmy cleaned up for lunch. I don't think John would be very interested in my hypothetical admirers," she said.

"Was that quite fair?" the doctor asked when the sound of her hurried flight up the corner staircase had died away, and Kate lowered her eyes.

"No, it wasn't," she said and stood to refill both their glasses, spilling a few drops of sherry because her hand was not quite steady. "I don't know what's the matter with me, John, unless this oppressive heat is getting us all down. Perhaps it's I and not Victoria who's in need of medical advice."

"Would you take it, Kate?"

"It would depend on the remedy, wouldn't it?"

"Perhaps the remedy is simpler and pleasanter than you think."

She sat down again, sipping her sherry quickly, and regarded him with troubled inquiry, but the old warmth was back in her eyes.

"I—I've been unfair to you, John," she said then. "Victoria took me to task, and we quarreled over you, since then we don't seem able to get back on the old footing.

She was right. Is it possible to be jealous but heartwhole at the same time, do you suppose?"

"One can feel possessive about a person without wishing to be possessed in return, I imagine. That might result in a sort of dog-in-the-manger form of jealousy," he replied with some dryness, and she made a wry face at him.

"Not a very attractive picture," she said. "I've always prided myself on being free of the more obvious weaknesses of my sex, but it seems I am wrong."

"Dear Kate, don't scorn your very natural imperfections—they make you so much more approachable," he said, and she looked at him with startled eyes.

"Approachable? But I'm the least self-satisfied of people!" she exclaimed, sounding quite hurt.

"Very true, but that's not quite what I meant. I was only implying that I find a touch of feminine inconsistency in you encouraging. Long associations, however unsentimental, have deep roots. Would you have married Farmer?"

"Perhaps," she said, sounding a little regretful. "It was such a pleasant, undemanding relationship . . . we made a family without the ties of necessity. It was so good for Timmy to have a man about the place. I just drifted."

"And now?"

She sighed, looking a little rueful. "And now there's Victoria, and I've no means of gauging how deep that's gone. Robert played a silly trick that had unfortunate results. Perhaps it jolted her out of a mood that was merely infatuation, in which case, it was just as well. The young have tender feelings, but not a great sense of proportion. It takes time to get one's emotional sights into focus."

"Not necessarily. That young woman, thanks to her unusual circumstances, has acquired quite a philosophy. Does Farmer know she's leaving you?"

"Not unless she told him when she wrote, and I don't imagine she did."

"H'm . . . interesting to observe the reaction."

"It will be more than interesting if he suspects his name has been introduced for the purpose of softening up Mr. Brown," Kate retorted with a brisk return to tartness. John got to his feet saying it was time he was off.

"Don't *you* lose your sense of proportion, my dear," he said with a twinkle. "It isn't likely Victoria would have given anything away other than her own feelings. She's hardly on confidential terms with her Invisible Man."

"No, I suppose not, I'm beginning to suspect he's really at the root of half the trouble," Kate snapped back impatiently. "If he'd declared himself in the first place and given the poor child some sort of anchorage for her starved affections, she wouldn't have fallen for the first man to take a flattering interest in her. Mr. Brown, whoever he may be, has a lot to answer for in my opinion. It would give me great pleasure to tell him so to his face."

"A sentiment I heartily endorse," he replied with a grin. "It seems unlikely either of us will get the chance, however, since I have a shrewd suspicion that he intends to remain a mystery to the end. Goodby for now, dear, troubled Kate, and whatever this weekend may bring, let things take their course. You know where to find me if I'm wanted."

As evening approached Victoria found herself listening for the sound of a car drawing up at the gates. That would give her time to make herself scarce and allow Kate to offer a welcome in private, but she was caught unprepared after all. She had run downstairs in her slip to retrieve the dress she had been ironing in the kitchen at the very moment Robert walked into the house.

"No need to be bashful on my account. It isn't the first time I've been greeted by a lady in her underwear," he observed as she turned to run back upstairs. At the remembered little flick of mockery in his voice she sat down abruptly on the bottom tread.

"I'm not the bashful type," she managed to retort with a comforting flash of the old spirit, "and I can well believe that you're fully acquainted with the details of feminine underwear!"

"I'm glad to see you haven't lost your gift for repartee. I'd feared I might be treated with cool disdain which would have been very dull," he said, and advancing farther into the hall, laid a florist's beribboned creation on the brassbound chest.

Victoria stared at the flowers in growing indignation and exclaimed, "Oh *no!*" then became aware of his brows raised in quizzical amusement while he stood looking down at her with eyes that were suddenly a little cool.

"Don't jump to unwarrantable conclusions," he said with a very slight drawl. "The flowers are for Kate, on whose behalf you thoughtfully drew my attention to too long an absence."

"Oh, I see. Well, if you'll excuse me, I'll find my dress and go and finish dressing."

"Find your dress? Are you in the habit of mislaying your garments, or am I to assume I've arrived at an inopportune moment and there's a follower lurking somewhere in hiding?"

"I wish I could truthfully say there was," she flung back at him, trying to struggle to her feet but finding herself slipping on the polished boards.

"Dear me! And what would Mr. Brown say to that?" he countered, then reached down a helping hand. "Allow me to assist you before that very brief trifle you're wearing rises any higher for decency, or the good of my blood pressure.''

He lifted her up, paying no attention to protests or resistance. He did not at once let her go and held her lightly but firmly between his hands while his eyes searched her upturned face with a disconcerting hint of tenderness.

"Dear, belligerent Victoria Mary . . . had you been bracing yourself against this moment?" he asked her softly. "You should know me better than to suppose I would take advantage of past indiscretions. I have my own way of dealing with awkward situations, so don't hold my manner against me."

The hostility that he had aroused in her so deliberately melted away, leaving her weak and once more vulnerable. If the past indiscretions he had mentioned were intended to refer to a mistaken infatuation on her part, or a perverted sense of humor on his she had no means of guessing. She knew now with depressing certainty that whatever the future held for her, she must go on loving him. Perhaps, she thought with a flash of saving humor, he would one day become just another image on which to feed her imagination, like Mr. Brown. Perhaps she had, from lack of masculine knowledge, already invented a personality for him that did not in fact exist.

"What are you thinking to cause those wrinkles of perplexity?" he asked, and she slipped neatly out of his grasp.

"Nothing of any consequence," she replied, recovering her composure. "Please go into the parlor and wait for Kate and allow me to finish dressing. Elspeth won't be pleased if I keep her very special dinner waiting."

"Oh! Is it a celebration?" he inquired innocently, but there was a look in his eye that boded no good. She stepped aside with relief as Kate came hurrying down the stairs, exclaiming, "Of course it's a celebration! You've neglected us for too long, Rob, and we've become browned off with each other's company. Have you forgotten to put on a dress in your haste to be first with a welcome, Victoria, or am I just out of step with the latest fashion?''

Victoria smiled mechanically without replying and escaped to the kitchen. As the door closed behind her she heard Robert say still with that note of mockery, "Do I detect a slight flavor of pussiness, dear cousin, or do I merely flatter my masculine ego?''

Kate made some laughing reply that Victoria did not catch and their voices died away as they went into the parlor and shut the door.

Upstairs in her room Victoria lingered over the finishing touches to her appearance in order to give Kate time for whatever she might have to say to Robert in private. It soon became clear that Timmy's demands had taken priority. A visit to the nursery was now in progress, judging by the squeals and laughter drifting down the passage, that would leave little margin for confidences before Elspeth sounded the gong for dinner. It was as good a way as any of bridging the gap, Victoria thought as she joined the nursery party. Timmy, sitting up in bed amidst a litter of string and paper wrappings, gave his mother no time for the tactful explanations she had doubtless reserved for a more propitious moment.

" *You* won't let my Toria go away, will you, Uncle Rob?'' he demanded.

"Is she going away?" Robert said after a brief pause, and his eyes rested for a moment on Victoria standing uncertainly in the doorway.

"She won't if you say she's not to. It's that Brown person making spells again. He's really a wizard, you know.''

"Don't be silly, Timmy, he's nothing of the sort,'' Kate

said sharply. "And if Victoria wants to leave us, Uncle Rob can't stop her."

"*Can't* you, Uncle Rob? But I heard you say—" the boy began bouncing up and down with excitement, but Robert interrupted, at the same time pressing him firmly back onto his pillow,

"Never mind what you thought you heard me say, young man. One doesn't repeat what isn't intended for one's ears. It's time you settled down and went to sleep, anyway."

Back again in the parlor, with drinks at their elbows he said to Kate, "Why didn't you tell me?"

"I've hardly had a chance since you arrived, have I?" she protested with some truth.

"No, but we've spoken on the telephone."

"Only to fix up this weekend. Besides, I imagined if Victoria wanted you to know, she would have told you herself."

"Did you, Kate? Well, it's of little consequence. When does she want to leave?"

"You don't sound very surprised. As usual, we are waiting upon Mr. Brown's pleasure."

"I see. And what if he continues to disregard his *protégée's* whims?"

"I don't think he will this time, since I've made my own wishes clear."

"I see," he said again. "Have you and Victoria fallen out?"

"In a manner of speaking, but I do honestly believe a change is called for. You're largely to blame, Robert. If you were really serious when you told me you wanted to marry her you've gone a very odd way about things. I don't imagine that's the impression she has given Mr. Brown."

"Oh? Do I take it then that I'm the villain of the piece?"

"I've no idea, I'm not in Victoria's confidence. You'd better ask John," Kate said shortly, and his eyebrows rose.

"Dear me! Am I to assume that the faithful doctor is in danger of transferring his affections?"

"I wouldn't know," she replied with an unconvincing air of indifference, "but she certainly took his advice in the matter of providing Mr. Brown with a more substantial reason for leaving. Whether he, or the lawyers, take a serious view of the situation is yet to be known, but I for one think it's time that gentleman took his responsibilities more actively. It wouldn't hurt him to pay us a casual visit without letting on who he is."

"Very true, but for all you know he may have done just that. Now I come to think of it I wonder it's never occurred to Victoria's lively imagination. You could both have gained much entertainment by inventing hidden identities for casual callers, or the vicar—or even the doctor with his fatherly interest and good advice. Now there is a man who might well feel impelled toward philanthropy without letting his noble intentions be known," Robert said with disconcerting enjoyment. She smiled, though without much amusement.

"Very likely," she retorted, "but John, though he's comfortably off and has a good practice, can hardly be described as a rich tycoon. Mr. Brown's little whim must have cost him plenty."

"No more than the keep and education of the daughter of any well-to-do parents, and you've no valid reason for inventing rich tycoons," he said, getting to his feet as Victoria came into the room.

"We were discussing the probable or improbable identity of your patron, Victoria. Has it occurred to you that the attentive Dr. Squires might well fill the bill?" he continued, pouring her a glass of sherry.

"For heaven's sake! Don't go putting fresh nonsense into the poor child's head!" Kate exclaimed, observing the gleam of interest that momentarily brightened the girl's eyes. Victoria was used by now to Robert's methods of getting a rise and became aware at the same time that Kate was not enjoying this latest flight of fancy.

"That of course would be a very happy ending if it were in any way likely, but even my fertile imagination hasn't grasped at that straw," she said and caught Robert's faint smile of appreciation as he handed her the sherry.

"I don't know that the worthy doctor would care to be likened to a straw, but we'll let that pass," he said, observing with interest the indignant glint in Kate's brown eyes. Victoria, also noticing, gave him a chilly glance.

"John Squires is good, kind, and worth ten of you," she said, and his eyes held a fleeting twinkle.

"I bow to your superior knowledge," he replied with mock humility. "And now let's settle for a pleasant weekend and a return to less controversial matters."

Once seated around the table, Robert steered the conversation into mundane channels with considerable skill. He insisted on Elspeth being summoned to the dining room to have her health drunk.

"Och, get away with you, Mr. Rab! Have you no better excuse for a toast than a plain body that's paid to cook your vittles?" she retorted with uncompromising bluntness. Her eyes dwelt for a moment on Kate, but lingered longest on Victoria, who sat, her face pale and politely attentive in the candlelight while she remembered the almost identical details of that last special occasion. As if he had guessed her thoughts, Robert said softly:

"Only the champagne is missing. I should have thought of that, shouldn't I, Elspeth?"

"Aye, you should, but one wine is as good as another for the purpose. Have you no other tricks up your sleeve, Mr. Rab?" Elspeth said. "It may be the last chance you'll have for wishing Miss Toria well."

"Thanks for the reminder," he replied casually, "but since I understand Miss Toria's departure still requires the sanction of authority, I will give you Mr. Brown—may his schemes prosper and his shadow never grow less!" He solemnly raised his glass and drank. Almost without volition, Kate and Victoria followed suit, but Elspeth set her glass down on the table unfinished and made for the door.

"And that's a toast I'll no' be troubling with! Shame on you, Mr. Rab, for making fun of an occasion that should be serious! Mr. Brown, indeed! If any such pairson exists, he's no better than a bogle to frighten the bairns with!" she exclaimed, her accent broadening in outrage, and she stalked out of the room.

For a moment there was an astonished silence, then Kate and Victoria succumbed simultaneously to giggles.

"Oh!" gasped Kate, wiping her eyes. "*Poor* Mr. Brown—just a bogle to frighten the bairns with!"

"Many a true word spoken in jest," observed Robert, whose laughter had been more perfunctory. "Haven't you been obedient to orders for too long, Victoria Mary?" He did not speak with any great seriousness, but her merriment was quenched.

"I've had no choice," she replied gravely. "Besides, debts have to be paid in whatever coin is stipulated and, bogle or not, I have nothing but gratitude for Mr. Brown."

"And to what extreme might that carry you?" he asked, his manner suddenly as sober as hers. Kate, conscious that she was momentarily redundant, murmured some excuse and left the room.

"Well?" said Robert, absently snuffing out a guttering candle between finger and thumb.

"I don't know," she said nervously, scooping up bread-crumbs into neat little piles beside her plate. "It would depend on what was asked, but as the demands have been purely functional all these years, I'm not likely to be put to the test, am I?"

"Oh, you never know! Even the most amiable of Shylocks has a habit of exacting his pound of flesh," he replied with a lightness that was far from reassuring. She looked across at him with widening eyes.

"Do you mean he might be a money-lender? I never thought of that," she said, and he pushed back his chair with an irritable little jerk.

"No, I don't," he replied, beginning to snuff out the remaining candles. "I was speaking figuratively, as you are quite intelligent enough to know. Now, we'd better abandon this unrewarding topic. Let's go and join Kate who, with the best of intentions, has made a tactful, if unnecessary withdrawal," he said and blew out the last of the candles.

The curtains had been left undrawn across the windows since the evening was very sultry and something of daylight still remained, but with the dousing of the candles the room seemed suddenly dark. Victoria, groping her way to the door, stumbled against Robert. He put out a hand to steady her, holding her against him for a moment, and she said a little breathlessly, "What are you after, Robert? Why are you treating everything as if it didn't matter?"

"Don't you know?"

"Not really—unless you're trying to let me down

lightly. I wasn't planning to treat you to—to sentimental recriminations when I asked you to come down."

"Weren't you? What a pity. Still, there's no reason why you should suppose I feared recriminations, was there? After all, it was you who turned *me* down."

"Yes . . . yes, I did, didn't I?" she said, sounding surprised, then confused memories of the insulting implication of that untimely proposal stiffened her weakening resolve.

"You could hardly," she said, trying to wriggle out of his suddenly tightened grip, "have expected me to fall into your arms with gratitude at an obvious attempt to soothe my feelings."

"I'm not the type to deal in soothing syrup, as you should know by now," he retorted, his voice a little rough above her head, "but you chose to be bloody-minded in order to save your silly little pride. You've only yourself to blame if the whole thing's backfired on you."

"What do you mean, backfired? Are you flattering yourself that I have regrets?"

"Well, haven't you? I should hate to think that all this sound and fury has no more reality than the one-sided imaginary scenes you probably indulge in with the absent Mr. Brown."

"How dare you mock at my dreams? How dare you mock at Mr. Brown who, if nothing else, has cared enough to give me the start in life my father had planned for me?" she burst out and heard him sigh as he gently released her.

"Dear, stubborn little ostrich—I would never mock at your dreams, but they're sometimes more pertinent than you think. As for Mr. Brown, I'm of the opinion that it's high time that gentleman revealed himself, or left the field to less exalted persons. I, for one, am beginning to find him a bore.''

As she lay tossing in bed that night, unable to sleep for the heat, and the conflicting emotions that troubled her spirit, Victoria bitterly regretted her impulse to make peace with Robert for Kate's sake. It was years since she had consoled herself with imaginary meetings with Mr. Brown and still more unlikely happy endings, but the subterfuge still worked. Her limbs relaxed and her eyelids grew heavy as she conjured up pictures of a faceless, old gentleman who listened gravely to her grievances and patted her kindly on the head. "There, there, my dear, it's all for the best. I never did like that browbeating barrister, so just forget him,'' he was saying comfortingly as she fell asleep. He must have continued talking right through her dreams for when she woke a voice was saying, "Forget your dreams, my dear. I've brought you a surprise.''

Victoria opened her eyes, still hazy with sleep, but it was only Kate standing by her bed with a breakfast tray, a quizzical smile twisting her lips.

"You were smiling most charmingly in your sleep,'' she said. "What were you dreaming about?''

"Mr. Brown. I thought you were him,'' Victoria answered, still only half awake, and Kate's eyebrows rose.

"Very curious,'' she observed a shade cynically. "Well, I hope the contents of your letter will match the promise of your dream.''

"What letter?''

"The long-awaited answer to yours, one must assume. That's the surprise.''

"Oh!'' Victoria struggled into a sitting position, snatching at the legal-looking communication, then held it gingerly as if she were afraid it might burn her.

"Aren't you going to open it?" Kate asked curiously, but Victoria slipped the letter under her pillow.

"Later," she said briefly. Kate smiled somewhat doubtfully and sat down on the side of the bed.

"Victoria—" she began a little diffidently, "I don't know whether this will be good or bad news, but whatever it is, try to be philosophical."

"Haven't you heard, too?"

"No, but I didn't put my own views very strongly, despite our unedifying little bout of mud-slinging. I'm very fond of you, my dear, and only want what's best for you. Remember that, won't you?"

Quick tears brightened Victoria's eyes for a moment, and she thrust out a willing hand.

"Oh, Kate," she said, "I've been so wretched thinking I must seem so ungrateful, after all you've done for me."

"I've done nothing but employ you, so don't go making mountains out of molehills. If it so happened that I also felt affection for you, there's no need to feel beholden for that," Kate answered with her more familiar briskness. Victoria gave her that slow, lifting smile that had been noticeably absent these past days.

"Dear Kate . . . " she said with lingering fondness, "I'm so glad to think you may miss me a little when I'm gone."

"Don't rush your fences! You won't know till you open that letter what the immediate future may hold. That's why I counseled philosophy. Do you really want to go, Victoria? Hasn't Robert talked any sense into you?"

"If you mean did he use persuasion when you so tactfully left us alone after dinner, no, he didn't. He was much too occupied sharpening his wits and his tongue at my expense to indulge in any helpful conversation," Victoria replied coolly and seemingly without concern. Kate said:

"Oh, dear, I had rather hoped . . . still, you should know Robert by this time. He has curious ways of bringing about his intentions," she said.

"His intentions, I think, were never very clear or very serious, dear Kate, so don't distress yourself on that count. Now, if you'll agree, I'd like to take Timmy for a picnic if the weather holds. That will give *you* time to have sense talked into you."

As soon as the door had closed behind her, Victoria pushed her plate away and snatched the letter from under her pillow. She did not know why she had felt such a strong desire to read it in private, but now that she was alone she could restrain her curiosity no longer.

Mr. Brown had been disturbed by the news conveyed to him in her letter of the 5th inst., Mr. Chapple had written. He considered it unwise, however, to seek fresh employment for so short a period, since his plans for the future had been cut and dried for some time. He was prepared to arrange a meeting at once in order to put certain propositions before her. Mr. Brown, Mr. Chapple pointed out with rather coy ambiguity, was neither senile nor in poor health, so he trusted that in view of past advantages she would look favorably upon his suggestions. If she would call at their city branch on Monday next, the 15th, at eleven-thirty precisely, Mr. Brown would make himself known to her and put forward his plans for their mutual consideration. They were, hers faithfully, etc. . . .

"Well, blow me down!" she exclaimed inelegantly and sprang out of bed. She couldn't wait to get dressed before imparting such momentous news to Kate and without troubling with dressing gown or slippers, raced downstairs in her pyjamas.

But Kate was nowhere about. It was Robert who ap-

peared in answer to her excited shouts, the morning paper
tucked under his arm.

"Dear me, what slovenly habits for this hour of day,"
he observed, eyeing her state of undress with interest. "Is
the house on fire?"

"Of course not, but I want to find Kate. I've had the
most extraordinary letter from Mr. Chapple," she replied.
"You wouldn't believe, Robert, what seems to have been
simmering in that man's mind!"

"What, old Chapple?"

"No, of course not—Mr. *Brown*! I'm to meet him on
Monday at half-past eleven to discuss certain
propositions."

"H'm . . . sounds fishy to me. He's probably a dirty old
man. May I see the letter?"

"No, you may not—not before Kate's read it, anyway.
You'll only make fun of it. Where is she?"

"At the bottom of the garden, I believe, pulling lettuces
for your lunch."

She found Kate in the vegetable garden, inspecting the
lettuces with a dissatisfied eye and bemoaning the fact
that most of them had been eaten by slugs.

"I don't know why I keep that boy on," she complained. "He's never here when he's wanted, and when he
is he skimps his work."

"Never mind the slugs—read this!" Victoria said,
thrusting Mr. Chapple's letter into her hands. "I always
told you I would meet Mr. Brown one day, and now it's
coming true."

"H'm . . . " Kate murmured, much as Robert had done
when she had reached the end. "Several conclusions could
be drawn from this. Well, Victoria, are you going? He
doesn't give you much time, I must say."

"But of course! Haven't I been waiting for this moment ever since it all began?"

"Yes, I suppose so. I didn't really think it would happen, you know. I've never quite been able to swallow Mr. Brown."

"Because you thought he was just a figurehead—something to represent a trust and nothing more."

"Yes, I expect I did. Victoria, do you think you're wise? You've made so many images, so many happy-ever-after endings . . . sometimes it's best to keep one's dreams intact." Kate sounded uneasy, and her eyes were grave. Victoria, although a little damped by this guarded reception was too excited to let doubts disturb her.

"Dear Kate, this *is* the happy ending," she said. "Whoever he may be, Mr. Brown has kept and educated me. Now it seems he has planned for me too. The least I can do is to listen to his proposals and fall in with them if I can."

"Listen, yes, but think twice before agreeing. However much you may have benefited by his generosity, he doesn't own you," Kate said a little dryly. "Has Robert seen this letter?"

"No. Anyway, it's nothing to do with him."

"He mightn't agree with that. Anyway, I think we'll let him read it. His advice on legal matters is to be respected."

But Robert had no advice to offer. Indeed he adopted a somewhat frivolous attitude when later, Victoria, bathed and dressed, joined the cousins on the patio for mid-morning coffee. He insisted on reading the letter aloud, interspersed with conjectures and speculations as wild and unlikely as any Victoria might have thought up, until she was reduced to giggles and Kate to exasperation.

"But seriously, Rob, don't you think she should insist on more definite details concerning these vague propositions before committing herself to an interview that might prove embarrassing?" Kate said. "I think she should have more time. It's extremely short notice considering the many opportunities there have been in the past. Call up and make another date, Victoria."

"Nonsense!" Robert said unhelpfully. "The gentleman might change his mind. Anyway, there won't be anyone in the office on a Saturday. As it happens I have an appointment with old Chapple myself on Monday, so Victoria can drive up with me. That will save her finding her own way."

"Oh, in that case I shall have fewer doubts. You can always insist on meeting the gentleman yourself, can't you?" said Kate, sounding relieved. Victoria, who did not take at all kindly to this unexpected turn of events, said quickly:

"I think you've just made that up, Robert. What business could you possibly have with Chapple, Chapple & Ponsonby?"

"Business that will, I trust, prove pleasantly lucrative. You must have forgotten that attorneys have to depend on lawyers for their cases," Robert replied with a touch of amusement, and she colored.

"Oh! Well, I'd just as soon go up by train."

"And I'd just as soon you didn't. No, no, my child, you must humor me in this. I can assure you I have no intention of cramping your style when we get there. It's making heavy weather, don't you think, to arrive at the same destination by separate routes just to be awkward—besides, it will clearly relieve Kate's mind," he said. She could do no less than give in, albeit with deep misgivings. If her anxiety to oblige Mr. Brown sprang largely from a desire to escape from Robert, it was not going to help her resolution to have him virtually handing her over.

"Well," said Kate briskly, "that's one thing settled to my satisfaction. I shall feel much happier knowing Robert will be keeping a lookout for you, my dear. He may seem to be treating this business casually, but he won't let you sign away your freedom. Now, if you want to find a quiet spot for your picnic before trippers get there first, you ought to be starting. Don't stay out too long, will you? It may be working up for a storm."

"Oh, no—not today!" Victoria exclaimed, springing to her feet with alacrity, glad that she could escape from them both and recapture in private the first fine flavor of her small miracle. "There's not a cloud in the sky, and nothing is going to spoil my red-letter day."

"Famous last words," Robert murmured as she ran into the house. "Let's hope Providence is too occupied with higher things to be tempted."

CHAPTER TEN

Alas for Victoria's confident predictions, the day was to end in near disaster. She had driven along by-roads and narrow lanes that were strange to her once the village was left behind before finding a suitable spot in which to picnic. She was governed by the age-old urge to find something better around the next corner. By the time hunger had driven them to stop by a stretch of woodland that promised shade and solitude she had little notion of where they were.

It was a delightful wood with grassy paths that enticed them farther and farther into its unknown depths. So isolated from the familiar world did it seem, Victoria would not have been surprised to come upon the gingerbread house that had lured Hansel and Gretel to their encounter with the witch. She felt quite relieved when the path opened out suddenly into a cheerful little glade that boasted a mossy carpet to sit on and sunlight filtering invitingly through the high trees. Even Timmy seemed glad to abandon exploration for the moment and eat his lunch in the safety of the less shadowy clearing.

By the time they had finished their lunch it had become very hot and still. The tracery of leaves and branches above them allowed glimpses of the sky too small for any warning signs of a change in the weather. Victoria lay back on the warm dry moss, stretching her limbs drowsily and closing her eyes to evoke more clearly the images she had fashioned for herself throughout the years. After

Monday there would be no need to dream, no need to wonder . . . no need, even, to remember that she had been fooled into false hopes on account of five dozen roses sent by another man. This was a train of thought, however, that led to mental pictures that only proved disturbing. Robert's image, she found, became superimposed on that other, reducing it to wraithlike proportions. She tried not to think of him, to comfort herself with the knowledge that Mr. Brown seemed to be offering a way of escape from the painful stirrings of first love. It was Robert's face she remembered last as she fell asleep, his voice following her into her dreams, saying with that mocking tenderness that meant so little, "Do you find it so difficult to see me in the light of a lover?"

A distant roll of thunder woke her. Perhaps it was the first chill drops of rain stinging her warm, bare flesh that startled her into awareness of the coming storm. The wood seemed to have undergone a frightening change while she slept; the little glade was no longer friendly and dappled with sunshine; the paths that led out of it were dark tunnels disappearing into a maw of blackness. Overhead, wind rocked the branches of the high trees in a frenzied dance of menace. Victoria looked around quickly for Timmy, wondering why he had not wakened her. He was nowhere to be seen in the small clearing, and she began calling impatiently as she packed away the picnic things. Progress was necessarily slow for a five-year-old with a slight limp. They were undoubtedly in for a soaking before the road and the car would be reached. Her annoyance grew as she heard no response; it was no time to be hiding and playing tricks on her. As the minutes passed and no answering shout rewarded her, annoyance turned to alarm. She did not know how long she had slept, and if the boy had wandered off to explore the wood on his own, he might well be lost or, even worse, have fallen and hurt himself.

She began running a little way down each path, calling his name, then thrust her way through the tangle of bushes and undergrowth that ended in the clearing, brambles tearing at her bare legs while whip-like branches snapped back in her face as she tried to part them. It seemed to her hours while she searched and called, running this way and that with panic mounting at every step. It was so dark now in the wood that it was difficult to recognize the outlines of paths. Although the rain still held off, the thunder grew louder and nearer while lightning streaked through the trees making grotesque shapes of their writhing branches. As she pushed her way back to the edge of the clearing, she stumbled over something that immediately fastened itself around her legs with such terrifying suddenness that she gave a scream.

"Did you think I was a bear?" said Timmy's voice with a complete absence of distress. She shook him quite roughly to ease her racing heartbeats.

"Have you been hiding here all the time?" she demanded furiously, and he gave her a complacent affirmative. "Didn't you hear me calling?"

"Yes, but I thought I'd give you a fright."

"Oh, for heaven's sake!" she answered impatiently, then hugged him to her as the storm broke in good earnest directly over their heads. Rain fell with a torrential violence, and in a moment they were soaked through; lightning seemed to run down the trunks of trees like fiery snakes and the noise was deafening. Even Timmy lost some of his brashness and clung to her, beginning to whimper. Although she was not normally affected by storms, she experienced a few seconds of atavistic terror.

The wood seemed alive with a primeval fury, threatening to crush them both for their wanton trespass. As though some unseen force could read her thoughts, there came an answering crack from the heavens, as a ball of fire descended, splitting the trunk of a fir tree from top to bottom. Victoria just had time to thrust the boy back into the bushes before the tree fell with a crash across the clearing, demolishing the picnic basket beneath its weight.

"Was that a thunderbolt?" asked Timmy, awed but still curious.

"I shouldn't think so, but a tree was struck. I think we'd better get out of here," Victoria answered, hoping her voice did not betray her fear.

There were several paths converging on the clearing, and for a moment Victoria stood in doubt. The tree that now lay across the open space altered its perspective, and in the noise and confusion everything looked different. She thought she remembered that clump of willows on the right as they had come out into the little glade, but half-way down the path she wasn't so sure. The wood seemed full of willow, and the path more twisting than she remembered, but she pressed on, hoping with every turn to come upon the road. The ground was already waterlogged beneath their feet, and every so often they stumbled and fell, trapped by unseen ruts and holes. The boy was beginning to flag, and his sense of adventure was already quenched.

"We're nearly there," she assured Timmy as she hastened her steps, but when they rounded the next bend she stopped dead with a little cry of dismay. The path straggled on for a little way, then petered out in a density of trees and bramble that stretched away on all sides as far as the eye could see. The path had led them back into the very heart of the wood.

"Where's the road?" asked Timmy blankly.

"Where indeed!" she replied with much bitterness.

"You *said* we'd find the road, Toria. Why isn't it here?" he persisted, beginning to whine.

"Because it's somewhere else," she replied with some tartness. "We'll just have to retrace our steps and try another path—this doesn't lead anywhere."

"It's all your fault—and you said you knew the way," wailed Timmy, beginning to cry, and sat down firmly in the mud.

"Well, I thought I did, but I chose the wrong path. Now be a brave boy, darling, and stop crying. We'll have a rest before we turn, but we have to go back. You wouldn't like to stay here all night, would you?" She had gone down on her knees in the muddy wetness to coax and comfort the child, feeling badly in need of comfort herself. Would Kate be worrying yet on account of the storm? Had she and Robert settled their affairs during the respite she had given them? Would anything ever be the same again after meeting Mr. Brown on Monday? But Monday seemed a long way off in her present predicament. Mr. Brown as strange and unfriendly as the dark, wet wood which threatened to imprison them. . . .

She had no idea how long it took them to retrace their steps, but back again in the clearing, she sat the boy down under the shelter of some bushes while she vainly tried to remember their direction. She had already lost a sandal and she took the other one off and threw it away, too tired by now to care whether her bare feet would carry her any farther.

"That's the way . . . a goblin's just made a face at me and run down there . . ." Timmy's voice came to her eerily from under the bushes. He was already half asleep, and she pulled him to his feet.

"All right, we'll follow the goblin," she said cheerfully. Short of tossing a coin, it was as good a way as any of deciding which path to take, but they had not been walking for long before the boy began to cry again.

"My leg's gone funny . . . I think it's broke. . . . Carry me, Toria," he whimpered.

"Oh, Timmy, I can't—you're much too heavy," she protested, wondering if, after all, they would have to spend the night in this horrible wood.

"You can—a piggyback, like Uncle Rob does," he said with a child's complacent disregard for an adult's difficulties.

"Your Uncle Rob is more used to your weight than I am," Victoria countered with some tartness. "All right, I'll try, but don't throttle me."

Progress was, naturally, slowed to a minimum, but she managed somehow. Every so often she trod on a stone that sent a sharp stab of pain through her numbed feet; the boy grew heavier and heavier astride her back. She spared a thought for St. Christopher breasting the torrent with his Burden, but the storm was retreating. Although the rain still fell with some violence, the lightning had become intermittent, and the thunder no more than a protesting grumble in the distance.

"Timmy, you must try and walk for a bit, now . . . I can't carry you much farther," she said at last, too weary to care any longer whether she had chosen the wrong path again. Timmy, already refreshed, slid unprotestingly to the ground and ran on ahead, shouting and splashing through the puddles. Presently he came running back to her, crying, "The road! The road! Only I think perhaps it's just a river."

"More likely a mirage," Victoria commented dryly, following in his wake with little hope that they had come to the end of their journey. Miraculously it was true, and she stood for a moment, staring with unbelieving eyes.

"What's a mirage?" Timmy inevitably demanded, but she hugged him to her half-laughing, half-crying.

"Something you imagine you see, though you weren't far wrong in mistaking the road for a river," she said. Indeed, the lane that sloped gently down to the next village was awash with a swirling torrent of water spewed out by ditches too blocked, or too shallow to hold it.

"Is it a flood, like Noah's Ark?" Timmy asked, sounding suitably impressed. She bundled him into the waiting car without stopping to embroider on this promising theme and wrapped him up in Kate's old rug that always reposed on the back seat.

"Are you cold?" she asked anxiously, very conscious, now that nightmare was behind them, of her responsibility concerning the boy's health. He shook his head and snuggled down beside her.

"No," he said, proffering a hand. "Feel me. This rug smells of mice."

She felt his hand then tucked it back under the rug, satisfied that he didn't appear to be chilled; aware that she was in less good shape herself, and her teeth were beginning to chatter. She turned the ignition, offering up a silent prayer that the aged Morris would not play one of its favorite tricks and refuse to go. After a few anxious attempts that produced nothing but ominous whirring noises, the ignition sparked and the car was in motion. It was a brief respite, however. The pedals felt strange and resistant without the support of shoes, and Victoria's bare feet kept slipping. She drove too fast down the hill and saw the minor flood at the bottom too late to slow up and take it cautiously. The Morris splashed recklessly through the water, sending up a spray that swamped the radiator. The engine promptly coughed and died.

"Damn, oh, *damn*! As if we hadn't had enough already!" she exclaimed. Had she been alone, she would have eased her frustration in a bout of weeping.

"We need an ark," observed Timmy, peering out at the water with interest, then settled comfortably into sleep.

"Yes, we need an ark," echoed Victoria bitterly. "Failing that, we'll just have to sit here and wait for some passer-by to give us a lift."

They waited for a long time. It was not a road much frequented by traffic. Early closing and the storm had kept tradesmen's vans and private cars at home. Eventually the driver of a truckload of manure rescued them, depositing them at the gates of Farthings very late in the afternoon, smelling strongly of dung. Kate, who must have been on the watch, rushed out of the house halfway between relief and anger, followed more leisurely by Robert who stood on the porch surveying the bedraggled pair with some amusement. Timmy, grasping very quickly that he was once more a satisfying center of attention, gave his mother such a highly colored account of their adventures that she rounded fiercely on Victoria.

"Hadn't you more sense than to stay in the wood with a storm brewing?" she snapped. "Don't you realize that when that tree was struck it might have fallen on the child?"

"It might have fallen on Victoria, too," Robert murmured from the background, but she ignored the interruption. "And dragging a five-year-old, let alone one that's lame, through mud and brambles because you hadn't the gumption to remember the way! And what about the car?"

"The truck driver promised he'd stop at the garage on his way to the village. I'm sorry, Kate, none of this was intentional, you know," Victoria said, sounding suddenly tearful. Robert, turning to go inside, said over his shoulder:

"Pull yourself together, Kate! Recriminations may relieve your feelings, but they serve no other purpose. Your son, quite clearly, is none the worse for his adventures, so forget your other grievances."

"I'm sorry, Victoria," Kate muttered, turning a little pink. "I only hope, though, that Timmy won't have caught a bad chill. I'll get him into a hot bath at once. You might call John in the meantime and ask him to come over."

She hustled the boy into the house and up the stairs, calling to Elspeth to have hot soup ready when the child was in bed. Victoria remained standing uncertainly in the middle of the hall, aware that her teeth were starting to chatter again.

"You could do with some hot soup yourself, I think, Victoria Mary. In the meantime, I would prescribe something stronger," Robert observed. She became aware that he had propped himself against the oak chest and was regarding her with an amused expression.

"Was Kate very worried?" she asked.

"My charming cousin tends to lose her sense of proportion where her ewe-lamb is involved, as you should know by now," he replied. She took immediate exception to his apparent air of unconcern.

"Well, at least you were here to boost her morale, or couldn't you be bothered," she snapped, and his eyebrows shot up.

"What an unsympathetic image you still have of me,"

he observed. "You don't need to be so up in arms. Kate and I understand each other very well."

"Does that mean that you've—settled your affairs?" she asked, and shivered, feeling suddenly very tired and cold.

"I don't know that I quite follow that question, but it's high time you removed those wet things," he said then, and moving suddenly, took both her hands in his. "You're icy, child, and your teeth sound like castanets. You'd better have the reversion of Timmy's bath in case the hot water doesn't last out. In the meantime go and put on a warm dressing gown while I fix you a good strong toddy."

The warmth of his hands, and the sudden warmth in his eyes were her undoing. His concern for her brought about a swift reaction, and she began to weep.

"There, now, my poor child . . . cry it all out . . . there was more in that wood to upset you than a thunderstorm, wasn't there?" he said. His voice held both tenderness and understanding.

"Yes, there was . . . you were all mixed up with Mr. Brown and I was being m-menaced . . . " she wept.

"Menaced?"

"By the wood . . . I can't explain . . . then Timmy went and hid to pay me back while I was asleep. Then we were lost and—and it was all a dreadful nightmare. . . . I don't think Timmy is any the worse, though. . . . I carried him piggyback the last part of the way . . . my b-back aches. . . . "

"I'm not surprised! You're hardly built for such feats of endurance. Don't take Kate's sharp words too much to heart, my dear—she was frightened. When one is frightened, one finds relief in hitting out."

She looked up at him with swift inquiry, wondering if

he intended the words to mean more than they said, and he smiled down at her and nodded his head.

"Yes," he said, "we all do it at times."

"Even you?"

"Even I. As for you, young woman, you make a positive art of the habit, but don't think you fool me."

"At least I haven't tried to *make* a fool of you, which is altogether different," she retorted, unable to resist an opportunity to renew hostilities in case he should imagine he had sufficiently weakened her defenses. He only grinned and gave her a mild shake.

"Now don't start all that nonsense again, Miss Hayes. One is taught to let bygones be bygones in more charitable circles, so stop bolstering up your ego with false grievances. Go on upstairs and get those wet things off."

When she came down again, she found Robert had switched on an electric fire. It was cooler now after the storm. She was glad of the extra warmth for her very bones felt chilled. She sat huddled up in her dressing gown sipping the whisky Robert brought her and staring at him with puzzled eyes. Every so often she sneezed, and he observed with gentle malice, "You, my child, are going to have the father and mother of a cold. I doubt you'll be keeping that appointment on Monday."

"Oh, but I must!" she exclaimed, feeling immediately guilty. "The chance may never come again."

"And would that matter?"

"Of course it would matter! Isn't it the one thing I've looked forward to for as long as I can remember?"

"But I fancy the image of Mr. Brown has suffered a sea change of late, or is that wishful thinking on my part?" he murmured gently, and she frowned.

"Why should it be wishful thinking? My feelings for

Mr. Brown can hardly matter to you," she retorted and wished he wasn't so adept at sowing doubts in her mind.

"If that remark was intended to provoke an impassioned denial, I'm afraid you'll be disappointed, Victoria Mary. I have no intention of competing with an imaginary hero," he said with that disconcerting ability to administer a sharp put-down just as matters were looking promising.

"It was no such thing!" she exclaimed indignantly. "I was merely stating an obvious fact. Why should I care if you minded or not?"

"Why, indeed? You've made it very plain that you prefer fiction to fact."

"I don't know what you mean. I may have built up an image for myself for want of anything better, but Mr. Brown is still a fact, however much you don't want to believe in him."

"Yes, yes . . . one can't, I'll agree, accuse poor old Chapple of cooking the whole thing up. I have no doubts concerning your Mr. Brown's existence, only the romantic notions he seems able to inspire in you."

"I've had no romantic notions. If I've thought of him as a father figure it was only natural in the circumstances."

"Ah, but it's been pointed out that he's neither senile nor in poor health. That strikes me as a hint that the suggestions he trusts you will look upon favorably are not necessarily paternal," Robert reminded her with an infuriating air of unconcern. She took another incautious gulp of whisky that made her choke and cough.

"You really should learn to treat spirits with more respect until you're accustomed to them," he reproved her, adding the final insult to his uncomplimentary innuendoes.

"I'm not a child!" she exclaimed angrily. "In France

we had wine with every meal as a matter of course and were taught to recognize a good vintage, too.''

"Let us hope, then, you also learned discretion in other matters.''

"If you mean affairs of the heart, there was little opportunity for learning discretion. There never has been much opportunity, now I come to think of it.''

She sneezed again and fumbled vainly in the pocket of her dressing gown for a handkerchief. Robert tossed her his. The small, intimate gesture accompanied by an indulgent smile made her want to weep once more and bid for the comfort he so obstinately withheld.

"And if you were me, would you let your head rule your heart or the other way around?" she asked him.

He gave her a long, considering look before replying, and the lines of his face settled into the unrevealing mask he had worn in court. She was carried back to that day and the same sensation of impatience when he said with cool finality, "That, in the circumstances, is a most improper question, Miss Hayes, and one I could not possibly answer with any certainty. You will have to make your own decisions, or, perhaps, Mr. Brown will make them for you.''

"Perhaps he will!" she answered on a rising note of angry disappointment. "Perhaps he'll settle my doubts and everyone else's, too, once and for all . . . and—and whatever he proposes, I shall be only too happy to oblige him. You needn't think a cold in the head will prevent me from keeping that appointment now.''

"What appointment?" John Squires asked unexpectedly from the doorway. She had heard him arrive some time ago and make his way up to the nursery. She turned to him now with relief at the interruption, but before she could reply Robert said with cool amusement:

"Haven't you heard the great news? Our little Victoria has been summoned at last to the Presence."

"Yes, Kate told me," the doctor answered rather curtly, turning a professional eye on the girl's flushed face and overbright eyes. "You look as if you're more in need of medical attention than that young man upstairs, Victoria. Are you running a temperature?"

"I don't know, but whether I am or not, nothing is going to stop me from going to London on Monday," she replied. He gave Robert a shrewd, appraising glance, then said briskly:

"In that case, the sooner you're tucked up in bed the better, and I suggest that you stay there tomorrow if you want to be fit by Monday."

"Now that, Victoria," said Robert approvingly, "is an excellent notion. It will give you time to prepare for this momentous occasion and consider the various ways in which you might be expected to oblige Mr. Brown."

"Run along, now," John said, ignoring the interruption. "I'll be up in a little while to take your temperature and prescribe something to tide you over the worst. Ah, here's Elspeth come to take charge with hot water bottles and a very determined expression, so away you go."

Victoria took herself off. Robert got up and poured a couple of drinks, saying the doctor might as well refresh himself while he waited. John accepted the offer absently, then asked, "Do you do it on purpose, or don't you care?"

"Do what, for heaven's sake?"

"You know very well. Making fun of the poor child's obsession with her illusionary benefactor."

"But the gentleman's far from being illusionary, as the latest development should convince you."

"But Victoria's conception of him may well be. It would be a pity if your vagaries drive her to extremes."

"My vagaries?"

"For want of a better definition. It's none of my business, I suppose, but it isn't very kind to let an inexperienced girl take your attention seriously if you mean nothing more than a mild flirtation."

For a moment the icy anger that leaped into Robert's eyes, and the hint of pain in the tightening of the muscles around his mouth took the doctor by surprise, but when he spoke his voice was quite controlled.

"As you say, it's none of your business," he answered coldly, "and since we're being personal, I would suggest you take a hand in working out Kate's problems rather than mine."

"Since Kate is involved with your problems, and incidentally, with mine, you can hardly expect me to be indifferent," John retorted. Robert's taut expression relaxed in surprise.

"But, my good chap! Surely you aren't laboring under the impression that Kate cherishes anything more than a cousinly fondness for me?" he exclaimed.

"I've never been sure, but Victoria certainly does," John replied a little stiffly, "and since she's a nice child with a strong sense of obligation it hasn't helped her to sort out her own emotions."

"Oh dear, oh, lord! What very unnecessary complications!" Robert observed, sounding at once both rueful and relieved.

"If," John said, finishing his whisky and putting down the glass, "you had been a little more explicit instead of indulging in provocation there need have been no complications. I think perhaps I may have misjudged you, Farmer, in the matter of your intentions, but don't carry this little game too far. Young girls have curious ways of saving their pride. I fancy you might have a serious rival in Mr. Brown.''

"Are you suggesting I should come clean, as the saying is, before allowing this eventful meeting to take its course?" asked Robert with a return to his sardonic manner. The doctor shrugged and rose to his feet.

"I would have thought it wise unless you have come to the conclusion that Mr. Brown would provide a convenient escape," he said, but did not have the satisfaction of stirring up that flash of anger again.

"That, of course, is a point of view," Robert observed amicably. "Still, one must take chances in this life, mustn't one? It would hardly be fair to my possible rival to use persuasion before he's had a chance to reveal himself."

For a moment John did not speak, but stood regarding the other man with hostile but puzzled eyes.

"You're a curious fellow," he said then. "I believe you're in love with that little girl after all. Why the hell don't you put your cards on the table and end all this Mr. Brown nonsense?"

"Because, nonsense or not, Mr. Brown has made his mark. Until she meets him Victoria will never be free of this image she has created for herself. I prefer to compete with flesh and blood rather than an imagined father-figure."

"And if those proposed suggestions don't turn out to be strictly paternal?"

"My dear chap, your guess is as good as mine. Suppose we leave such contingencies until they materialize—and don't, I beg you, offer well-meaning as well as professional advice when you go upstairs."

"And what of the possibilities of coercion from another quarter? I doubt if your elderly rival will be quite so particular in view of past benefits,'' John retorted with some impatience. Robert merely shrugged and smiled a little enigmatically. The doctor turned on his heel.

''Well, I'll go up now and take a look at her,'' he said a shade gruffly, ''after which I would like a word with Kate in private.''

''Yes, you do that. I will diplomatically take myself off to the nursery and amuse my godson, so don't hurry away unless you have to,'' Robert said, observing with wry amusement the dull flush creeping up the back of the doctor's neck as he left the room.

After John had visited her, Victoria lay in her bed listening to the comings and goings in the house and trying to guess what they portended. She heard Robert come up to the nursery where he seemed to remain for some time; and, later, Kate's voice on the stairs followed by the sharp little click the parlor door made when it was shut because the latch was faulty.

She must have dozed off, for the daylight was nearly gone when she heard John drive off. She hoped Kate would come up and tell her how he had taken the news, forgetting that there had been no chance as yet to have her own surmises confirmed. Kate did not come.

She turned her face to the wall, feeling as she had at school when parents came down for special occasions and everybody seemed to have someone belonging except her. She remembered how Mr. Brown had gradually become a myth in whom no one believed very seriously, and her own hurt feelings at his continued disinterest. Well, she thought with renewed confidence, that was all changed now. Mr. Brown was not only about to declare himself, but clearly had definite plans for her future. It was distinctly comforting to know that although the Trust was coming to an end, it was possibly the beginning of a new relationship. . . .

It was dark before anyone visited her. Elspeth had brought up a light supper and remained for a while to chat, but her thoughts must have been elsewhere. She answered at random and did not even notice that Victoria's wet clothes still lay in a sodden heap on the floor. When Kate finally came it was only to say good night and inquire a little apologetically if there was anything she needed.

"How's Timmy?" Victoria asked, remembering that Kate must still hold her responsible for any harm that might have come to the boy, but Kate only laughed and replied absently that Timmy was making the most of his situation. She was afraid she had created rather a fuss about nothing.

"In fact, my cunning son seems to think he was clever to hide and give you a fright, because it would make you change your mind," she added, sounding suddenly mischievous. Victoria sent her a puzzled glance. There was something different about Kate tonight; it was almost as if she was a schoolgirl again, nursing a secret that she had been forbidden to tell.

"Change my mind?" she said guardedly.

"About leaving us. I tried to explain about Mr. Brown, but he seems to think he's a kind of wizard who's put a spell on you, and in a sense, I suppose, he has. Poor Timmy! This will be his first lesson in playing second fiddle, but we all have to learn, don't we?"

Victoria eyed her uneasily. "Kate, you're being very unlike yourself. Have you something you want to tell me?"

"Nothing more momentous than a decision to adopt

John's advice and keep you in bed tomorrow. Whatever happens you must keep that appointment on Monday."

Victoria blinked. It was Kate who had been suspicious, counseling postponement—and now here she was speeding on an eventual parting with uncomplimentary haste.

"You and Robert have come to an understanding, I imagine," she said tentatively, and Kate smiled.

"Oh yes. He's quite convinced me that the sooner you meet your peculiar patron, the better. Since he's going with you, I'm quite satisfied that you won't be persuaded into anything foolish."

It was not the answer Victoria wanted, but short of putting her question more bluntly she would have to be content to wait until Kate was ready to confide. As if she had guessed her thoughts Kate sat down on the side of the bed and said suddenly, "Victoria, you remember I told you I had been in love with another man before I married Jim?"

"Yes. He was engaged to someone else, so you did the noble thing and cut your losses. When you both were free you met again. Well, I know all that, so what?" Victoria replied, trying to sound casual and adult. Kate smiled.

"But you don't, my dear. I only met him again quite by chance that weekend I was in London. He hadn't changed a bit, but thank goodness, I had. I thought you might like to know."

Victoria was silent from sheer surprise, then she remembered Elspeth's acid remark about bad pennies turning up again, and her relief was mixed with pain.

"You thought it was Robert, didn't you?" said Kate softly.

"Did he tell you that?"

"I don't think he even suspected. No, John told me."

"Oh! Well, it's of no consequence now. I'm glad all the

same, Kate, that I wasn't poaching. It worried me dreadfully."

"Silly child! Don't you think in the circumstances that you should reconsider before casting in your lot with Mr. Brown?"

Kate made the question sound like a casual afterthought, but her eyes were warm and a little anxious. Victoria had to fight an impulse to succumb to the luxury of confessing to the sorry state of her own heart, but it was too late now for reassurance, neither did she fancy the possibility that Robert might still be offering to make insulting amends.

"There's nothing to consider. I took too much for granted, that's all. It was really very fortunate that Robert's silly trick misfired," she said and began to sneeze.

"Those blasted roses!" Kate exclaimed, getting up and smoothing down the bedcover. "Oh well, perhaps the real Mr. Brown will remedy that, once he's made his intentions plain. Would you like Robert to come up and say good night?"

"No!" Victoria answered so vehemently that she started coughing. Kate stood looking down at her with an odd expression, then she firmly tucked in the bedclothes and went away.

Victoria spent Sunday in feverish anticipation of the morrow. Fears that she might not be fit enough to travel were mixed with a sneaking desire for the opposite, for although her temperature was normal, there was no denying that her cold was in its most unbecoming stage. Robert had thoughtfully sent up a supply of masculine handkerchiefs. By the time he put in an appearance himself to inquire, her nose was pink from repeated blowing, and she was inclined to be tearful.

"Isn't it too humiliating?" she said when he commiserated tactfully with her situation. "The only time in my whole life that I want to make an impression, and I have to look like a half-boiled rabbit!"

"Oh, hardly that . . . just a frail young thing with a re-grettable addiction to the bottle," he replied gravely, making her giggle. "Your ears are pink too, which on second thoughts does suggest a rabbit on account of their size."

"You," she said, "are very rude, and it will serve you right if you catch my cold." She added casually, "I think after all, it might be better if I postponed that meeting tomorrow. It wouldn't be very tactful to pass on a cold to Mr. Brown as a token of esteem."

"Nonsense!" he retorted cheerfully. "Weren't you taught that procrastination is the thief of time? For all you know the poor old gentleman may be on his last legs and thinking of making his will. You surely wouldn't want to disappoint him after all this time?"

"There you go again—mocking poor Mr. Brown!" she exclaimed, welcoming a bracing return of hostility. "Why do you always have to provoke me just when I'm trying to be friendly?"

"Possibly because I'm heartily sick and tired of Mr. Brown and all his works!" he replied. "You, I might add, are surprisingly touchy on the subject, considering the gentleman in question is a stranger."

"Well, after tomorrow he won't be a stranger any more, so you can stop amusing yourself at my expense," she snapped. His eyebrows rose with a quizzical air of indulgence.

"At Mr. Brown's expense, not yours, my purblind child," he said.

"Purblind?" she echoed between sneezes, and he took a

clean handerkerchief from the pile on the table beside her and tossed it into her lap.

"Yes, purblind," he said gently, "but there's some excuse for you, I'll admit. I tend to forget your youth and inexperience when we wrangle so merrily."

"Merrily?"

"Yes, merrily, and a good thing too. Relations would have become insupportable if there hadn't been a lighter side to our disputes. Now take your medicine and keep warm. By tomorrow you'll feel more like putting on your best bib and tucker to dazzle Mr. Brown. When the interview is over I'll take you out to lunch to celebrate."

She saw no more of him until the evening when Kate thought it wise, in view of tomorrow's trip, to get dressed and join them for Sunday supper. Perhaps because John Squires had joined the party, Robert seemed to be in a mood to tease. Since he appeared to be accepting the doctor's presence with unusual equanimity, Victoria bore with his mischievous attentions for Kate's sake. Even Kate, who every so often exchanged knowing smiles with John, finally rounded on him and told him to behave.

"You can hardly accuse me of improper conduct while you and Squires provide such admirable chaperonage," he protested innocently, and she gave him a look that was strongly reminiscent of Elspeth.

"You know very well what I mean," she retorted briskly. "You're an expert at tripping up witnesses and getting them confused, but you're not in court now."

"Are you confused, Victoria Mary?" he inquired with mock anxiety. Victoria who was beginning to long for the privacy and solace of her bed gave him a withering look.

"Not in the least," she replied, somewhat tartly. "Such confusion as I may once have felt was only to be expected since I was very green and unaccustomed to charming insincerities, but things are crystal clear now, so you don't need to keep on pressing your point in this tedious fashion.''

"Well said," the doctor murmured with an appreciative grin. "I think you asked for that, Farmer."

"Yes, perhaps I did," Robert answered, and his eyes were suddenly grave. Kate, looking surprised and a little unhappy, said quickly:

"Why don't we all play Consequences or something instead of talking a lot of nonsense?" Both John and Victoria smiled sympathetically though they did not second the suggestion, but Robert exclaimed irrepressibly:

"Now *that's* an idea! I haven't played Consequences since I was a boy. Think what fun we could have with sinister Mr. Brown meeting gullible Miss Hayes in a lonely wood. He said to her: 'How will you repay me for past favors?' She said to him—''

"That's enough!" Kate broke in quite sharply, but Victoria got to her feet and, looking Robert straight in the eye, finished for him:

"She said to him: 'In any way you choose that will settle affairs once and for all.' Now, if you don't mind, Kate, I'll say good night and go to bed. I wouldn't want to keep Robert waiting in the morning."

She crossed the room and unhurriedly mounted the corner staircase that had played such an unhappy part in her affairs, and John remarked gravely, "I think she meant that. Are you trying to drive the child into the arms of a total stranger who may or may not be on the level, Farmer?"

"Perhaps," Robert answered with tantalizing prevarication, and the doctor frowned impatiently. Kate touched his hand sympathetically, but she, too, seemed surprisingly unperturbed.

"Dear John," she murmured softly, "Robert isn't as hard-boiled as he sounds. Even if he goes about things in a peculiar fashion, he knows his own business best."

"Thanks, my comely cousin. I suggest we all have a nightcap to restore relationships and talk of cabbages and kings," Robert said and got up to dispense the drinks.

Victoria slept heavily as a result of her cold and the strain of standing up to Robert's provocations. Although Kate called her with a breakfast tray in plenty of time, she fell asleep again and was obliged to dress with more haste than she had planned for such a momentous occasion. Kate came back as she was trying to decide which dress to wear, thankful that the weather at least was being kind. She could dispense with the summer coat that had been chosen for utility rather than smartness.

"Would you think the candy-stripe pink, or the black sheath? The print is gay and was quite expensive, but the black is towny and more sophisticated," she said, her head on one side. Kate took a navy-blue linen with crisp white collar and cuffs off its hanger and replied without thinking:

"No, wear this, it's Robert's favorite. He says it gives you the air of a demure schoolgirl that is most intriguing and reminds him of the day he first saw you in court."

"Well, that's a day I have no wish to remember, and since it's Mr. Brown I want to impress and not Robert, I'll wear the black," Victoria retorted, snatching back the dress and throwing it on the bed. When later, she came downstairs, ready to go, Kate observed with amusement that she had evidently changed her mind. She thought the girl looked delightful in the plain navy dress that made her appear so incredibly slender. She was too tactful to comment and merely observed that she approved of the broad headband that did duty for a hat and was distinctly becoming.

For a moment as they left, Victoria had a cold feeling of finality, the sensation of boats too hastily burned, the point of no return too suddenly reached.

"It isn't really goodbye, is it, Kate?" she said as the older woman kissed her.

"Of course not, you goose! Robert will see you safely onto the train after lunch, and Elspeth's preparing your favorite dinner."

"If, that is, Mr. Brown doesn't spirit her away to his hidden lair before she can change her mind," observed Robert from the open front door.

"Now, Rob, don't tease," Kate admonished him. "Pay no attention to him, Victoria, if he tries to provoke you all the way to London. He's probably only jealous of his unknown rival."

It was not very kind of Kate to make fun of her, too, Victoria thought as she followed Robert out to the waiting Bentley. Whatever his intentions may have been, he seemed undisposed for chatter. He drove with his usual speed, and she sat beside him, every so often glancing at the hard, unrevealing lines of his profile and wondered what he was thinking about. Her own efforts at small talk having met with little response, she relapsed into an uneasy silence and wished she were not filled with so many last-minute doubts. Now that she was actually to come face to face with her benefactor she was aware of a strange reluctance. The mysterious Mr. Brown had been an accepted part of her background for so long that she had not paused to consider that one day there might be a reckoning. She remembered those other summonses to the office of Messrs. Chapple, Chapple & Ponsonby, and her sharp disappointment at Mr. Brown's failure to appear. She would, she reflected unhappily, have been journeying to London today in a state of excited anticipation had it not been for the regrettable change in her situation. She wished Robert would make a last-minute appeal for further reflection before committing herself to the dictates of a stranger, but his disinclination to treat the subject seriously was even worse than his teasing. He seemed all at once like a stranger.

He braked violently to avoid a car that turned off without giving signals, swore under his breath, then gathered speed with fresh vigor, at the same time placing a hand on her knee.

"Nervous?" he asked.

"Not of your driving," she answered, edging away, and saw him smile with amused comprehension.

"Having cold feet for other reasons," he said, but his tone was not conducive to a sympathetic hearing, and she made no answer.

All too soon the country was left behind them, and the Bentley was forced to a crawl as it joined the incoming stream of traffic. The rows of ugly little houses with their sooty backyards depressed Victoria unutterably, and she thought with longing of the Sussex lanes and woods and the familiar grace of Farthings. How much longer would she have to think of the place as home after today's interview? She wondered disconsolately what would be decided; had perhaps already been decided for her immediate future?

"I'm not, of course, obliged to agree to anything," she told herself reassuringly, aware too late that she had spoken aloud. She glanced a little nervously at Robert, hoping he had not heard, but he, with his usual promptness to pounce on an ill-considered remark, said a little mockingly:

"And what of those brave resolves of Saturday? Whatever your benefactor had in mind you would do your best to oblige him, you said. It's hardly becoming in a beneficiary to have second thoughts after accepting so much."

"You," she exclaimed, rejoicing in a temporary return to normal, "are the last person to preach gratitude and duty. If it hadn't been for you I wouldn't have been summoned to the Presence now."

"But that, surely was what you wanted," he pointed out with infuriating logic. She gave an angry little bounce that shot her purse onto the floor, spilling out its contents.

"Will you please shut **up**, Robert Farmer, or better still, let me out here and I'll take a bus," she said, diving under his legs for an escaping lipstick.

"That would make you late for your appointment, which wouldn't make a good impression—do stop fiddling about with my ankles, my dear child, you might cause an accident," he said, sounding inappropriately restored to good humor. She surfaced once more, quite pink in the face.

"I was *not* fiddling about with your ankles—I was retrieving my lipstick, and if you had an ounce of decent feeling you'd be giving me a little c-confidence instead of s-slapping me down!" she retorted. He glanced down at her with a quizzical little lift of one eyebrow.

"Are you in need of confidence, then, Victoria Mary?" he inquired quite gently, and she blinked rapidly and looked hastily out of the window.

"Naturally," she replied in slightly muffled tones. "It's most important that Mr. Brown should like me and—and I'm already handicapped by having a c-cold in the head."

"Poor Victoria! Never mind, you can have a good blow before we get there and powder your nose. I don't suppose anyone will notice a slight pinkness around the edges," he said.

After that they drove on in silence, but soon Victoria managed to ignore the slight sinking feeling in the pit of her stomach in renewing acquaintanceship with the exhilarating bustle of the London streets.

They were passing the Law Courts, and she gazed upon them, remembering the last occasion when she had journeyed so expectantly on top of a bus to a meeting that had never taken place and had, instead, been packed off abroad to finish her education.

"Unpleasant memories?" asked Robert suddenly, as they waited in a traffic jam. Because for the moment her thoughts were divorced from the immediate present, she gave him that slow, lifting smile.

"Not all unpleasant," she answered. "I was thinking of the times I came this way expecting to meet Mr. Brown only to be fobbed off with a stuffy lawyer. Twice they sent for me and twice I was disappointed, but third time lucky, they say, so this must be it." She sneezed twice and suddenly looked anxious. "You don't think this is another let-down do you, Robert? They wouldn't have come out with all those queer hints and suggestions if Mr. Brown wasn't going to turn up, would they?"

"Who knows what eccentric clients may think fit to do at the last minute?" he replied as the traffic moved on. "Anyway, we'll soon be there, so have a good blow, powder your nose, and prepare yourself for the worst."

Robert parked the Bentley in an adjacent cul-de-sac behind the office premises and told Victoria to go on up while he locked the car. She hurried up the dark staircase with its familiar musty smell, hoping that he was tactfully giving her time to make herself known without his supervision. She could hear his leisurely steps on the bottom stair just as she reached the top and quickly slipped into the outer office, letting the door swing shut behind her.

Like the recurrence of a dream the same old clerk came forward to meet her; a little grayer, a little more bent, but as primly incurious as he had appeared three years ago.

"Please take a seat, Miss Hayes, Mr. Brown has not yet arrived," he said, conveying a touch of reproof in that she herself was too early.

"Then he really *is* coming?" she said, aware that she had been half expecting excuses for unavoidable absence.

"Naturally," the old man replied with a slight air of disapproval, then allowed himself a fleeting expression of surprise as Robert opened the door and came in.

"Good morning, Mr. Farmer. Your appointment was for eleven-fifty-five, if I am not mistaken. Would you care to come back later?" he said.

"I know I'm early, but I don't mind waiting," Robert replied, sitting down on a hard, uncomfortable chair and stretching out his long legs before him.

"I will just ascertain whether Mr. Chapple is free," the clerk said. Robert gave Victoria a most undignified wink as the old man knocked on the door of one of the private rooms and vanished inside.

"You needn't try to upset my dignity by making me giggle," Victoria said, sitting down on another hard chair. "Anyway, he hasn't arrived yet, so it looks as if you'll have a long wait for your own appointment. Wouldn't you like to take a walk and come back?"

"Not at all. I promised Kate to see you safely bestowed before attending to my own business. Besides, I'm not entirely devoid of curiosity concerning your Invisible Man," Robert replied and gave her another disconcerting wink.

Before she had time to retort, the door opened. Mr.

Chapple came bustling out, rubbing his hands together and exuding an air of roguish bonhomie that forcibly reminded Victoria of their first meeting.

"Well, well, well! So you have already introduced yourselves," he said. "But of course I'm forgetting, Mr. Farmer, that you're a cousin of Mrs. Allen's, so you are hardly strangers to one another."

"Mr. Farmer drove me up from Sussex as he already had an appointment with you. I don't mind waiting if you would care to see him first. Mr. Brown hasn't yet arrived," Victoria said politely as she shook hands, hoping that Robert would take the hint and leave her to get over the first introductions alone.

For a moment Mr. Chapple looked surprised and a little put out as if he suspected an impertinence. Then he caught Robert's eye, went a little red in the face, and cleared his throat with a series of explosive little pops.

"Well, well, well . . . " he said again, ushering them toward his private room. "No need for hurry . . . no need at all . . . you must both of you wait in the greater comfort of my own office, so come along in. I have a very tolerable sherry decanted in honor of this occasion, so I trust you'll join me in a little celebration."

Victoria hung back, feeling slightly bewildered, but the two men were waiting for her to precede them, and she could do no less than make the best of the situation. It seemed to her a little premature to start drinking before the principal participant had joined them, but Mr. Chapple was already handing around glasses and making coy little jokes that she thought ill became him. Robert seemed to find nothing odd in the procedure.

"Well now, before we get to business, may I propose a toast to the—er—winding up of a project that I will confess caused me grave misgivings at the time. Mr. Farmer—

Miss Hayes—I drink to the happy conclusion of this affair.''

He raised his glass on the last words, took a slow, appreciative swallow and nearly choked when Victoria suddenly stamped her foot at him and burst out, "It's all another hoax, after all! I don't know why you've staged this ridiculous scene, Mr. Chapple, unless you've been put up to it by your learned friend who has, I've cause to know, a very odd sense of humor. It wasn't very kind, was it, to pretend when you knew all the time Mr. Brown wouldn't be c-coming?''

Mr. Chapple's jaw dropped visibly, and he favored Robert with an outraged glance before turning an offended eye on Victoria, remembering his impressions at that first meeting. He had been prepared to admit on this occasion that judging by appearance, the experiment had paid off. But it seemed that Grahame Hayes's daughter was no less likeable at 20 than she had been at 14.

"Well, upon my soul, young lady! A respectable firm of lawyers hardly lends themselves to the perpetrating of hoaxes!'' he snapped. "It would seem that it is I who should demand explanations, not you.''

Victoria had taken refuge in blowing her nose, thankful that her cold gave her an excuse for concealing a humiliating threat of tears. She heard Robert murmuring something she could not catch, followed by a dignified snort from Mr. Chapple, then the sound of a door opening and shutting. She turned slowly, thinking that Robert had gone, but he was still there, propped against Mr. Chapple's imposing desk and regarding her with a cool and unconcerned eye.

"Would you care for the loan of my handkerchief?'' he asked conversationally. "Your own doesn't appear to be very adequate.''

"No, I wouldn't," she replied ungraciously. "Why are you still here?"

"To keep an appointment," he replied with the indulgent air of an adult humoring a child.

"Your appointment was for a quarter to twelve and has nothing to do with mine, anyway," she pointed out, wondering at the same time, what could be occupying Mr. Chapple's attention.

"Hasn't it?"

"Well, only in a nosy kind of way, but as Mr. Brown isn't here, your curiosity will have to go unsatisfied, won't it?"

"Who says he isn't here? Not poor old Chapple dispensing bonhomie and his best sherry. You really did cut him to the quick with those most improper suggestions."

She stared at him dumbly for a moment, only conscious that she might have jumped too hastily to conclusions. It would be just like Mr. Robert Farmer to have the last laugh.

"You mean he's gone to fetch him?" she said; then, "He was here all the time, waiting in another room?"

"Here all the time, certainly, but not waiting in another room. Can't you guess, Victoria Mary?" he replied, and, had she not known him so well, Victoria could have sworn he seemed suddenly anxious.

"What are you trying to tell me? That you've thought up another good practical joke for your entertainment?" she said, clinging to proved facts. Her voice was not as steady as she would have wished, and her legs felt suddenly as if they were made of cotton-wool.

"No joke, I assure you," he replied wryly. "Neither were those perishing roses a joke, since they really did come from Mr. Brown. Aren't you ever going to forgive me for that?" he said. For a moment the room seemed to spin around her, and the rows of file boxes looked in imminent danger of falling on her head.

"I think I'd better sit down," she said, groping wildly for the nearest chair. Robert said nothing, but poured out some more sherry and placed her fingers firmly around the glass. She took a long swallow while the room slowly righted itself, then blinked up at him propped once more against the desk and regarding her with tender amusement.

"Are you disappointed?" he asked, and she took a deep breath.

"That Mr. Brown turns out to be only you? I suppose, knowing the peculiar way your mind works, I should have guessed there was something fishy going on," she retorted, recapturing her self-possession with an aplomb that made him smile.

"Something fishy? Oh, surely not."

"Yes—decidedly fishy if I'd stopped to think. Mr. Brown, always so adamant on the subject of jobs and possible admirers, showed a remarkable tolerance where you were concerned. In fact, though he set his face firmly against followers, he never took exception to you."

"Well, naturally one tends to be broadminded where one's own interests are concerned," he replied, quite unabashed. She looked at him wrathfully.

"Then the whole thing was engineered from the start—Kate offering me the only job I was allowed to accept; you coming down to find out how your experiment was working. No wonder I never had a chance to make a life of my own! I suppose Kate was in on the joke, even if she did play up to the extent of firing me."

"Kate knew nothing until yesterday when, in view of pending change, it seemed only right to put her in the picture. She was aware that I had retained an interest in

Grahame Hayes's daughter and was glad to offer you a job on my recommendation. It never crossed her mind that the invisible Mr. Brown, and her by no means invisible cousin could be one and the same person.''

"Why did you do it? Make yourself responsible for a stranger you had only seen in the witness-box, I mean?'' she asked curiously. He ran a hand absently over his lean jaw as if unsure of the answer.

"I don't really know," he said then. "There was something about you that stuck in my mind and produced quite irrational feelings of remorse since my cross-examination was wholly justified. . . . There was no one to pick up the pieces and I had an impulse to play providence . . . perhaps because I'd been let down myself and was in the mood for a little gratitude. . . . Who knows on looking back what prompts one to certain actions? It may be that I was no less eccentric and careless of my money than Mr. Brown appeared to be. It could, I suppose, be judged the height of eccentricity to go to such lengths to provide oneself with a suitable marriage partner.''

She stared at him disbelievingly, not very sure if he wasn't still enjoying a private joke at her expense. He added with sudden gentleness, "Don't look so incredulous . . . that, to you, must seem an unromantic way of going about things, but as I'd fallen out of love with a resounding crash, it seemed quite sensible then to insure against the future.''

"I see. Wrapping the next possible contender in cotton wool until you were ready.''

His smile was a little wry, and he momentarily hunched his shoulders as though he felt a draught from the open window.

"Well, not quite so cold-blooded as that. I was always prepared for my plans miscarrying, hence the cotton wool. You see, my child, as I once told you, even brow-beating attorneys have their pipe-dreams, and there was no more harm in my fantasies than in yours relating to Mr. Brown.''

She considered this gravely, then said with that sudden capitulation to reason that always surprised him, ''No, there wasn't, was there? I don't, in any case, see anything odd in wanting to fashion someone to your specification should the opportunity arise. The only thing is one's dreams don't always work out as one expects. Look how I've been let down by Mr. Brown.''

''Very true, if all you expected was a substitute papa who would make no embarrassing demands, which brings us back to the point of this long-delayed meeting,'' Robert said with a sudden alarming change of manner. Sitting down in the chair Mr. Chapple reserved for inter-viewing clients, he fixed her with a cool, forensic eye. ''However mistaken you were in your private fantasies, the fact remains, Miss Hayes, that you made certain state-ments before witnesses that I now propose to hold you to.''

''What statements?''

''You know very well. In return for past considerations, you were willing to oblige Mr. Brown to the best of your ability.''

''Well, I didn't know he was you, then,'' Victoria pro-tested indignantly, but she felt herself coloring as she re-membered Robert's outrageous suggestions, and her own rash commitments.

''The fact of his identity makes no difference,'' he re-plied with something of his courtroom manner, and she blinked but was not silenced.

''Yes, it does. You obtained that assurance under false

pretenses, so it cancels out!" she said with renewed confidence. He grinned, suddenly shedding his legal mask.

"A good try, but it won't hold water. The fact that your unknown patron happens to be me and not a gouty, old gentleman with slightly improper intentions in no way alters the case. That you were prepared to meet the demands of a total stranger as a means of escape from me in no way releases you from obligation, so hadn't we better end this farce once and for all? Old man Chapple will be back any minute to offer congratulations and draw up contracts."

"Draw up c-contracts?"

"Figuratively speaking, of course, since I trust that will be the vicar's privilege. Still and all, it might be as well to have everything down in writing in case you're thinking of ratting on the agreement."

"There hasn't *been* an agreement!" she shouted at him, nearly in tears. "What are you trying to do to me, Robert? Get your own back because I turned you down? You know very well you have only yourself to thank for that. I could hardly be expected to take you seriously after your silly prank with the roses."

His eyebrows went up in that familiar expression of fastidious inquiry.

"I thought I'd explained away that bone of contention," he remarked. "Don't you understand that I wasn't ready then to confess to a dual personality. Neither were you in a mood to take kindly to relinquishing those father-figure fantasies. I'm prepared to fill that role upon occasions, but not to the exclusion of the normal demands of the flesh. Did you really think I asked you to marry me as a kind of consolation prize?"

"It wouldn't have been any c-consolation, so you

needn't f-flatter yourself," she flung back at him, and quite suddenly found herself in tears.

He was around the desk and kneeling beside her chair before she even had time to turn away.

"There, my poor, bedevilled sweetheart . . . stop fighting me . . . it's a losing battle, you know," he murmured as he gathered her into his arms. "You try so hard to convince me you couldn't care less, but you're forgetting those revealing letters to Mr. Brown."

"You did read my letters, then?"

"Every one. Such stiff, dutiful, little effusions, Victoria Mary Hayes—until that last *cri de coeur*, which certainly gave me encouragement."

"Why did you never answer?"

"I don't really know—unless it was a reluctance to shatter the paternal image that you seemed to set such store by. Now, will you please dry your eyes and attend to me seriously? I can't offer better proof of sincerity than to propose once more on my bended knee, so please, dear, militant Victoria Mary, don't send me away again with a flea in my ear."

She began to smile at him, but tears and a cold in the head stifled responses. She snatched the handkerchief from his breast pocket and blew her nose with some violence.

"Do get up, Robert," she said then, clutching at the remnants of her composure. "It doesn't become you at all to kneel and be humble."

"No? But then you've still a great deal to learn about me, haven't you—between the traditional browbeatings, of course," he said, but he obediently rose to his feet, pulling her up with him. "You haven't answered me, yet.

"If you're really sure—" she began a little shyly, and he gave her a shake.

"Of course I'm sure. I've been sure ever since that day in the orchard when you thought you'd fooled me and stood under an apple tree shaking down blossoms and stealing my heart away."

"Did I? Did I really, Robert—as long ago as that?"

"Yes, you did, and merely disliked me intensely in return, which was ungenerous of you."

"You could hardly expect me to feel kindly toward you in the circumstances," she pointed out, and he grinned.

"Well no—perhaps you have a point there. You still haven't answered me or, for the matter of that, given me any assurance of a return of affection."

"I don't need to—I told Mr. Brown," she answered demurely, and he grinned again.

"So you did. Well, I suppose I must be content with that for the time being. At least you no longer labor under delusions concerning Kate!"

"Kate?" For the moment she had forgotten Kate, and her eyes grew troubled.

"No," she said. "She explained about that other man, only you couldn't very well turn her and Timmy out of Farthings, could you, Robert?"

"Oh, I see. Without the bribe of Farthings, you'd think twice before committing yourself," he countered so severely that she looked quite horrified. Then he laughed and pinched her ear. "You don't need to worry about Kate's future, you prevaricating goose! I fancy it won't be very long before the worthy doctor succeeds in persuading her to move down to the village."

The last remaining scruple melted away, and her face lit up.

"Oh, I'm so *glad*! John is so kind and dependable. He'll make a far better stepfather than you ever would!" she exclaimed, and he gave her another shake.

"Very possibly," he replied dryly. "For myself, I prefer to father and bring up my own brats than be a stand-in for someone else's."

"Yes," she agreed a little smugly, "it wouldn't suit you at all to play second fiddle."

"No, it wouldn't, so please remember that in the future, Miss Hayes. No followers, however respectable, or there'll be trouble."

"You see?" she said as he bent his head at last to kiss her. "I'll never quite get away from Mr. Brown. He had very old-fashioned views about followers."

"Oh, damn Mr. Brown and his old-fashioned views! I'll have enough to contend with without that gentleman being thrust down my throat when it suits!" Robert exclaimed and tilted up her face to his with some impatience.

"You'll catch my cold," she murmured, and he administered one last shake before imprisoning her firmly between his hands.

"Don't change the subject," he said severely and proceeded to ensure her silence for quite some time.

"Isn't it strange?" she said when finally she could speak, peering over his shoulder at the gloomy rows of fileboxes that probably held secrets and even scandals long since forgotten. "It all began in this ugly musty room, and now it all ends here. . . . Do you suppose records of the Hayes Trust are buried in one of those boxes?"

"Most certainly, since this is a most reliable and trustworthy firm, but don't let skeletons in cupboards rattle their bones at you, sweetheart. Remember that sinister Mr. Brown has already been written off as only a bogle to frighten the bairns with," Robert said, ignoring a discreet tap on the door.

"He said to her, 'How will you repay me for past favors?' " Victoria murmured.

"And kindly remember the lady's reply," he promptly retorted. "What a pity we never got as far as the consequence."

"The immediate consequence will probably be an explosion from Mr. Chapple if you don't tell him to come in," Victoria retorted as a more peremptory knock sounded on the door. She straightened his tie with a proprietorial air before putting a decorous distance between them.